THARN'S HUNT
A FATED MATED ALIEN ROMANCE

BARBARIANS OF THE DUST
BOOK TWO

AG WILDE

PETRONIE
PUBLISHING

For every reader who has ever looked at their life's problems and thought, "You know what would fix this? A giant, possessive alien." This one's for you.

CHAPTER 1

HOW TO GET LOST IN 10 EASY STEPS (A SURVIVAL GUIDE BY JACQUI "SHOULD'VE STAYED HOME" PARKER)

JACQUI

The desert holds twenty-seven ways to die. Dehydration? Check. Heatstroke from the hateful glare of this planet's massive sun? Oh, we're well acquainted. Spontaneous combustion? Give it an hour. But today, I'm aiming for something more creative. Like composing a scathing one-star review in my head. *'Ambiance is oppressively hot, and the staff is nonexistent. 0/10, would not die here again.'*

It's the petty victories that keep you going.

But hey, at least the view's great. If you like sand. And despair. And more sand.

My sister, Justine, had vanished into this orange-hued wasteland weeks ago. I'd followed, of course, because that's what I do. She's the trailblazer; I'm the sarcastic cleanup crew. The rest of the crash survivors thought I was insane to leave the relative safety of the transport bus, but they didn't know Jus. Stubborn doesn't even begin to cover it.

AG WILDE

"Jus," I croak, my voice scraping past a throat full of sand as I shade my eyes. The massive sun above continuously bakes the sky a permanent shade of bruised yellow, indifferent to my pain. "If you're alive—and you better be—I'm going to strangle you *with my bare hands*."

I reach the rock formation she'd set out for and collapse in its shade. "Justine? Jus!"

Silence.

The only answer is the whisper of wind over dunes. Of course. Because why would my life be that easy?

My legs tremble. My lungs burn. The air is so thin and dry it feels like I'm breathing in glass dust. And my brain is too fried to think of anything except how good it feels to stop moving.

I scan the area, turning my head left and right, hoping to see Justine waltz around the corner with her usual "I've got this" grin.

"Jus?" My voice croaks out again. Still nothing.

Great. Just fantastic. I press my palms to my face, the sting of tiny sand grains making me want to scream. I do scream, but it's a silent, energy-conserving one, my head thrown back.

"Fucking COME ON! Why don't you just fuck me and be done with it?!" I don't know who I'm talking to. The sun? The planet itself? All I know is I didn't walk all this way for more sand. At least give me a mirage. A hot alien with a water bottle would be nice. I'm not picky!

"Justine!" I shout for real this time, the name swallowed by the vast emptiness. The silence that follows is so absolute it feels heavy. Just me and the stupid desert.

I press my palms to my eyes again, forcing the tears back. Crying won't help. Justine wouldn't cry. She'd keep going. She'd find me if the roles were reversed.

So that's what I'll do. I'll find her.

I push myself to my feet, legs wobbling like overcooked spaghetti. The shade of the rock formation is tempting me to sit back down and play dead for a while, but I can't.

Then comes a dark thought. *Justine's been out here alone for weeks—*

Nope! Not today, Satan. My sister isn't dead. She's annoyingly resilient. Like a cockroach, but prettier because hey, we're family.

I shuffle around the rock formation, scanning the ground for any sign she was here. But there are no footprints. No discarded ration pack. No alien skeleton with a note pinned to its ribs saying, "Your sister went thataway."

"Cool. Love this for me," I mumble, kicking a tiny rock that barely moves because even my kicks are pathetic now.

But then, something catches my eye. A tiny glint in the sand. I freeze, my heart thudding in my chest. It could be nothing. It probably *is* nothing. But I'm desperate enough to investigate.

I drop to my knees, brushing away the sand with trembling fingers, and there it is. Tiny. Pink-and-gold.

My breath halts in my chest.

Justine's earring.

The little butterfly one that belonged to Mom. The one with the impossibly flimsy clasp.

I clutch it in my hand and press it against my chest. Relief crashes over me so hard I gasp. She was here. She was alive. She made it this far. But the relief curdles into dread. *Why would she leave this?* She'd sooner leave a kidney.

I glance around, my eyes darting between the rocks and the endless waves of sand. She wouldn't just drop it for no reason. Not Justine.

"She's smarter than this," I whisper to myself. "She wouldn't just... leave."

Panic creeps in, threading along my spine, but I shove it down. Focus, Jacqui. *Think.* What would Justine do? If she had to leave, she'd leave... something. A sign. A clue.

I force myself to stand, tucking the earring into my bra for safekeeping. The movement makes my head swim, and for a second, I think I might pass out right here in the sand. But no. Not yet. I've been fighting this heatstroke, dizziness, and occasional weird dreams thing for weeks now. What's a few more hours?

I stumble around the rocks, one hand bracing against the striated stone to keep myself upright, and scan the ground again, looking for anything out of place. A shoe. A water sachet. Maybe a middle finger carved into the stone.

That's when I see it.

Etched into a flat stretch like a Post-it note.

"BRB," I read aloud. My laugh comes out as a choked wheeze, part relief, part pure disbelief. Only Justine would casually leave a "be right back" note in the middle of an alien desert. Like she just stepped out for coffee or something. "An arrow. Just an arrow, Jus? Couldn't spring for a map, huh? Lucky for you, I love your stupid face."

Still, it's enough. A direction. A sign she was thinking clearly, at least when she left it.

I squint into the distance, shielding my eyes from the last rays of sunlight. Far ahead through the heat haze, I can just barely make out another rock formation. That must be where she went.

The muscles in my legs burn at the thought of walking any further, but I don't care. I'll crawl if I have to.

But not tonight.

The desert's already growing darker, the sun sinking below the horizon to leave behind a sky streaked with orange and purple. Soon, it'll be pitch black, and traveling at night without a light source is just another way to add "fall into a hole and die" to my catalog of desert deaths.

I stagger back to the shade of the rocks, my legs giving out beneath me. My body hits the ground with a thud. The stars overhead blur as exhaustion pulls me under. "Tomorrow," I whisper, clutching the earring to my chest. "I'll follow her trail tomorrow."

It was a good plan. A sensible, human plan. It never occurred to me that on this planet, the things that hunt don't need light to see.

CHAPTER 2
IS IT TOO LATE TO CALL FOR BACKUP?

JACQUI

My eyes snap open at a sound.

Justine?

No...no...not Justine.

A dry, clicking sound slices through the night. It's not the wind. It's not a rockslide. It's rhythmic. Chitinous.

I freeze, every muscle screaming in protest as I push myself up into a crouch. My heart hammers against my ribs as I clutch the jagged piece of metal Mikaela had ripped from the bus for me, her words echoing in my head: *"This is a suicide mission, Jacqui."*

For a few long moments, nothing happens. No sound. No movement. Then, ahead, a flicker of movement in the pitch-black. A shape detaches itself from the deeper shadows. I squint, but there's barely enough light to see my own hand. Two greenish-yellow pinpricks of light blink open, like a cat's eyes catching a flashlight beam. Then they're gone.

I imagined it. My brain is fried. In all our time here, we've seen nothing. It's all just sand and rock.

But then the clicking sound returns, closer now. And not from one source. There are multiple. Like echoes on stone.

Oh.

Oh shit.

Run.

My legs move before my brain catches up, powered by sheer panic and whatever scraps of energy I have left. My pack slams against my hip as I stumble forward, nearly tripping over my own feet. The screech that follows freezes my blood. It's a dry, bone-deep sound that vibrates through my ribs, like metal scraping against raw nerve endings.

I don't look back. Can't. My lungs burn, my legs scream, but I push harder, ignoring the dizziness threatening to consume my vision.

Ahead looms a darker mass against the night sky—a small rock formation. Higher ground. A chance.

I scramble toward it, tripping, falling, and scrambling to my feet again. Behind me, the clicking gets louder, closer. A hungry crescendo.

When my hands finally connect with solid stone, the impact almost sends me backward. I grip it like a lifeline, swallowing down nausea as I haul myself up.

"Come on. Come on!"

Pain explodes in my calf. Something sharp rakes across my leg, tearing into skin. I scream, nearly losing my grip.

No.

My leg is on fire, hot blood quickly soaking into my boot. But I can't stop. If I stop, I'm dead.

I climb blindly, hands scrambling for purchase on the jagged stone. Below, the creatures circle like sharks, their glowing eyes and clicking sounds sending chills down my spine.

I press myself against the rock face, willing my heart to quiet, praying they can't climb.

Universe: Bitch, do I look like I give out favors?

Claws scrape against stone as the first one begins its ascent.

"Oh, you have got to be kidding me," I sob, scrambling higher.

The creature gains on me, its breathing a wet, hungry rasp. I scramble higher, blindly reaching out when my hand closes around a rock, loose in its position in the striated stone. Without thinking, I wrench it free and hurl it down.

A satisfying thunk followed by an outraged shriek tells me I've hit my mark. The creature tumbles back to the ground, buying me precious seconds.

That's when my hand finally slaps against a wide, flat surface. A ledge. I haul my screaming body onto it, pressing my back against the cliff face, chest heaving. Pain sears up my leg as I kick out at another ascending creature, sending a shower of pebbles down. It retreats, but I know it's only temporary.

"Back off, you *fuckers*," I growl, searching along the ledge for another loose rock. "I'm 90% gristle, anyway."

Fuck.

Dawn feels like a century away.

I spend the night in a hellish game of King of the Mountain, keeping the creatures at bay with some choice words and desperate kicks. By the time the first hint of light touches the horizon, my arms are leaden, my throat raw, and my leg a throbbing mess of pain.

But I'm alive. Somehow.

Then, something strange happens.

The sand below shifts. Not from the creatures, but a deeper vibration, a swell beneath the surface as if something massive is stirring. As one, the shadow creatures scatter, melting back into the darkness as if fleeing something far worse than them.

I don't wait to find out what. When the sun is high enough to see, I look down. My leg is a bloody, throbbing disaster. And as I turn my head, my heart sinks. I'm completely disoriented. I have no idea which way Justine's arrow was pointing. I am utterly and completely lost.

The thought doesn't feel dramatic anymore. It feels like a fact.

I'm going to die out here.

And Justine...Poor Justine...

I wipe my eyes, but the tears keep coming down. Numb, I push myself up and start walking. When I lift my water sachet to my lips and just a single drop falls on my tongue, despair almost consumes me whole.

The cave appears like a cruel joke at first. Just a dark smudge halfway up a crumbling rock face. I stare at it for a long moment. Can I even reach?

But hope is a hell of a drug.

I crawl toward it. Dragging my mangled leg, I haul myself up the rock face one agonizing inch at a time. When I finally pull myself inside, the cool, dark air feels like heaven.

"Jus?" I croak, knowing it's useless. My voice echoes back. I sound...desperate. Lost.

I collapse into the cool shade, ready to let the darkness take me. And that's when I hear it.

Not voices. Not footsteps. Not the sound of my sister calling my name.

Pitter...patter.

I freeze before slowly lifting my head.

9

That soft, echoing drip might as well be a symphony. My body moves, harsh gasps of air grating past my throat as I crawl deeper into the darkness, following the sound like a lifeline. When my fingers finally brush against the slick stone and the shallow pool gathered there, I nearly sob.

I drink like a dying woman. Because that's exactly what I am.

The water is cool and clean, a stark contrast to the fire spreading through my veins from the gash in my leg. It doesn't quench the fever, but it gives me a moment of gut-wrenching clarity.

I'm not going to make it out of here. But Justine might. Someone else might follow.

I have to leave a sign. A sign that there's water.

The thought is a lightning bolt in the fog of my pain. It's not a plan; it's a compulsion.

Ignoring every screaming nerve in my body, I turn and drag myself back toward the blinding light of the cave entrance. Getting down the rock face is a controlled fall. Fiery agony that makes black spots dance in my vision.

Then I walk.

Or stumble. I don't know. My brain is on fire, and my only thought is to put distance between the cave and the sign, to leave a trail someone might cross. Every step is a fresh wave of nausea. The landscape is a blurry, swimming mess of orange and purple. I have no idea how far I've gone—maybe a hundred yards, maybe a mile.

Finally, my legs give out for the last time. I collapse onto my knees in the open sand, the impact jarring through my whole body. This is it. This is the spot.

With a shaking hand, I drag my finger through the sand, carving the symbols that have bound me and my sister together our whole lives.

J + J
4 EVER

Tears mix with the dust on my face. My movements are clumsy, my hand barely obeying. I add the last vital piece of information: a crude arrow pointing back in the vague direction I came from.

H_2O →

It's done. My last duty.

The journey back is a new kind of hell. It's a crawl. An inch-by-inch agony, my mind set on that dark smudge of the cave entrance, the only promise of shelter in this entire gods-forsaken world. I follow my own pathetic trail back, my body a dead weight I have to haul.

By the time I pull my broken body over the threshold and back into the cave's cool shade, there is nothing left. The last of my adrenaline vanishes, leaving only the deep, throbbing pain and the suffocating heat of the fever. I collapse near the water, unable to move another inch.

Back in the cave, I press a hand to my forehead. It's damp, even though my throat is so dry it aches. My stomach churns, the edges of my vision blurring as the fever overtakes me. My limbs feel heavy, my breaths shallow, and the world tilts, slipping in and out of focus.

Time...slows.

When something shifts at the entrance of the cave, the sound is so faint I could have imagined it. My head rolls as I lift it, my heart pounding weakly in my chest.

There's a shadow there.

"Jus?"

But the shadow is too tall. Too broad. Motionless as carved stone.

Maybe it's another fever dream. Maybe I'm already dead.

But one truth cuts through the delirium:

I am not alone here.

And perhaps, neither was my sister.

CHAPTER 3
NOT PREY, BUT POSSIBLY STILL LUNCH-SIZED (A HUNTER'S DILEMMA)

THARN

I have never hunted a female before.

Mere sols ago, I did not believe they existed outside the clan's ancient stories. Now I stalk one across the dust, and the very air feels different.

She moves with a clumsy urgency that is neither prey nor predator. Not the careful prowl of a shadowmaw. Not the heavy trudge of a rock-beast. Something new. Something fascinating.

Something potentially dangerous.

I crouch, studying the marks in the sand. Small prints, too perfect to belong to any creature native to Xiraxis. No claws. No tail-drag. Just neat impressions, each one placed one in front of the other, if unsteadily.

My claw traces the edge of one print. Smaller than mine by half. How can something so small be a thing of legend? How can something this delicate be real?

Rok's female, Jus-teen, had spoken of this female with such

longing. Her clumsy mental images had been clear: "*Find her. Please, Tharn. Find my sister.*"

Jah-kee.

Rok is my clan-brother. Finding Jus-teen's sister-female was my duty. But the clan has changed. Since Rok returned with Jus-teen, every male walks with a new tension. We watch him. We watch his female. We wonder.

But there is more. Another reason I took the hunt.

Since the females came, my blood runs hot. My sleep is thin. There is a hunger that has no name, because meat does not kill it. My body is a stranger to me.

To track another female... it is not just a rescue. It is a hunt for a cure to this new madness.

Shaking these thoughts away, I return to the trail. For solmarks, I've been tracking her, following her increasingly erratic path across the dust. She travels by Ain's light, and sometimes too far past when Ain retires.

Her trail leads toward a cluster of stone spires reaching up from the dust. I quicken my pace, eager to close the distance. But as I approach the spires, I notice something that makes me freeze mid-stride.

A red tinge. Dark against the orange rock. The ever-shifting dust tried to hide it, but the truth is clear to a tracker's eye.

Lifeblood.

My dra-kir gives a hard, steady thump as I crouch, touching one claw to the mark. It's dry, but recent.

My head snaps up as I scan the area, nostrils flaring. The scent is faint but unmistakable.

Shadowmaw.

She was hunted.

I follow the trail, alarm growing with each new evidence of the dark liquid against the dust. There is too much.

The lifeblood leads upward to a rocky outcropping where

signs of struggle mar the stone. Claw marks. More lifeblood. Loose rocks. The unmistakable pattern of a desperate climb.

She did not just run. She fought back. And she climbed.

A smart move to escape the pack. But as my eyes scan the base of the rock again, a cold dread settles deep in my gut, heavier than any fear of shadowmaws.

Circular patterns trace through the sand, barely visible even to my trained eye.

The sister-female didn't just face shadowmaws. She attracted the attention of something far worse.

And she survived.

The lifeblood trails away from the outcropping, staggered, but definitely made by something still alive.

A sharp flicker of respect cuts through my alarm. This is no simple, fragile thing to be coddled. This female has a fighter's spirit that burns brighter than Ain's own light. She's proven herself worthy of the hunt.

No. Not hunt, Tharn. *Rescue.* I must remember she is not prey, despite how the tracking of her makes my lifeblood sing.

Her trail leads to a rock face, cracked and weathered by countless cycles of Ain's wrath. At first, I see no sign of the female. Then I notice a dark opening halfway up the stone—a cave mouth, perfectly positioned to catch Ain's last light while providing shade during the harshest hours.

And there, leading up to it...more lifeblood.

She is in there. I can feel it.

I scale the rock face easily, claws finding purchase where her small hands must have struggled. At the cave mouth, I pause, scenting the air. Yes, there is her strange smell, mixed with the metallic tang of lifeblood.

And there, curled against the far wall beside a tiny pool of water, lies the sister-female.

Jah-kee.

She is smaller than Jus-teen, though similar in form... dressed in similar torn hide coverings. And she's damaged. Badly. Her breathing comes in short, sharp bursts. Her body trembling with each inhale, each exhale.

"*Do not fear,*" I project into the silence of her mind. "*I am ally. Not foe.*"

When I move closer, a wave of heat rolls off her small body. Too much heat. This is not just venom-fire.

The wound on her leg is deep. Swollen. Angry. My eyes see this. My mind knows it is the threat.

But my eyes betray me. They wander.

Her face. It is... soft. No sharp angles. No battle lines carved into the jaw. Just smooth curves. Her mouth is full. Her head-fur, dark like deep canyon sand, is tied back, but strands cling to her skin like dark vines.

No scales. No hard hide. Only skin. So soft, it looks like a thorn could tear it. Her legs are long, but thin. Not shaped for a strong stance. Not made for this world.

How did my ancestors come to worship such fragile beings?

And yet... a strange feeling twists in my gut. A tightness. This softness... it is beautiful. Not like the dawn. It is the beauty of a new, sharp spear tip. The beauty of a shadowmaw's eyes before it strikes. Dangerous.

Something inside me stirs. A deep growl. It is a feeling I do not know. It tells me to back away. It tells me to stay. It tells me to... guard this place. This female.

By Ain's light... *What is this madness?*

I force my gaze from her face to the wound on her leg. The wound is the only thing that matters.

She needs water. Sustenance. Care for her wounds. The dried lifeblood on her leg concerns me most. Shadowmaw venom festers quickly, even when not directly bitten.

I reach for my waterskin, uncorking it with ease. Her condition worries me. Even Jus-teen wasn't this damaged when Rok found her. Fire isn't meant to be trapped within.

I reach forward, careful to be gentle as my claws brush her head fur. The moment my claw makes contact, light explodes beneath my skin. A violent, golden radiance erupts from my hand, searing up my arm in a blinding wave. I jerk back with a startled snarl, claws unsheathing as I stare at my hand. The light pulses, a frantic, silent beat that matches the sudden, wild hammering of my dra-kir. It races across the patterns on my shoulders like a fire with no heat, consuming me.

What—by the Giving Stone—*what is this?*

The female moans. It's a soft, yearning sound. Her back arches slightly, her lips parting as if my light has seeped into her dreams.

And dust take me, my *member* twitches in its pouch with a life of its own.

What—in the dust?

Is this what happens when males and females touch?

I go utterly still, as if movement might worsen the sensation. This has never happened before. Rok never mentioned this with Jus-teen. Never described light, warmth, or this tightness in the chest that accompanies it. Perhaps it's unique to this female. Or to me.

Or to the combination of us both.

The thought sends a thrill of pure terror through me.

The glow intensifies as I reach for her again. My claws tremble as they brush her head-fur—dust and stones, it's so soft—and I force myself to focus. Her condition is critical. Whatever is happening to me must wait.

"*Jah-kee,*" I project through the distraction, the thought weaker than it should be as my concentration fractures. "*Drink.*"

She doesn't respond. Her lips remain slack, her mind closed.

I try again, fighting to steady myself as the light pulses brighter.

"*Female. Water. Drink.*"

Still nothing. Only the shallow rise and fall of her chest.

With a single digit that now trembles with both the glow and uncertainty, I part her lips and trickle water between them.

Mouths are not particularly interesting. They're for eating. But hers...

Her lips are soft, pliant. Nothing like mine or my brothers'. The sensation makes my claw shake harder, and I nearly spill the water.

Water is precious. Every drop spilled is a small death on Xiraxis.

Despite my care, some water trickles down her chin. I catch the escaped drops with my free hand and take them within my own mouth, unwilling to waste even this small amount. The clan would be horrified at my inefficiency, but I cannot keep my claw from trembling.

When her throat moves in a weak swallow, I release a breath. Thank Ain, some got through.

It's a painfully slow process, but I continue feeding her, hoping she will take more. All the while, the glow never dims. It pulses softly beneath my skin, as if it has a will of its own. That thought terrifies me. That part of me that has always been in perfect control of my body, my instincts, my dra-kir.

By the time a quarter of the waterskin is empty, I am both relieved and unsettled.

Relieved because her breathing has steadied slightly. Unsettled because every moment I spend tending to her, I feel myself being drawn deeper into her strangeness.

Perhaps the light affects my mind as well as my body.

Now, the wound.

The gash is deep. She continued through the dust with such an injury? The pain would have been searing...and still she carried on.

I marvel at this. The tales spoke of the Daughters of Ain as wise, powerful beings who commanded the elements. This small creature before me seems neither wise about Xiraxis nor particularly powerful. Yet she survived where most would have perished.

I retrieve my satchel, selecting firebloom leaves that will fight the shadowmaw venom. Crushing the leaves in my palm, I squeeze until they form a paste.

As I apply the mixture to the wound, the female's body jerks, a small sound escaping her lips. Not vocalizations. This sound is soft. High and vulnerable.

"*I am sorry, small female.*" I work more gently, trying to minimize her discomfort. "*I do not wish to harm you.*"

I do not expect her to respond. Her mind is closed, her body weak. But then her hand suddenly shoots out.

Small, soft, clawless digits close around my wrist.

I flinch, nearly dropping the paste. My dra-kir hammers against my chest, and for a moment, I freeze. My first thought is that she has attacked me, but... no. Her grip is weak, trembling against my skin.

I stare at her hand, then at her face. Her eyes remain closed, her breathing faint. She has not woken.

"*What are you doing?*" I project, glancing at her face as if she might answer. "*I am not... something to catch.*"

I try to pull my wrist free, but her fingers tighten slightly, as if even in her unconscious state, she refuses to let go.

And where our skin touches...

More light.

But where before it was merely bright and pulsing, now it swirls.

I stare at our joined hands, at the patterns of light dancing beneath my skin. The sensation of a bone lodging in my throat makes me swallow hard.

I am a hunter. I am controlled. *I do not crave strange sensations.*

And yet, I do not remove her hand. I am ever aware of the sensation of her touch. There is warmth there, as if her small grasp is burning an imprint into my flesh. I finish treating her wound, gaze shifting to her hold on me even as I wrap the wound with fresh leaves to keep the poultice in place.

Through gentle movements, almost as if I don't want to disturb her hold on me (which is ludicrous), I settle back on my haunches, considering my options.

I cannot leave her alone here while I venture far for assistance. Worse, I cannot take her with me. In her condition, she might not survive the trip. Better to stay, to help her recover enough strength for travel.

And perhaps, whispers a thought, to discover more about this light between us. About why my dra-kir beats differently in her presence. About why I'm drawn to study the lines of her face when I should be focused only on her survival.

"*Jah-kee,*" I project again. "*Rest. Tharn will protect you.*"

But rest does not come. I sit guard, a sentinel between her and the dangers of the dark, her touch a burning imprint on my skin. When Ain's first light begins to touch the horizon, I check her condition. The fire has not quelled, but it has not worsened. She needs meat. I must hunt.

Prying her fingers from my wrist feels like tearing away a part of my own hide. The absence of her touch is immediate and unnerving. Growling at my own foolishness, I descend from the cave.

The hunt is fast, efficient. A sand runner, its meat tender enough for a weakened body. Laden with fresh meat and a full waterskin, I make my way back, my mind focused on the strange, vulnerable female.

But as I approach the base of the rock face, I pause. There's something in the sand. Crouching, I peer down at the tracks. Shadowmaw. They must have arrived after I departed. I'm studying their passage when something prickles at the back of my neck.

I'm being watched.

My head snaps up...and there she is.

Jah-kee.

Ain. She is there. Looking at me.

My dra-kir, always so reliable and steady, does an unreasonable flip in my chest.

She's awake.

Perched at the cave's entrance, the dying light of Ain catches in her wild, tangled hair, haloing her in gold. But it's her eyes that stop me dead. Wide, unblinking, the whites showing all around that strange blue.

She doesn't blink. Doesn't move. Just stares down at me, wide-eyed and trembling, like I've already torn her limb from limb. Her strange blue eyes burn with a mix of fear and fury that tightens my chest in a knot.

And I realize with a jolt that shakes me to my core: she does not see a rescuer.

She sees a monster.

CHAPTER 4

HALLUCINATIONS 101: PLEASE TAKE A SEAT

JACQUI

My palms tingle where I clutch my weapon too tight. I press myself deeper into the shadows of the cave, my heart slamming against my ribs.

Before me, at the base of the rock face, is a hallucination. It has to be.

Because I'm looking at an honest-to-God man.

A *naked* man.

I squeeze my eyes shut, then open them again like a reboot will somehow help.

He's tall. Impossibly muscled. With golden-bronze skin that looks so rich, he must be painted.

My dehydrated, half-starved brain can't decide if he's a very creative hallucination my dying mind conjured to seduce itself, an actual threat who inexplicably moisturizes, or proof I've been alone in this desert exactly three days too long.

Jacqui, you're losing your marbles. Officially. That tall shadow

I saw before I passed out must have been the opening act, because this is the main performance.

At least the predators I ran into had the decency to be horrifying in a traditional way. This? This is worse. This is confusing.

My head pounds, but the raging fire of the fever has lessened. My throat isn't a desert of its own anymore, just raw. And the wound on my leg... it throbs, but it doesn't scream. It feels... different.

The hallucination crouches, examining something on the ground. My tracks, probably. I hadn't been careful. But does it matter if this is all in my head?

Jacqui, you fool, hallucinations don't kick up sand when they walk. They don't cast shadows. And they definitely don't tilt their heads like wolves scenting prey.

My breath ceases as his head snaps up.

Golden eyes lock onto mine, piercing through the shadows like he's found the only source of water in this entire wasteland. The look is so intense, so focused, it steals the air from my lungs.

Oh, fuck. Predators aren't supposed to look at you with that much... hunger. And it doesn't feel like the "I want to eat you" kind.

My heart plummets as he begins to climb, his massive form ascending the rock face with an ease that makes my own desperate scramble feel laughable. I raise my weapon, the pathetic shard of metal trembling in my grip.

He appears in the entrance, his massive form blocking the light. His copper auburn hair casts his face in shadow, but I can see the sharp glint of fangs. The memory of the shadow creatures, of their claws and screeches, slams through me.

Survival instinct overrides everything. I lunge, swinging

the warped metal with all the strength my exhausted body can muster.

He doesn't even flinch.

The weapon connects with his arm—and bounces off like I've just hit solid rock.

He moves then, faster than anything his size should be capable of, catching my wrist in a grip that's firm, almost crushing.

"No!" I thrash. Wildly. Kicking and scratching. I even try biting him. I use every dirty trick I've ever learned. But it's useless. He restrains me with insulting ease, pinning me to the cave floor with my arms above my head, his weight distributed so I can't move but can still breathe. Pain lances in my wrist.

"Get...OFF me!" I scream, knowing it's useless but unable to stop fighting. "Let...me...go!"

There's a grunt in his throat, a wince as he turns his head away from me. His brows furrow as if *I'm* the one causing *him* pain. And in that moment of pinned desperation, my frantic eyes catch sight of my own leg.

There's something stuck to my calf. A poultice of dark, crushed leaves, clinging to my skin right over the gash.

My fevered brain stumbles, short-circuiting.

I didn't do this. I was delirious. Bleeding out. I don't know these plants. Someone—or something—tended my wound while I was unconscious.

The thing currently pinning me to the floor... also played nurse?

The thought is so absurd, so impossible, that my struggles cease for a single, stunned second.

And in that second, it happens.

I open my mouth to scream again when, like an easily distracted infant, my eyes catch on something impossible.

Light.

Where his skin touches mine...light blooms. It's subtle at first. A faint golden glow that pulses between us where his clawed fingers grip my wrists. Then it intensifies, spreading up his arms like a firework, illuminating the cave like a signal fire.

He jerks back as if he's been burned, releasing me and stumbling to his feet. His pupils blow wide, swallowing the amber of his eyes until there's almost none left.

For one terrifying heartbeat, I recognize his expression. It's the same look I had when I first saw this godforsaken desert. Pure, animal shock. The kind that bypasses language and culture and whatever evolutionary tree he climbed. A low, guttural sound escapes him. Clearly distressed.

I scramble backward, too stunned to run. *What the hell was that?* Alien static shock? Some kind of defense mechanism? My frazzled brain serves up the absurd image of golden pollen, except made of light instead of plant matter. Which is ridiculous. There are no flowers in this wasteland. Just death and dust and whatever he is.

And why is he acting like *he's* the one who got zapped? *I'm* the one who should be clutching her chest and making wounded noises. Not him—all seven feet of sculpted alien menace currently looking at me like I just rearranged his DNA with a touch.

I grip my wrist, barely aware of the blood there as I shuffle farther away from him, knowing that if he lunges for me again, there's nothing I can do. I'm clearly too weak to harm him, and even if I were at full strength, my efforts would be pointless.

Think of something, Jacqui. Think of a plan.

My eyes flick over the cave floor, searching for something, anything, and that's when something else catches my eye—a small object sitting on the cave floor. Something that glints in his fading light. Something familiar. Something impossible.

A butterfly earring. Golden and pink crystal.

Justine's earring. The twin of the one currently burning a hole against my breastbone.

The air leaves my lungs.

We both notice it at the same time. His body goes rigid. My vision narrows to that single, tiny object on the dusty floor.

For a moment, we just stare at it. Then, with terrifying slowness, he reaches down.

I flinch, but he only retrieves the earring, holding it between clawed fingers like it might dissolve. His eyes flick to mine, searching. Then slowly, he places it on the ground between us.

He's...not keeping it. He's offering it?

What...the...

My mind races with possibilities. He's killed her and taken it as a trophy. No, he wouldn't offer it back. He's found her body. No, he wouldn't look so purposeful, so intent.

"Justine?" I whisper, her name scraping past my raw throat. "Where did you get this? Is she...is she alive?"

Something flickers across his face. Pain? Regret? He doesn't answer. He just tilts his head, those piercing golden eyes locked on my lips as if he's trying to decipher the very shape of my words. It's disturbingly close to how my neighbor's dog used to watch me when I offered it a treat.

But this isn't a dog.

This is a seven-foot-tall alien warrior who glows when he touches me. And he knows where my sister is.

CHAPTER 5

MY CAVEMATE IS A NUDIST (AND OTHER PROBLEMS)

JACQUI

My entire being feels suddenly weak. I slide down the cave wall, eyes still fixed on the earring. After so long searching, waiting. Of alternating between hope and despair. Of imagining the worst...

And now this... exhibitionist. This giant, golden, terrifying... exhibitionist... has Justine's other earring.

Her earring.

I'm swimming in too many emotions to process. Relief collides with fear, hope tangles with confusion, and somewhere deep down, a flicker of gratitude burns hotter than I want it to.

He's the one who tended my wounds while I was at death's door, wasn't he.

He hasn't attacked me; only reacted to defend himself.

I raise my eyes to him, really taking him in now that the shock has temporarily replaced fear. His proportions are almost human, but *wrong* in ways that keep setting off alarms in my brain. His shoulders are too broad, his limbs too long, and his ears are not rounded like mine, but sweep up to elegant, knife-like points. His features are just alien enough to unsettle me without fully crossing into monstrous.

And those eyes.

Golden, unblinking, and too intense. They study me with a predator's focus, like they're cataloging every breath I take, every micro-expression I make.

And yet...

He placed the earring between us like an offering. A message?

The alien shifts, gliding like some kind of giant jungle cat, which is just plain unfair for something that big. He watches me with this intense stillness, like I'm a scared little bunny and he's afraid I'll bolt. Buddy, look in a mirror. I am not the one people run from here.

Lifting one clawed hand, he points first to the earring, then in a direction over his shoulder. I blink at him, almost too afraid to acknowledge what he's trying to tell me. But the message is clear: *She's that way. I can take you to her.*

My throat constricts around words I'm afraid to voice. If I speak them, if I let myself believe...

"Justine?" I finally croak. "My sister. Is she alive?"

He winces when I speak. Actual physical pain flickers across his face, but he doesn't reply.

"Do you know where she is?"

No response. But his eyes remain fixed on mine with unmistakable intelligence. Unnerving, in fact.

Slowly, he reaches for something tied to his waist—some kind of pouch—and pulls out...is that a stomach? A dried animal bladder? It sloshes.

He extends it toward me, carefully, like he's offering treasure instead of what looks like a grotesque science experiment.

Water.

It has to be water. Nothing else would make that sound.

I don't care if it's camel piss or recycled colon juice at this point. My fingers shake as I reach for it, the promise of liquid overriding every survival instinct screaming *don't trust alien beverages.*

The moment my fingers close around the waterskin, his entire body tenses. For a split second, as our knuckles brush, I think I see a faint spark, like static electricity on a dry day. He pulls his hand back quickly, a low grunt rumbling in his chest, but my grip is already ironclad.

Okay, so the hot alien is a little jumpy. Noted.

But that's not as important as the liquid in my grasp.

I don't care about decorum. Don't care if I'm gulping like a dying animal at an oasis. The container smells faintly of herbs and something earthy, but the water itself tastes clean. Better than the metallic tang of our emergency rations.

It's cold. Perfect.

I'm halfway through draining it when I notice him still watching me.

He's standing so absolutely still, staring at my throat with something between fascination and alarm.

When I drain half the skin in one go, a strangled sound escapes him. Like I've just committed a crime against his entire species.

"What?" I rasp, wiping my mouth. "You offered it to me."

His claws twitch like he wants to snatch it back.

Maybe his people sip.

Maybe the undignified burp that escapes my throat gives him the ick. All I know is he's looking at me like I've just performed a magic trick by doing the most basic mammalian function.

29

I thrust the waterskin back at him, and this time, our fingers lock for a solid second.

Light doesn't just spark. It explodes.

A brilliant golden fire erupts between us. It races up his arm, mapping veins and patterns under his skin that I shouldn't be able to see. He jerks away with a sharp hiss, stumbling back a step and cradling his hand to his chest as if I've physically burned him. The violent pulse of light subsides, but it doesn't disappear. It settles, leaving a soft, steady glow beneath his skin.

For a moment, we just stare at each other. His nostrils flare wide as he inhales deeply, his golden eyes wide with pure, animal shock. My skin does a strange prickling thing that I'm not sure is actually from fear.

I swallow hard, gesturing to my calf. "You did this?"

His gaze snaps to the plant matter stuck to my wound. Something unreadable passes across his face. Then he looks at me again, like he's trying to tunnel through my skull and into my brain.

I break eye contact, pushing myself up straighter. "I'm going to take that as a yes. You're the only thing I've encountered in this wilderness apart from those shadow creatures that wanted me for dinner." I pause, swallowing hard. "Thank you."

My wrist aches where his claw had pricked me earlier, but the pain feels distant. Unimportant.

All that matters is the earring between us, and what it means.

"And if you've helped me...that means maybe you helped my sister, too."

When I meet his gaze again, he's looking at me in that same way. Still clutching his chest as the glow pulses beneath his skin, even as he stares at me so hard I actually feel a dull sensation behind my eyes.

I don't wait for whatever silent conversation he wants to have. My legs tremble as I force myself upright, swaying slightly with the effort. Weakness and hunger pull at me, but determination pushes back. I wipe the blood from my wrist onto my already filthy clothes without a second glance.

Steadying myself against the cave wall, I point at the earring, then toward the desert beyond the entrance. My voice comes out hoarse but determined: "Take me to her."

He doesn't move.

His expression shifts in subtle, alien ways that are hard to describe. The tightening around his eyes. The slight flaring of his nostrils. I can't interpret it, but it clearly means something.

I take a shaky step forward, then another. My body betrays me with a stumble, but I catch myself.

"Come on," I say, each word pulled from somewhere deep. "Show me where you found her."

The alien's expression shifts. The muscles in his jaw tighten. A low, sharp grunt escapes him. A sound of pure negation.

My gaze snaps to his. "What do you mean, *no?*" I take another shaky step forward. "If my sister is alive," I say, each word pulled from somewhere deep. "I need to go to her. Now."

The moment I stagger toward the exit, he moves faster than I can track, blocking the cave entrance with his massive body.

I freeze as his glowing skin illuminates the space between us.

Who the hell is he? How did he meet Justine? And where did he come from?

I freeze, glaring up at him. "Move."

He doesn't. Instead, he simply points one long, clawed finger at my leg. At the wound. Then he gestures to me, his hand making a slow, falling motion, mimicking my earlier collapse. His meaning is brutally clear.

You are too weak. You will fall.

"I don't care," I lie, my voice trembling with a mixture of fury and frustration. "I'll crawl if I have to. I'm excellent at crawling. I did it for a whole year when I was a baby."

He meets my glare, his golden eyes unwavering. Then he points to himself, taps his own broad chest, and points to me again. The gesture is so simple, so primal, it bypasses language entirely. *I will care for you. I will decide when you are ready.*

Oh, hell no. *'I will decide when you are ready'?* Excuse me? Has he met me? I've been successfully ignoring unsolicited advice from men my entire life; I'm not about to start taking it from a seven-foot-tall *naked* one who thinks a grunt is a complete sentence.

He then gestures to the back of the cave, where I'd been resting. An order. A clear, non-negotiable command. *Rest.*

I should argue. Should scream and throw rocks. Should insist we leave immediately. But my legs wobble beneath me, my vision spotting with exhaustion.

He's right.

And damn him, knowing he's right is the most infuriating part of all. I haven't eaten anything proper in days. I'm tired. Hungry. Even with the water he's provided, my body is running on empty. I wouldn't make it a hundred yards.

My shoulders slump. For once, I listen to my body instead of my stubbornness. It's the rational choice, I tell myself. No point in getting eaten by desert monsters when I'm this close to finding Justine.

As I slump against the cave wall, sliding down until I'm seated on the cool stone floor, my gaze slides back to him. This golden-skinned, copper-haired, naked alien who's appeared out of nowhere with my sister's earring and water to share.

Who somehow made light appear between us.

Who wants to take me to Justine.

The earring still lies between us, a tiny fragment of my world in this alien place. He notices me looking at it and, with those careful movements, as if he's trying not to startle me, he picks it up again.

This time, he extends his hand, offering it to me directly.

Close enough to feel the heat radiating off his golden skin. Close enough that the air between us prickles with static.

He goes utterly still, not breathing, not blinking, as if waiting for a detonation.

I snatch the earring without contact.

His exhale is audible.

Mine burns in my chest.

Even though I just took a drink, my throat goes dry and I clench my teeth, watching as he eases back.

The earring is heavier than I remember, the cool metal biting into my palm. My chest tightens, tears threatening behind my eyes, but I blink them away before they can fall.

For the first time since I'd set out to find Justine, hope warms me more effectively than this planet's blazing sun.

Justine is alive.

This strange being knows where she is.

And tomorrow, he'll take me to her.

The desert holds twenty-seven ways to die.

But as his golden eyes lock onto mine in the deepening twilight, a new thought takes root. Maybe, just maybe, I've finally found the one way to survive. *And he is it.*

CHAPTER 6
INSTRUCTIONS NEEDED. THE FEMALE IS AWAKE (NOW WHAT?)

THARN

The female rests now.

I crouch at the edge of the cave, careful to keep my distance, watching the rise and fall of her small chest. So small. Small but loud. Dust, so *loud*.

Jah-kee. Sister-female of Jus-teen. A *miracle*.

She shifts in her rest, making a small pained sound that grates against my ears even as it makes me instantly alert. Her face tightens, brows drawing together. Pain? Hunger? Thirst?

I reach for my waterskin. Surely, she couldn't need more so quickly. She'd consumed the water I offered like a creature dying of thirst, gulping so quickly I'd feared she might choke. Already, she's consumed enough to last me seven sols.

Female? I project the thought carefully, keeping it gentle. *Jah-kee? Are you in pain?*

Nothing. Not even a flicker of recognition in the mindspace.

I try again, louder.

34

JAH-KEE. HEAR THARN?

She doesn't stir. Dust! Jus-teen could hear me. She could hear Rok. What am I doing wrong? How did he get her mind-space to open?

I shift closer, carefully. When she first became aware of me, she attacked. An attempt that would have been amusing if not for the terror in her scent. Then when I'd restrained her...

My skin prickles at the memory. That strange light. It had filled me, racing through pathways I didn't know existed in my own body. And it had *hurt* this time. Hurt, yes, but also... *felt good*? It awakened something. Something I feel deep down but can't quite grab hold of.

I settle back on my haunches, sniffing the air, cataloging the scents clinging to her. Fear. Exhaustion. Pain. Hunger. The sharp tang of injury...

Wait. *Lifeblood?*

Fresh lifeblood.

She is bleeding.

I shift closer, panic thrumming with every beat of my dra-kir. If she is injured, I must find the wound. I have firebloom left; I can crush the leaves again. I'm already reaching for it when the female cracks one eye open.

The moment she spots me, she scrambles upright like a startled rock jumper, her back hitting the cave wall with a painful *thunk*. Her hand claws for her pathetic weapon—that jagged scrap of metal she'd tried to stab me with earlier—as her mouth spits sounds at me. Loud, sharp sounds.

Like a dust crab snapping at a predator ten times its size.

Ain.

My poor ear holes.

Still heavy with exhaustion, her gaze darts wildly around the cave before landing back on me. Then, inexplicably, drops lower.

Her nose wrinkles.

Ah.

She's looking at my pouch.

My member is not visible. Not like Rok's now is. He has... changed after claiming Jus-teen.

A hot rush of something sharp floods my veins.

Is that why Jah-kee doesn't recognize my mindspeak? Because I haven't... presented properly? Jus-teen entered the mindspace because Rok claimed her. I found Jah-kee in the dust, so now she is mine. The mere act of my finding her means I have claimed her. That is the law on Xiraxis. As simple as Ain rising each dawn and going to sleep before the dark.

But perhaps I need to claim Jah-kee in a way she understands. Perhaps that is how she will enter the mindspace.

Hmm. Females are strange; their customs even stranger. I am still learning. *We all are.*

Perhaps the sight of my member is... reassuring? Or maybe it's an offering? A gesture of goodwill? I've seen Jah-kee clutch the strange creature trapped in crystal for comfort. Perhaps females need to see things to trust them.

I tilt my head, considering. That would explain why her gaze lingered there, why her nose wrinkled. Perhaps she finds my lack of... presentation offensive. Or disappointing.

I stiffen, spine straightening. The thought of disappointing this strange soft thing is one I *DO NOT* like.

How do I do this? Do I need to... display it, like a gift?

I huff softly. This is complicated.

But if laying eyes on my member will bring Jah-kee into the mindspace, I must try. For her sake. For... understanding.

I curl my claws around the edge of my pouch, ready to slide it free, when a pained whimper cuts through my thoughts.

Her face tightens as she shifts, the movement pulling at a

wound along her wrist. One still weeping faint streaks of rust-scented blood.

I go still.

I've ripped apart many a kill to know the look of a wound made by my own claws.

No.

My gut twists.

I lean forward without thinking—

"Stay on your side, Goldilocks!"

—and freeze when she brandishes her weapon, her arm trembling but her glare searing.

I don't need mindspeak to understand that.

Slowly, I retreat, settling back on my haunches. She eyes me for another breath before slumping slightly, her grip on her weapon loosening. But not releasing. Never releasing.

Angry, stubborn, *loud* little thing.

Her vocalizations, thank the dust, go lower. She's still angry, still stubborn, still *loud*, but at least my ear holes aren't ringing anymore.

"Thanks for your help, but we're not friends, okay. You're still a stranger. Still a male—" (another glance at my pouch) "—kinda."

Her words may be meaningless, but her actions are clear enough. She doesn't trust me. Of course, she doesn't. She doesn't understand me, and she cannot hear me in the mindspace.

And that... that is my failure.

She must be claimed. Perhaps exactly like her sister-female was.

I recall the moment all too clearly. Jus-teen broadcasted it. The image of Rok crouched between her thighs, his tongue moving. The wet slurping sounds.

She shared water with him...from between her thighs.

The entire clan had seen it.

Water-sharing is sacred. If I drink from Jah-kee, she will be claimed. She'll hear me. Understand.

Or perhaps I must do both. Present myself first, *then* share her water.

Hmm. This is logical.

I square my shoulders. "*JAH-KEE*," I project, gesturing first to my pouch, then emphatically at her thighs. "*THARN WILL PRESENT AND LICK. FOR CLAIMING.* YOU WILL ENTER THE MINDSPACE AS YOUR SISTER-FEMALE HAS."

She blinks at me blankly.

Dust.

"JAH-KEE. THARN CLAIM NOW. MAKE YOU HEAR."

Nothing.

I huff. Clearly, I must demonstrate. I crouch abruptly, claws retracting.

"*I'll lick you now*," I announce. Uselessly, because she only blinks at me. Which is why I need to do this. "*Open.*"

When I gesture firmly at her thighs, her eyes do an alarming bulging thing.

"EXCUSE ME?!"

Ain's wrath. I'm sure her exclamation just burst a vessel in my ears.

She scrambles backward so fast her elbow cracks against stone.

"Oh my God, no. NO. Whatever the hell you're thinking —*stop.*"

The shiny weapon is back in her grip, jabbing the air between us.

I tilt my head. *Is she not producing water there?* Perhaps if I reveal my member, hers will produce water, and I can lick—

"I WILL STAB YOU IN THE EYE."

The vocalizations, though strained, don't miss their mark.

She points her weapon at me, close enough that it's directly in line with my right eye.

Why is she rejecting this?

Strange female. Does she truly mean to pierce my eye? Rok did not mention this as a possibility.

I pause, reassessing.

Perhaps I cannot go about it like this. Perhaps she needs to understand that belonging to me will be good. I will feed her and shelter her. I will make sure no harm comes to her in the dust.

"*Relax, female. I will not harm you.*"

It's clear she doesn't hear even a shadowy imprint of my thoughts. Even with my directing them straight at her. Her weapon remains raised, and she rubs at her wrist with a hiss, her fingers coming away smeared red.

Dust and bones.

I've hunted injured prey before. But this? This tiny, bleeding female glaring at me like I'm the threat when she can barely keep her eyes open?

This feels...wrong.

This is harder than tracking a sand serpent through the plains. At least then I know what to do. Track. Hunt. Kill. Simple. This... this is not simple. My claws dig into my thighs. Hunters don't apologize. Don't fret over scratches. But...*I hurt a female.* This miraculous, precious thing. And the way her scent sours with pain only feeds the guilt. I must fix this. Somehow.

I snatch my waterskin and toss it at her feet.

She jumps, then squints at me.

What does Rok do with Jus-teen again? Right, he has this new thing of baring his teeth at her, but not in a snarling way. Females do not like it when you snarl at them.

So I bare my teeth at Jah-kee, careful not to snarl.

She pales.

Dust. Wrong expression.

I try again, forcing my features into something softer.

She eyes me like I've grown a second head.

"Nope. Nope. Still terrifying." She weakly waves the shiny weapon. "Cave's big enough for two, okay? You stay over there, I'll stay here, and we'll have a staring contest until you're ready to take me to my sister."

Then she does the most curious thing. Her mouth stretches wide, revealing small, blunt teeth and a pink tongue. A long, wavering sound escapes her, and her jaw snaps shut with a click. Her whole body slumps as if the act has drained what little energy she had left.

"...*Did...did you just unhinge your jaw?*"

I watch, fascinated, as her head bobs. Once. Twice.

Then she's slumped against the wall again, weapon still clutched in her limp hand.

Resting. Mid-threat.

A fascinating, impossible creature.

Now, without her glaring at me, I shift ever so slightly closer, peering at the wound on her wrist. Shame fills me. *I* did that. It wasn't intentional. I'm not some untrained fool who can't control his strength. But females are so fragile...

My chest feels strange again, tight and uncomfortable. Is this... concern?

Hunters don't feel concern. We feel hunger, satisfaction, pride in the kill. Not... whatever this is.

Bones. I will make it up to her. I will make it right. As soon as I can, I will hunt. Bring her fresh meat. And not a small sand runner next time. I must bring her something bigger. Make a poultice to help her heal. And then we will head to her sister-female.

Whatever you find in the dust is yours. That's our way.

I found Jah-kee, so she is mine. But... not like a kill. Not something to throw over my shoulder and drag back to the clan caves.

No, females are different. Special.

This is a lesson my brothers will have to learn, too. Rok had no time to explain much, but I had observed. Jus-teen stayed with him willingly. Walked beside him, not behind or in front. Touched him without fear. Communicated with him.

"*I'll protect you,*" I project, more to myself than to her. "*I'll bring you to your sister-female Jus-teen. To my clan. I will keep you safe.*"

A strange mixture of pride and... something else rises within me.

Something that makes me want to hunt every shadowmaw on Xiraxis just to see if she would make that sound again. The one she made when I handed her the creature trapped in crystal. That small gasp of hope.

I've never cared about sounds other than those that help me hunt. Never cared about the reactions of others unless they affected the clan's survival.

But I want to hear that sound again.

Want to be the cause of it.

I settle in for the long dark ahead, watching over the small, fragile female who somehow makes me feel both powerful and completely helpless at the same time.

I've never felt helpless before. Never had reason to.

I am Tharn, second hunter. First tracker. I take what I want. I find what I seek.

I do not fail.

Jah-kee.

Precious female.

My new hunt.

The strangest hunt of all.

CHAPTER 7
IF LOOKS COULD KIDNAP

JACQUI

I wake to find golden eyes directly in front of my face.

"Jesus!" I jerk back, skull cracking against stone. "Ouch!" Pain explodes behind my eyes, turning my vision white for a terrifying instant. It only highlights the already harsh pounding in my head.

When my vision clears, he's still there. Seven feet of naked alien crouched barely an arm's length away.

My head throbs with each heartbeat, a vicious pounding that makes even blinking hurt. I thought I was getting better. It's gotten worse again. Hunger, dehydration, or maybe just the stress of having a giant gold man staring at me like I'm the most fascinating bug he's ever found.

Whatever the cause, it feels like someone's drilling through my temples with rusty screwdrivers.

I fumble for my weapon, fingers closing around the familiar metal. My arms feel like lead, but I manage to lift it between us. The movement makes my vision swim.

"Hey," I rasp. "Remember yesterday? This is just business. Keep your... whatever that was... to yourself."

The alien tilts his head, those eerie eyes unblinking. Does he even need to blink? This close, I can just about see that they're a beautiful amber-gold, speckled with white flecks that make it look like there's a whole universe in there.

It's beautiful.

But then the memory of him gesturing toward my thighs comes rushing right back, and I scowl. That was universal speak for 'can I see your panties?', wasn't it?

"Some things transcend species, apparently—like being a creep."

My weapon wavers even as I gesture at him to back up. He doesn't move, just watches with that unsettling intensity. Then, slowly, he shifts backward, giving me space.

Wait. He understood that?

I squint at him through the hammering pain in my skull. He's...respecting my boundaries? That would be hilarious if I weren't so tired. A naked alien wild man actually listening to what I say when human men find that simple task challenging? An Earth-shattering concept, I'm sure.

I slump back against the wall, suddenly aware of how vulnerable I've been. I fell asleep again. I actually fell asleep with this... alien...in the cave. He could have done anything to me while I was out. Killed me. Eaten me. Attempted whatever he was suggesting with that thigh gesture.

But he didn't.

The waterskin sits within reach, as if he put it there so I could reach it as soon as I woke. Despite wanting to grab it and quench my thirst, my gaze slides past it to what lies beyond.

Laid out on flat stones is... food. A *lot* of food.

Dominating the makeshift table is what can only be described as a nightmare with fins. It looks like someone crossbred a manta ray with a porcupine, resulting in a flat, wing-like body topped with a massive spiny fin running along its length. Its mouth is mercifully closed, but even dead, the thing looks ready to snap at any fingers that venture too close.

Beside this monster are several smaller creatures, lizards of some kind, with scales that shimmer with an iridescent blue-green sheen that would be beautiful if they weren't, you know, *dead alien reptiles*.

"You brought food..." My gaze shifts back to the alien. His eyes are locked on mine. Unreadable—but there's something there. A brightness. A spark.

Excitement?

My stomach twists. Why is he excited?

Before I can figure it out, he moves, his massive frame gliding with that frightening grace. He's heading toward the horrifying sand ray thing. I stiffen, but he doesn't seem to notice. Or care.

His claws unsheathe as he crouches beside the carcass, the deadly curve of them catching the light. For one terrifying second, I think he's about to attack me. But then he turns his attention fully to the creature.

The clicking sound comes again, softer this time, almost... pleased.

I stare, heart pounding, as he leans over the thing, his claws working with care. He's *opening* it. Peeling back layers of tough skin like he's done this a hundred times before.

My stomach churns.

And then it hits me.

Oh my God. He's preparing it.

For me.

He separates meat from bone, extracting a pale strip of flesh, free of spines and skin, and holds it out to me.

The reverence of his offering is unmistakable. Like he's

presenting me with the rarest delicacy, not a chunk of raw alien desert fish.

I stare at the glistening meat, then at him. His posture has changed. Back straight. Shoulders squared. Chin slightly raised. *Pride.* He's proud of this kill. He hunted this for me specifically, it seems.

"Um, thanks?" I say, reluctantly accepting the offering. Our fingers brush briefly, and that strange light phenomenon flickers beneath his skin before he jerks his hand back.

He watches with laser focus as I examine the meat. I sniff it cautiously. It smells... not terrible. Just raw.

My stomach rumbles, deciding for me. I take a small bite and chew. The texture is firm, almost like a very dense scallop. The taste is mild.

"Not bad," I admit, taking another bite.

The alien's eyes brighten. Literally. The amber-gold intensifies like the sun. He immediately returns to his butchering, carving more precise strips from the creature's back.

I point to the iridescent lizards. "What about those?"

He follows my gesture, then makes a dismissive motion with one hand, nudging them slightly away from the main spread.

"Not good?" I mime eating, then make a face, pointing at the lizards.

He hesitates, then reaches for one of the lizards. With swift precision, he slices into it, extracting a small portion of meat. He gestures to the manta-ray thing, then to the lizard, then back to the ray. His preference is clear.

"The ray is better?"

He just stares, and again, the focus in his gaze is so intense it feels like he's burning thoughts into my brain.

"Right," I mutter. "You don't understand a word I'm saying."

Of course, he doesn't understand. He's an alien.

Not like the Xyma who came to Earth with their universal translators and diplomatic smiles. This is a wild alien on a wild planet. Different rules entirely.

Wait. *Translator*.

My hand flies to my ear, feeling for the small device that should be there. The universal translator the Xyma provided us before we arrived on this hellscape.

It's gone.

"Shit," I hiss, patting my pockets. My gaze lands on my handbag, lying discarded against the cave wall. I lunge for it, upending the contents onto the stone floor. An empty chicken biscuit packet falls out, followed by an empty water sachet. Evidence of how close to death I'd actually been when Goldilocks found me.

Then there. It hits the cave floor and rolls down to my boot. I reach for it like it's gold.

"Please, God. I haven't asked for much this whole time. All I ask is for this to work." I push the thing into my ear, my gaze flying to the alien expectantly.

I'm not even sure how to turn it on. I give it a few taps before swallowing hard and looking at the alien again.

Of course, for it to work, he actually has to speak. Which he hasn't done since he found me here. To be honest, I'm not sure he *can* speak. Maybe his species is mute. Or maybe just him.

I clear my throat, pointing to myself. "Jacqui." I tap my chest. "Jah-kee."

That glow that appears beneath his skin flickers now. He makes a soft sound—not quite a word, more like a rumble deep in his chest.

"Your turn," I prompt, pointing to him.

Nothing. Just that unblinking stare.

"Fine, I'll call you Goldilocks, you know..." I gesture from his copper-red hair that gleams like metal to the rest of his golden-bronze body. "Because you're just right."

Wait, what? No. *Because of the hair. Just the hair.* Wait. His hair is red-copper, not gold, and wasn't she blonde? God, my head hurts. Thank God he can't understand me.

I take another bite of the ray meat, watching him as he continues his butchering. Every time I look away, my gaze keeps sliding back to him, and I tell myself it's because there's nothing else to look at.

He's scarred. Not just in a few places, but everywhere. Long slashes across his ribs. A puckered circle on his shoulder that looks like it might have been a puncture wound. A jagged line running from his collarbone down across his chest.

But despite his fearsome appearance—or maybe because of it—I find myself oddly at ease.

He had the twin of my sister's earring. If he wanted to hurt me, he's had plenty of opportunity. Instead, he's brought me water. Food. Treated my wound.

Annnd, he's watching me again, those amber eyes tracking my every movement with that strange intensity that should be unsettling but somehow isn't anymore. Not completely, anyway.

"It's morning," I mutter, gesturing toward the cave entrance where light streams in. "We need to go. You need to take me to Justine."

No response.

"Justine," I stress her name. "You do know who I'm talking about, right?"

I fish into my bra for the earring. His gaze follows my movements. Not my hand, but the way my boob shifts in the bra. His head tilts almost imperceptibly.

I clear my throat. His gaze flies to my neck instead. His

head tilts the other way. A strange little shiver goes through me. Good Lord. I really need to get rid of this delirium.

"This." I show him the earring. "You'll take me to her now, yeah?"

I put the earring away again and try to stand, but the cave tilts alarmingly. I brace myself against the wall, willing the dizziness to pass. Fuck.

Don't pass out. Don't pass out.

Blood rushes to my temples, making my skull pound harder.

Goldilocks is there instantly, one massive hand hovering near my elbow without quite touching me. Those deadly claws just inches from my skin, yet so carefully restrained.

"Thanks," I say, taking deep breaths as I sit back down, "But I'm fine."

He makes that clicking sound again, then reaches for something else—a small pouch. From it, he extracts a set of leaves that he crushes in his palm. The scent that rises is strongly herbal, and I recognize it as the same plant matter he'd put on my leg. He gestures to my head, then to the paste.

"Medicine?" I ask, pointing to my temple where the headache pounds the hardest. Maybe it will help the fever, too, which seems to be rising again.

He tilts his head to the side in a way that comes off not as confusion but as affirmation, and I realize with a start that while he may not understand my words, he's been under-standing plenty.

"Okay," I say cautiously.

I watch as he dips a finger into the paste, then pauses, holding it toward my mouth, not my temple.

I recoil slightly. "Wait, I'm supposed to *eat* that?"

He makes a soft, insistent sound, still offering the paste-covered finger. The hesitation in his eyes is unexpected. He's... asking consent with his gaze.

I sigh. "Fine. But if I croak, I demand a tombstone that reads: 'Here lies Jacqui — should've stuck to trust issues.'"

He doesn't get my joke, of course, and I'm just too weak and woozy to laugh.

I open my mouth, and he carefully places the medicine on my tongue. The moment his finger brushes my lips, that strange light ripples beneath his golden skin, pulsing outward from the point of contact. His jaw tightens, but he doesn't pull away this time. If anything, his movements become even gentler, more precise.

The paste is bitter and earthy, with an underlying spice that burns slightly. I swallow quickly, fighting the urge to gag. Almost immediately, it tingles pleasantly down my throat, then a cooling sensation spreads through my entire being.

"I probably shouldn't have eaten that," I murmur, resting my head back. "If I die, it will be my own damn fault."

The alien watches me intently, his golden eyes shifting over my face. I brace for worse pain, for my stomach to revolt...

Instead, second by second, the jackhammer in my temples slows its rhythm, until it's a bearable throb.

"Wow, it's..." I blink in surprise. "Actually helping."

He studies my face, searching for confirmation. I nod, offering a small smile of gratitude.

The moment my lips stretch, his gaze snaps to the movement. For a moment, he stills, then the transformation in his expression is unmistakable. His shoulders relax, the severe line of his mouth softening.

He's pleased by my approval.

The sight almost makes me chuckle.

I reach for the waterskin, needing to wash away the taste of that bitter medicine. The water is still cool, and I drink deeply.

When I lower it, I find him watching me with that same fascinated intensity. Another one of those strange shivers goes through me.

"You're staring again," I point out, wiping my mouth with the back of my hand.

He doesn't look away. Instead, he points to the ray meat, then to me, then makes a motion like he's growing stronger.

"Yes, I need to eat more," I agree, accepting another strip of the pale flesh. It's better than it looks, and my body is desperate for the energy.

As I bite in, I notice the way he keeps checking that I'm eating, that the paste is helping my head.

This isn't just a random alien who found me in the desert. This is someone who's made a decision to help me. To care for me, even.

Why?

The question burns in my mind as I finish another strip of meat. What does he want?

"We need to go," I say again, gesturing to the cave entrance. "Justine. My sister." I point to myself, then mimic another person next to me. "Sister."

He tilts his head, considering. Then he points to the food, to me, and makes a motion like drinking.

"Yes, I get it. Eat, drink, get stronger." I sigh. "But we need to find—"

A low, sharp click cuts through the cave, echoing off the stone walls. My eyes widen on him, even when some part of my brain knows it's not from Goldilocks.

His entire body snaps rigid, claws unsheathing to full lethal length. His pupils slit to needle-thin black lines in the amber-gold, every muscle locking as he whirls toward the cave entrance.

For one terrifying heartbeat, he's transformed.

The creature before me isn't the same one who carefully offered water. Who hunted and prepared food for me. Who treated my wound with such gentleness.

No—this is what he looks like when he means it.

That wasn't him being aggressive with me earlier.

That was him playing nice.

Every inch of him screams violence. His shoulders tense like coiled springs, and he snarls, giving me full view of his razor teeth.

The sound comes again, closer this time, before it branches into a staccato rhythm. It's a sound that makes a cold tendril of fear wrap itself around my spine.

I remember that sound. From the night I was chased by the shadow creatures.

It's them. They've found me here.

Goldilocks moves with shocking speed, positioning himself directly between me and the entrance. His body blocks my view completely, a living shield of muscle and lethal intent.

I grab my weapon, fingers tightening around the handle. My headache is still there, the fever is still there, but fear sends fresh adrenaline surging through me.

"D-do you think it can get up h-here?" I whisper, hating how my voice trembles.

He doesn't answer. Doesn't need to. The shadow that falls across the cave entrance tells me everything I need to know.

It's here.

And it's hungry.

CHAPTER 8

HOW TO KEEP YOUR FRAGILE, SCREECHING FEMALE ALIVE (A HUNTER'S GUIDE)

THARN

The sound comes first.

The clicking. High and sharp. Splitting the air like a bone spear against raw stone. My claws flex as I whip toward the entrance.

And there it is.

A shadowmaw.

Sleek and low to the ground, its body ripples with hard, black plates that catch the light as it moves. Its head is long and narrow, lined with serrated teeth. It slinks into the cave with those unnaturally smooth movements that make them terrifying in the dark.

It shouldn't be here. Not while Ain's light still shines. It has scented Jah-kee, but something has driven it here—hunger perhaps, or something worse. It lunges, bouncing off the wall, but it can't get to her. Not without going through me.

Behind me, Jah-kee releases a piercing scream. The sound cuts through me, but it only heightens my determination.

She is unwell with the fire raging beneath her skin. Unwell with the wound on her leg and the one I myself inflicted on her wrist. She cannot defend herself.

I will not let her come to harm.

I bare my fangs, lowering myself into a crouch. *"You will not have her,"* I tell the shadowmaw, the thought vibrating hard in the mindspace. The shadowmaw tenses, its long, sinewy tail flicking behind it. Then it lunges.

Its weight slams into me, sending us both crashing into the cave wall. Teeth snap inches from my neck, its breath hot and foul. I snarl, twisting my body to pin it down, but it's fast. Too fast. It slithers free, claws raking across my side, and I hiss as lifeblood slicks my skin.

Behind me, Jah-kee screams again, her voice raw and terrified. I can hear her scrambling, her back hitting the wall. She's trapped. The cave is too small. There's nowhere for her to go.

The shadowmaw moves toward her again. What an annoying ka'vrakt. It is relentless.

I lunge, catching its hind leg and dragging it back. My claws dig deep into its scaly hide, and it screeches in fury, whipping around to snap at me. I take the blow, its teeth sinking into my shoulder, hot pain flaring as lifeblood flows.

I don't stop.

I drive my claws into its flank, twisting hard. The shadowmaw thrashes, trying to dislodge me, but I hold firm, snarling as I force it away from Jah-kee. My lifeblood splatters the stone, but it doesn't matter.

I will bleed for her. This small, angry, loud little thing that I have come to care for the moment I knew of her existence.

The creature lunges again, its jaws aiming for my throat. I duck low, slashing upward with all the strength I have left. My claws rip through its neck, severing something vital.

The shadowmaw thrashes, its sounds growing frantic. Lifeblood spills over my claws.

I do not release my grip.

Not until the screeching stops. Not until the body goes limp. Not until I am certain, absolutely certain, that it poses no threat to Jah-kee.

For a moment, the cave is silent except for the ragged sound of my breathing.

I turn to Jah-kee.

She is pressed against the far wall, her strange weapon clutched in her hands. Her eyes are wide, pupils dilated with fear. And she is trembling.

Something cracks in my chest.

She is afraid. Of the shadowmaw? Of me?

I lower myself slowly, sheathing my claws as I huff softly. The movement pulls at the torn flesh of my shoulder, but I ignore it. I keep my movements slow, calm, despite the battle-blood still singing in my veins.

Alarm goes through me when her eyes lose the blue, rolling over to display pure white before she fights to steady herself again. Still fighting to remain vigilant. She is very unwell. Her breathing too rapid. The fire beneath her skin too much.

We cannot stay here. Shadowmaws are never alone. This shelter is no longer safe.

I need to take her somewhere secure. Somewhere I can protect her while her body fights the illness that has claimed her. Somewhere with water, with healing herbs.

Home.

I will take her home.

"Jah-kee," I project. Her gaze flickers to my face, then to the corpse of the shadowmaw, then back to me. Her body trembles like something caught in the cold.

"We must go now," I try again, the thought heavy with

urgency. This place is no longer safe. The shadowmaw's presence here—it defies the laws of Ain. It's a warning. A sign.

I reach for her, moving slowly, cautiously, not wanting to frighten her further. She watches me, those water-blue eyes fixed on mine. For a moment, I think she understands.

Then her eyes roll back once more. Only this time, they don't right themselves. Her weapon clatters to the stone floor, and she crumples.

I catch her before she can hit the ground, cradling her overheated body against my chest. The light in my skin roars to life where we touch, racing across my skin and sinking into hers.

There is no time to wonder at it now.

I gather her close, securing her against me with one arm while I collect the waterskin and medicinal pouch with the other. The food I must leave behind. Perhaps the shadowmaws hunting this female will sate themselves in what is left of the sandfin and cease their pursuit of her.

With Jah-kee held securely against my chest, I step over the shadowmaw's corpse and out into Ain's harsh light. Her body is limp. A small, burning weight in my arms. Her life-force feels thin, a flickering flame threatening to be extinguished by the slightest breeze.

I press my nose to her temple, inhaling her scent, and my dra-kir thunders in my chest. She is small. Fragile.

And she is mine.

I must move quickly.

I must get her home.

I must save her.

JACQUI

The sun beats down. It feels like it's trying to crush me into the sand, turning me into nothing more than dust.

Perhaps that's why this planet is so desolate. Maybe it's not covered in sand...maybe it's the remains of crushed bones from unfortunates like myself.

But I'm not on the ground.

I'm being carried.

His arms are solid around me, holding me close, his skin cool where it touches mine. My head lolls against his chest, and I can feel the steady thrum of his heartbeat beneath my cheek.

It's faster than I'd expect, frantic even, but the rhythm of it is...comforting.

Something to focus on as my consciousness wanes in and out.

Where his arms meet my fevered skin, his golden glow pulses softly, like trapped sunlight. It's beautiful. If I weren't so weak, I'd lift my hand to touch it.

But I can't.

I'm so, so tired.

A sob slips out before I can stop it, barely a sound, but enough to shake my chest. The tears abruptly follow, spilling down my cheeks despite how I try to hold them back.

I don't want to die.

Not here. Not like this.

Not until I've seen my sister again.

The alien stiffens beneath me, his muscles bunching suddenly. The movement presses me tighter against his chest.

"*No*," he growls, not in my ears, but *in my skull*. The vibration of it is a shock.

So...he *can* talk. His hand moves awkwardly to my face,

clawless now as he clumsily tries to...wait...what is he...is he trying to *push the tears back* into my skin? *"No, precious one. Do not do this."*

A desperate thumb tries to force a particularly large tear back into my eye.

"You must conserve your water. Do not lose hope. You must hold on a little longer."

His voice scrapes something raw inside me. A place so vulnerable it aches. Because this alien, this stranger, is now the only thing standing between me and death in this wasteland.

A sob rips free before I can choke it back.

His reaction is instantaneous. Almost frantic. A calloused palm smears against my cheek, catching tears before they can vanish into the dust. Like each one is a drop of water he can't afford to lose. Like *I'm* something he can't afford to lose.

"Stop that," I murmur. "You can't just... push them back in."

He speeds up. The world around us blurs as he moves faster, his breathing ragged, his heart hammering wildly beneath my jaw. I snuggle closer to it, letting its rhythm soothe me even as my body burns with fever.

It's nice. His heartbeat.

Strong. Steady. Powerful.

Like him. This strange golden being that somehow exists.

I smile. This has been a dream, hasn't it. He's not really here, and I'm...

"I'm dreaming of someone holding me. Someone golden," I murmur.

The world drifts, liquid and hazy. I'm struck by the strange sense of things floating, drifting. Him. Me. The world around us. Everything soft and blurred at the same time.

"Jah-kee," his voice—or something like it—cuts through the haze. So deep. So full of command but still not in my ears.

In my head. Ah, fuck. I'm dreaming about him talking to me. *"You will not die. I will not allow it."*

The words hang in the space between us, vibrating through me, and I blink slowly, trying to focus on his face. It's hard to think, to breathe.

"You're so dramatic," I murmur.

It's so easy to communicate. As if the barrier between my mind and the world has thinned. As if I am closer to the center of the universe. A part of me notices this, some part tucked away in the back of my fever-riddled mind, but it feels inconsequential. Just a detail in this strange dream that I won't question until I wake up.

Like his dark, metallic blood. Wait. He's bleeding. It catches my eye, seeping from the wound on his shoulder and running down his arm in slow, glistening rivulets.

"Hey," I slur, my head lolling against his chest. *"I don't... I don't want you to die either."*

His gaze snaps to mine, and he stumbles, the disbelief in his eyes crystal clear.

For a moment, I think he's about to drop me, but his grip tightens.

"You..." He sounds stunned. *"Can hear me?"*

"Of course I can hear you," I say, struggling to keep him in focus. The world tilts drunkenly, and his face swims in and out of my vision, golden eyes flickering like lit candles through the haze. *"I'm not deaf. Just... a little dumb."*

His steps falter. The light in his skin flares brighter. *"This is not possible,"* his voice is ragged. *"I have not... claimed you. I have not even licked you yet."*

He...what?

I'm hearing things that don't make sense. I really am not well.

"How did you enter the mindspace?"

"*Mindspace?*" I repeat, frowning. "*I don't know what that is. I'm just talking to you. With my mouth. You know, like normal people?*"

The way he's looking at me, it's like he's searching for answers I don't have. "*Your mouth is not moving.*"

I blink slowly. "*Huh. Weird.*"

My head swims, the fever pulling me under in waves, but I cling to the sound of that deep, steady, grounding voice.

"*Jah-kee,*" he says again. My name comes out so thick with emotion it's almost unrecognizable. "*Do not leave me. Stay awake.*"

I manage a weak laugh. "*Wouldn't dream of it, Goldilocks. You're kind of growing on me.*"

But I don't hear his response, if any. The world tilts, the heat and exhaustion finally dragging me down. The last thing I remember is his heartbeat, frantic but steady beneath my cheek, and the faint glow of his skin lighting the darkness behind my eyelids.

CHAPTER 9
DYING IS A BITCH (BUT SO IS WALKING THROUGH THE DESERT)

JACQUI

Pain. Heat. A deep, rhythmic jolting.

Consciousness comes in waves. Some strong enough to pull me under, others weak enough to let me float. My skin is on fire. My throat is a wasteland of its own.

A sound drills into my skull. A desperate, repeated chanting.

"Live, Jah-kee. Live."

It's a voice, but not a voice. A feeling. A frantic prayer being hammered directly into my brain. The sheer force of it is an anchor, and I cling to it, pulling myself back into my body one agonizing inch at a time.

He's still carrying me.

The realization tugs at the edges of my awareness, but everything feels distant, like I'm floating in a dream. I can't tell how much time has passed. Minutes? Hours? Days? The sun is much farther across the sky than it was before.

"Live, Jah-kee."

His voice hums through my mind, and I blink my eyes open with effort, the world tilting sharply before settling into the same endless stretch of blasted sand and stone. The sun hangs lower now, painting everything in hues of amber and purple. This fucking desert. It's beautiful in that brutal, unforgiving way that reminds you it could kill you without a second thought.

And then there's him.

Goldilocks.

He's not just walking; he's running. His movements a desperate, jarring rhythm. His face is a mask of grim exhaustion. Dark streaks of blood mar his golden skin. And he's glowing, a frantic, flickering light pulsing beneath his skin with every panicked beat of his heart.

He looks... terrified.

And it's because of me.

My gaze meets his, and his frantic steps falter for a single heartbeat. The desperation in his golden eyes hits me like a punch to the gut. He looks at me like I'm a precious water source evaporating before his very eyes.

"Why...?" The thought is a weak, broken thing, but it's all I can manage. *"Why are you looking at me like that?"*

Relief crashes over his features. *"You are awake,"* his voice sounds ragged, breathless. *"You came back."*

"Barely." I manage a weak smile. *"You didn't answer my question."*

His jaw tightens. *"You are..."* He searches for the word, the effort visible on his strained face. *"...wondrous."*

I blink at him, certain I misheard. *"Wondrous? Me? What, because I'm really good at almost dying?"*

His chest rumbles faintly beneath my cheek. Not quite a laugh. It's too raw with relief.

"No. Because you exist."

That sobers me. "*Uh, thanks? I hate to break it to you, but I'm not that special. I'm just a girl. One of billions.*"

"*Not on Xiraxis.*" His voice is quieter now, almost reverent, but laced with an undercurrent of panic. "*There were no females here...until now.*"

That gets my attention. "*Wait, what? None? Like... zero?*"

"*None.*" The word carries such weight, such longing, that it makes my chest tighten.

I try to imagine it. Earth without men. For a moment, the thought sparks something giddy in me. No catcalling, no "not all men" lectures, no unwashed gym socks fermenting in bachelor apartments. *Marvelous.*

But then...

My fever-muddled brain conjures an inconvenient truth: *I'd miss the cocks.*

Not the men. Definitely not the men. But the glorious, thick-as-my-wrist, functional parts of them? The ones that could turn me into a boneless puddle with the right angle and rhythm?

Hypothetically.

What the hell is wrong with me?

"*There is nothing wrong with you, precious one.*"

His words make my eyelids flutter open. With all my strength, I angle my head to see him better, wincing at how heavy it feels. He's watching me with an intensity that sends that same strange shiver through me.

"*Your thoughts are... strong,*" he says, his voice tinged with a new, deep curiosity.

"*Oh God, did I say all that out loud?*"

I blame the fever. Or the desert.

"*The imagery was...*" He pauses, and something flickers across his face. His jaw tightens, and when he speaks again, his voice *feels* quieter. "*Vivid. A...marvelous design.*"

Heat rises in my cheeks, rivalling the burning in my veins. *"Uh, thanks?"*

"And yet..." His voice lowers even further, and I sense something sharp and raw that vanishes almost as quickly as it appears. *"It is not at all like what I possess."*

I blink up at him, confused. It takes my fever-addled brain a moment to process what he's just said. And the way his tone shifted, like he was mourning some deep, personal failing. Before I can puzzle it out, another realization hits me.

"Wait." I squint, trying to focus on his face. *"You've been able to talk this whole time?"*

"Yes." The answer is simple, matter-of-fact.

"And you didn't think to start with that?" My indignation is a weak, sputtering flame.

"You did not hear me before." He adjusts his hold on me, his speed slowing. The passing desert comes a bit into focus again. *"Your mind was closed. Now... now I can feel you."*

"Yeah, well, you were busy glowing at me and gesturing at my thighs like a creep."

"I was not creeping," his voice is sharp, laced with genuine confusion. *"My steps were strong. I did not crawl on my belly. I was crouching. There is a difference."*

I blink slowly, trying to process his literal-minded defense. He thinks "creep" means... actually creeping around on the ground. The absurdity of it is so profound it almost makes me laugh, but I don't have the energy.

"Right. My mistake." My words slur with exhaustion. *"You were performing a... crouching, non-creepy thigh-gesture. Totally normal."*

"I was attempting to offer a claiming," he explains. *"To bring you into the mindspace so you could hear me."*

"Oh, is that all?" My thoughts are getting fuzzy around the

edges. *"And here I thought you were just really, really interested in my panties."*

I let out a sigh that turns into a shuddering breath and snuggle back against his chest. Arguing with a giant, literal alien is officially beyond my pay grade today. Especially when he's the only solid thing in this tilting, burning world.

My eyes flutter closed. So tired. I just want to sleep.

"No." The command is a physical jolt in my skull. Sharp. Terrified. *"Jah-kee. You must stay awake."*

"I'm trying." My lids flutter, but it's so much easier to just close my eyes. *"But it's hard."*

"You must," he demands, the intensity of his voice pulling me toward consciousness once more. *"You will not leave me."*

There it is again. That overwhelming wave of longing that crashes into me. It's so raw, so desperate, that it almost drowns me.

CHAPTER 10

MY HUNT LEAKS WATER AND TALKS OF NON-EXISTENT FOOD

THARN

S he is burning alive in my arms.

The fire beneath Jah-kee's skin rages hotter with each step I take across the dust. Her small body curls against my chest, her face buried in the crook of my neck. Her breath comes in quick, shallow pants that make my dra-kir twist with worry.

I have hunted many creatures across Xiraxis. I have tracked beasts that could tear a hunter in half. I have faced dust serpents that lurk beneath the sand, waiting to drag unwary prey to their deaths.

But I have never felt fear like this.

The female in my arms is *dying*.

And I do not know how to save her.

"*Jah-kee,*" I project, desperate to keep her in the mindspace. "*Tell me of your world. Tell me of the place that made you.*"

Her mind brushes against mine, weaker now than before.

The connection that flared so unexpectedly between us flickers like a flame being smothered by the dust.

"*Earth?*" Her thoughts are disjointed, slippery. "*It's...blue. So much water. Too much sometimes. Cities with lights that never go out. Forests that stretch forever. And people. So many people.*"

I try to picture this strange world she speaks of. A place of endless water. Of *forests*. The concept is as alien to me as she is.

"*And food,*" she continues, her mind wandering. "*God, I miss food. Real food. Not just... whatever that spiny thing was.*"

The thought hits me harder than the shadowmaw's teeth. The sandfin was a good kill. Its meat is rich with strength. I hunted it *for her*. And she did not like it.

A sharp ache, one I have never felt before, tightens my chest. Not anger. Not pride. It is the feeling of... failure. I have failed to provide her with something that brings her pleasure.

"*You did not like the sandfin?*" My thought is soft, laced with this strange new ache.

"*Don't get me wrong. It was great considering. But I'd kill for a burger. Or pizza. Or chocolate...*" Her thoughts fade, then return sharper. "*Do you have chocolate here?*"

"*I do not know this cho-co-late.*"

"*It's sweet. Dark. Melts on your tongue. Makes everything better.*"

I cannot picture this strange food, but the way her thoughts warm at the memory of it makes my chest tighten. I want to give her this cho-co-late. I want to give her anything that would make her eyes brighten the way they did when I handed her the crystal-trapped creature.

But I have only myself to offer. My strength. My determination. My will that she shall not die.

"*We will find water soon,*" I promise, adjusting my grip on her small form. "*And shelter from the dark.*"

Her response is a weak pulse of gratitude that brushes

against my mind like a sand moth's wing. Too gentle. Too fragile.

I tighten my hold on her, careful not to press against the wound on her calf. The skin around it is still an angry red.

"*I know it hurts,*" I tell her, my thoughts gentler than I knew they could be. "*But you must fight it.*"

I feel her trying. I feel the struggle in her mind. The way she pulls herself back from the darkness that threatens to swallow her.

"*That's it,*" I encourage. "*Strong female. Fight.*"

She vocalizes something, her head lolling against my chest. The firebloom paste I gave her earlier should have helped more than this. But her body is different. Foreign to this world. Perhaps it fights the very medicine meant to heal it.

My wound throbs where the shadowmaw's teeth tore into my shoulder, the lifeblood dried to a tacky mess along my arm. I ignore it. The pain is nothing compared to the fear gripping my dra-kir.

I have never feared death. Not my own. It is the way of things on Xiraxis. We hunt. We kill. One day, we fall. Our bodies return to the dust, and the clan brings us to the Giving Stone, so Ain may welcome us into the next cycle.

But the thought of Jah-kee's death...

It tears at me like nothing I have known.

"*Live,*" I project, forcing the thought through our flickering connection. "*Your sister-female awaits. Jus-teen needs you.*"

Her consciousness flares at the mention of her sister.

"*Justine...*" The thought is like a faint murmur. "*I need to find her.*"

"*Yes. And you will. But first, you must live.*"

Ain hangs low on the horizon now, her light bleeding into the sky in shades of red and gold. Soon, darkness will claim the land, and with it will come the predators that hunt in the dark.

I must find shelter before then. A cave. A rock formation. Anything to keep us safe while Jah-kee recovers enough strength to continue.

I scan the horizon, searching for somewhere to take her. The dunes stretching out before us? None offer the protection we need.

Ahead, barely visible, a dark line breaks the monotony of sand. Rock formations.

Shelter.

I quicken my pace, ignoring the burning in my muscles, the throbbing of my wound. Jah-kee's breathing has grown more labored, her small form still limp in my arms. Her mind flickers against mine, faint and erratic.

"*I see shelter ahead,*" I tell her, hoping she can still hear me. "*Hold on, precious one.*"

No response.

"*Jah-kee?*"

Nothing.

Panic surges through me. I press my palm to her face, tilting it toward mine. Her eyes remain closed, her skin burning beneath my touch. The glow beneath my skin flares where we connect, pulsing with a desperate intensity.

I do not understand this light. Do not know why it appears when I touch her. But in this moment, I cling to it like a lifeline. If it still burns between us, she still lives.

"*Do not leave me,*" I demand, pushing the thought at her as if I could order her back from the edge of death through sheer will alone.

She stirs slightly, a small sound escaping her lips. Relief floods through me, so intense it nearly brings me to my knees.

She lives.

But for how long?

The question haunts me as I push onward, the rock formations growing larger with each stride. The light is fading quickly now, Ain's retreat casting long shadows across the dust. In the distance, I hear the first clicks of shadowmaws emerging from their hiding places.

They will hunt this dark. They will scent us on the wind.

And they will come.

I reach the rocks as the last light bleeds from the sky. The formations tower overhead, weathered by countless cycles of wind and dust. Ancient. Unyielding. I scan them quickly, looking for openings, for shelter.

There—a narrow gap between two massive slabs of stone. I approach cautiously, alert for signs of predators already claiming the space. But the air is clean, undisturbed. Nothing has made this place its den.

Yet.

I slip sideways through the gap, Jah-kee cradled close to my chest. The space opens into a small chamber, the ceiling high enough that I can stand upright. The stone walls will keep out the night chill and shield us from prying eyes.

Perfect.

I lay Jah-kee down carefully on the smooth stone floor, positioning her away from the entrance. Her skin glistens with tiny beads of water, and my gut clenches. This is waste. Her body is spilling what little water remains inside her, as if surrendering to the dust. But her chest rises and falls in shallow, rapid movements.

I place my hand on her brow, and the glow flares between us, casting eerie shadows across the chamber walls. She is too hot. Too still.

"*Water*," I murmur, reaching for the waterskin at my side. "*You must drink to replace what you are losing.*"

I lift her head gently, cradling it in my palm as I bring the waterskin to her lips. Most of the water spills down her chin. I find I don't care this time, as long as some passes between her parted lips. I watch her throat work, relief flooding through me as she swallows.

"*Good*," I praise, stroking her face with my thumb. "*Strong female.*"

The glow intensifies where I touch her, and with it comes warmth. A warmth that has nothing to do with exertion or the wound in my shoulder. A connection that defies understanding.

I pull my hand away, unsettled by the strength of it.

Outside, the clicks of shadowmaws grow louder. Closer. My muscles tense, and I move to the entrance, peering out into the gathering darkness. I can see them, sleek black shapes moving across the sand, their scales gleaming in the faint starlight.

They have caught our scent.

They are hunting us.

I bare my teeth, a low growl rumbling in my chest. Let them come. They will find only death if they try to take what is mine.

A soft moan pulls my attention back to Jah-kee. She stirs, head turning restlessly from side to side, lips moving in silent words I cannot hear. I return to her side, crouching beside her small form.

"*Jah-kee,*" I project, reaching for her mind. "*Can you hear me?*"

Her consciousness brushes against mine, weak but present. She doesn't respond with words, just a confused tangle of emotions and fragments of memory. Images flash between us —a world I cannot comprehend, full of strange structures and machines. People with faces like hers. And pain. So much pain.

"*You are with me,*" I tell her, my thought gentle. "*Tharn is here.*"

I reach for my medicinal pouch, retrieving firebloom leaves. My stash is dwindling quickly. There are only a few left. I crush them between my palms; the scent rising as I apply the fresh poultice to the wound on her calf.

I work carefully, spreading the medicine over the inflamed skin. When I finish with her leg, I turn my attention to her wrist—the wound *I* inflicted. It is smaller, less severe, but guilt claws at me, nonetheless.

I made her bleed.

I, who have sworn to protect her, hurt her with my own hands.

I spread the paste over the cut, my touch feather-light. The glow follows my fingers, sinking into her skin like liquid. I do not understand it, but I welcome it now. Perhaps it helps her somehow. Perhaps it fights the fire consuming her from within.

When I finish tending her wounds, I settle beside her, my back against the stone wall. I position myself between her and the entrance, a living shield against anything that might try to enter.

Outside, the shadowmaws continue to circle, their clicks a constant reminder of the danger. But they do not approach the entrance. Not yet. Perhaps they sense my presence. Perhaps they have heard of the fate of their brother in the cave.

Jah-kee whimpers again, her small body trembling. Without thinking, I gather her into my arms, cradling her against my chest. Her head fits perfectly beneath my chin, her weight barely noticeable against my frame.

So small. So fragile. So utterly precious.

"*Rest,*" I murmur as I press my face into her head-fur, the fine strands tickling my chin. "*I will keep watch.*"

She sighs, her body relaxing fractionally against mine. Her mind, when it brushes mine, is calmer now. Less frantic.

71

This small, injured female trusts me.

The realization settles in my chest like a weight, both heavy and somehow precious. I have never been trusted like this before. Relied upon, yes. Respected for my skills as a hunter and tracker. But this...this is different.

This feels like responsibility. Like duty. Like...something I have no word for.

Outside, a shadowmaw screeches, the sound echoing across the stone. Others answer, their calls forming a discordant chorus that sets my fangs on edge. They are coordinating. Planning.

Hunting.

I tighten my hold on Jah-kee, my claws extending slightly in response to the threat. They will not have her. I will tear apart any creature that tries.

"Goldilocks..."

Her voice in the mindspace is so faint I almost miss it. It takes me a moment to realize she is referring to me. She has named me.

"I am here," I respond immediately, searching for her consciousness in the swirling storm of fire and pain.

"Don't leave me," she pleads, the thought achingly vulnerable.

"Never," I promise, and mean it with every fiber of my being.

I feel her relax against me, her consciousness slipping away once more. But this time, it doesn't feel like she's fading. Just resting. Gathering strength.

Fighting.

Hesitantly, I press my face to her head fur again, inhaling her scent. Even through the fire and fear, her scent is vivid. It calls to me in ways I cannot explain. Calls to me in ways that make me want to hunt the stars themselves if it would keep her safe.

I do not understand what is happening. Do not know why this female affects me so. Why her presence in my arms feels like coming home after a long hunt. Why her pain feels like my own, tearing at my dra-kir with each labored breath she takes.

I only know that I must save her.

Whatever the cost.

Whatever it takes.

Jah-kee will live.

I will accept nothing less.

CHAPTER II
WHEN YOUR ALIEN KNIGHT IN SHINING GLOW STARTS TO DIM

JACQUI

I wake up smothered in golden warmth.

For a blissful moment, I'm floating in that perfect space between dreams and reality. My body feels heavy, worn out, but the raging fire that had been consuming me from the inside has subsided to a dull warmth. My head is pillowed against something firm but comfortable, and there's a steady rhythm beneath my ear that lulls me back toward sleep.

Then memory crashes through the haze.

The shadow creature. The fight. Goldilocks bleeding as he defended me. The fever taking hold. Being carried across endless dunes. The light beneath his skin when he touched me. The conversations we had.

My eyes fly open.

I'm curled against his chest, my body tucked between his arm and torso like a child's stuffed animal. His copper-red hair falls across his face, his breathing shallow but steady. The wound on his shoulder looks angry and swollen, dark streaks extending from it like tendrils reaching for his heart.

That doesn't look good.

I try to move, but my limbs feel like they're filled with sand. But the fever has broken. I can tell by the way my skin no longer feels like it's trying to crawl off my body.

"Goldi?" I whisper, my voice a ragged scrape.

He doesn't stir.

I manage to push myself up slightly, wincing at the protest from my muscles. "Hey. Alien guy. Wake up."

Nothing.

Panic flutters in my chest. I press a hand to his face, feeling the cool, smooth texture of his skin. Too cool.

"Oh God," I mutter. "Don't you dare die on me, you big, golden idiot." *Because I need you,* my brain supplies. *To get to Justine,* I add quickly, as if that's the only reason my heart is trying to beat its way out of my chest.

I check for a pulse, my fingers fumbling at his neck. It takes me a moment to find it. Thank God his anatomy is similar to a human's. When I finally locate the steady thrum of his heartbeat, relief washes through me so intensely that I slump against him.

Not dead. Just unconscious.

But not good. Definitely not good.

I need to help him. He's saved my life multiple times now; the least I can do is return the favor. But how? I don't know the first thing about alien medicine. The paste he used on my wounds seemed to work, but I don't know what plants he used or how to prepare them.

Water. Water is a good start.

I spot the waterskin nearby and reach for it, my arm feeling like it weighs a thousand pounds. The effort leaves me dizzy, but I manage to grasp it and bring it to Goldi's lips.

"Drink," I murmur, tipping a small amount into his mouth.

Most of it spills down his chin, but his throat works slightly, swallowing some. I take it as a good sign.

The irony isn't lost on me. Not long ago, he was doing this for me, and now our roles are reversed. I guess we're taking turns saving each other.

"Okay, big guy," I say, setting the waterskin aside. "What next?"

The wound. I need to clean the wound.

I shift closer, examining the angry gash on his shoulder. The shadow creature's teeth had torn deep, and though the bleeding has stopped, the wound looks infected. Dark streaks radiate outward, and the skin around it is hot to the touch.

"This doesn't look good," I mutter. "Like, at all."

I scan the small cave, looking for his medicinal pouch. There it is; attached to his hip with what looks like dried sinew. I crawl toward it, every movement an effort, but determination pushes me forward. When I reach it, I fumble with the ties, my fingers clumsy from weakness.

Come on, Jacqui. Focus.

Inside the pouch, I find a few remaining leaves, and by a few, I mean two. Surely, this won't be enough. They're crumpled and dry, too, but they'll have to do. I crush one between my palms like I'd seen him do. It takes a lot of work; my weak fingers barely manage to create a paste. I add a few drops of water to help.

As the scent rises, it reminds me of lemon just mixed with something spicier, like pepper. I hope I'm doing this right.

I return to Goldi's side, carefully applying the paste to his wound. My hands shake with the effort, but I work slowly, covering every inch of the angry flesh.

"There," I whisper when I've finished. "That should help. I hope."

I sit back, exhaustion washing over me in waves. Even that small effort has drained what little energy I had. I take a small sip from the waterskin, savoring the cool liquid as it soothes my parched throat.

The cave is dim, lit only by the faint glow emanating from him. Outside, I can hear the distant sounds of the desert night. Strange calls and clicks that make my skin crawl. We're safe in here, for now. But for how long?

I look at Goldi again, at his still form and the wound I've done my best to treat. He risked everything to keep me alive, to bring me to safety. And now he might die because of it.

The thought sends a surprising pang through my chest.

"Don't you dare die on me," I mutter, crawling back to his side. "We had a deal, remember? You were taking me to my sister."

He doesn't respond, but I wasn't really expecting him to. I settle beside him, drawing his arm around me partly for warmth and partly because... well, it feels right somehow. Safe.

And...I'm being a bit selfish right now, aren't I?

"Thank you," I whisper against his chest. "For saving me. For carrying me. For not leaving me to die out there."

I close my eyes, exhaustion pulling me under once more. The last thing I remember is the steady beat of his heart beneath my ear, a rhythm that promises he's still fighting.

Still with me.

I WAKE TO THE SENSATION OF MOVEMENT.

Goldi's chest rises and falls beneath my cheek, his breathing stronger than before. I blink awake, lifting my head to find golden eyes watching me.

"Hey," I croak. "You're alive."

His gaze flickers with what might be relief, though it's hard to tell with his alien features. He shifts slightly, wincing as the movement pulls at his wounded shoulder.

"How are you feeling?" I ask, pushing myself up to a sitting position. The world tilts briefly before stabilizing.

He doesn't answer, just watches me with those intense amber eyes. The disconnect is jarring after what felt like such clear communication during my fever. The memory of his deep and commanding voice is so vivid.

My heart starts to pound with a nervous uncertainty. "Goldi?" I try, keeping my voice soft, the way his felt in my mind. "Can you... understand me? The way you did before?"

His brow tightens, his head tilting in that curious, animal-like way. He's studying me, but he doesn't respond.

A cold knot of dread forms in my stomach. I try to push past it. "Remember?" I search his gaze. "We talked. You called me 'precious one' and told me I wouldn't die. It was all very dramatic."

I search his face for any sign of understanding, but his expression only grows more strained. The muscles in his jaw clench, and a low growl of frustration rumbles deep in his chest. He looks... annoyed. Like I'm a buzzing insect he can't swat. The line between us, which felt so clear and open, is now a wall of silent, angry confusion.

Oh God.

It wasn't real.

Great. So I hallucinated the whole thing. The connection, the comfort, the raw desperation in his voice... all of it. Just a side effect of my brain getting cooked, served up with a side of wishful thinking.

Fuck.

I slump back against the stone, the disappointment a cold,

heavy weight in my gut. "Never mind," I sigh, the word feeling hollow. "Let's just focus on getting you better."

I pass him the waterskin, and he accepts it with that slight head tilt that's becoming familiar.

Too familiar.

I shouldn't be noticing how his throat moves as he drinks, the way his jaw flexes with each swallow. Shouldn't be cataloging the exact shade of gold that tints his skin where it stretches over muscle. Our fingers brush as he returns the pouch, and suddenly his entire arm ignites with golden light, veins lighting up like molten rivers under his skin.

The glow pulses once, twice, searingly bright, before settling into a steady hum.

I can't decide if I'm staring because the phenomenon is so strange...or if I'm just that desperate for something beautiful to look at in this hellscape.

When he reaches for me, I automatically stiffen, eyes wide, my heart suddenly beating a little too hard. He pauses, amber-gold eyes flicking to me, watching my reaction. When I remain still, throat bobbing with a swallow, his arm completes the movement. His hand comes up to my forehead, checking my temperature. His touch is still cool, almost too cool. A niggling thought in my mind tells me something's wrong.

"How much longer until we reach Justine?" I ask, my voice echoing softly against the rock around us.

He doesn't answer, just continues his gentle assessment. Those impossibly gentle fingers trail from my forehead to my cheek, then lower, pressing against the frantic flutter of my pulse.

And damn him, because I notice everything. The corded strength in his arms, muscles shifting like steel wrapped in velvet. The way his touch lingers just shy of possessive. The traitorous shiver that skates down my spine—one I barely suppress.

I should pull away.

I don't.

"Hey," I try again, speaking a little louder. "How long?"

Still no answer. His eyes meet mine, narrowing on a slight wince, but he doesn't reply. Is my voice that croaky? Or is he just too exhausted to respond?

Panic flutters in my chest. I reach for his satchel, fumbling with the ties. "You need to take some of that paste. For your wound."

He catches my hand, pushing the satchel back toward me.

"Don't be stubborn," I say, frustration sharpening my tone. "You're hurt. You need medicine too."

He makes a soft, rumbling sound—not words, just a noise that might be meant to reassure. It doesn't work. If anything, it makes me more afraid, because it means he either can't or won't speak to me anymore.

"Goldi, please." I try to sit up, but the world spins violently, and I collapse back against the cave wall. "Say something. Anything."

He blinks slowly, watching me with those amber eyes. Then he shifts, positioning himself beside me, his larger body curled protectively around mine. One arm wraps around my waist, drawing me against his chest where I can feel the too-rapid beat of his heart.

Oh God.

Had I *really* imagined it all? Our conversations? The connection I'd felt? Was it just fever dreams and delirium?

"We're not going to die here," I whisper, though I'm no longer sure if he can hear me. "I won't let us."

His only response is to tighten his hold slightly, his breath warm against my hair. His glow flickers, dimming further until it's barely visible in the darkness of the cave. Like a battery dying.

Fear grips me then. I press my hand to his chest, feeling the rhythm of his heartbeat. Still there, still fighting, but weaker now. How much blood has he lost? How far has he pushed himself beyond his limits?

"Please," I whisper into the darkness. "Please don't leave me."

He makes that soft rumbling sound again, and I feel the lightest pressure of his arms around me as if he's willing to protect me from the rock and the cold even while dying.

I curl against him, as much for his warmth as for my own comfort. If we're going to die, at least we won't die alone. That has to count for something, right?

As his eyes flutter closed and his breathing grows shallow, I press my face against his neck and let the tears fall freely. The silence of the desert settles around us, and the tears come harder.

CHAPTER 12
DON'T CALL IT HEROIC (I'M JUST KEEPING SCORE)

JACQUI

P ain is the first thing I register. A dull, aching throb that pulses through my entire body.

The second is movement. A slow, rhythmic, agonizingly determined lurching.

I blink, my vision swimming. Fucking sand. An endless, rolling sea of it. The sun is a merciless hammer in a bruised yellow sky. And beneath me... the solid, unyielding muscle of Goldi's shoulder.

He's carrying me. Again.

But this is different. Every step he takes is a visible struggle. His breathing is a harsh, ragged sound in the silence of the desert. The golden glow that usually shimmers under his skin is basically gone. He's not walking; he's forcing one foot in front of the other through sheer, stubborn will.

He's dying. And he's still carrying me.

"Goldi?" I whisper, my voice a dry crackle.

He doesn't turn his head. Doesn't react. Every ounce of his energy is focused on moving forward.

"Hey," I try again, pushing up with what little strength I have. I'm still weak, still aching. The fever's left a hollowed-out exhaustion in its place. I manage to shift my position, sliding from his shoulder until I'm looking at his face instead of his ass.

He finally glances at me, and what I see in his eyes makes my own breath catch. Raw pain. Bone-deep weariness. And a fierce, terrifying determination that seems to be the only thing holding him together.

"Put me down," I say, my voice firmer now. I slap his back, the impact jarring but necessary. "I can walk."

He lets out a low growl, a sound of pure refusal, and his arm tightens around my thighs.

"No," I insist, pushing against his chest, trying to create some leverage. "You're going to kill yourself!" In my struggle, my hand slips, my knuckles brushing against the edge of the angry wound on his shoulder.

He flinches violently, a sharp hiss of pain escaping him, but his grip on me doesn't loosen.

"Oh god, I'm sorry," I say, instantly retracting my hand. "Damn it, Goldi, just *stop!*"

He doesn't.

I sigh, frustration and a terrifying wave of concern warring within me. Fine. If he won't listen, I'll make him. I start to squirm, to wriggle, to make myself as difficult to carry as possible. It's a pathetic struggle, but it's enough.

With a final, frustrated growl, he reluctantly lowers me to the ground.

The moment my boots touch sand, the world sways violently. I stagger, stars exploding behind my eyes as blood rushes from my head. Goldi's hand shoots out, steadying me before I can face-plant into the dunes.

"Okay," I admit, clutching his forearm. "Maybe walking was ambitious."

A dry, exhausted huff escapes him, and his gaze fixes on my mouth. It's a look of desperate focus, as if he's trying to read my lips to gauge if I'm about to collapse again.

"Hey, my eyes are up here," I say, the joke falling flat even to my own ears. "You don't have to watch my mouth for a weather report. I'll let you know if I'm going to pass out."

He doesn't respond, of course, just continues that unblinking stare. Then his gaze shifts, scanning the horizon, muscles tensing beneath my hand. Even with his shoulder still clearly bothering him, he's on high alert. The constant vigilance of someone who knows danger is always one heartbeat away.

I take the moment to really look at him. His skin has lost some of its luster, the golden glow dimmed to a faint shimmer that pulses irregularly. The wound on his shoulder looks better than it did in the cave, but not by much. Dark streaks still radiate outward, though they've faded from black to a dull, bruised purple. His breathing is a shallow, controlled rhythm, but it's the tightness around his eyes that tells the real story. He's in agony.

He's not well. Not at all.

"Hey," I say softly, tapping his arm to get his attention. "We need to stop. You need to rest."

His eyes flick to mine briefly before returning to scan the horizon. No response.

"Goldilocks," I try again, stepping in front of him to block his path. "You're going to die if you keep this up. And then I'll die. So, for purely selfish reasons, I am ordering you to stop."

He catches my wrist in a gentle grip, the gesture almost

absentminded as he continues his surveillance. When he finally looks back at me, there's a determination in his eyes that brooks no argument. With careful movements, he lifts me again, this time cradling me in his arms rather than slinging me over his shoulder.

"Oh, come on," I protest, though it's halfhearted at best. "I can walk. Really."

He ignores me, adjusting his hold before resuming his steady pace across the sand. I sigh, resigning myself to being carried. At least this position is more dignified than the previous one.

"Fine," I mutter, laying my head against his chest. I can feel the frantic, shallow beat of his heart. "But just so we're clear, this isn't you being heroic. This is you being a stubborn, thick-skulled idiot. And when we find my sister, I'm telling her you were a terrible patient."

He finally glances down at me. The weariness is still there, but for a moment, it's overshadowed by a look of profound, searching curiosity. His golden eyes trace the lines of my face as if trying to memorize them, before his gaze lifts back to the horizon.

The look lasts only a heartbeat, but it leaves me feeling strangely breathless.

We travel in silence for what feels like hours. The sun beats down mercilessly, and even with Goldi's body partially shielding me, sweat soon plasters my hair to my forehead. I watch him for signs of fatigue, of the infection worsening, but his face remains impassive, his stride steady despite the burden of my weight.

Eventually, the monotony gets to me. "So," I say, "do you come here often? To this charming wasteland of death and despair?"

He glances down at me, brow tightening slightly.

"I'll take that as a yes," I continue. I'm fucking desperate to fill the silence. "Great vacation spot. Love the ambiance. The constant threat of horrible death really adds to the exotic appeal."

His expression doesn't change, but something in his eyes softens. It's subtle. The barest easing of tension. But it makes him look softer somehow. Less like a warrior and more like a ... something else. Something I shouldn't really focus on.

"You're actually pretty handsome when you're not snarling or, you know, bleeding to death," I muse, then immediately regret the words. Heat floods my cheeks. "Not that I... I mean, obviously you're... God, why am I still talking?"

His brow tightens again, this time in what looks like concern. His pace slows slightly as he shifts his attention fully to me, amber-gold eyes scanning my face with that unsettling intensity.

"I'm fine," I assure him, waving a hand dismissively. "Just babbling. It's what humans do when they're uncomfortable. Or nervous. Or, you know, being carried across an alien desert by a golden god with amazing physique and a shoulder wound."

He doesn't react to the joke. At all. His head tilts, and a low, questioning sound rumbles in his chest. But it's short, sharp, and laced with an edge of something that sounds like a warning. His golden eyes narrow, scanning my face, my neck, my chest, as if searching for the source of a new injury.

The intensity of his scrutiny makes the heat in my cheeks burn hotter. He clearly doesn't understand my words, but he has sensed the sudden shift in my emotional state. And whatever conclusion he's drawn, it isn't a good one.

As we crest a dune, I notice his glow flickering more noticeably, almost stop-starting beneath his skin. His breath stutters, a barely perceptible hitch that sends alarm bells ringing in my head.

"Hey," I say, suddenly serious. "Put me down. You need to rest."

He ignores me, his jaw set in stubborn determination as he continues forward. The flickering intensifies, his breathing growing more labored with each step.

"Goldilocks," I insist, pushing against his chest. "Stop. Please."

Nothing. He just keeps moving, his eyes fixed on some distant point I can't see.

Frustration builds in my chest. How am I supposed to communicate with someone who won't listen and can't understand me? I need this damn translator to work. I need...

I reach up to check if the device is still snug in my ear. It is. The small metallic curve has molded perfectly to fit my ear as if I was born with it. So why isn't it working? It should be translating his language, his gestures, *something*.

I tap it gently, wondering if it's malfunctioned. Maybe damaged in the fall, or when we crashed here. Hell, maybe alien tech just isn't compatible with whatever Goldilocks is.

I'm about to demand he put me down again when I hear him murmur something. The sound is so faint I almost miss it, a whisper carried away by the desert wind.

"...*need more firebloom...*"

I freeze, eyes wide. Wait. What? I just heard him speak. In English. Clear as day.

But his lips didn't move.

I tap my translator frantically, suddenly unsure of what's happening. "What did you just say?"

He glances down at me, doesn't respond, but at least he isn't wincing anymore when I talk.

"You just said something," I insist, pointing to his mouth. "About firebloom. I heard you."

His expression shifts to something I can't read. Surprise? Alarm? Hope?

Am I losing my mind? Did I imagine it? No. No, I definitely heard him. But if his lips didn't move...

Oh God. It was in my head. The voice was in my head.

I tap the translator again, harder this time, as if that might fix whatever reality glitch is happening. "This can't be... I'm not..."

"Jah-kee."

There it is again. His voice. But not in my ears—in my mind. Like when I was fevered and delirious, when I thought we were having conversations.

But I'm not delirious now. I'm clear-headed, conscious, fully aware.

"I'm going crazy," I whisper, more to myself than to him. "That's it. I've finally snapped. The desert has won."

Goldi's arms tighten around me, in a gesture that might be comfort or concern. He looks down at me again, and this time there's something like frustration in his eyes. He opens his mouth as if to speak, but only a soft clicking sound emerges.

"Great," I mutter, dropping my hand from the translator. "So I'm hearing voices. Specifically, *your* voice. In my head. That's normal, right? Totally not a sign of an impending psychotic break."

His stride falters slightly, and for a moment, I think he might actually stop. But he pushes on, his determination evident in every line of his body.

"Firebloom," I hear again.

"Firebloom," I whisper. Realization makes my eyes widen. I gesture to the pouch tied to his waist. "Are you talking about those plants? The ones you used on my leg?"

His gaze snaps to mine, sudden awareness in those amber depths.

"Let me check," I say, reaching for the pouch tied at his waist. "There was one left."

He shifts me in his arms, allowing me access to the pouch. I fumble with the ties, finally managing to open them and peer inside. Just as I suspected—there's only one leaf left, crumpled and dry.

"There's only one," I tell him, holding it up. "Is that enough?"

He studies the leaf before his gaze shifts to my leg, to the healing wound there, then back to the leaf. With careful movements, he adjusts me on one arm only to use the other to take the leaf from my hand. Without any hesitation, he tucks the leaf back into the pouch.

"Hey," I protest. "Don't you need that? For your shoulder?"

He ignores me, securing the pouch and resuming his steady pace across the sand. But now I understand what's happening. He's saving it. For me. In case my wound gets worse again.

The realization makes me...deflate. This stubborn, golden alien is willing to suffer through his pain, his infection, to make sure I have medicine if I need it?

"You self-sacrificing idiot," I mutter, torn between gratitude and frustration. "You need it more than I do."

He doesn't respond, just continues trudging forward, his breathing growing more labored with each step. The glow beneath his skin flickers, dimming further until it's barely visible even in the shade of his arms.

We continue like this for what feels like eternity, the sun crawling across the sky, the sand shifting beneath his feet. I watch him with growing concern as his condition visibly deteriorates. His skin grows paler, the gold taking on an ashen quality. Every step he takes seems to draw all the energy from him.

He's going to collapse soon. I can feel it in the increasingly erratic rhythm of his heartbeat against my side, in the trembling of his arms as they struggle to support my weight.

"Please," I whisper, not caring if he understands or not. "Please stop. Rest. Before you kill yourself."

But he doesn't stop. Doesn't even slow down. His eyes remain fixed ahead, locked onto a series of flat-topped rocks ahead.

And then, without warning, his knees buckle.

We go down hard, but he somehow manages to twist his body so that he takes the brunt of the impact. Sand flies up around us as we hit the ground, his arms still locked protectively around me, even as his chest heaves with labored breaths.

"Goldilocks!" I scramble out of his grip, kneeling beside him in the sand. "Hey, hey, look at me."

His eyes find mine, pain clear in their amber depths. He tries to sit up, but his arms shake too badly to support his weight. He collapses back onto the sand, a frustrated growl rumbling in his chest.

"Stop," I command, pressing a hand to his uninjured shoulder. "Just... stop. Rest."

He grunts, gesturing weakly toward a point in the distance. I follow his gaze, squinting against the setting sun. There, the rocks that form a plateau. A cave, maybe. Shelter. About the length of a football field away.

"Is that where we're headed?" I ask, pointing toward it. "That cave?"

He grunts, then he tries to rise again, determination etched into every line of his face.

"Oh no, you don't," I say, pushing him back down. "You're staying right here. I'll go."

For a second, it's clear he doesn't understand. Not until I turn in the direction I need to go.

Goldi's eyes widen, alarm filling their depths. He grabs my wrist, a growl in his throat.

"Look," I say, meeting his gaze. "You're in no condition to walk. Let alone carry me. I'm feeling better, and that cave isn't far. I can make it."

He growls a warning and his grip on my wrist tightens enough to make his point clear. *Don't go.*

"I have to," I insist, trying to pry his fingers loose. "If there are more of those plants you need, I can bring them back."

His expression darkens. He points to the sand around us, then makes a slithering motion with his free hand. Danger. There's danger out there.

"I know," I say softly. "But we have no choice. You can't make it, and we can't stay here in the open."

For a long moment, we just stare at each other, locked in a silent battle of wills. Then, slowly, reluctantly, his grip on my wrist loosens.

"Thank you," I murmur, giving his hand a gentle squeeze before pulling away. "I'll be careful. I promise."

I push myself to my feet, swaying slightly as my legs adjust to bearing weight again. The world tilts briefly before steadying, and I take a tentative step forward. Then another. My muscles ache, protesting after so long being carried, but they hold.

"I'll be right back," I tell him, trying to project a confidence I don't feel. "Just... stay alive, okay?"

He watches me with those intense amber eyes, his chest rising and falling in rapid, shallow breaths. When I turn to go, he makes a sound—half growl, half whimper—that tears at something in my chest.

But I force myself to keep walking. One foot in front of the other. Sand shifts beneath my boots, making each step a challenge, but I push on. The rocks grow slowly larger in my vision, a dark smudge against the orange-tinged sky.

Behind me, I hear movement. I glance back to see Goldi attempting to follow, dragging himself across the sand with dogged determination. He makes it barely a meter before collapsing again, one hand clutching at his chest as if in pain.

And strangely, impossibly, I feel an answering twinge in my chest. A phantom ache that has no business being there.

I almost turn back. Almost. But the darkening sky and the memory of those shadow creatures keep me moving forward. We need shelter. We need those plants. And Goldi can't get them himself.

So I steel my nerves and continue, even though, ridiculously and nonsensically, each step feels like I'm leaving a part of myself behind. Each meter of distance between us makes that phantom ache in my chest grow stronger, a dull throb that matches the desperate look in his eyes as I walk away.

By the time I reach the rocks surrounding the cave, my legs are trembling with exhaustion, and sweat drenches my clothes despite the cooling air. I pause, catching my breath before venturing closer.

The cave mouth is smaller than I expected, barely large enough for someone Goldi's size to squeeze through. But that's good. It means the shadow creatures will have a harder time getting in, too.

I approach cautiously, alert for any signs of creatures already claiming the space. Because, as I have been reminded time and time again now, this desert is alive. But the area seems deserted, quiet except for the soft whisper of wind across sand.

As I push through the entrance, it takes a moment for my eyes to adjust to the dimness inside. It's damper in here, even though I can't hear any dripping water. Slowly, I move forward, scanning the walls when something catches my eye. A splash of vibrant blue-orange against the dull beige of rock and sand. Plants. Small, spiky things growing in clumps in one corner.

Firebloom. It has to be.

Relief floods through me so intensely my knees nearly buckle. I hurry forward, reaching for the nearest plant with eager hands. No sooner do I touch the first one than pain lances through my palm as dozens of tiny thorns sink into my skin.

"Shit!" I snatch my hand back, staring at the blood welling from countless pinpricks. "Okay, so you're not friendly."

I glance back toward the cave entrance. I can't see Goldi, but I can almost feel his eyes on the cave, watching. Waiting. Worrying.

"Right," I mutter, turning back to the plants. "Let's try this again. More carefully this time."

I pull the hem of my shirt up, creating a makeshift basket. Then, using a loose stone nearby, I carefully sever several plants at the base, letting them fall into the fabric. The thorns catch on the material, but it's thick enough to protect my hands.

When I've gathered as many as I can carry, I knot the fabric to secure my harvest. Blood drips from my injured hand, leaving a trail of dark spots in the sand as I turn to head back to Goldi.

Exiting the cave, I spot him immediately. Those amber-gold eyes lock onto me like I'm the only thing alive in this wasteland.

And damn if that look doesn't send a rush of something unfamiliar through me.

I hold up the makeshift basket of my shirt, displaying the spiky, life-saving plants. A grin splits my face. *I did it.*

I got the firebloom. *Me.* Not Justine charging ahead, not Goldilocks carrying my half-dead weight. Just my own stubborn legs and shaky hands.

The pride hits hard, swelling like a warm, foreign thing in my chest. I've spent my whole life following—my sister's plans, Earth's collapse, the Xyma's lies. Always a step behind, always the one being protected. But this? This choice, this risk, this victory... this is mine.

I start walking toward him, my steps more confident than they've been in weeks. I can almost feel the phantom ache in my chest ease with every meter I close between us, and the relief in his gaze is a palpable thing, a reward more satisfying than I could have imagined. I'm not just a burden he has to carry. I'm a partner. *I can help.* I can save him, too.

I'm halfway there, my mind replaying the small victory, when I feel it.

A subtle vibration beneath my feet. A shifting of sand that doesn't match my footsteps.

I freeze, the triumphant smile wiped from my face. My heart, which had been swelling with pride, now fills with a familiar, sickening dread. Slowly, I turn to look behind me.

At first, I see nothing. Just endless sand, painted orange and gold by the setting sun. Then I notice it. Subtle as a breath, the sand shifts twenty paces behind me. A tiny ripple, barely visible, moving beneath the surface. Like something large swimming just under the sand.

It pauses where my blood dripped earlier.

The spot vanishes as if swallowed whole.

Oh shit.

I don't wait to see what it is. I run, clutching my bundle of plants in my skirt, blood dripping faster now as exertion forces it from the wounds on my hand.

The vibration increases, the rippling growing larger, faster, as whatever it is gives chase. I push myself harder, legs burning with the effort, lungs screaming for air I don't have time to gulp down.

Goldi comes into view, his body tense as he tracks something behind me. He's managed to push himself into a half-sitting position, but his face is contorted with pain.

"Run!" I scream, though I know he can't understand the word. "There's something—"

The sand erupts behind me, a fountain of golden particles exploding upward as something massive breaks the surface. I risk a glance over my shoulder and immediately wish I hadn't.

It's like the manta ray thing from the cave, but larger. Much larger. Its flat, wing-like body ripples as it moves, and the massive spine running along its back quivers with what can only be anticipation.

Well, shit. I guess we ate the baby.

I'm not going to make it. The realization hits me with cold clarity. I'm still too far from him, and even if I reach him, what then? He's too weak to fight, and I've got nothing but a handful of spiky plants and my own stubborn will to live.

But I keep running anyway, because what else can I do?

Twenty meters. Fifteen. Ten.

I can hear it now, a terrible whooshing sound as it glides through the sand behind me, gaining with each passing second.

Five meters.

Almost there.

And then I'm falling, my foot catching on something hidden beneath the sand. I hit the ground hard, the bundle of plants scattering as my grip loosens. Pain explodes in my knee, my palms, as I try to break my fall.

The creature is right behind me. I can feel its presence, a cold weight of dread pressing down on my spine. This is it. This is how I die. Not from fever or dehydration or even shadow creatures, but from a giant, spiny manta ray in an alien desert.

I roll onto my back, determined to at least face my death head-on. The creature looms above me, its body half-emerged from the sand, mouth opening to reveal rows of needle-like teeth.

Really, *really*, preferring it when it was dead with its mouth closed.

And then something moves, faster than I can track. A blur of gold and bronze as Goldi launches himself past me, claws extended, a snarl ripping from his throat that makes the hair on my neck stand on end.

He collides with the creature mid-air, claws sinking deep into its hide. They crash back into the sand, a tangle of thrashing wings and slashing claws. Then it hisses.

Not a shriek. Not even a sound, really. More like pressurized air escaping a rusted pipe. A thin, keening vibration that splits my skull. My hands fly to my ears, but it's too late. The noise lodges in my molars, rattles my eye sockets, turns my vision white with pain.

By the time it fades, Goldi's already torn its throat out.

Silence falls across the desert, broken only by his ragged breathing. He remains crouched over the creature's body, chest heaving, blood—both his and its—dripping from his claws.

"Goldi?" I whisper, barely daring to move.

His head snaps toward me, and for a terrifying moment,

there's something wild in his eyes, something untamed and dangerous. Then recognition flashes, and he's scrambling toward me, moving with a desperate urgency that belies his injuries.

He reaches me in seconds, hands hovering over my body, searching for wounds, for damage. His touch is gentle despite the blood still staining his claws, his eyes wide with concern as they scan my face.

"I'm okay," I assure him, though I'm not entirely sure that's true. My knee throbs where I fell, and my hands sting from the firebloom thorns. But I'm alive, which is more than I expected a minute ago. "Thanks to you."

The pride I felt just a moment ago dims.

The alien makes a soft, distressed sound, his fingers tracing the blood on my hands. I follow his gaze to the scattered plants around us, understanding dawning.

"I got them," I say, reaching for the nearest clump of fire-bloom. "The plants you need. They're a bit spiky, but—"

He catches my hands, stopping me before I can touch the thorns again. With a growl, he carefully gathers the plants himself, the thorny bits not seeming to bother him.

"Show-off," I mutter, but I feel only gratitude. And something else I'm certainly not going to mention. Not even to myself.

With the plants secured, Goldi turns his attention back to me. His hands cradle my face, those amber eyes searching mine with an intensity that steals my breath. Once more, the glow beneath his skin pulses where we touch, stronger now than it's been since his collapse.

"I'm really okay," I whisper, my voice catching slightly. "You saved me. Again."

He makes that soft rumbling sound in his chest, the one that's becoming strangely familiar. Comforting, even. Then, to my surprise, he drops to one knee before me, head bowed low.

The gesture is so... formal. So out of place, it completely knocks me off balance. It's like something out of a fantasy novel—the knight pledging fealty to his queen. It's the last thing I'd expect from a seven-foot alien who was, just moments ago, redecorating the sand with a monster's internal organs.

But the meaning is unmistakable, even across species. Gratitude. Respect. And maybe... something deeper.

I stare down at him, momentarily speechless. His copper-red hair falls forward, and my eyes snag on the decorations woven into the strands. They're vertebrae from the spine of some desert creature, their rounded bases threaded through by locks of his shiny hair. They suit him perfectly, these wild adornments. Predator wearing the trophies of his hunts.

"Hey," I say softly, reaching out to touch his shoulder. "You have nothing to thank me for. I'm the one who keeps getting into trouble, remember?"

He lifts his head, those amber eyes locking with mine, and there's something in them that makes my breath catch. Something that transcends our language barrier and speaks directly to something primal inside me.

I help him to his feet. He's heavy, a dead weight of exhausted muscle, and he leans on me for a moment to find his balance. When he's steady, I gesture to the medical pouch where he's stored the fresh blooms.

"You should use those," I tell him, pointing to his wounded shoulder. "That's why I went for them."

He hesitates, eyes flicking between the pouch and my injured hands. Before I can protest, he's taking my palms in his, turning them up to examine the countless tiny punctures from the firebloom thorns.

"I'm fine," I insist, trying to pull away. "They're just scratches. You're the one who—"

He silences me with a single look. A flat, unblinking stare that couldn't say "shut up and let me help you" any clearer. Opening the pouch, he selects one of the freshest blooms, carefully removing the thorns before crushing it between his fingers.

"Seriously," I begin, but he's already applying the medicine to my palms, his touch impossibly gentle for someone with claws that just tore through a sand creature's spine. "I didn't get these for me. I got them for you."

He ignores my protests, focused entirely on tending to my wounds. When he's satisfied with my hands, he produces another bloom, removing the thorns and crushing it into a different consistency before offering it to me.

"I don't need it." I shake my head. "I made that trip for *you*, not me. I'm fine. You're the one who's been half-dead all day."

Another look, this one somehow both pleading and commanding at once. His fingers press the paste closer to my lips, insistent.

I sigh, defeated. "Fine. But you're taking some too. Right after me."

I accept the medicine, grimacing at the bitter taste as it spreads across my tongue.

Only when I've swallowed does Goldi finally prepare some for himself. He applies a generous portion to his wounded shoulder, his face tightening briefly in pain before relaxing as the medicine takes effect. Then he consumes a healthy dose, his eyes never leaving mine as if making sure I witness him fulfilling his end of the bargain.

The change is almost immediate. Color returns to his skin, the golden glow beneath it strengthening, pulsing more steadily. His breathing eases, the tension in his shoulders loosening.

"Now—oh!"

Without warning, he gathers me into his arms again, this time with renewed strength. The other arm grabs the narrow tail of the desert ray. Before I can protest, he's moving. Not the careful trudge of an injured male, but an explosive, powerful run, his legs eating up the sand.

I clutch at his chest, startled by the sudden speed.

He's showing off. The big, golden idiot is showing off for me.

"Show-off," I mutter into his neck, the grin I can't stop from spreading muffled against his skin.

CHAPTER 13
THE GLOW ISN'T THE ONLY THING THAT'S RISING

THARN

The firebloom works its magic quickly.

My wound still throbs, the shadowmaw's poison not entirely purged, but the burning has subsided. The dark tendrils creeping toward my dra-kir have retreated, leaving only a dull ache where fangs tore flesh. I am healing. Not fully restored, but strong enough to hunt. Strong enough to protect.

Strong enough to continue our journey to Jah-kee's sister-female and Rok.

... If that is what I truly want.

I sit at the cave entrance, watching Ain's light fade from the sky. The stars emerge, burning cold and bright against the endless dark. In the clan tales, the patterns are the great hunters of old, their spirits forever tracking their legendary prey across the sky. We trace their hunts, telling the stories of their strength so young Drakav learn the ways of the clan.

This dark, their light feels heavy. A judgment on my own hunt. On my... hesitation.

Behind me, Jah-kee rests. Her breathing is even now, her small body curled on the soft sand I gathered for her. Rest came quickly for her after taking the firebloom paste.

I shift, adjusting my position to see both her and the cave entrance better. My duty is clear: guard her through the dark, then continue our journey at first light. Where Rok and her sister-female wait lies three sols to the northwest. It will be a curving path from here.

And all because I diverted.

I told myself the diversion was necessary. That we needed the firebloom to heal. That the extra sol or two it would add to our journey was a small price for our survival.

These are true thoughts. Good, hunter's thoughts.

But under them, something else moves. A truth I do not wish to see.

I do not want to reach Rok.

I do not want to give Jah-kee back.

My gaze drops to my claws, to the faint golden glow that pulses beneath my skin even now. It is always there since finding her, but stronger when she is near. Stronger still when we touch. I flex my claw, watching the light follow the movement, tracing the path of veins and muscle beneath my skin.

What is this connection? This light that binds us?

A soft sound from the cave's depths pulls my attention back to Jah-kee. She shifts in her rest, brow furrowing slightly before smoothing again. Even unconscious, she makes noises. Strange, soft vocalizations that should irritate my sensitive ears but now somehow... don't.

When did her noise stop being noise? When did it become... necessary? Like the warmth of Ain after a cold dark. Like the taste of blood after a long hunt.

Like something necessary.

My chest tightens at the thought, an echo of the pain I felt earlier when she walked away from me across the sands. That had been... unexpected. Alarming. A physical agony that went beyond the shadowmaw's poison or the fatigue of our journey. It felt as if she were pulling my very dra-kir from my chest with each step she took away from me.

The pain had eased only when she returned, firebloom clutched in her hide covering, determination in those water-blue eyes. The relief had been so intense it momentarily over-whelmed my alarm at the sandfin pursuing her.

Even now, with barely the length of the cave between us, I feel a faint tugging sensation. A pull toward her that makes my skin hum with awareness.

We are tethered somehow, bound by whatever strange force creates this light between us.

And I do not know how to break free.

Or if I want to.

The sandfin I killed earlier lies just outside the cave entrance, its corpse already stiffening in the cool night air. I should prepare it now, while Jah-kee rests. The meat will restore our strength, and we can save portions for the journey ahead.

I rise silently, moving outside to where the creature lies. Its scales gleam in the light of my glow as I crouch beside it, unsheathing my claws to begin the careful work of separating meat from bone. The flesh parts easily under my touch, pale and rich with nutrients. But even over the scent of fresh blood, I can smell her. She is close. Awake.

A soft shuffling confirms it. The whisper of feet on stone.

I stiffen, glow brightening as I turn to find Jah-kee standing in the cave entrance. Her head fur is mussed from sleep, her eyes heavy-lidded but alert. She sways slightly, still not fully recovered, but there is determination in the set of her jaw.

"*Jah-kee*," I project, forgetting for a moment that she can no longer hear me. The frustration of our severed connection burns anew. "*You should be resting*."

She vocalizes something, the sounds soft and slurred with sleep. Her small hand gestures vaguely toward the darkness beyond the cave, then down at herself. I tilt my head, trying to decipher her meaning.

She sighs, then repeats the gesture more emphatically, adding a squeezing motion with her thighs.

What is she trying to tell me?

Oh. Dust. Is this what I think it is? A request for me to present myself? My dra-kir thrums hopefully—

But no.

Jah-kee turns toward the darkness beyond the cave, and my claws extend on reflex. The dark belongs to shadowmaws and dust stalkers. Even a healthy hunter would hesitate to venture out alone.

When I move to accompany her, her face heats with color. The pale skin of her cheeks flushes deep pink, almost red. Is she ill again? Has the fire returned?

I reach for her brow, but she steps back, making that strange squeaking sound she emits when startled. The color deepens. Not the fire then. Something else.

She gestures more urgently now, pointing to herself, then the darkness, then making a shooing motion at me. Her meaning is clear: she wants privacy.

But privacy is a luxury afforded only within the safety of clan caves. Out here, in the open, during the dark? It is a death sentence.

She makes a frustrated sound, then more vocalizations that

rise in pitch before dropping to a resigned grumble. Whatever argument she was making, she seems to have abandoned it.

She pins me with a final, sharp look, then turns and steps past me into the dark. I drop the sandfin immediately, rising to follow her. Her shoulders hunch when she realizes I'm behind her, but she doesn't try to send me away again.

She moves a short distance from the cave. I follow, stopping a few paces behind her. The soft breeze brings the scent of the open dark to me. From here, I can see everything. Hear everything. She is a warm, small point in the center of the world. Nothing will reach her.

"Fine," she vocalizes, the sound sharp but quiet. "It's not like you can see in this pitch black anyway."

The sharp sounds she makes mean nothing to me. It is the movement that follows that steals my breath. She lifts the strange hide covering her lower half. It rises, revealing pale thighs that gleam like polished bone in my glow.

My glow, which had been a soft, ambient shimmer, suddenly flares with the intensity of Ain herself. The entire area is instantly bathed in brilliant golden light, turning the sand white and the shadows to sharp, black spears. It is, for all intents and purposes, a beam of solid light. Pointed directly at her.

She freezes, a startled, squeaking sound escaping her. Her entire body goes rigid, caught in the beam of my traitorous light.

For a long moment, she doesn't move. A strange look crosses her face. The lines around her eyes tighten, her small teeth dig into her lower lip, and her body gives a small, involuntary shudder. She presses her thighs together again.

"Oh no, no, no, not now," she mutters, the vocalization a low, strained sound. A soft groan rumbles from her chest. It is the sound of a body fighting a battle it is about to lose.

What is she doing? I should scan the surroundings for any threat, but I cannot tear my eyes from the sight of her.

The curve of her backside, round and soft. The smooth expanse of her thighs. The glimpse of something between them, hidden in shadow but unmistakably different from my own anatomy.

Heat floods my veins, pooling low in my gut with an insistence I've never experienced before. My member stirs in its pouch, pressing against the confining tissue with growing urgency.

And then her body gives one final, sharp tremor, and the tension breaks.

At the first hint of water leaving her being, I freeze, alarmed. But then the scent of her fills my nostrils. *Dust.* So *rich.* Not just the waste she's expelling, but something deeper. Muskier. It stirs something in me, something that makes my claws itch to extend, my fangs ache to descend.

It is like Rok's scent after he claimed Jus-teen. That same heady musk that clung to him for sols afterward, marking him as changed. As...a male who claimed a female.

By Ain. I dig my claws into the meat of my thigh to keep them sheathed. *Control, Tharn.* Jah-kee is vulnerable, exposed. You are meant to be guarding her, not... whatever this is.

The thought flickers through my mind that there are no goldweeps here to reclaim her water. The round, thirsty plants cluster in the clan caves, hungrily absorbing what we give them to be purified. Because the dust swallows everything. Precious moisture vanishes in uncaring sand.

A poor trade. Jah-kee's water is precious.

Yet my focus isn't on wasted water. It's fixed on the differences between our kinds. The water Jus-teen shared with Rok wasn't this waste Jah-kee is expelling now. How can there be two waters from the same source? One for waste, and one for... sharing? From some hidden wellspring I've never seen but now can't stop thinking about? A soft, hidden place between a female's thighs that my body now aches to touch. To taste.

Jah-kee finishes quickly, lowering her hide-covering and rising. Her face is still flushed, her gaze avoiding mine as she hurries back toward the cave entrance.

I remain where I am, needing a moment to collect myself. To wrestle my suddenly unruly body back under control. My member strains against its pouch with a strange, unfamiliar readiness, as if it prepares for a hunt I do not understand. It is a demand, but for what, I do not know.

I command it to be still. It does not obey.

With intense focus, I slow my breathing. Center my thoughts on duty, on protection. On anything but the curve of Jah-kee's behind or the scent that still lingers in the air around me.

When I finally return to the cave entrance, Jah-kee has already retreated inside. I retrieve the partially cleaned sandfin, resuming my work with single-minded determination. My claws move. They slice. They clean. This is a thing I know. It is a quiet, steady thing in the noise of my head.

By the time I've finished preparing the sandfin, my member has settled, my breathing steady once more. I gather the meat and head into the cave, moving quietly in case Jah-kee has fallen back into rest.

She hasn't. She sits near the back of the cave, knees drawn up to her chest, watching me with those water-blue eyes that seem to see too much. Her face is still flushed, but less intensely now.

I do not look at her yet. I can already smell her. I can hear the soft sound of her breath. A low rumble starts in my chest as

I move to arrange the meat on the stone shelf that runs along one wall of the cave. This place is known to me. An established camp, one marked with dust stalker waste to warn away other predators. It has firestones and offers good shelter, though the water source is small.

It is not the clan caves, but it will keep us safe through the dark.

I retrieve the firestones, arranging them carefully within a circle of smaller rocks. Jah-kee watches with undisguised curiosity as I strike them together, creating the spark that ignites and spreads between them.

"Ooh," she breathes as flames leap to life, casting dancing shadows across the cave walls.

The sound she makes pulls my gaze to her face, and my dra-kir gives a strange, tight thump. Her eyes reflect the fire-light, turning them from water-blue to something deeper, richer. Her mouth is parted, and I watch the movement of her lips, the shape of them. The curve of them. The fullness that only her lips possess.

Jah-kee is pleasing to look at.

The thought is like a smooth, round stone in my claw. I turn it over and over. I have never thought this of another living thing. A kill is a kill. A brother is a brother. There is strong, and there is weak. There is threat, and there is prey. There is no... *pleasing.*

But Jah-kee...

Ain's light. She is a new thing in my world. A new thing in my head.

I cannot pull my gaze from her. From the light on her face. From the way her small hands gesture as she vocalizes. I try to listen to the night, to the fire, but the only thing my ears find is the sound of her voice.

My focus is broken. She has broken it.

"What are these stones?" she asks, leaning forward to examine the firestones more closely. "I don't think we have anything like this on Earth. This is like a camper's dream."

Her meaning is clear in her wide, curious eyes. Her interest is fixed on the firestones. Not true stone, but something else. The hardened lifeblood of things that lived and died. When struck, they bleed not water, but fire.

I select one of the smaller firestones, dousing it with sand before holding it out to her. She hesitates only briefly before accepting it, turning it over in her hands with careful movements.

"It's warm," she says, those water eyes bright as she looks up at me.

Taking the stone back, I demonstrate again how to strike it against another to create spark and flame. Bleeding fire for her.

Her face lights up with understanding. "Instant fire. God, my sister would love these. Justine's always been the one with survival skills. Me? I once set my hair on fire trying to light a gas stove."

She mimes something that might be flames rising from her head, then laughs at her own gesture. The sound catches me off guard. So bright and clear, like water tumbling over stones. It makes something warm unfurl in my chest, a sensation as strange as the fact she is here with me.

I realize with a jolt that I want to be the one who brings her joy like that. I want to be the reason she is happy.

It is not like my life as a hunter. My purpose has always been to track, to hunt, to provide meat. Protect the clan. To survive. The happiness of another being has never been a goal.

Until now.

I don't know when her presence became comfort rather

than duty. When her safety became more important than the hunt itself.

No. Her safety *is* the hunt now.

The thought is a simple, hard truth. Like stone. Like bone.

She continues vocalizing, pointing to various aspects of the cave, asking questions I cannot answer but feel compelled to try anyway. I show her the small water source at the back of the cave. It's barely more than a seep between rocks, but her reaction is like watching a rare spine-flower unfurl its petals after a storm. Her smile when she cups her hands beneath it to catch the precious drops is a heat that radiates. It makes my skin hum.

It makes the air in my lungs feel thin.

It makes my dra-kir beat a wrong, stuttering rhythm.

"This is perfect," she says, drinking deeply before wiping her mouth with the back of her hand. "Thank you. For finding this place. For..." She gestures vaguely, encompassing the cave, the fire, perhaps our entire journey together. "Everything."

I tilt my head, accepting her approval though I don't deserve it. Not when part of me secretly, *selfishly* wishes to extend our journey. To keep her to myself a little longer before returning her to her sister-female.

Because Jah-kee belongs with her sister-female, with her own kind. And I belong with the clan, with my brothers, with the life I've always known.

Don't I?

The glow beneath my skin pulses, as if in answer to my unspoken question. It illuminates the space between us, casting everything in soft golden light.

Jah-kee's eyes widen slightly as she notices it. She points to my chest, then to her own skin where no such light exists.

"Why does that happen?" she vocalizes. "That glowing thing. Is it... normal for your kind?"

She sees it. She wonders at it.

Her sounds are questions. Questions I do not have the words for, even in my own mind. How can I explain this to her? That the soft, controlled glow of a calm Drakav is nothing like this? That this wild, brilliant fire under my skin is a betrayal. A light that has its own will, that answers only to her presence, to her touch. That my skin burns with this light only for her. That it both terrifies and fascinates me.

She inches closer. When she's near enough, she reaches out, her fingers hovering just above my skin, not quite touching.

"May I?" she vocalizes, voice soft.

My body leans toward her hand before my mind realizes I've moved. Her touch, when it comes, is breath-light against my forearm. The glow flares instantly, brightening to almost painful intensity where her skin meets mine.

We both gasp at the sensation—a jolt of something electric that races through my veins. It doesn't hurt. Quite the opposite. It feels... *good*. Like completing a circuit I didn't know was broken.

She doesn't pull away. Instead, her fingers trace a slow path up my arm, following the glow as it spreads. Her touch is curious, exploratory, without fear or hesitation.

"It's beautiful," she whispers, her gaze fixed on the patterns of light beneath my skin. "Like... like you've swallowed the sun."

The wonder in her voice makes my chest tight. Makes me want things I cannot name, let alone understand.

Makes me want *her*.

The need to have her should send me away. Should make me put stone walls between us. But I do not move. I let her touch. I let her stay close.

She looks up at me then, her water-blue eyes locking with

mine. In that quiet, a spark jumps between us. Not the light under the skin. Something else. Something that does not need words or mind-thoughts to be understood. It is a feeling of... *rightness*. A quiet in my blood that I have never known.

My claws ache to answer her touch. To trace the lines of her face, to feel the softness of her skin. But I keep them sheathed. My claws are made for hunting, for fighting, for breaking things. She is small. Soft. I could tear her skin with a careless move.

The thought is a spear in my gut.

I cannot risk it. Cannot risk *her*.

So I remain perfectly still as her fingers continue their journey, mapping the contours of my arm, my shoulder, careful to avoid the healing wound. When she reaches my chest, just above where my dra-kir thunders beneath bone and muscle, she pauses.

"Your heart," she vocalizes, splaying her fingers over the spot. "It's racing."

The air freezes in my lungs. I cannot draw a breath. I cannot let one out. The glow under my skin pulses in time with my dra-kir, a frantic, silent betrayal of the control I pretend to have.

Her fingers press a fraction harder, as if she could feel the thunder of it, and something in me tightens to the point of breaking.

She is too close. Her scent is a storm in my head, wiping out all other thought. My claws slide from their sheaths. My fangs ache, a deep, sharp pressure in my jaw.

A fire ignites in my gut, and it is *not* the clean fire of the hunt. This is a greedy, molten heat that pools low. Heavy. Demanding. It is not pain. It is... purpose. A truth that lives in my blood.

It *wants*.

It wants to drag her into my lap. To bury my face in the soft curve of her neck and breathe her in until I am full of her scent. It wants to sink my fangs into the swell of her shoulder. To *mark* her. To taste the heat of her skin.

It wants to push her down onto the sand, part her soft thighs, and find the secret heat between them. Find that hidden spring and push into it. Push and push until she is full of me, overflowing with me, until every part of her screams *mine*.

The vision is a fire in my blood. My body clenches, a pleasure so sharp it is almost pain. My member strains, hard as stone, a singular, focused ache. Yes. This is what it wants. This is what *I* want.

Then, through the red haze of need, a second vision forms. My strength against her softness. My claws, my teeth, my weight... I would tear her apart. I would break her. This starving beast inside me would devour her.

She is not prey.

The thought shatters through me like cracking stone. It breaks whatever spell her touch has cast, sending me flying backward so suddenly that she topples with a startled yelp.

"Sorry," she says, catching herself on her palms. "Did I hurt you?"

Dust.

Dust and bones.

I turn away, putting the fire between us, my body trembling with the force of a need I have only just tasted and must now deny. The ache has not faded. It is a hot, coiling serpent in my gut.

I force my claws to sheathe.

Focus. Provide.

The meat. The fire. A memory surfaces like a

lifeline. *Rok.* He held Jus-teen's meat to the fire. Held it until the red was gone, until it was tough and dry.

Females are delicate.

The thought is simple. A fact. A solid rock to stand on in the middle of this madness. Jah-kee has suffered much. The meat I have given her has been raw, the way of a hunter. That is wrong. For her.

I will prepare the meat the way she needs it.

The task gives me something to focus on besides the dangerous heat in my veins. I arrange the meat carefully over the fire stones, using the sandfin's quill to pierce the flesh. The smell fills the cave, rich and savory.

"That smells amazing," Jah-kee says, moving to sit across from me, the fire between us like a barrier. Perhaps she senses my sudden distance. Perhaps she welcomes it.

Frustration burns hot in my gut. It is a fire I cannot put out with sand. I keep my attention fixed on the task at hand.

When the meat is held to the fire until it is tough and dry—almost charred in places—I transfer it to a flat stone and offer it to her. She accepts with a smile, and my member strains against its pouch once more.

"Thank you," she says, taking a cautious bite. Her eyes widen in surprise, then what looks like pleasure. "Oh wow. This is good. Like, *really* good. So much better than when I first ate it. Mm!"

A sound escapes her—something between a moan and a hum—as her pink tongue darts out to run over her lips.

I stare, transfixed.

At this rate, I won't need to ever light a signal fire for my clan. The glow under my skin could guide them here from three territories away.

Pride swells in my chest at her approval. I select a piece for myself, though I prefer the taste of raw meat, its juices rich with lifeblood. But sharing this meal with her, prepared as she prefers it, feels right somehow.

We eat in companionable silence for a time, the fire crackling between us. When we've finished, Jah-kee wipes her hands on her hide-coverings then looks at me with renewed curiosity.

"I just realized," she vocalizes slowly, "I don't know your actual name. You came out of nowhere. Saved me. And...I've just been calling you 'Goldilocks' this whole time."

She points to herself. "Jacqui," she says clearly, then points to me, raising her brows in question.

Ah. She's tried this before. She wants my name. Something so simple, yet it has never occurred to me to offer it. In the mindspace, a name is the echo of a soul's shape, not...this. Not sounds forced through throat and lips.

I press a claw to my throat, feeling the vibration of my dra-kir beneath. How does one carve a feeling into noise?

My first attempt is pure silence. Just lips parting on air. The second produces a growl so crude I wince.

Jah-kee doesn't laugh. She leans forward, her water-filled eyes wide. Waiting.

I try again, shaping my tongue as I've seen hers move.

"Thhh—" A hiss of air.

"—aaarn." The ending rattles like rocks tumbling.

Tharn.

Graveled. Broken. But there.

For a moment, she doesn't move. Then, suddenly, she launches herself at me, her arms lock around my neck so tightly I feel her dra-kir pulse against my chest. Her voice is muffled against my skin.

"Th-aaarn."

My name. Worn smooth by her lips.

I should push her away. This closeness is too much. The scent of her head-fur, the heat of her skin...

Instead, I press my forehead to hers and try again:

"Tharn."

"Tharn."

Clearer this time.

Dust.

Her smile could burn brighter than Ain at dawn.

CHAPTER 14
SURVIVAL 101: DON'T DIE; DON'T FALL FOR THE ALIEN

JACQUI

It turns out that traveling with a seven-foot alien has its perks.

For one, I don't have to worry about carrying water. Tharn's got that covered. For another, I can see danger coming from miles away because he suddenly freezes like a cat spotting a laser dot.

Like right now.

We've been walking for hours, the morning sun already climbing high in the yellow sky, when Tharn stops so abruptly I nearly slam into his back.

"What?" I ask, stepping out from behind him to scan the endless dunes. "What is it?"

He doesn't answer, of course. But his entire body has gone rigid, head tilted back, nostrils flaring as he scents the air. His amber eyes track something in the sky I can't see yet.

Then I spot it—a shadow passing over the sand, growing larger by the second.

Before I can even process what's happening, Tharn moves. One moment I'm standing beside him; the next, he's in front of me, body angled to shield mine, one arm extended backward to keep me in place behind him.

The shadow resolves into something that looks like a—and I shit you not—a ducking pterodactyl. Its leathery wings stretch wide, a long, whip-like tail trailing behind it. It soars overhead, circling once before continuing on its way, apparently uninterested in us.

Just like the last three threats Tharn's protected me from this morning.

"It's gone," I say, still wide-eyed. There are flying things here? Not just things hiding under the sand or shadow creatures from the underworld. This really is hell.

Tharn glances down at me, golden eyes scanning my face as if checking for signs of fear. Finding none, he relaxes marginally, though he keeps scanning the sky for several long moments before resuming our trek.

I fall into step beside him, a small smile playing at my lips. His protectiveness is endearing, if occasionally over-the-top. He positions himself between me and literally everything. From actual dangers like that sand manta ray thing, to even a harmless tumbleweed that rustled in the breeze.

He reminds me of Justine, in a way. My sister was always the shield between me and the world's sharp edges. But where Justine's protection was emotional, his is intensely physical. Primal. Like he's made a blood oath to keep my fragile human body intact, even if it means throwing himself in front of anything that moves.

"You know," I say, "on Earth, we have these animals called dogs. Big, furry things that are fiercely loyal to their humans. They guard them, protect them, follow them everywhere."

Tharn glances at me, head tilting in that curious way that's become so familiar.

"You remind me of a dog sometimes," I continue, grinning. "A big, golden guard dog. All growls and protective instincts."

His brows furrow slightly, as if he senses I'm teasing him but isn't quite sure how to respond.

"It's a compliment," I add, reaching up to pat his shoulder. "Dogs are the best."

He looks thoroughly confused now, but there's a softness around his eyes. As if he knows I'm not mocking him, even if he doesn't understand the words.

We walk in companionable silence for a while, the rhythmic crunch of sand beneath my feet oddly soothing.

It should be monotonous, this endless walking. But something about Tharn's presence makes it... not unpleasant. There's a comfort in having him nearby, in the steady cadence of his breathing, in the occasional rumble of satisfaction he makes when he spots something familiar on the horizon.

"So," I say, breaking the silence again, "on a scale of one to 'we're totally screwed,' how are we doing? Are we getting closer to Justine?"

He glances at me, then points toward what looks like a distant mountain range barely visible through the heat haze. His expression is reassuring, though I'm not sure if that's intentional or just my desperate need to find something positive in this situation.

"That's where we're headed?" I ask, following the line of his finger. "Where Justine is?"

His head snaps toward me at the name, pupils flaring.

"Jusss-teen," he repeats, the syllables rough and halting, like his tongue can't quite shape itself around human sounds.

God. Just hearing her name in that gravelly voice makes my throat tighten.

I point to the mountains, then hold up my fingers one by one. "How. Many. Days?"

He stares at my hand, gaze shifting to the digits with intense focus. After a beat, he mirrors me—three fingers raised.

"Three days?" I guess, and he tilts his head back. "Okay. Three days. I can do that."

I can do that. The thought feels strange, unfamiliar. Since when am I the type of person who can trek across an alien desert for days on end? I'm Jacqui Parker. Perpetual follower, professional younger sister, queen of bad decisions.

And yet, here I am. Still walking. Still breathing. Still stubbornly refusing to die despite this planet's best efforts.

Maybe Justine isn't the only stubborn one in the family after all.

The thought brings a small smile to my lips. What would Justine think if she could see me now? Walking side by side with a golden alien warrior across an endless desert, surviving shadow creature attacks and devil manta rays, and blistering heat?

She probably wouldn't believe it. Hell, I barely believe it myself.

"Hey," I say, a sudden idea striking me. "Want to learn something fun?"

Tharn looks at me curiously.

"Human gestures," I explain. "Like... this."

I hold up my thumb in the universal sign for 'okay' or 'good job.' Tharn stares at it before hesitantly mimicking the gesture. His thumb is nearly twice the size of mine, tipped with a retracted claw that glints in the sunlight.

"Perfect!" I beam at him. "That means 'good' or 'I approve' or, you know, 'thanks for not letting me die horribly.'"

His lips twitch, almost a smile, and he repeats the gesture with more confidence.

"Now try this one," I say, raising my hand in a wave. "This is how humans say hello."

He copies me, his massive arm moving stiffly, the gesture somehow both regal and absurdly awkward on his large frame.

I can't help it—I laugh. Not a small chuckle, but a full-bodied laugh that bubbles up from somewhere deep inside me. When was the last time I laughed like this? Before the crash, certainly. Maybe even before we left Earth.

Tharn tilts his head, watching me with those intense amber-gold eyes. Then, to my surprise, he repeats the wave, this time with exaggerated awkwardness, his arm flailing slightly as if he's intentionally making it comical.

He's... joking with me?

My laughter redoubles, tears springing to my eyes. I'm so caught up in the moment that I don't notice the uneven ground ahead. My foot catches on a rock hidden in the sand, and suddenly I'm pitching forward, arms windmilling uselessly.

Before I can face-plant, strong hands catch me, steadying me effortlessly. I find myself pulled against Tharn's chest, his arms around me, his leathery warm scent filling my nostrils.

Our eyes meet, and something electric passes between us. His glow brightens where our skin touches, pulsing in time with what feels like both our heartbeats. For a moment, I can't breathe, can't think, can't do anything but feel the solid warmth of him against me.

His eyes drop to my lips, just for a second, but long enough to send a jolt of... something... through my entire body.

Oh. Oh no.

I pull away quickly, brushing sand from my clothes with more force and focus than the situation warrants. "Thanks for the save," I say, my voice a slightly higher thing than normal. "Good reflexes. Very... helpful."

He watches me, something unreadable in his expression.

I force down a swallow.

"We should, um, keep moving," I say, gesturing vaguely ahead. "Places to go, sisters to find and all that."

His gaze lingers on me a beat too long before he turns to lead the way once more.

Well, that was... something.

Something I absolutely do not have time to think about right now. Or possibly ever.

We continue walking, the silence between us different now. Charged with an awareness I'm not ready to acknowledge. I focus instead on the horizon, on putting one foot in front of the other, on the goal that's driven me since I left the transport wreckage.

Find Justine. Survive. Go home.

Simple. Straightforward. Definitely not complicated by whatever just happened.

By the time the sun begins its descent, we've reached the base of a cliff formation that rises abruptly from the desert floor. Tharn leads me to a narrow fissure in the rock face, barely visible until we're right in front of it. He gestures for me to go first, his expression clearly saying, "This is where we'll camp."

I squeeze through the opening, which widens into a small cavern—more of an alcove, really—sheltered from the wind and hidden from view. The floor is sandy but level, and the ceiling is high enough that even Tharn can stand upright.

"Nice find," I say, hoping my voice communicates my appreciation. "Cozy."

Tharn does that chin tilt of his head. Before I can decipher what he means, he's leaving. I watch him go, a strange twinge in my chest at even this brief separation.

Get it together, Jacqui. He's just getting firewood or something. Not abandoning you in the desert.

I busy myself arranging our sleeping area, clearing away larger stones, and smoothing the sand as best I can. By the time Tharn returns, arms laden with what looks like the carcasses of those small, lizard-like creatures, I've created a reasonably comfortable spot.

"Dinner?" I ask, pointing to the dead animals.

He does the chin tilt, setting to work immediately. I watch, still fascinated by the careful precision of his movements as he prepares the creature. For someone with claws that can tear through a living thing's spine, he's remarkably delicate when the situation calls for it.

Once the fire is lit and the meat is cooking, Tharn settles beside me, his larger body radiating heat in the cooling evening air. We sit in silence, watching the flames dance, the familiar routine of camp-making somehow grounding despite the alien surroundings.

"We make a good team," I say softly, more to myself than to him. "Who'd have thought, right? Human girl and alien warrior, surviving the desert together."

He glances at me, the firelight reflecting in his amber eyes, turning them to molten gold. Something in his expression makes my heart skip a beat. There's warmth there; an intensity that goes beyond simple companionship.

I look away quickly, focusing on the cooking meat. "Food's almost done," I say, though I have no idea if it is or not. "Smells good."

When we eat, the flavors are rich and savory. I suppose I've gotten used to alien cuisine now. Surprisingly (or it could just be the fact I'm a foodie), I like it.

After we've eaten, I move to the entrance of our shelter, gazing out at the desert night. The sky here is nothing like Earth's. The stars are different, arranged in patterns I don't recognize, and there are three moons, each a different size and color, hanging low on the horizon. Despite that, their light hardly reaches the surface.

It's beautiful, in a haunting, alien way.

Tharn joins me, his presence warm at my back. He points to a cluster of stars, then traces a pattern with his finger, making a soft rumbling sound in his chest.

"A constellation?" I guess. "That's what we call them on Earth. Patterns in the stars. Stories written in the sky."

He rumbles, seemingly pleased that I understand. He traces another pattern, this one resembling something with many legs. A spider, maybe, or a crab.

"What's that one called?" I ask. I know he can't answer, but I can't stop myself from asking anyway.

To my surprise, he attempts to vocalize something. His voice is a low rumble that sends a skitter down my spine and straight to the bottom of my belly, where it settles. I swallow hard. He's trying to share his world with me.

"It's beautiful," I say, gesturing to the entire sky. "All of it."

His gaze shifts from the stars to my face, and the intensity in his eyes steals my breath.

"Bee-yooo-tiful," he repeats, the word rough, broken, and aimed directly at me.

Heat floods my cheeks, and I drop my gaze. "How..." I pant. "Do you even know what that means?" He doesn't. It's just a coincidence, and I'm here getting all flustered over it.

God, Jacqui. Whatever's happening, end it.

"We should, um, get some rest," I mutter, retreating into the shelter. "Big day tomorrow. More walking. Yay."

I settle onto my designated sleeping spot, hyper-aware of Tharn as he moves around the small space, banking the fire for the night. When he finally sits, it's with him facing the entrance, his side profile visible to me as he guards me even in rest.

"You don't have to stay awake all night," I say, though I know he probably won't sleep deeply anyway. "We can take turns keeping watch or something."

He tilts his head at me before gesturing for me to sleep. His meaning is clear: he'll keep watch, I should rest.

"Stubborn," I mutter, but am I actually scolding him? No. Truth be told, I'm exhausted; the day's journey weighs heavily on my limbs.

As I drift toward sleep, my thoughts wander to Justine. Is she safe? Is she wondering where I am, if I'm alive? Does she think I'm still back at the transport, waiting for rescue with the others?

Or does she know, somehow, that I came looking for her?

Justine has always been the strong one, the capable one. While I was busy partying through college, she was securing internships and planning her future. When our mother died, she handled everything—the funeral arrangements, the paperwork, the endless details that grief makes impossible to focus on. And I...

I went into myself. Lost my ability to speak.

We were only kids. She shouldn't have had to deal with that alone while I...

I swallow down the pain.

She's been taking care of me for as long as I can remember. Always the protector, the guide, the one with the plan.

And I've been... what? The follower? The burden?

No, that's not fair. Justine never made me feel like a burden. But I've always been aware of living in her shadow, always a step behind, always a little less capable.

Until now.

Because out here, in this alien desert with only Tharn for

company, I've had to find my own strength. My own capability. My own will to survive.

And I have.

I've survived shadow creature attacks and more. I've trekked across endless dunes under a merciless sun. I've gathered poisonous plants with my bare hands and faced down death more times than I can count.

Maybe I'm not just Justine's little sister anymore. Maybe I'm becoming someone else. Someone stronger. Someone who doesn't need to be saved.

The thought follows me into dreams filled with golden light and amber eyes. Dreams where we do more than just trek the desert. More than just survive. We *explore*. His hands learn the map of me, my body sings under his touch, and when our skin meets—

Oh.

I wake with a silent gasp in the predawn dark, the desert air cool against my flushed skin. My pulse thrums in places I'm trying *very hard* not to think about.

Tharn sits where I last saw him, but something's different. His posture, usually so alert, seems... softer somehow. Less guarded.

He's staring into the dead fire, his expression distant, almost melancholy. The glow beneath his skin is dimmer than I've seen it before, pulsing slowly like a fading heartbeat.

He looks... lonely.

The realization makes something in my chest ache. Of course, he's lonely. He's stranded out here with a being he can barely communicate with, diverted from his path, injured, exhausted. He's probably missing his tribe, his home, his people.

And yet, he's never complained. Never shown frustration at

having to care for me, protect me, guide me. He's just... done it. Willingly. Patiently.

Why?

Duty? Honor? Some alien code of ethics I don't understand? Or something else?

I watch him silently, the question turning over in my mind. His profile in the dying light is striking—the strong line of his jaw, the slope of his forehead, the copper-auburn hair that falls in loose waves to his shoulders. He's unlike anything I've ever seen, and yet, in this moment, he seems so... human. So vulnerable.

I almost call out to him, almost break the silence with his name. But something stops me. This feels like a private moment, a glimpse of Tharn when he thinks no one is watching. A side of him I'm not sure he'd want me to see.

So I remain quiet, my breathing even, pretending to sleep while my mind races.

What am I to him? A burden? A duty?

And the question that makes my own heart ache in the darkness...

What is he becoming to me?

CHAPTER 15

SHE...THINKS ABOUT MY MUSCLES

THARN

My dra-kir beats too quickly for a hunter at rest. Many sols have passed since we left the cave of fireblooms. Many sols of constant vigilance, of scanning horizons for threats, of watching Jah-kee's small form for signs of weakness or pain. Many sols of growing awareness that something inside me has fundamentally changed.

The tether between us grows stronger with each passing moment. It is no longer just the light beneath my skin that responds to her presence. It is *everything*. My senses heightened to catch the faintest change in her scent, my ears tuned to the rhythm of her breathing, my body instinctively positioning itself between her and any potential danger.

I find myself watching her when she does not notice. Watching the way Ain's light catches in her head-fur. Observing how her water-blue eyes narrow when she concentrates, how her small teeth catch her lower lip when she's uncertain.

These details should mean nothing to a hunter. Yet I catalogue them as carefully as I would track prey across the dust.

It is... unsettling.

More unsettling still are the glimpses I've begun to catch of her thoughts. Not true mindspeak, but flashes. When she looked at the stars, I felt her wonder. When she stumbled and I caught her, I felt her gratitude. These moments are brief, but I have begun to hunger for them.

And now, as we begin another sol's journey, I find myself searching for more. Hungering for them in a way that makes my instincts bristle with warning.

This is not the way of a hunter. Not the way of the clan.

I push the thoughts aside as I guide Jah-kee through the dust. Ain is already high overhead and Jah-kee moves beside me, her stride shorter than it was at dawn. Her breathing comes quicker. Her skin pushing those tiny beads of water from her pores.

She is weakening, and the waterskin is nearly empty. She will suffer because I failed to provide.

I scan the horizon, searching for signs of water, of shade, of anything that might ease her burden. The dunes roll endlessly before us, broken only by a dark line in the distance—a ravine cutting through the desert floor.

Beyond it, the land rises into rocky foothills. A better place. Higher ground often holds water, and the rocks will offer true shelter from Ain's light. Good. But to reach it, we must first cross the scar on the land.

I gesture toward it, catching Jah-kee's attention. She follows my gaze, chin jerking in understanding.

"Is that where we're headed?" she vocalizes, her voice thin with tiredness or maybe thirst.

I tilt my head, pointing to the waterskin at my side, then to the ravine.

"*Water.*" Maybe. I hope.

She smiles, the expression brightening her face despite her exhaustion. "Lead on, Tharn."

My dra-kir speeds up at the sound of my name on her tongue. By the time we reach the edge of the ravine, Ain has climbed to her zenith, her light brutal and unforgiving. I scan the steep walls of stone dropping away before us.

The path across is barely wide enough for my feet, the ground unstable with loose rock and shifting sand. My instincts scream to find another way. But I know this is the only path. For me, it is a risk. For her, it is a death sentence if she falls.

Jah-kee steps forward, peering down. "Well," she vocalizes, "that's going to be fun."

I gesture for her to stay close, pointing to the path and then to myself to indicate I will guide her. She should follow behind me, where I can best protect her from what lies ahead.

But she shakes her head, jaw setting stubbornly. She points to herself, then to the path. She wants to go first.

Worry tightens my chest. My dra-kir pulses an urgent warning. She is tired, weakened by heat and thirst. Her steps have been unsteady for the last half-sol. If she slips—

But the determination in her eyes stops my protest before it forms. There is pride there, and something else. A need to prove herself, perhaps.

I cannot deny her this. Not when I feel the strength of her will pulsing across the strange connection between us.

So I tilt my head in affirmation, though every instinct rebels against it. I gesture for her to proceed, but indicate I will stay close behind her.

She takes a deep breath and steps onto the path. I follow so close my chest almost touches her back.

The ground crumbles slightly beneath her first step. She steadies herself, her breathing quickening, before continuing forward. One careful step after another, her arms slightly extended for balance.

We make slow progress, the ravine yawning wide beneath us. The wind picks up, whistling through the stone corridors below, tugging at Jah-kee's garments. She sways slightly but continues forward.

A section of path gives way beneath her foot, loose rocks skittering down into the ravine. She lurches forward, arms flailing as she tries to regain her balance.

My body moves before thought, an instinct faster than reason. My arm wraps around her waist, pulling her hard against my chest as her feet slide out from under her.

For a single dra-kir beat, we teeter on the edge, my own balance precarious from the sudden movement. Planting my feet, my claws dig into the stone, anchoring us.

Jah-kee gasps, her small hands grasping my arm where it holds her. Her dra-kir races against my forearm in a frantic rhythm.

The thought of her falling, of her fragile body shattering on the rocks below, sends a surge of pure fear through me. She looks up at me, her water-blue eyes wide, her breath coming in short gasps. Her scent fills my senses—fear, yes, but also trust. Complete, absolute trust that I would not let her fall.

She trusts me. With her life. With her safety. With everything.

The glow beneath my skin pulses brighter, responding to the surge of... something... that floods through me at this understanding.

I set her carefully back on the path, though my hands

linger on her shoulders longer than necessary. She's trembling slightly, the fear she hid now visible in the fine shaking of her limbs.

"Thanks," she vocalizes. "Guess I should watch where I'm stepping, huh?"

I rumble softly, a sound of comfort, and move closer still, my arm a ready shield as we finish the crossing.

When we reach the other side, she collapses onto a flat rock, her face pale beneath the flush of heat.

I offer her the last of the water. She refuses, gesturing for me to drink. Her stubbornness burns bright.

I growl low in my throat and press the pouch firmly to her lips. She drinks, draining it. It is not enough.

She needs more water. Now. I must leave her to find it.

I scan our surroundings, searching for any sign of moisture. The ravine floor below might offer better chances. Water often finds the lowest point, and the shade of the ravine walls would protect any seeps from Ain's evaporating light.

But reaching the floor means leaving Jah-kee alone, exposed on the ridge. The thought makes my dra-kir twist painfully.

There is no choice. She needs water. I must find it.

I help her move to the shade of a rock outcropping, gesturing for her to stay put while I search. She frowns, her brow furrowing.

"Where are you going?" she vocalizes. She tries to sit up. "Tharn, please, don't leave me here."

The distress in her tone is clear. I place my claw over hers, rumbling softly in reassurance. I point to the ravine, then mime drinking.

Her eyes widen in understanding, but she shakes her head. "I'll come with you."

She tries to stand, but her legs wobble dangerously. I push

her gently back down, my expression firm. She cannot make the climb down the ravine wall in her current state. She would fall. She would die.

"Fine," she mutters, crossing her arms across her chest. "But hurry back. I don't want to be shadow creature bait."

I rumble again, this time with a note of promise. I will return. She will be safe.

I move quickly to the edge of the ravine, seeking a path down its steep wall. The descent is treacherous, loose rock sliding beneath my feet, but I make my way down with the sure-footedness of a hunter born in the dust.

The floor of the ravine is cooler, sheltered from Ain's direct light by the high walls on either side. I move swiftly, scanning the base of the rock walls for any sign of moisture.

And there—a darker patch of sand near the base of the eastern wall. I approach cautiously, hope rising in my chest. Yes. A small seep of water trickles from a crack in the rock, forming a tiny pool no larger than my claw before disappearing back into the dust.

It's not much, but it's enough. Enough to fill our waterskin, enough to cool Jah-kee's overheated skin, enough to keep her alive until we reach the next water source.

I fill the pouch carefully, making sure to capture every precious drop.

The climb back up the ravine wall is harder, hampered by my need to keep the waterskin secure, but the thought of Jah-kee waiting above drives me onward.

When I crest the ridge, my dra-kir pulses with relief at the sight of her still sitting where I left her. Her head rests against the rock, eyes closed, face turned away from the sky. For a terrifying moment, I fear she has fallen unconscious.

But at my approach, her eyes flutter open, finding mine immediately.

"You found water," she breathes, her gaze fixing on the pouch in my hands.

I kneel beside her, offering it immediately. She drinks greedily, her movements clumsy with exhaustion. Water spills down her chin, dampening the front of her hide-covering, but she doesn't seem to notice or care.

When she's drunk her fill, she sighs, eyes closing in obvious relief.

"That feels amazing," she murmurs, resting back against the stone. But the fire in her skin still burns.

I look at the waterskin. Then at my claw.

To waste even a single drop on the dust is a deep offense. Water is life, meant only for the throat, to sustain the body from within. What I am about to do... it is wrong. A hunter does not waste.

But the heat from her skin is a silent scream, and it overrides every law I have ever known.

With a resolve that feels like a betrayal of my kind, I pour a small amount of the precious water into my palm. Before I can second-guess the waste, I press my wet claw to Jah-kee's brow.

She sighs, a deep, shuddering sound of pure relief, her body leaning into my touch. The simple sound shatters something inside me.

I move my claw to her cheeks, her neck, the exposed skin of her arms where Ain has created an angry red. Each time my claw runs dry, I pour more water, ignoring the voice of my ancestors screaming in my head at the sacrilege. I am letting life itself drip onto the dust, all for the soft sounds she makes.

And Jah-kee allows this tending without protest, a sign of just how deeply the heat has taken her.

As I press my damp palm to the fast, frantic pulse at the base of her throat, it happens. A strange pulse of thought reaches me. It is not my own.

It is a warmth. A feeling of safety. And something else, a thought so clear it is like a whisper in my own mind:

—*gentle... for someone so dangerous*—

The fragment slips in, gone before I can grasp it. My claw stills on her skin.

Did she...?

Is the mindspace opening between us? I stare at her face, but her eyes are still closed, her expression peaceful. She is unaware. The thought was hers, but she does not know she sent it.

I help her to her feet, focus on her face. Hoping for more. As we walk, slower now, more fragments come, brief flashes of her thoughts breaking through.

—*wonder what Justine will think of him*—

—*the way his muscles shift when he walks*—

That last thought is not just an observation. It carries a warmth that makes my member stir. She finds my form... pleasing? The thought is a strange, hot stone in my chest. I find myself suddenly aware of my own body.

The water from the ravine gives her strength. For a time. We walk for the rest of the sol, her steps more certain, her mind quieter. We camp in the shelter of tall rock formations. Jah-kee seems to be regaining some strength. I allow myself to believe the worst is over.

But the dust is relentless. And Ain is unforgiving.

Another sol of walking under the burning sky begins to strip away the strength she had regained. The water is once again a few precious, sloshing drops at the bottom of my waterskin.

I slow my pace, allowing Jah-kee to match it without strain.

"I'm fine," she vocalizes when she catches me watching her. "Just a little hot."

The barely there impression of her thoughts in the mind-space tells me what she means. But she is not fine. Her steps grow increasingly unsteady. Twice already this sol she has stumbled on perfectly flat ground. Her skin has taken on a strange flush, different from the reddening caused by Ain's light. And there is something else. A subtle shift in her scent that triggers an ancient warning in my hunter's instincts.

Something is wrong.

That dark, as she rests, I watch the too-rapid rise and fall of her chest. Her face appears flushed even in the darkness, and occasionally she mutters words I cannot understand, her head turning fitfully from side to side.

I press a careful hand to her brow, alarmed by the heat radiating from her skin. Not the normal warmth of her alien body, but something hotter, dangerous.

That fire beneath her skin is returning.

Is it the shadowmaw's poison still? A new sickness? Something in the water or meat I have been feeding her?

I do not know. And not knowing fills me with a fear I have never experienced before—not in the face of shadowmaws or dust storms or rival clans.

This fear has no target to fight, no strategy to overcome it. There is only Jah-kee's small body, burning with an invisible fire I cannot extinguish.

My dra-kir pulses frantically, reaching for hers across whatever strange connection binds us. I feel... something. A flickering response, weaker than before. Like a light dimming.

I do not rest that dark.

CHAPTER 16
I DO NOT WANT TO GIVE HER BACK

THARN

The third sol begins badly.

Jah-kee wakes late, her movements sluggish and uncoordinated. Her eyes, usually so bright and alert, appear glassy and unfocused. When I offer her water, she drinks mechanically, without the usual eagerness.

"I don't feel so good," she vocalizes, voice hoarse and distant.

I help her to her feet, alarmed by how heavily she leans against me. The heat from her body strikes me like a lance. Too hot. Too much heat for a living being.

She tries to take a step forward and immediately sways, her knees buckling. I catch her before she can fall, lifting her easily into my arms.

She doesn't protest. Doesn't squirm about being carried again. Doesn't vocalize anything at all.

That, more than anything, tells me how serious her condition has become.

137

I press my palm to her brow again, a low growl of distress escaping me at the burning heat I find there. Her skin is dry now, not leaking those tiny droplets of water as it usually does. Her breathing is unsteady, too.

"'m fine," she mumbles, her eyes struggling to focus on my face. "Jus' need to rest a minute."

I rumble softly, trying to convey reassurance I do not feel. We need to find shade, water, coolness. I need to bring her temperature down before it cooks her fragile human brain.

But we are in the open dust, the next proper shelter at least half a sol's journey ahead. Ain's light will only grow stronger, hotter, as the sol progresses.

"Jus..." she mumbles, her head rolling against my chest. "Need to find Jus..."

Jus...her sister-female, Jus-teen.

"*Yes,*" I project into the mindspace. "*We will find her.*"

But her eyes have closed, her body going limp in my arms. She hasn't lost consciousness completely—I can see her eyes moving beneath their lids, her lips occasionally forming silent words—but she's no longer fully present.

Fear claws at my chest. This is beyond my knowledge, beyond my skills as a hunter. A tracker. She needs help that I cannot provide.

She needs her sister-female. She needs Rok.

And they are still at least a sol's journey away.

I adjust my hold on her small form, cradling her against my chest where I can feel each too-rapid beat of her dra-kir. Then I run.

The dust shifts beneath my feet, Ain beats mercilessly upon us both, but I do not slow. My muscles burn with the effort, my lungs working hard to keep pace with my exertion, but these discomforts are nothing compared to the fear driving me forward.

As Ain climbs higher in the sky, Jah-kee's condition worsens. Her breathing grows more labored, her body alternating between terrifying stillness and sudden, violent shivering. The few times her eyes flutter open, they stare past me, seeing things that aren't there.

"S'all burning," she murmurs once, her voice cracked and dry. "Justine... fire everywhere..."

Then, unexpectedly, the mindspace opens between us.

It happens without warning. One moment, I am carrying her burning body across endless sand, the next I am plunged into a whirl of chaotic images and sensations.

A place called *Earth*. A world of green and blue, so different from the dust. Tall structures reaching toward the sky. Crowds of humans, moving in unfathomable patterns.

Fear—a lurch, the scream of twisting metal, gravity tilting unnaturally. Jah-kee's terror rips through me: the taste of copper, her sister-female's crushing grip, and the detached voice of the metal beast: *'Payload compromised.'*

The images shift faster now. The transport we found in the dust with all the other females. Images of Jus-teen.

And then, abruptly, *me*.

I see myself through her eyes. Golden skin glowing in the darkness, copper-red hair gleaming in the sunlight, amber eyes watching her with an intensity that startles me.

With the image comes a flood of emotions so powerful they nearly overwhelm me. Fear, yes, but also fascination. Gratitude. *Trust.*

And something else. Something warm and sweet and sharp all at once. Something that makes my dra-kir pound harder, faster.

Beautiful.

The thought drifts through the mindspace, tinged with wonder.

I see more images of myself—carrying her across the sand, fighting the shadowmaw, tending her wounds with gentle hands. Each memory pulses with that same warmth, growing stronger with each one.

—*safe with him.*

—*never looked at anyone this way before.*

—*want him to—*

The last thought cuts off abruptly, leaving behind an impression of desire so powerful it steals my breath. It is not a hunter's desire for prey, or a warrior's desire for victory.

It is something else entirely. Something I have glimpsed only in the way Rok looks at Jus-teen.

The realization rocks me to my core.

Before I can process this revelation, the mindspace shifts again, darkening at the edges. Jah-kee's presence grows fainter, more difficult to sense.

She is slipping away.

"*No!*" I project into the mindspace, reaching for her with everything I have. "*Live, Jah-kee!*"

It is weak, but I feel her stir, drawn by my voice even in her delirium.

"*Tharn?*"

Her mental voice is faint, confused, but she knows me. Recognizes me across the barrier of unconsciousness.

"*I am here,*" I project, pouring reassurance, strength, determination into the words. "*I will not let you go.*"

"*So tired.*"

"*Hurts.*"

"*Sorry.*"

Each thought comes more faintly than the last, her presence in the mindspace flickering like a dying flame.

"*No,*" I project again, more forcefully. "*You will fight. You will live.*"

I push my will into the mindspace, wrapping it around her fading presence like a physical shield. I pour every ounce of strength I possess into the connection between us, willing her to take it, to use it, to hold on.

In the physical world, I run faster, my muscles screaming in protest. All my focus is on Jah-kee. On her burning body in my arms, on her fading presence in the mindspace.

I will not lose her. Not now. Not when I have only just begun to understand what she means to me.

Solmarks bleed into solmarks, the landscape changing gradually as we approach the foothills leading to our destination. The mindspace flickers erratically, sometimes clear enough that I can feel Jah-kee's strange dreams, sometimes so faint I fear I've lost her completely.

By the time Ain begins her descent toward the horizon, my legs are numb, my lungs burning with each breath. But I do not slow. Cannot slow. The foothills rise before us, familiar territory at last. We are close. So close.

And then, as I crest a ridge overlooking a small valley, I see them.

Two figures in the distance, one tall and golden like myself, the other small like Jah-kee. They move together across the valley floor, apparently searching for something.

Searching for us.

Rok and Jus-teen.

Relief floods through me, so powerful it nearly brings me to my knees. They are here. Help is here. Jah-kee will be saved. Somehow.

I draw breath to extend my mindspeak, to alert them to our presence, but something stops me. A sudden, visceral reluctance that makes no sense in the face of Jah-kee's dire condition.

I do not want to give her back.

The thought rises again, unbidden and unwelcome. Selfish. Dangerous. *Wrong*.

Jah-kee stirs in my arms, a small whimper escaping her parched lips. Her skin burns against mine, her breathing shallow and rapid. She needs help. Now.

I force the selfish thought away and push my mind across the dust.

Rok's head snaps up immediately, his body tensing as he scans the ridgeline. When he spots me, he gestures urgently to Jus-teen, pointing in my direction.

They begin running toward us, Rok easily outpacing the smaller human despite his obvious effort to match her stride.

I start down the ridge, moving as quickly as I dare with Jah-kee's fragile form in my arms. The mindspace between us has gone silent, her presence faded to the barest whisper. Fear tightens my chest, makes my steps clumsy with haste.

"Jacqui!" Jus-teen's voice carries across the distance, high and desperate. "Oh my God, Jacqui!"

The female reaches us first, her water-blue eyes—so like Jah-kee's—wide with shock and fear as she takes in her sister's condition.

"What happened?" Her vocal screech would have once hurt my ears. It does not now. "*Tharn*," she mindspeaks, her hands reaching for Jah-kee even as I instinctively tighten my hold. "*Is she—*"

"*Fire*," I project. "*Under her skin. Help.*"

Rok's golden eyes assess the situation quickly. "*Brother*," he greets me, his gaze moving from my face to Jah-kee's still form. "*You found her.*"

I tilt my head in affirmation, unable to form more complex communication in the mindspace. Every fiber of my being is focused on Jah-kee, on the weak pulse of her life against my arms.

Jus-teen's hands hover over Jah-kee, trembling. "*We need to get her to the shelter*," she projects, her mental voice steadier now, though fear erupts from her into the mindspace. "*Hurry, Tharn.*"

My grip tightens slightly. The thought of relinquishing Jah-kee, even to her sister-female, sends a wave of resistance through me.

Rok's gaze shifts to the glow beneath my skin, understanding dawning in his eyes. "*Follow us, brother*," he projects quietly. "*It is not far.*"

Jus-teen leads the way, frequently glancing back at her sister's limp form in my arms, her pace urgent. Rok walks beside me, his protective stance mirroring my own as we approach a small cave entrance partially hidden in the rock.

Inside, the air is cooler. Jus-teen moves quickly, dusting sand from a flat surface.

"Here," she vocalizes, gesturing to the area. "Set her down. I need to examine her."

But I am already there, standing over the area where she wants me to put Jah-kee down. And...I hesitate, my arms tightening around her. The thought of letting her go claws at me, but I force myself to lower her onto the prepared bed.

The moment our bodies separate, the pain in my chest flares.

Jus-teen immediately kneels beside her sister. "*Rok, the fire-bloom.*" There's a ripping sound as she tears hide from her already torn hide coverings. "*And water. We need more water.*"

Rok dips his chin to his chest, moving quickly to retrieve what she needs. I stand motionless, suddenly adrift without Jah-kee's weight in my arms. My body feels numb with exhaustion now that the desperate drive to reach help has been fulfilled.

I watch as Jus-teen tends to her sister, as Rok assists with quiet efficiency, their movements synchronized like hunters who have tracked together for many seasons.

I remain at the edge of the small cave, my purpose fulfilled yet feeling strangely incomplete. The relief of finding help wars with a hollow ache, the pain, in my chest.

I have done my duty. The hunt is over.

There should be satisfaction. Pride.

There is only a hollow space in my chest where her weight used to be. There is only loss.

Rok approaches a short time later as Jus-teen continues her ministrations, his expression grave. "*Jus-teen knows how to treat the fire,*" he tells me.

"*Will she live?*" The question tears from me, raw with fear I don't try to hide.

Rok studies me for a long moment before answering. "*She is strong, this small one. Like her sister.*"

Relief weakens my knees, forces me to brace against the rock wall for support. Jah-kee will live. She will recover. She will...

She will no longer need me.

The thought strikes with unexpected force, leaving a cold emptiness in its wake.

"*Brother,*" Rok projects softly, "*what has happened between you and this female?*"

I look up, meeting his golden gaze directly. There is no judgment there, only curiosity. Understanding.

"*I do not know,*" I answer. "There is a... something. A tether. I can feel her thoughts sometimes. Her emotions. And when we touch..." I gesture helplessly to the golden glow that still pulses beneath my skin, though fainter now with distance from Jah-kee.

Rok does that chin jerk thing—something he has no doubt

learned from Jus-teen. *"It was the same with Jus-teen and me,"* he projects. *"This light. This connection. It grows stronger with time."*

I stare at him, shock momentarily overriding exhaustion. *"You experienced this, too? The glow? The... pull?"*

"Yes." His expression softens, something like contentment passing over his features. *"This light, this connection...it is rare, brother. Special. It is Ain's gift, marking her as yours to protect, as Jus-teen is mine. I fought it once, too. I tried to tell myself it wasn't real, but the light does not lie".*

I follow his gaze, watching as Jus-teen carefully bathes Jah-kee's feverish face. The tenderness in her movements mirrors the fierce protectiveness I've felt since finding Jah-kee in the dust.

"A Daughter of Ain...mine?" The thought filters into the mindspace.

Rok's mouth quirks in what might be amusement. *"Jus-teen does not like when we call them that."* He places a hand on my shoulder, his grip firm and reassuring. *"Rest now, brother. Regain your strength. There will be time to understand what this means later."*

At his words, my legs, steady through three sols of relentless travel, finally surrender. I slide down the cave wall until I sit on the cool stone floor, my gaze never leaving Jah-kee's still form.

Even as Jus-teen works, as my brother stands guard, I remain connected to her in ways I cannot fully comprehend.

Mine to claim. Mine to protect.

I do not want to give her back.

CHAPTER 17

SHARING WATER, CLAIMING, AND OTHER THINGS I SHOULD NOT DISCUSS AROUND JUS-TEEN

THARN

I do not like the way Jus-teen touches Jah-kee.

This is an unreasonable thought. I know this. Jus-teen is Jah-kee's sister-female. Their bond is ancient and deep. Deeper than clan-ties, deeper than lifeblood. And Jus-teen's hands are skilled, gentle as they wipe the fire-sweat from Jah-kee's brow, as they tip water past her cracked lips, as they check the pulse at her throat.

Yet I cannot stop the low growl that builds in my chest each time she leans close to Jah-kee, each time her fingers brush the strands of head-fur from Jah-kee's face.

The growl dies before it reaches my lips. But barely.

"*She will be well, brother,*" Rok projects, his mindspeak rippling with amusement. "*Jus-teen knows what she does.*"

I force my claws to retract, my shoulders to relax. "*I know this,*" I project back, not taking my eyes from where Jah-kee lies still on the stone pallet. "*I merely... observe.*"

"*Is that what you call it?*" Rok settles beside me against the cave wall, his frame also casting shadows across the floor. *"Strange. I would call it 'watching her like prey about to escape a trap.'"*

My gaze snaps to his face, a snarl building in my throat before I recognize the teasing light in his eyes. Rok, amused by my discomfort. As always.

"I brought her here," I project stiffly. *"I am responsible for her recovery."*

"Mmm." Rok's mental hum vibrates with doubt. *"And that is why your skin glows where her scent lingers? Why your dra-kir pounds when her name crosses the mindspace? Why you have not taken your eyes from her since you arrived?"*

Heat floods my face. It is an unfamiliar sensation that irritates me further. *"I am concerned,"* I insist. *"The Giving Stone was waiting. She nearly died in my care."*

"Nearly died while you carried her across half the territory to reach help," Rok corrects. *"There is a difference, brother."*

I have no response to this, so I return to watching Jah-kee. Her color is better this sol, the unnatural flush of *fever*—as Jus-teen calls it—fading from her cheeks. Her breathing comes easier, deeper.

I know she will live. This knowledge alone should ease the tight knot of fear that has sat in my chest since her collapse. Yet tension still coils through me, making me restless, irritable.

Jus-teen rises from Jah-kee's side, wiping her hands on her strange hide coverings. Her water eyes—so much like Jah-kee's, yet lacking the same pull on my dra-kir—meet mine across the cave.

"She's stable," she projects, her mindspeak clear in the mindspace. *"The fever's broken. She needs rest now, and more fluids when she wakes."*

I dip my head in the way Rok has now taught me means affirmation. *"You have my gratitude,"* I project.

Jus-teen's lips quirk in what might be amusement at how formal I sound. "*I didn't do it for you, big guy. But you're welcome.*" She crosses to Rok's side, her small form fitting neatly against his larger one as she settles beside him. "*You look like shit, by the way. When's the last time you slept?*"

I blink. "*...Like excrement?*" My gaze flicks to Rok, seeking confirmation. But I sense no insult here. "*Is this a human compliment?*"

Jus-teen chokes on air. Rok's amusement rises in the mindspace.

I nod, solemn. "*Then you also look like... shit.*" I gesture between them. "*Very... healthy.*"

Jus-teen collapses against Rok, gasping. "*Oh my god. Never change.*"

I tilt my head. Change what? My appearance? My scent? Before I can ask, she adds: "*And for the record—no, it's not a compliment. Just a human phrase that means you don't look so well.*"

"*I am not tired,*" I lie.

Her water eyes set on me with disbelief.

"*Riiiight,*" Jus-teen projects, stretching out the word unnaturally. "*That's why you're swaying on your feet. Very convincing.*"

The casual way she addresses me unsettles my instincts. She speaks as if we've shared a hearth for many cycles, not mere sols. Yet when Jah-kee's clumsy thoughts brushed my mind, it felt... different.

Natural.

Everything about these females defies understanding.

"*You should rest, brother,*" Rok adds, his mental voice gentler. "*Jah-kee will not wake for some time. Her body heals.*"

I resist, unwilling to close my eyes even for a moment. Not while Jah-kee remains vulnerable.

"*I will watch,*" I insist, settling more firmly against the wall. "*In case she wakes.*"

Jus-teen and Rok exchange a look, and I wonder if they are having some private conversation.

"*Suit yourself,*" Jus-teen finally says, turning back to me with a shrug. "*But if you face-plant on the cave floor, I'm not picking you up.*"

I do not know this "face-plant." Is it a plant with a face? A hunter plant that bites?

My gaze sweeps the cave floor. My claws flex. If this face-plant is a threat to Jah-kee, I will tear it from the stone.

"*What is this face-plant?*" My thought echoes sharply with suspicion. "*A predator?*"

Jus-teen snorts, the sound loud in the quiet cave. A clear image flashes from her mind to mine: a creature made of nothing but black lines. Two for legs, two for arms, a circle for a head, swaying with exhaustion, suddenly tripping over nothing and landing flat on its face with a silent thud. The line creature has my distinctive tracker's markings on its back.

"*It means you will fall,*" Jus-teen projects, her thought laced with deep amusement. "*On your face.*"

My posture straightens. My gaze shifts to Jah-kee's sleeping form, then back to Jus-teen. My exhaustion is a betrayal I will not admit.

"I will not fall," I project, the vow a solid, steady thing.

A small smile plays on Jus-teen's lips, and she shakes her head slowly. A wave of fond exasperation washes from her mind into mine. "*Okay, big guy,*" she projects, the words soft with amusement. "*Whatever you say.*"

Rok's amusement ripples through the mindspace like wind over the dust, and I get the distinct impression he approves of how his female teases me. "*Come, Jus-teen,*" he says, rising to his feet and extending a claw to help her up. *"Let us give my brother space to prove he is as sturdy as he claims."*

They move deeper across the cave and I watch them go, noting the easy way they move together, the casual way Rok's hand settles at the small of Jus-teen's back.

And I wonder.

What is it like to be so comfortable with another being? To have such ease between you? To feel the light connecting you, strong and unbreakable?

My gaze returns to Jah-kee's sleeping form. Will she ever want that? With me? Or will she, once recovered, wish to return to her own kind, her own world?

I have seen images of her planet. So much water. Why would any being want to remain here, in the dust, where every drop is scarce and precious?

The thought sends a spike of pain through my chest so sharp I nearly gasp aloud.

I do not wish to contemplate such things. Not now. Not while the memory of her burning skin against mine, her fading presence in the mindspace, is still so fresh.

Instead, I settle more comfortably against the wall, my eyes never leaving her face, and prepare for a long vigil.

I MUST HAVE SLEPT AFTER ALL, FOR I WAKE WITH A START TO FIND THE cave dimmer, Ain's light barely streaming through the entrance. My neck aches from the awkward angle, my muscles stiff from too long in one position.

But these discomforts fade to nothing when I see Jah-kee's eyes are open, watching me.

"Hey," she vocalizes, her voice weak but clear. "You look terrible."

The sound of her voice sends a wave of relief through me so powerful I nearly sway with it. My dra-kir pounds against my ribs, the golden glow beneath my skin flaring brighter in response to her wakefulness.

"*Jah-kee!*" I am by her side in an instant.

"I'm here." She smiles faintly, the expression lighting her pale face. "Alive, too. Thanks to you." She tries to sit up, wincing with the effort. "Though I feel like I've been run over by a truck."

Faint images. So faint as she vocalizes. A hulking thing of unnatural angles and shrieking metal, rolling on circular limbs that crush everything in their path. *Dust.* What world breeds such monstrous moving things? One of my hands hovers near her shoulder as if to protect her from it, but I am uncertain if I should touch her.

"Care-ful," I vocalize as best as I can, having heard Jus-teen say the same in the many solmarks that she bent here tending to her. But the human word is still awkward on my tongue.

Jah-kee looks up at me, surprise flickering across her features. "You're getting better at talking," she vocalizes. "I understood that perfectly."

Is that…approval?

Pride swells in my chest, though I know such a simple accomplishment hardly merits it.

Jah-kee's smile widens, and my dra-kir stumbles in its rhythm. Has her smile always affected me this way? Or is it merely relief at seeing her recovered?

"Where are we?" she asks, glancing around the cave. "Is this where Justine's been? Is she here?"

I recognize Jus-teen's name and lift my head, scanning the cave as if she might appear at the sound of it.

"Did we make it?" Jah-kee breathes, her eyes widening. The hope there is unmistakable, fragile but blazing. "You brought me all the way here. Through the desert. While I was..." She trails off, her gaze dropping to her hands, which tremble slightly against the stone beneath her. "I don't remember much. Just... the fever. And dreams."

I tilt my head, her thoughts still that hazy imprint in the mindspace. Perhaps only facilitated by the fever fog that consumed her. It has not fully cleared.

Her cheeks stain pink as she flushes slightly, the color creeping up her neck. "Weird ones. Probably just the fever."

Before she can say more, footsteps echo from the cave entrance. I tense automatically, my claws flexing instinctively before I catch the familiar scents. Jus-teen. Rok.

But Jah-kee does not know their scents.

Jah-kee startles as Rok steps into the cave. Her entire body stiffens, her eyes going wide as they lock onto his tall, lean form. Her trembling hand instinctively reaches out toward me. "*Tharn?*"

Before she can continue, another figure appears behind Rok, smaller and quicker.

Jus-teen steps into the cave, her face shadowed at first but quickly brightening when she sees Jah-kee awake. Her eyes widen, and then her expression crumples, her lips parting with a sharp inhale.

"Jacqui!" she exclaims, rushing forward in a blur of movement.

Jah-kee barely has time to sit upright before Jus-teen drops to her knees beside her and throws her arms around her— tightly, desperately, like a hunter clutching a kill. No. Not like a hunter. Like someone holding the most precious thing in the dust.

Emotions ripple through the cave. Raw and sharp, impossible to ignore even for one like me. Jus-teen shakes as she holds her sister, her entire body trembling with relief, with the weight of fear finally lifting.

"I thought you were dead," Jus-teen chokes, her voice breaking. "I thought—" Her words cut off, swallowed by a sob that echoes through the mindspace like a distant storm.

Jah-kee's arms come up slowly, as if she doesn't trust her own strength, but then they tighten around Jus-teen with equal ferocity. "I thought you were dead too," she whispers. "I came looking for you... and I—I didn't know if I'd make it. I didn't know if you were even alive."

Jus-teen pulls back just enough to look at her sister's face, her hands framing Jah-kee's cheeks as if she needs the physical proof that she's here, alive, breathing.

"You stupid, stubborn idiot," Jus-teen says, her vocalizations thick. "Why didn't you stay with the group? Why didn't you wait?"

Jah-kee lets out a trembling laugh, one that sounds wet, as if she might choke. I stiffen but force myself to remain still. "You left first, remember? What was I supposed to do? Just sit there while you wandered off into this deathtrap of a desert?"

Jus-teen shakes her head, laughing and releasing wetness from her eyes at the same time. "Of course, you came after me. It's what you do. God, Jacqui..." Her voice cracks again, and she pulls her sister back into a fierce embrace, clutching her like she's afraid she'll disappear.

Water swells in Jah-kee's eyes, too, spilling over to streak her cheeks. The sight makes me stiffen some more, but Rok's steady *"Do not be alarmed"* holds me still.

"I'm alive," Jah-kee murmurs. "I'm alive."

"But you almost weren't," Jus-teen vocalizes fiercely, pulling back again to scan her sister's face, as if memorizing every detail. "You almost—" Her voice stops, and she presses her forehead to Jah-kee's, her hands still cupping her cheeks.

"Don't you ever do that to me again. Do you hear me? Don't you ever scare me like that again."

"I won't," Jah-kee whispers, the vocalization breaking. "I promise."

She smiles faintly, but the expression falters as her water-filled gaze flickers past Jus-teen's shoulder to where Rok stands near the cave entrance. Her hands tighten on her sister's arms.

"You sent an alien to find me," she vocalizes. "You made friends with them. Are there more?"

Jus-teen pulls back, glancing toward Rok and then back at her sister, her lips twitching faintly. "Yeah, there are more of them. They're called the Drakav, and they're the reason we're all still alive."

"All?" Jah-kee's eyes search her Jus-teen's, almost as if they have a mindspace of their own. "The others?"

Jus-teen does that chin-to-chest thing, more water swelling in her eyes, and they embrace once more.

For a moment, the cave is silent except for the sound of their breathing, the quiet sniffles as they hold each other. Even Rok stands quietly at the edge of the space, his expression solemn.

I step back, giving the females space for their reunion, though every instinct screams to remain close to Jah-kee. Rok joins me, his expression knowing as he observes my obvious reluctance.

"*Your female awakens,*" he projects privately, his mental voice tinged with satisfaction. "*Good. The bond will strengthen now that she recovers.*"

I bristle at his phrasing. "*She is not '**my** female,*'" I project back sharply. "*At least, not in the way of the Law of the Dust. She is Jah-kee. She is...*"

I falter, unable to define exactly what she is to me. Not prey. Not clan. Not... anything I have words for.

Rok's smug knowing floods the mindspace. *"Yes, brother. I recall similar protests when Jus-teen first arrived."* His gaze shifts to where the two females embrace, his expression softening. *"At first, I thought her a brazen male scouting to destroy us and I, too, denied what the light revealed."*

I follow his gaze, watching as Jus-teen fusses over her sister, checking her temperature, helping her drink water. They look *so* similar yet different. Jus-teen's features sharper, her manner more open. Jah-kee, even weakened by fever, is more guarded.

"The light," I project hesitantly, keeping my mental voice private between Rok and myself. *"What does it mean? Truly?"*

Rok is silent for a long moment, considering. Finally, he replies. *"A marking. A blessing. I believe the light chooses those who are meant to bond across worlds."*

"And this... bond. It causes pain when separated?"

Rok's gaze sharpens, focusing on me with sudden intensity. *"You have felt it already? The pain of separation?"*

I think of the hollow ache in my chest when I was forced to set Jah-kee down, and when she left me to go to the firebloom cave. *"Yes."*

"Tharn," Rok projects grimly. *"If the light has chosen, the pain will grow until the bond is completed."*

"Completed?" I repeat, my unease growing. *"How is a bond... completed?"*

Rok's amusement returns. *"You truly do not know what comes next?"*

This smug-faced ka-vrakt.

I look away, uncomfortable with my ignorance. Hunters learn the ways of tracking, of fighting, of survival. We are not taught about... whatever this is that happens between male and female.

"How could I know?" I project defensively. *"Until Jus-teen*

arrived, we had never seen females. There are no teachings about this."

"*As there were none for me,*" he acknowledges, his thoughts gentler now. "*I learned as the bond grew. As my body changed.*"

My gaze drops involuntarily to Rok's loincloth, where the evidence of his successful adaptation is difficult to miss. The impressive bulge there is unlike anything I have seen on other hunters. Then my eyes fall to my pouch, still flat and unremarkable.

Drak.

Rok follows my gaze and makes a sound suspiciously like a snort. "*It changes, brother,*" he projects, his mindspeak rich with mirth. "*When the time comes. When the bond demands it.*"

"*And until then?*" My gaze slides to Jah-kee. Still hugging her sister-female, her eyes find mine. My dra-kir does a hard thump.

"*Until then, the light calls. The pain grows when separated. The body prepares.*" Rok shrugs, the motion fluid and unconcerned. "*It is not comfortable. But it is necessary.*"

With Jah-kee's eyes still on me, the next question feels the most important.

"*And...*" I hesitate. "*How did you convince Jus-teen to... stay? To accept the bond?*"

Rok's expression turns thoughtful. "*I did not convince her,*" he projects slowly. "*She chose. As all females must. I merely... showed her what could be between us.*"

"*How?*"

A slow, satisfied look spreads across Rok's face. "*I shared her water,*" he projects, his mental voice dropping to a lower, more intimate register.

I blink. I know this. I have been preparing for this.

Rok's gaze slides toward Jus-teen. "*Water comes from many places in a female's body. The sweetest flows when pleasure peaks.*"

My gaze shifts back to Jah-kee. Rok speaks of the moisture between a female's legs, and the memory of her that night, when she pulled her hide-coverings away and I saw the temptation that is her smooth curves—

"This... water sharing," I project carefully. *"It pleases females? Makes them wish to stay?"*

"Oh my GOD," Jus-teen's mental voice cuts sharply into our private conversation. *"Are you two seriously discussing oral sex right now?"*

I jerk my head up, startled to find both females staring at us—Jah-kee with confusion, unable to hear the mindspace conversation, and Jus-teen with a mixture of horror.

"Oral?" I project, confused by the term. *"Is that what you call it?"* The word feels wrong.

Jus-teen makes a strangled sound. *"Please stop talking about going down on my sister while I'm trying to help her recover from nearly dying."*

"Going down?" I repeat. This is also a strange phrase. *"Another odd term."*

"I prefer 'water sharing,'" Rok adds in. *"It is accurate and... reverent."*

Jus-teen's face flushes bright red. "Oh my God, I can't with you two," she vocalizes loudly, throwing her hands up in frustration.

Jah-kee's gaze flicks between the three of us, her confusion growing.

"Wait... wait, wait, wait," she stammers, her voice hoarse but gaining strength. "You're communicating with them? Like...how? They're not even talking!" Her brow furrows. "What's going on?"

Jus-teen hesitates, her gaze darting to me, to Rok, then back to her sister. She presses her lips together like she's debating whether or not to explain.

"I..." Her words trail off as she glances at Rok, who rises and takes a step closer, giving his silent support. "Okay, fine. Yeah. They're talking. To me. In my head. Telepathically." She waves her hand around. "Consider it alien brain magic or something."

Jacqui blinks, her mouth falling open. "What." Her gaze shifts to me. "Tharn too?"

"Yes," Jus-teen continues. "He's probably been projecting at you this whole time. But since you're not in the mindspace, it just looks like he's staring at you like a creep."

Jacqui's jaw drops further, her gaze snapping to me. "Wait. WAIT. He's been—so when he just stares at me like that, he's actually—?"

"Talking," Jus-teen confirms. "Yup. Like, full-on sentences. It's a good thing I'm here to play translator, or you'd assume he's just zoning out and plotting your demise."

Jah-kee's cheeks flush, her hands gripping the edge of the stone beneath her. "And... what exactly has he been saying?"

Jus-teen pauses, her lips twitching. It's not hard to catch the flow of conversation from what she's projected back into the mindspace. She glances at Rok, her expression clearly asking, '*Do I tell her?*'

I stiffen, my claws flexing against the stone floor. "*Her recovery,*" I project firmly, my voice directed at Jus-teen in the mindspace. "*Tell her I was speaking of her recovery.*"

Jus-teen arches a brow. "Her recovery?"

"*Yes.*"

"Not, for example, water sharing?" she vocalizes out loud.

Jah-kee brightens suddenly, her expression softening. "What about water sharing?" she says, glancing between Jus-teen and me. "Oh no, he's been the one sharing his water with me this whole time." Her expression crumples. "Is he saying I've been drinking too much?"

She groans, her cheeks coloring as she meets my gaze in earnest. "I'm sorry, Tharn, I really tried not to. Once I'm on my feet, I'll share my water with you anytime if you need it."

Jus-teen freezes mid-breath. Her eyes widen, and then she claps a hand over her face with a loud groan. "Oh God," she mutters, her voice muffled behind her fingers.

Jah-kee's brow crumples. "What? What did I say?"

"*I was speaking of her recovery*," I project sharply, my projection tight and strained.

Jus-teen lowers her hand, her face now bright red, too. "That's not—Jacqui, that is not what he meant by water-sharing."

"What?" Jah-kee asks, her gaze darting between us. Her confusion only deepens when she notices Jus-teen's flushed face. "Seriously, what did I say? I meant it! Tharn kept me alive, didn't he? I'd share my water with him anytime!"

Jus-teen groans louder, burying her face in both hands now. "Oh my God, Jacqui, stop talking."

But the echo of her words moves through Jus-teen and into the mindspace. The tension in the cave seems to expand, pressing heavily against my chest, and my dra-kir stumbles painfully. Her words echo relentlessly, vivid and impossible to escape.

She would share her water with me.

My claws scrape against the stone. My breathing quickens. The implications flood my thoughts, and I can barely contain the surge of emotions crashing through me.

A sudden sense of warmth touches my mind, as if sensing my rising panic. It is Jus-teen. "*Tharn.*"

I don't respond. My thoughts whirl uncontrollably, my pulse roaring in my ears.

"*Tharn,*" Jus-teen projects again, her mindspeak more insistent this time.

159

But it's too late. I turn abruptly and stride toward the far side of the cave, my claws flexing and unflexing as I try to calm the storm within me. My movements are stiff, uncoordinated, and I hear Jus-teen groan again behind me.

"Oh great," she mutters. "Now you've broken him."

"Broken him?" Jah-kee's voice is startled, concerned. "What? What did I say? What's wrong with him?"

"Nothing," Jus-teen says, dragging her hands down her face. "He's fine. He just... needs a minute. Or an hour. Maybe a day."

I press my back against the cool stone of the cave wall, inhaling deeply and trying to steady my racing thoughts. But Jah-kee's words linger, impossible to ignore.

She would share her water with me. Anytime.

CHAPTER 18

MY SISTER CAN READ ALIEN MINDS, AND I'M JUST SITTING HERE, DUMB

JACQUI

"And... what exactly has he been saying?"

I'm staring at my sister, who's suddenly developed the ability to communicate telepathically with aliens. Because of course she has. Justine has always been the overachiever. I barely survive a crash landing, nearly die (multiple times), and get dragged across a desert by a giant golden alien. Meanwhile, Justine's out here making interspecies alliances and developing psychic powers.

Typical.

Justine pauses, glancing at Tharn with an expression I can't quite read. "Her recovery?" she finally asks. But her focus is on Tharn, and her tone is odd.

I frown. Something in her voice tells me that's not the whole truth. My suspicion deepens when she adds, "Not, for example, water sharing?"

Oh.

My face softens with understanding. Water sharing. Of

course. Tharn's been sharing his precious water with me this whole time, keeping me alive in this hellscape of a desert. And what have I done? Probably drunk way more than my fair share.

"What about water sharing?" I say, guilt washing over me. "Oh no, he's been the one sharing his water with me this whole time. Is he saying I've been drinking too much?" I look at Tharn apologetically. "I'm sorry, Tharn, I really tried not to. Once I'm on my feet, I'll share my water with you anytime if you need it."

Justine makes a strangled noise and claps a hand over her face. "Oh God," she mutters.

"What?" I ask, confused by her reaction. "What did I say?"

Justine's face is bright red now. "That's not—Jacqui, that is not what he meant by water-sharing."

"What?" I demand, brows diving. Why is everyone acting so weird? "Seriously, what did I say? I meant it! Tharn kept me alive, didn't he? I'd share my water with him anytime!"

Justine groans louder, burying her face in both hands. "Oh my God, Jacqui, stop talking."

I look between her and Tharn, completely lost. What's the big deal about water? It's just water.

Something in Tharn's posture changes. His shoulders stiffen, his claws scrape against the stone floor, and his breathing quickens visibly. He stares at me with an intensity that makes my skin heat up, and then he abruptly turns and strides to the far side of the cave.

"Oh great," Justine mutters. "Now you've broken him."

"Broken him?" I echo, alarmed. "What? What did I say? What's wrong with him?"

"Nothing," Justine says, dragging her hands down her face. "He's fine. He just... needs a minute. Or an hour. Maybe a day."

I stare after Tharn, who's now pressed against the far wall of the cave, his claws flexing and unflexing like he's trying to calm himself down. His chest rises and falls rapidly, and there's that golden glow pulsing beneath his skin still. I glance at the other alien. He's just as impressive as Tharn, but he doesn't glow.

And suddenly, I have the sinking feeling that "water sharing" might mean something very different to aliens than it does to humans.

<hr/>

IT'S BEEN HOURS, AND MY HEAD IS STILL SPINNING.

Justine has filled me in on some of what's happened since the crash. How she was rescued by Rok (and yes, that's his real name), how he kept her alive, brought her to his tribe, and how they rescued the other survivors. But my brain keeps snagging on one unbelievable detail: Tharn has been talking to me this whole time. Or at least, trying to.

I stop breathing, a new, horrifying thought dawning. "Wait. When I was sick... when I had the fever... I thought..." I press my fingers to my temples. "I thought we were having conversations. I could hear his voice in my head. He told me I wouldn't die. He called me 'precious one'." I look at Justine, my heart hammering. "I told myself it was just a dream. A hallucination. Was it...?"

Justine's expression softens with a sympathy that is almost worse than her mockery. She gives a small, hesitant nod. "If you heard him, Jacqui... it was real."

The air leaves my lungs in a rush.

It was real.

All of it. His desperation as he carried me. His commands for me to live. His clumsy attempts to push my tears back into

163

my face. My own slurred, delirious confession that I didn't want him to die, either. He heard it all. He felt it all.

The embarrassment I felt before is nothing compared to the wave of heat that floods me now. It's a full-body blush of pure, unadulterated mortification.

I groan and press my hands over my face, wishing I could just disappear. "Oh my god. He must think I'm a complete lunatic."

Justine snorts. "If it makes you feel better, he can't understand *everything* you say. The connection isn't there yet. And he doesn't think you're a fool. He carried you across half the desert while you were dying, remember? That's not something you do for someone you think is an idiot."

My brain latches on to another detail she dropped casually earlier. Too casually. Like it wasn't world-shattering.

She and Rok are a thing.

My brain stumbles over the thought, sputtering like a broken engine. *My sister is fucking an alien.*

A sentence that would have been utterly ridiculous—hell, impossible—just weeks ago. But now... my gaze shifts to Tharn, who is, surprise surprise, watching me with the focus of a predator. Suddenly... it doesn't seem so ridiculous.

Oh no. *Shoot me now.*

"Great," I say, pulling my gaze from Tharn and swallowing past the shiver his attention sends down my spine. "So he just thinks I'm a helpless damsel who can't survive two minutes without him saving me. Much better."

Justine rolls her eyes. "Stop catastrophizing. It's not a good look on you."

Easy for her to say. She's somehow managed to become best friends with these aliens, develop telepathic powers, and probably learn their entire language while I've been busy trying not to die. Even in an alien apocalypse, Justine manages to thrive while I'm barely surviving on good looks and dumb luck.

I push myself up to a sitting position, wincing as my muscles protest. I'm still weak from the fever, but at least I'm not burning up anymore. Small victories.

My gaze drifts automatically to Tharn once more. He's been hovering for the past few hours. Near enough to watch me but far enough to maintain some kind of distance. He's pacing now, moving back and forth along the far wall of the cave like a caged animal. Every few steps, he pauses, his hand going to his chest as if something there pains him.

It's not the first time I've noticed him doing this. Ever since I woke up, he's been rubbing at his chest, sometimes clutching it like he's having heartburn or something. Is he sick, too? Did he catch whatever I had?

I watch as he stops again, wincing slightly as his hand presses against his sternum. His glow pulses beneath his skin, brightest where his palm rests. It's almost beautiful, the way the light ebbs and flows like sunlight on water.

Wait. What if...

I narrow my eyes, focusing intently on Tharn. If my sister can telepathically communicate with these aliens, why can't I? Maybe I'm just not trying hard enough.

I concentrate, staring at Tharn with everything I've got. "*Can you hear me?*" I think as loudly as possible, imagining the words shooting from my brain to his.

Nothing. Not even a twitch of acknowledgment.

I try again, squinting harder. "*HELLO? THARN? THIS IS JACQUI'S BRAIN CALLING THARN'S BRAIN. OVER.*"

Still nothing. Tharn continues his pacing, oblivious to my mental shouting.

Fine. Maybe I need to be more direct. I take a deep breath

and try once more, visualizing a direct line between us, like a golden thread connecting my mind to his.

"What's wrong with your chest? Are you sick? Are you allergic to me or something?"

Tharn pauses mid-step, his head snapping up to look at me. For a second, my heart leaps—did it work?—but then I realize I've been staring at him so intensely that he's probably just noticed my attention.

His amber eyes lock with mine, and something passes between us. Something that makes my skin prickle with awareness. He looks... pained. Conflicted. His hand is still pressed to his chest, and his claws flex against his skin as if he's trying to dig out whatever's bothering him.

"Oh my God, is it the water thing?" I blurt out, unable to contain my frustration any longer. "It's the water thing, isn't it. You're mad I drank too much. I knew it!"

Tharn blinks, clearly startled by my outburst. Across the cave, Justine chokes on a laugh.

"It's not the water, Jacqui," she says, shaking her head. "Trust me on that."

"Then what is it?" I demand, my patience wearing thin. "Why does he keep clutching his chest like he's having a heart attack? Why won't he come closer? Why does he look at me like I'm... like I'm..."

I trail off, not even sure how to describe the way Tharn looks at me sometimes. Like I'm something dangerous but fascinating. Like I'm...

"It's complicated," Justine says, her voice gentler now. "Alien biology is... different. And their connection to us is... well, it's not exactly like anything we have on Earth."

"Great," I mutter. "More cryptic answers. Just what I needed."

I flop back against the stone, frustration bubbling under

my skin like a pot about to boil over. My muscles ache, my head throbs, and there's this weird, restless itchiness I can't seem to shake. Maybe it's just the aftermath of nearly dying. Or maybe it's the fact that everyone seems to know what's going on except me.

"Look, Jacqui," Justine starts hesitantly, and I glance over at her. She's fidgeting, which isn't like her. She's usually so composed. "It's not like I have all the answers, okay? Half the time, I'm just trying to figure this out as I go."

I sit up again, wincing at the soreness in my body. "Figure what out, Justine? Because from where I'm sitting, it sure looks like you've got this whole alien telepathic survival thing down. Meanwhile, I can't even tell if Tharn hates me or if he's just constipated."

Justine snorts, but there's no humor in it. She runs a hand through her hair, staring at the fire with a furrowed brow. "Look, I know this is going to sound insane, but... I think the planet is alive."

My lashes flutter as I blink at her. "*Alive?*" I laugh, but the serious look on her face wipes the mirth from my lips. "Like... what? A giant brain under the sand or something?"

She shoots me an unimpressed look. "No, smartass. Not like that. But there's something here—particles or... I don't know, spores or something—that's doing things to us. To me. To you."

I stiffen, because I saw those particles. Early on, when I met Tharn and saw his glow. I thought I saw pollen in my mind.

"Doing what to us?" I whisper.

Justine hesitates, and for a moment, I think she won't answer. But then she sighs and rubs the back of her neck. "When I first got here, I was sick too. Fevers, dreams... vivid ones."

I straighten, my pulse quickening. "Dreams?" I've had those too. Vivid as she says.

Her eyes flick to mine, and there's something guarded in her expression. She nods slowly. "Yeah. At first, I thought they were just fever dreams. I'd see these... particles floating in the air. They'd sink into my skin, my mouth, my lungs. It felt... strange, but not bad. Like they were changing me somehow."

I shiver, suddenly hyperaware of the air we're breathing in.

"And then," Justine continues, her voice quieter now, "there were other dreams. Dreams where I'd see Rok. Only... it wasn't just seeing him."

Her cheeks flush pink, and she clears her throat, glancing away.

Oh no.

My stomach drops as I realize where this is going.

"And?" I prompt, even though I'm not sure I want the answer.

"And..." She gestures vaguely, her hand flapping in a way that's supposed to mean something but just leaves me more confused. When I don't respond, she groans and tries again. "You know. Dreams. *Those kinds of dreams.*"

Oh God.

I slap a hand over my face, groaning. "Justine, I swear to God, if you're about to tell me you had sex dreams about an alien—"

"It wasn't just dreams!" she blurts out, her voice rising defensively. "Okay? It was... more than that. I think he imprinted on me or something when we met. He was glowing, like Tharn is now, and then..." She trails off, her hands gesturing awkwardly toward her lap before she widens her eyes meaningfully.

It takes a second for her implication to sink in.

Oh.

Oh no.

Rok has been wearing a loincloth that hardly hides the massive thing beneath it. But Tharn isn't wearing a loincloth. I've gotten used to his lack of sexual bits, but now Justine is telling me something impossible.

"Are you saying he... changed?" I ask, my voice rising in pitch as my brain tries to process this information.

Justine nods, her face redder than I've ever seen it. "Physically. Yes. And it was... noticeable."

Kill me. Just kill me now.

I groan loudly, lying back on the stone and covering my face with both hands. "I didn't need to know that, Justine. I really didn't."

"You're the one who asked!" she snaps, clearly embarrassed.

"Not for that! I didn't need the visual of your alien boyfriend... you know... upgrading himself for you!"

"Well, get used to it," she says, her voice tart. "Because it's probably going to happen to you, too."

That makes me sit bolt upright again, my heart pounding. "Excuse me?!"

Justine shrugs, avoiding my gaze. "I mean, I don't know for sure, but... Tharn's glowing. None of the other males glowed when they met the other women. I think the glowing is a sign."

"A sign of what?" My throat goes dry.

"That he's bonding with you," she says flatly, as if it's the most obvious thing in the world.

I stare at her, my brain short-circuiting. "Bonding with me? What does that even mean? Is he going to start... changing too?"

Justine shrugs again, but there's a knowing look in her eyes that makes me want to scream. "Probably."

My gaze snaps to Tharn's groin against my will. Nothing. Still just... smooth.

Oh God. Probably.

Bonding. Changing. My brain latches on to the words like a lifeline, but the more I think about them, the less sense they make. Or maybe they make too much sense, and that's what terrifies me.

Because if Tharn is bonding with me—if his glowing, his pacing, his constant hovering is part of some alien ritual—I'm not sure I'm ready for what comes next.

What does that even look like? Am I supposed to... bond back? Is there some alien mating dance I'm about to completely screw up? And what happens when he starts changing? Will I wake up one day to find him... upgraded, like Rok? Do I get a say in the design specs?

The thought makes my stomach flip.

"Great," I mutter finally, trying to shove the swirling mix of panic, confusion, and... something else down where I don't have to deal with it. "More cryptic answers. Just what I needed."

Now I find I can't even look in Tharn's direction.

I fall back against the stone, exhaustion washing over me again.

Maybe it's just the aftermath of nearly dying. Or maybe it's the frustration of being the only one who can't seem to get on board with the whole telepathic alien communication thing.

I close my eyes, trying to block out the strange tension in the cave. Through my lashes, I catch glimpses of Tharn still pacing, his focus on me, and another shiver goes from my throat to the pit of my belly. Suddenly, the stone beneath me is too hard. Every sensation seems heightened, more intense. I shift, trying to get comfortable, but it's like my body has forgotten how to relax.

"You should rest," Justine says, misinterpreting my restlessness. "You're still recovering."

"I'm fine," I insist, though I'm not entirely sure that's true. "Just... antsy."

Justine studies me for a moment, her expression unreadable. "Uh-huh," she says finally. "Well, try to get some sleep anyway. Rok and I are going to go hunting soon, and you need to conserve your strength."

"You're leaving?" I ask, a spike of anxiety shooting through me. "Both of you?"

"We need food," she says simply. "Fresh food to eat now, not to carry. Tharn will stay with you."

My gaze flicks to Tharn again, who seems to stiffen at Justine's words. His hand goes back to his chest, pressing hard against the glow there.

Great. Just me and the telepathic alien who may or may not be allergic to my existence. Or changing because of it. What could possibly go wrong?

"Fine," I sigh, squeezing my eyes shut. "Go hunt. Bring back something that doesn't taste like sand, if possible."

Justine laughs, the sound echoing in the cave. "I'll do my best. Sleep well, Jacqui."

I don't plan on sleeping. I'm too wired, too overwhelmed by everything that's happened. But as Justine and Rok prepare to leave, my eyelids grow heavy.

Despite my best efforts to stay awake, sleep pulls me under, dragging me down into dreams laced with gold.

CHAPTER 19
MY ALIEN ABDUCTION WAS AN INSIDE JOB

JACQUI

I'm in the desert, but it's different somehow. The sand beneath my feet isn't harsh and burning, but soft and yielding, almost like silk. The sky above isn't the merciless yellow of the day or the star-studded black of night, but a strange, golden twilight that casts everything in a warm, hazy glow.

I'm alone, but I don't feel afraid. There's a sense of anticipation in the air, like the desert itself is holding its breath, waiting for something—or someone.

And then I hear it—my name, but not quite my name. "Jah-kee."

The voice is deep, resonant, and it comes from everywhere and nowhere at once. It wraps around me like a physical touch, making my skin prickle with awareness.

"Where are you?" I call out, turning in a slow circle. The desert stretches endlessly in all directions, beautiful and smooth.

"Here," the voice says, and suddenly he is. Tharn, standing before me where nothing was just a moment ago.

But he's different in this golden dream-desert. His skin glows brighter. His amber eyes are molten, burning with an intensity that should frighten me, but instead makes something low in my belly tighten with anticipation.

"Tharn," I breathe, and the name feels right on my tongue, like I've been saying it all my life.

He moves toward me with the fluid grace of a predator, but I don't feel like prey. Or if I am, I want to be caught.

"Jah-kee," he says again, and this time I hear it not just with my ears but inside my head, a mental caress that makes me shiver. "You hear me now."

"Yes," I whisper, though I'm not sure if I speak aloud or just think the word. It doesn't seem to matter here, in this golden place between reality and dream.

He stops just before me, so close I can feel the heat radiating from his body. His scent fills my nostrils. Wild and alien. Leather and heat. It's intoxicating.

"I have waited," he says, his voice rough with emotion. "So long, I have waited for you to hear me."

"I'm sorry," I say, and the thought is an ache. I'm sorry for all the times I didn't understand, all the times I thought he was just staring at me, all the times I failed to hear what he was trying so desperately to tell me.

His hand rises, hovering just beside my face, not quite touching. "May I?" he asks, and the gentleness in his voice, in his eyes, makes my heart ache.

I nod, unable to speak past the lump in my throat.

The moment his fingers brush my cheek, my thoughts shatter. A jolt of pure heat races through me as the glow beneath his skin flares. I can feel it pouring into me like a thick, warm honey that pools low in my belly and makes my knees weak. "Beautiful," he murmurs, his eyes roaming my face like he's memorizing every detail. "Your light calls to mine."

His touch trails down my jaw, down the sensitive column of my neck, to the hollow of my throat where my pulse hammers. Everywhere he touches, my body comes alive, hypersensitive and trembling. I should be afraid. His claws are sharp, dangerous, but his touch is impossibly gentle, reverent even.

"Tharn," I whisper, his name catching in my throat as his hand slides around my waist, pulling me closer.

"You are mine," he says, his voice rougher now, filled with a hunger that sends a jolt of heat straight to my core. "And I am yours."

My breath catches as his body presses against mine, solid and impossibly warm. My heart pounds, a frantic rhythm that echoes in my ears, and I suddenly notice the glow at his waist.

Oh.

I can't look away.

The light beneath his skin is blindingly bright there, obscuring the details of what I see, but even through the glow, I can make out... *enough.*

I swallow hard, my mouth suddenly dry. My blood roars in my ears, and a desperate part of me wants to see more, to know exactly what I'm dealing with.

But then he steps closer, and the glow intensifies, and when he presses against me, I forget how to think at all.

His claws skim over my thighs, light as a whisper, and I gasp, my body arching instinctively toward him. His touch leaves trails of fire in its wake, and I'm burning now, consumed by a need I don't even know how to describe.

"You are mine," he growls, his voice vibrating through me as his hand slides higher, impossibly gentle yet so commanding it makes my knees weak.

"Say it," he urges, his lips brushing against my ear, sending a shiver down my spine. "Say you are mine."

"I'm yours," I gasp as his fingers find the most sensitive part of me, teasing with a touch so light it almost drives me mad. "I'm yours, Tharn."

The sound he makes is a raw, satisfied snarl. His hands are on my hips, lifting me as if I weigh nothing. He hikes my legs, wrapping them around his waist, and my world tilts. I am open to him, vulnerable, my core aching and needy.

I feel the blunt, hot pressure of his tip against me, just before he thrusts forward, filling me in one powerful motion.

I cry out, clinging to him as pleasure and pain mix in a way that's almost unbearable. He's so big, stretching me in a way that feels like too much, but at the same time, it's exactly what I need.

The glow between us flares impossibly bright, and I lose myself completely.

"Mine," he growls one last time, and then I'm shattering, coming apart in his arms as waves of ecstasy crash over me. Golden and perfect and endless.

***

I WAKE WITH A GASP, MY BODY STILL THRUMMING WITH THE aftershocks of what was definitely not just a normal dream. My skin is flushed and damp with sweat, my heart racing like I've run a marathon, and there's an ache between my thighs that has nothing to do with my recent illness.

Oh...my God.

I lie perfectly still, trying to calm my breathing, trying to make sense of what just happened. It was a dream. Just a dream. A very vivid, very... specific kind of dream about Tharn, but still just a dream.

Right?

Except it felt so real. His touch, his voice in my head, the golden light that connected us. The sensations were too intense, too detailed to be just my imagination.

But that's ridiculous. Aliens don't invade your dreams and give you the best orgasm of your life. That's not a thing that happens in reality, even in a reality where aliens exist and your sister can talk to them telepathically.

I squeeze my eyes shut, trying to banish the lingering images, the ghost-sensation of his hands on my body, his mouth on mine. It doesn't work. If anything, closing my eyes just makes the memories more vivid.

I need to get a grip. It was just a dream, brought on by stress, and nearly dying, and finding out my sister can communicate psychically with aliens. Perfectly normal under the circumstances. Nothing to freak out about.

Except...

Except Justine said she was having dreams too.

Fuuuuuuck.

I crack one eye open, scanning the cave for Tharn. He's still there, on the far side, but he's not pacing anymore. He's sitting with his back against the wall, his legs stretched out, his arms resting on them. And he's watching me.

His amber eyes are fixed on me with an intensity that makes my breath catch. His chest rises and falls rapidly, as if he's been running.

Does he know? Can he tell what I was dreaming about? Is that even possible?

I tear my gaze away, heat flooding my face. This is mortifying. I just had the most erotic dream of my life about an alien who's probably been trying to talk to me about perfectly normal, non-sexual things this whole time, and now I can't even look at him without blushing like a teenager.

"Jacqui?" Justine's voice startles me so badly I nearly jump out of my skin. I hadn't even realized she was back. "You okay? You're looking a little... flushed."

"I'm fine," I say quickly, my voice coming out higher than usual. "Just... just a dream. Not a big deal."

Justine pauses, her eyes narrowing ever so slightly as she studies me. Her expression is casual, but I know her too well. That slight furrow between her brows, the way her lips press together for half a second before she speaks. It's worry. She's trying to hide it, but it's there.

"A dream," she repeats, her tone light, almost teasing. Too light.

"Yes, a dream," I snap, looking up at the stone ceiling as if it can shield me from her gaze. "People have them all the time. It's perfectly normal."

"Right," she says slowly, leaning against the cave wall. Her arms cross over her chest, but there's no mistaking the flicker of unease in her eyes. "Perfectly normal."

I narrow my eyes at her. "Don't you have hunting to do or something?"

She laughs, the sound echoing in the cave. "Already done. Rok caught dust crabs. They're actually pretty good."

As if on cue, my stomach growls loudly. Despite the lingering embarrassment, I realize I'm starving. How long has it been since I've had real food?

"Should we really be eating these things?" I hesitate. "If what you think is true..."

"Well..." Justine says with a shrug. "We don't have a choice. And you need to get your strength back. There's a long journey ahead of us."

Right. To the clan caves. Where all the other women are. Where more of Tharn's people are.

I swallow hard.

Justine turns to prepare some of the meat, and I take the opportunity to steal another glance at Tharn. He hasn't moved, but his glow seems to have settled into a steadier rhythm, less frantic than before.

Maybe he doesn't know about the dream after all.

But then his eyes meet mine, and my stomach drops.

There's something in his gaze—sharp, focused, like he's peeling back my defenses layer by layer. Like he knows.

I force myself to look away, but it's too late. The sensation lingers, crawling under my skin and making my pulse race. My fingers tighten on the stone, trying to ground myself, but the memory of his touch in the dream feels too real to shake.

And then I feel it again—that warmth blooming in my chest, spreading through me like a live wire, sparking every nerve it touches.

"Jacqui," Justine says, her voice cutting through the tension. I flinch, startled, and turn to her. She's holding a piece of cooked crab out to me, concern flickering in her eyes again.

"You sure you're okay?"

I nod too quickly, grabbing the meat just to give my hands something to do. "I'm fine," I say, even though my throat feels tight and my voice sounds hollow.

But I'm not fine.

Because when I glance back at Tharn, his eyes are still on me, glowing faintly in the firelight. And for just a moment, I swear I feel it—his presence brushing against my mind.

A warning, maybe.

Or a promise.

"Hey..." Justine kneels by my side, her voice soft but steady, like she's trying not to startle me. "If you're feeling over-whelmed... if you really want to understand him..." She hesitates, her gaze dropping to the sand for a moment before lifting to meet mine. "Try pressing your forehead to his. It's... grounding. It helps you hear them. Really hear them."

I blink at her, startled by the sincerity in her tone. "You've done it?"

She nods, her lips quirking faintly. "Yeah. It's strange at first, but it helped me. It might...it might help you too."

My eyes drift to Tharn, the firelight casting flickering shadows across his face. He's sitting so still, almost like he's holding himself back.

His throat moves, and I swallow hard, my pulse pounding in my ears as I force myself to look away again.

It might help you, too.

I don't know what's happening to me. But I'm starting to think it's not a bond I can choose to form.

It's a door that's already been kicked wide open.

CHAPTER 20
NO, I WILL NOT PLANT-FACE. STOP ASKING

THARN

I am a hunter.

Pain means nothing. Pain is merely a warning to the body. Avoid that which hurts. Step away from danger. Withdraw from the sharpness of a spear, the heat of flame.

But what do you do when the pain comes from within? When every beat of your dra-kir feels like a blade twisting beneath your ribs? When the agony has no source to escape, no threat to avoid?

What do you do when staying near what hurts is the only way to survive?

I press my hand against my chest, claws flexing involuntarily as another wave washes through me. The glow pulses beneath my palm. Once, I found the light beautiful. Now it mocks me with its intensity, a visible reminder of what binds me to Jah-kee.

Of what tears me apart when she withdraws.

"*Brother.*" Rok's mental voice slides into the mindspace, his concern poorly masked. "*The pain... I sense it is increasing.*"

I drop my claw from my chest immediately, squaring my shoulders against the cave wall where I've been standing guard while Jah-kee rests. "*I am fine.*"

Rok's topaz eyes narrow, his head tilting in that way that means he sees more than I wish him to. "*You are not fine,*" he projects, keeping his thoughts private between us. "*The pain grows worse. I see it in the way you move, in how you wince when you think no one watches.*"

I bare my teeth in warning. "*It is nothing.*"

"*It is not nothing,*" Rok insists, his mental voice sharpening. "*It is the bond. Unresolved, incomplete.*"

I turn away, unable to face the knowing in his gaze. Of course, he understands. He felt this too, once. Before Jus-teen accepted him. Before they sealed their bond.

My eyes find Jah-kee where she rests across the cave, her small form curled into itself. She looks peaceful now, the fever gone from her cheeks. Her breathing comes easy and deep. She will recover fully.

And then what?

"*She avoids my gaze now,*" I project, the admission torn from me against my will. "*Since the dark when she woke from her dream.*"

Rok steps closer, his presence steady beside me. "*She is confused. Afraid. The bond is new to her, as it was to Jus-teen.*"

I remember all too clearly the way Jah-kee had gasped awake, her skin flushed, her scent heavy with something that made my dra-kir pound painfully. She'd looked at me with wide, startled water eyes, as if she'd seen me for the first time.

Then she had turned away, and has not looked at me directly since.

"*I do not wish to frighten her further,*" I project, my claws clenching into fists at my sides. "*She has suffered enough.*"

"*And so you suffer instead,*" Rok observes, his mental tone softening. "*As I did.*"

I say nothing. What is there to say? I am caught in a trap of my own making. The closer I stay to Jah-kee, the more her presence soothes the ache in my chest, yet the space between us still tears at me. But to move away, to widen that space...

I tried that once, when I stepped outside the cave to check for threats. Three steps beyond the entrance, and the pain dropped me to my knees, stealing the breath from my lungs and the strength from my limbs. Only crawling back to where I could see her sleeping form had eased the agony enough for me to function.

"*She will come to you,*" Rok projects with quiet certainty. "*When she is ready.*"

"*And if she is never ready?*" The question escapes before I can stop it. So raw and desperate. Not like me at all. "*If she chooses to return to her world? If she rejects the bond?*"

Rok is silent for a long moment, his gaze turning to where Jus-teen rests beside Jah-kee. The softness in his eyes when he looks at her makes my chest ache with a different kind of pain.

"*Then you will have a choice to make, brother,*" he finally projects. "*As I did.*"

I do not ask what choice he means. I am not sure I want to know.

Instead, I return my attention to Jah-kee, watching the gentle rise and fall of her chest, listening to the soft sounds of her breathing. For now, she is safe. She is healing. It is enough.

It has to be.

THREE SOLS PASS IN THE CAVE, EACH MORE AGONIZING THAN THE LAST.

Jah-kee grows stronger, eating the meat Rok and Jus-teen bring back from their hunts, walking short distances without assistance. Her water eyes are clear now, her movements more certain. Soon, she will be well enough to travel to the clan caves.

And I will still be trapped in this pain that never ends.

The bond has changed. It no longer eases when I am near her. Now the pain is constant, gnawing at me from within, whether I stand at her side or across the cave. It lessens slightly when our eyes meet. Those rare, fleeting moments when she forgets to look away. But even that small relief is temporary.

My body is breaking apart, yet I cannot let her see.

I am a hunter. I am strong. I will endure.

"We should leave tomorrow," Jus-teen vocalizes as we gather around the small fire for the evening meal. *"The others will be worried about us."* She releases a breath from the center of her chest. *"And I have a lot of explaining to do."*

ROK RUMBLES IN AGREEMENT, HIS HAND RESTING LIGHTLY ON JUS-teen's smaller one. *"Yes. We must reach the clan caves soon."*

Jah-kee shifts slightly, her gaze lowered to the food in her hands. "How far is it?"

Jus-teen glances at Rok for confirmation before vocalizing. "Four or so days' journey," she answers. "If we move quickly."

"And the others?" Jah-kee asks, her voice stronger now than it was three sols ago. "You say they're with more of Tharn's people?" Her gaze shifts to me just briefly.

Jus-teen does the chin jerk movement. "They are safe."

I watch the tension ease from Jah-kee's shoulders, relief washing over her features. She cares deeply for her kind, worries for their safety. It is an admirable trait, one that stirs something warm in my chest despite the constant pain.

"Are you ready for such a journey, Jah-kee?" I project without thinking.

Jus-teen glances at me, then turns to her sister. "Tharn wants to know if you're ready to travel that far."

Jah-kee's gaze flicks to me before skittering away again. "I'll be fine," she says, her voice firm despite the flush that creeps up her neck. "I'm stronger now."

I get the hazy image of her vibrant and strong. Of her facing the dust and travelling far.

She is stronger, yes. But is she strong enough? The dust shows no mercy to the weak, and four sols' journey is no small challenge even for one in perfect health.

Yet I say nothing. It is not my place to question her assessment of her strength. And perhaps... perhaps the sooner we reach the clan caves, the sooner this pain will end. One way or another.

"Then we leave at dawn," Rok declares, rising to his feet. *"We should rest while we can."*

As the others prepare for sleep, I take my customary position near the cave entrance, standing guard. It is easier this way. Easier to maintain the distance Jah-kee seems to prefer. Easier to hide the tremors that occasionally shake my frame as the pain crescendos.

I do not expect sleep to find me. It rarely does anymore. But as the others' breathing deepens and the fire burns low, my exhaustion finally overtakes me, dragging me into fitful dreams laced with golden light and Jah-kee's voice calling my name.

THE JOURNEY BEGINS AT DAWN, JUST AS ROK DECREED.

We move in formation across the dust—Rok leading, Justeen and Jah-kee in the middle, and me taking up the rear. This positioning is strategic, Rok explained in the mindspace before we left. It allows me to watch for threats from behind while keeping Jah-kee in my sight at all times, minimizing the pain of separation.

It was a thoughtful arrangement. But it does nothing to ease the agony that has become my constant companion.

Each step feels like walking on shattered stone, pain shooting up from my feet through my entire body. My chest burns as if a firebloom has taken root between my ribs, blooming with each breath I take. The glow beneath my skin pulses erratically, sometimes flaring so bright I fear it outshines Ain's light.

Still, I walk. I keep pace. I show nothing.

I am a hunter. I endure.

The females walk ahead of me, their heads bent close in conversation. The edge of Jah-kee's sleeve is frayed, a single thread dangling as she gestures while she speaks. It is such a small thing, but I cannot stop watching it, wondering if the hide will unravel further. I do not know why I notice these details about her, only that I do.

The thought comes unbidden, as it often does when I look at her. And with it comes a flicker of something else—a faint echo in the mindspace, not my thought but hers.

It happens more frequently now. These ghostly impressions of Jah-kee's mind touching mine. Never words, exactly. More like... feelings. Images. A hazy glimpse into her thoughts that vanishes as quickly as it appears.

This time, the flash is of me. Golden skin in the dark. My eyes watching her. And the feeling that comes with it... it is not fear. It is a warmth. A quickening. Like the air before a storm.

The glimpse fades as quickly as it came, leaving me wondering if I imagined it. But the flutter in my dra-kir tells me I did not.

She thinks of me.

"*Brother.*" Rok's mental voice cuts through my distraction. "*The path narrows ahead. We must cross single file.*"

I shake myself back to alertness, scanning the terrain. Rok is right. The smooth dust gives way to rougher ground, a rocky pass that will funnel us between two tall stone formations. A dangerous place. Perfect for an ambush.

"*I will go first,*" Rok projects, already moving toward the passage. "*Then the females. You follow and watch our backs.*"

I tilt my head in affirmation, dropping to a crouch to examine the dust for signs of recent passage. Nothing. No tracks, no disturbance in the fine particles that would indicate others have been here recently. Still, my instincts prickle with unease.

Rok leads the way through the narrow path, Jus-teen following close behind. Jah-kee hesitates at the entrance, her eyes scanning the high stone walls with obvious apprehension.

"*It is safe,*" I project automatically, forgetting again that she cannot hear me. The pain flares sharper in my chest, a reminder of the disconnect between us.

She glances back at me, as if she felt something, her brow furrowing slightly. For a heartbeat, our eyes meet, and the pain in my chest eases just a fraction.

Then she turns away, squaring her shoulders and following Jus-teen into the passage.

The moment she disappears from view, the pain explodes through me with such force that I nearly double over. My vision blurs, darkening at the edges, and my legs tremble beneath me. I catch myself against the stone wall, claws scraping against rough rock as I fight to remain upright.

I cannot fall. Cannot show weakness. Cannot let her see.

Gritting my teeth, I force myself to straighten, to place one foot in front of the other, to follow where Jah-kee has gone. Each step is agony, but I keep moving. I must keep moving.

By the time I emerge from the other side of the passage, my breathing comes in short, my chest expanding and contracting uselessly. Rok's gaze fixes on me immediately, his expression tightening as he takes in my condition.

"*Brother*—" he begins, his projection laced with concern.

"*I am fine.*"

Rok's jaw clenches, but he says nothing more. Instead, he turns to the females, who have paused to drink from the waterskin. "*We continue,*" he announces. "*There is shelter ahead where we can rest during the hottest part of the sol.*"

I am relieved at the prospect of rest, though I know it will bring little relief from the pain that consumes me. Still, for Jah-kee's sake, we must stop.

As we resume our journey, I catch Jah-kee watching me from the corner of her eye. There is something in her gaze. A question, perhaps? Or concern. I perk up, squaring my shoulders and puffing out my chest, but she looks away quickly when she realizes I've noticed her attention.

She knows. She senses something is wrong, though she cannot know what. My female is no fool.

My female. The phrase echoes in my mind, both right and wrong at once. She is mine in the way of the dust. But she has not chosen me. Has not accepted what grows between us.

May never accept it.

The thought brings a fresh wave of pain, this one having nothing to do with the law of the dust and everything to do with the tightness in my chest when I think of her leaving.

I push the thought away, focusing instead on placing one

foot in front of the other. On scanning the horizon for threats.
On being the hunter I was born to be.

I am a hunter. I endure.

Even as I break apart.

CHAPTER 21

MY MOUTH IS FOR BITING, NOT FOR WORDS

THARN

By the middle of the sol, the shelter Rok promised comes into view—a small cave set into the side of a tall rock formation. It is not very deep, but it will provide shade from Ain's harshest light.

"*We rest here,*" Rok announces, already moving to secure the area.

I remain on alert, scanning our surroundings one final time before following the others into the shade. I can tell the relief from Ain's direct light is immediate, the cooler air of the cave soothing against Jah-kee's overheated skin.

She sinks down against the rear wall, exhaling softly. She looks tired but not exhausted, her color good despite the exertion of the morning's travel. She is stronger than I feared, adapting to the harsh conditions of the dust with surprising resilience.

Pride swells in my chest, momentarily overshadowing the

pain. She is impressive, my Jah-kee. Strong in ways that have nothing to do with physical might.

The females share a waterskin, speaking softly in their strange language. I catch Jah-kee glancing at me occasionally, her expression unreadable. The flickering impressions from her mind brush against mine again. Fractured images, fleeting sensations. A strange heat. A longing for... something.

Rok settles beside me at the cave entrance, his projections pitched low and private. "*How bad?*"

I don't pretend to misunderstand. "*Manageable.*"

He makes a sound that clearly conveys his disbelief. "*It does not look manageable, brother. You move like one wounded, though you hide it well.*"

I say nothing, my gaze fixed on the horizon where heat waves distort the view. Of course, Rok can tell. He is our best scout after all. He sees things others would not.

"*You must tell her,*" Rok continues after a moment. "*She should know what happens between you.*"

"And frighten her further?" I project sharply. "*Make her feel responsible for pain she did not ask to cause?*"

"*She is stronger than you think,*" Rok argues.

Before I can respond, Jus-teen approaches, settling cross-legged beside Rok. Her expression is serious, her gaze flickering between us with suspicion.

"*What are you two talking about?*" she projects into the mindspace.

"*Nothing of importance,*" I answer quickly.

Jus-teen's eyes narrow. "*Right. That's why you both look like you're planning a funeral.*" She turns to Rok. "*He's getting worse, isn't he?*"

Rok hesitates, his gaze meeting mine briefly before he nods. "*Yes.*"

"*Rok.*" The thought is like a growl, a low warning.

"*She knows, brother,*" Rok projects, unmoved by my displeasure. "*She has seen this before.*"

Jus-teen's expression softens slightly as she looks at me. "*When Rok and I first met, he went through the same thing,*" she projects. "*The pain. The separation sickness.*"

I look away, uncomfortable with her scrutiny. I do not wish to discuss this. This tearing inside me. This separation from skin and bone.

"*Jah-kee deserves to know what's happening,*" Jus-teen continues, her mental voice gentler now. "*She's confused. Scared.*"

"*No,*" I project firmly. "*She has enough to adjust to without my... difficulties.*"

Jus-teen sighs, frustration evident in the sound. "Men," she mutters under her breath before switching back to mindspeak. "*Alien or human, you're all the same. Keeping everything bottled up inside like it makes you stronger.*"

"*It is not about strength,*" I project, the thoughts tight with restraint. "*It is about what she needs. What helps her.*"

"*You know what would help her?*" Jus-teen argues, leaning forward. "*Being able to understand what's happening around her. I've been thinking about the translator. If we could get it working, even a little...*"

"*Trans....lator?*" I project. The image I get isn't something that makes sense. A stone in Jah-kee's ear.

"*Well,*" Jus-teen begins, "*Jah-kee has a device in her ear —a translator. It helps humans understand different languages.*" Her hands gesture as she explains, a habit I've noticed when she speaks of things from her world. "*Right now, it's useless because you all communicate through mindspeak, but if we spoke aloud in your language, it might start to work.*"

My gaze shifts to Jah-kee, to the small stone barely visible

AG WILDE

in her ear. I had noticed it before but assumed it was a decoration.

"*A stone that teaches language?*" I project. "*Your kind has strange powers.*"

"*Not us and not powers,*" Jus-teen corrects, her lips quirking. "*Just technology. But if we can get it working, Jacqui might be able to understand at least some of what you say.*"

"*Drakavian is not spoken aloud after one emerges from the Giving Stone,*" I remind her.

"*But you remember it, right?*" she presses. "*You can still form the words.*"

I hesitate, uncertain. The thought of speaking aloud feels strange, uncomfortable. Hunters communicate through the mindspace, have done so for generations. Vocalizing is... primitive. Inefficient.

"*It would help Jacqui feel less isolated,*" Jus-teen adds, clearly sensing my reluctance. "*She's struggling, being the only one who can't understand what's happening.*"

That argument strikes deeper than she knows. The thought of Jah-kee feeling alone, cut off from understanding while everyone around her communicates freely... it claws at something protective in my chest.

"*I will try,*" I project reluctantly. "*Though I make no promises about my skill.*"

Jus-teen's expression brightens, a smile curving her lips. "*Great!*" She turns and calls to Jah-kee, who looks up from where she's been pretending to examine a small stone. "Jacqui, come here a minute."

Jah-kee approaches cautiously, her gaze flickering to me before settling on her sister. "What's up?"

Jus-teen pats the ground beside her, indicating Jah-kee should sit. "We're going to try something with the translator. Maybe help it calibrate to Rok and Tharn's language."

Jah-kee's eyebrows rise in surprise. "It can do that?"

"Worth a try," Jus-teen says with a shrug. "Beats having to play charades for the rest of our lives."

I don't understand what "charades" means, but Jah-kee's soft laugh makes the pain in my chest ease momentarily.

"So how does this work?" she asks, settling beside her sister. "Do they just... start talking?"

Jus-teen nods, then turns to Rok. "You first. Just a few words. Nothing complicated."

Rok inclines his head, then opens his mouth. The sound that emerges is strange to my ears. Rough, guttural, yet with a rhythmic quality that speaks of our ancestors' time when the Daughters of Ain roamed the dust.

"Teka..." Rok struggles, throat working, but he pushes on. "Vhan rath...kul doreth sa."

I stiffen at the sound of the old language, memories stirring from deep within. It has been so long since I heard these words spoken aloud. Many revolutions ago. The last time Kol, our leader, visited the Giving Stone. When the dust claimed one of our clan.

Jah-kee jumps slightly, her hand flying to her ear where the small stone device sits. "It beeped," she says, her eyes wide with surprise. "It's doing something!"

"What does it say?" Jus-teen asks eagerly.

"Nothing yet," Jah-kee answers, her head tilted as if listening. "Just—"

"ARCHAIC LANGUAGE DETECTED. DRAKAVIAN. CALIBRATING."

I freeze, my claws unsheathing instinctively. Something is speaking in Jah-kee's ear. But it is not her voice, not Jus-teen's, not anything I can see. A hidden thing is speaking in her head. A parasite.

"*What is this?*" My gaze locks on Jah-kee, whose eyes are

wide with surprise, her hand still pressed to the side of her head. *"Who speaks to her?"*

"It's fine!" Jus-teen says quickly, stepping into my path with both hands raised. *"Relax, Tharn. It's not an enemy."*

I do not relax. My claws twitch at my sides, my chest throbbing. *"It is a voice."* My gaze narrows. *"It hides. It speaks from nowhere. What is it?"*

"It's the translator," Jus-teen vocalizes. Her mental voice is steady. *"It's not alive. It's a device. A tool. It will help her understand you."*

I glance at Jah-kee again, my gaze drawn to the tiny stone lodged in her ear. It is too small to hold a voice. It is unnatural. Dangerous.

Jah-kee must sense my unease, because she takes a small step back, her free hand lifting defensively. "It's okay," she says softly, her water-blue eyes meeting mine. "It's just... technology. It's supposed to do this."

I want to believe her. But my instincts scream otherwise.

"It will not harm her," Jus-teen says firmly, stepping closer to Jah-kee as if to shield her from my suspicion. *"I promise, Tharn. It's meant to help. Let it calibrate."*

The word means nothing to me. My gaze flicks between the females, then to Rok, who stands silently beside Jus-teen, his expression calm but watchful. He tilts his head slightly, projecting reassurance into the mindspace. *"It is safe, brother. Trust her."*

Trust. The word feels heavy in my mind, but I force myself to still my claws and step back. My dra-kir does not settle.

"Try again," Jah-kee says after a moment, her voice hesitant but curious. She looks at Rok, her hand still hovering near her ear. "Say something else."

Rok goes still, his throat working. I see the effort it takes. The strength for him to speak another phrase in Drakavian. I watch Jah-kee's face closely, noting the way her expression shifts from concentration to excitement when the translator responds.

"CALIBRATION AT 15%."

"It's working," she beams. "But it's *really* slow."

"Better than nothing," Jus-teen says, then turns to me. *"Your turn, Tharn. Try saying something to Jacqui."*

I hesitate, suddenly aware of all eyes on me. The thought of speaking aloud, of using my voice rather than the mindspace, feels foreign. Uncomfortable. But for Jah-kee...

I clear my throat, the sensation strange after so long communicating only through the mindspace. When I speak, the words feel awkward on my tongue, rusty from disuse.

"Jah-kee. Dov'ah. Khem'sa'kahn. Dov'ah."

Jah-kee's eyes widen slightly, her lips parting in surprise at the sound of my voice.

"CALIBRATION AT 20%."

Her eyes meet mine directly for the first time in sols. "Tharn, your voice...your language...it's beautiful."

Her gaze is steady, curious, lingering on my face as if seeing me anew.

The pain in my chest recedes slightly, replaced by a different kind of ache—one that pulses in time with my dra-kir and sends heat flooding through me. My member twitches in its pouch, the sensation so unexpected and overwhelming, and I stagger under the weight of it.

I drop to my knees, claws digging into the sand as I fight to keep myself from unraveling completely. The rush of pleasure is too much. It is consuming.

My gaze shifts to Jus-teen.

There is no time for this. No time for the strange teaching stone to work or for the slow, clumsy process of speaking Drakavian.

I need Jah-kee to understand me now.

I project the thought sharply into the mindspace, directly at Jus-teen, my voice a low growl that rumbles through her thoughts. *"Teach me one word."*

She blinks, startled. *"One word?"*

"One word she will understand. One word I must say to her."

Jus-teen hesitates, her gaze flicking between me and Jah-kee. I can feel her unease, her doubt. But she knows I will not be swayed.

"What word, Tharn?"

CHAPTER 22

WHEN IN DOUBT, PRESS YOUR FOREHEAD TO THE HOT ALIEN

JACQUI

One minute, Tharn is on his feet, his voice resonating with that strange, alien beauty, and the next, he's on his knees, claws digging into sand, his massive body shuddering like he's being torn apart from the inside.

"Tharn!" I'm moving before I can think, heart pounding as I drop to my knees beside him. "What's happening? What's wrong with him?"

Justine hesitates. I see the pain, the worry, the uncertainty about what to do in her eyes.

"It's... complicated," she finally says, which is becoming her standard answer for everything on this godforsaken planet.

"Uncomplicate it," I snap, my patience evaporating as Tharn's breathing grows more labored, his claws digging deeper into the sand. "He's in pain!"

"It's the bond," Justine says, her voice dropping lower.

AG WILDE

"He's been fighting it, but it's... progressing. The pain gets worse until..."

She trails off, but I don't need her to finish. Until what? Until he breaks? Until he dies? The thought sends ice through my veins.

Without thinking, I slide closer to Tharn, my hands hovering uncertainly over his trembling form. He's so big, so intimidating even on his knees, that I'm not sure where or how to touch him. But I can't just sit here and watch him suffer.

"Hey," I say softly, reaching out to touch his shoulder. "Tharn, it's okay. Just breathe, all right?"

The moment my fingers brush his skin, his head snaps up, those amber eyes locking onto mine with an intensity that steals my breath. There's pain there, yes, but something else too. Something hot and desperate that makes my heart stutter in my chest.

Before I can pull away, his breathing changes, the shuddering easing slightly under my touch. It's working. Whatever's happening to him, my touch is helping.

I shift closer, moving my hand to his face, cradling his jaw in my palm. His skin is burning hot, almost feverish, the glow pulsing beneath my fingertips like a second heartbeat.

"That's it," I murmur, forgetting everything else—Justine, Rok, the alien world around us. It's just me and Tharn, connected by my hand on his face and his eyes fixed on mine. "Just breathe. In and out. See? Easy."

His breathing gradually steadies, the glow beneath his skin dimming slightly as his shuddering subsides.

"What the hell kind of bond is this?" I wonder, but even as I think it, I know. Deep down, I know. The dreams, the way he looks at me, the way my skin heats under his gaze—it's all connected. This isn't just some alien biology thing. It's about us.

198

He's in pain because of me. Because, somehow, he's imprinted on me.

Guilt washes through me, followed quickly by determination. I'm not going to let him suffer like this. Not when there's something I can do about it.

"You're okay," I whisper, my thumb tracing the hard ridge of his cheekbone. "You're strong. You've got this."

His eyes close briefly, his head tilting into my touch like a cat seeking more contact. The gesture is so unexpectedly vulnerable, so human in its need for comfort, that my throat tightens with emotion.

This alien—this massive, intimidating hunter who's saved my life multiple times—is leaning into my touch like it's the only thing keeping him anchored. Like I'm the only thing keeping him together.

It's terrifying. And kind of amazing.

But the moment of calm is shattered when Rok suddenly stiffens near the cave entrance. His nostrils flare, and a low growl rumbles from his chest, the sound primal and threatening. Beside him, Justine immediately tenses.

Tharn reacts instantly, despite his condition. His head snaps up, his body going rigid beneath my touch. A growl builds in his chest, vibrating against my palm, and then he's surging to his feet with surprising strength, shoving me behind him.

"Hey!" I yelp as I stumble backward. "What the—"

But Tharn isn't listening. He's focused entirely on the cave entrance, his massive body positioning itself between me and whatever threat Rok has sensed. His claws flex at his sides, the glow beneath his skin brightening again as adrenaline overrides his pain.

Great. Just what we need. Another crisis.

Rok and Tharn exchange growls, clearly communicating

silently while Justine moves closer to them, her expression tense but determined. I'm left standing there, completely clueless, watching as they prepare for... something.

I hate this. I hate not knowing what's being said—or thought, or projected, or whatever. It's like being stuck in the middle of a conversation where everyone's speaking a language you don't understand, and you're just standing there hoping you don't get punched in the face.

"What's happening?" I whisper, stepping forward despite Tharn's obvious attempt to keep me back. "Is it something dangerous? Another one of those shadow creature things?"

But they're not even looking at me. They're focused entirely on whatever's outside the cave, their bodies tense and ready for action.

That's when I remember what Justine told me earlier. About how pressing my forehead to Tharn's might help me hear him. Understand him.

It sounds insane. It probably is insane. But what choice do I have? I need to know what's happening, and the translator is still stubbornly stuck at 20% calibration, occasionally beeping but otherwise useless.

Before I can second-guess myself, I step forward, grab Tharn's arm to turn him toward me, rise on my tippy toes, and press my forehead directly to his.

The moment our skin connects, it's like touching raw electricity. Heat explodes through me, racing from the point of contact down my spine and settling low in my belly. The sensation is so intense, so unexpected, that I almost pull away.

But then I hear it. His voice. In my head.

"Jacqui."

It's faint and distorted, like he's speaking underwater, but it's unmistakably him. His mental voice is so darn deep, rich and resonant in a way that makes everything between my legs respond without my input.

I squeeze my eyes shut, focusing as hard as I can on that faint connection. *"Tharn? Can you hear me?"*

There's a sensation of surprise, almost like a jolt through our connection, and then his voice again, clearer this time.

"Yes. You... hear me now?"

"Yes!" I could cry with relief. *"What's happening? What's out there?"*

"Intruder," comes the immediate response, sharp with tension. *"Not clan. Rival."*

"Rival? Like... enemy clan?" I press, trying to understand. *"Are they dangerous?"*

I feel rather than hear his growl, a rumble of confirmation that makes the hairs on my arms stand up. *"Yes. Will take you. Will take Justine. Will take...all females."*

Oh. Great. Space alien territorial disputes. Just what we needed to make this day complete.

"What do we do?" I try to keep back my fear, try to hide it and be brave, but I'm sure he hears it anyway. *"Hide? Fight?"*

There's a pause, and then I feel his hands cup my face, his touch impossibly gentle despite the deadly claws at the tips of his fingers. The connection between us strengthens, his mental voice becoming clearer.

"I protect. Always protect you, Jacqui."

The conviction in his voice, the absolute certainty, almost bowls me over. He means it. With every fiber of his being, he means it.

When I open my eyes, I find his face inches from mine, those amber eyes burning with determination despite the pain I know still grips him. My heart does a strange flip in my chest, and for a moment, I forget how to breathe.

"*Safe*," he projects, the word rough but unmistakable. "*I keep you safe.*"

And then he's pulling away, straightening to his full height despite the tremor I can still see running through his massive frame. He turns toward the cave entrance, where Rok is already positioned defensively.

"Wait!" I grab his arm, panic surging through me. "You can't go out there. You're not well!"

But he doesn't even look at me. He just shrugs off my grip like I weigh nothing, his focus entirely on the threat outside.

"Tharn!" I try again, but Justine catches my arm, pulling me back.

"He has to go," she whispers urgently. "Rok can't—they'll smell me on him. They'll see his loincloth and know something's... different."

I stare at her, momentarily distracted from my panic. "Wait, you're saying Tharn's the only one who can go because he's still... normal?!"

Justine shrugs, her expression a mix of embarrassment and resignation. "More or less."

Right. Because amid all this chaos, I'd almost forgotten that my sister is having sex with an alien who apparently grew new parts just for her. Fantastic.

"But he's in pain," I argue, keeping my voice low as Tharn moves steadily toward the cave entrance. "He can barely stand!"

"You have no idea the strength of these men," Justine says, her grip on my arm tightening when I try to pull away. "Trust me, Jacqui. He knows what he's doing."

I want to argue more, to demand that someone else handle this, that Tharn stay here where it's safe. But a part of me knows it's useless. He's already made his decision. He's going to face whatever's out there, pain or no pain, because he thinks it's his job to protect me.

The realization makes my chest ache with a strange mix of frustration, fear, and something very close to admiration.

I watch as Tharn steps into the fading light at the cave entrance, his massive form casting a long shadow across the sand. Despite the weakness I saw just moments ago, he moves with predatory grace, his shoulders squared and his head held high.

Through the gathering dusk, another figure approaches. He is Drakav, tall and golden-skinned like the others, but where Tharn is solid strength and Rok is lean muscle, this one is pure, brutal mass. His shoulders are broader, his neck thicker, and his face is a mask of jagged scars and a permanent scowl. He doesn't walk; he stalks, his movements radiating an arrogant, violent energy that makes the hair on my arms stand up.

Tharn's growl fills the cave as he shifts slightly to block the newcomer's view of the inside. Even wounded, even in pain, he's a wall of muscle and fury, his claws flexing at his sides as he faces down the intruder.

Not for the first time since I've met him, I'm actually glad he's terrifying.

Tharn faces the intruder, and I realize with growing frustration that they're communicating telepathically. Having an entire conversation—or confrontation—that I can't hear or understand. It's maddening.

Rok herds Justine and me deeper into the cave, positioning himself between us and the entrance where Tharn faces the stranger. Blocking my view of Tharn and everything else.

"What are they saying?" I whisper to Justine, who's watching Rok's face intently.

"Hold on," she murmurs, her voice barely audible. "It's coming through Rok and then to me."

I wait, impatience gnawing at me.

"It's not good," Justine finally whispers, leaning close to my ear. "The other guy is furious. Says their water sources are drying up."

"Water sources? What does that have to do with us?"

"They think our clan is taking too much," she explains quickly, her eyes darting between me and Rok. "Draining the watering holes across the desert."

Our clan? When did it become our cl—. Nevermind.

"Is that true?" I whisper, though I already know the answer. If there's one thing I've learned about Tharn, it's that he respects the harsh balance of this world.

Justine shakes her head. "No. But they need someone to blame."

My heart thunders in my chest, and I focus on keeping silent.

"What now?" I whisper after a few moments.

"It's a threat," Justine translates, her expression growing more worried. "He's warning Tharn that his clan won't tolerate being cheated of water. Says if they don't get what they need..."

She trails off, glancing at Rok, whose growl rumbles low in his chest.

"If they don't get what they need, what?" I press.

"They'll take it," she finishes grimly. "By force if necessary."

Great. Just what we need—a water war. And not the fun kind.

For several long minutes, Rok is silent and still above us, and then his shoulders suddenly relax. When there's finally movement at the cave mouth, my heart lurches. But it's Tharn. His expression is grim, his glow pulsing erratically beneath his skin.

He's still in pain. Maybe even more so after that confrontation. But he's hiding it better now, his movements controlled and his face carefully blank. My palms itch to reach out and touch him.

"The water," Justine says out loud. "They think you're using too much of the water."

Tharn's jaw ticks, his displeasure still clear.

"Could it be because of us?" My gaze shifts to Justine. "We drink more than they do. Maybe..."

She shakes her head. "Rok said we don't drink enough to cause a problem."

"So..." I continue, searching her face. "So why are their water sources drying up?"

Justine looks at Rok, even moving closer to him, though I don't know if she's even aware she's doing it. The utter trust in her eyes. The peace...

I look at Tharn, who's still watching me with that intense, unreadable expression. Despite everything, despite the danger and the confusion and the fear, I find myself stepping closer to him, drawn by something I can't explain.

Maybe because these past few days I've been watching him, watching Rok, watching Justine...and Justine is happy. Like, actually happy. I can't recall the last time I saw my sister without worry lines creasing her brow.

"Are you okay?" I ask softly, my eyes searching Tharn's face for signs of the pain I know he's still feeling.

He nods once, a jerky motion that doesn't convince me at all.

I reach out and take his hand, my fingers wrapping around his much larger ones.

The contact sends a jolt through me, like static electricity but warmer, more pleasant. His skin is still hot, almost feverish, but soothing. Strangely soothing.

"Thank you," I say, my voice steadier than I feel. "For protecting us."

His expression softens slightly, something flickering in those amber eyes that makes my heart beat faster. He squeezes my hand gently, careful of his claws, and nods again.

And despite everything—the danger, the confusion, the fear of what comes next—I believe him. Completely and without reservation.

Because one thing is becoming increasingly clear: on this alien world, with its rival clans and dangers lurking in every shadow, Tharn might be the only thing keeping me alive.

And I'm starting to think that I might be the only thing keeping him together.

CHAPTER 23
I WASN'T LOOKING FOR AN ALIEN HUSBAND. BUT HE'S LOOKING AT ME

JACQUI

Tharn is kneeling before me, his massive frame somehow less intimidating in this dream-space.

"Jah-kee," he rumbles, his voice both in my ears and inside my head, "let me share your water."

I don't question the words. Dream-logic makes them the only thing that has ever made sense. I nod, a wave of heat washing through me as his large hands slide up my thighs, his thumbs brushing the insides as he pushes the fabric of my clothes aside.

His touch is fire. I gasp as his claws skim over the sensitive flesh of my inner thighs. Teasing. Promising.

"Please," I whisper, voice husky with a need that makes me tremble.

He looks up at me, his amber eyes molten, burning with a hunger that mirrors my own. Then he lowers his head between my thighs.

My back arches off the ground as his hot breath ghosts over

my folds. His scent is intoxicating. I whimper, my fingers fisting in the soft sand, waiting, begging.

And then his tongue touches me.

A broad, hot, purposeful stroke, right over my clit. A shockwave of pure pleasure rips through me. My whole body jolts. The universe implodes.

He makes a low, satisfied sound against my skin, a rumbling growl that vibrates through my entire being. His hands grip my thighs, holding me steady as he licks again, slower this time, learning my shape. He tastes me, his tongue tracing patterns that make my hips buck, chasing the pleasure he's creating.

One of his claws traces a line from my hip bone down to the wet curls between my legs, dipping into my slickness. He brings the finger to his mouth, tasting me, his golden eyes never leaving mine. The look in them is pure, savage possession.

Mine. The thought is his, a brand on my soul.

He goes back to work, his tongue now relentless. Lapping, sucking, flicking. He finds a rhythm that has my vision going blurry, my moans turning into shameless, breathless cries. I'm close, so close, the pleasure coiling tight in my gut, a breath from release.

"Tharn," I gasp, my body shaking.

He answers by pressing the hard ridge of his nose against my clit while his tongue continues its assault, adding a deep, perfect pressure that shatters my control.

I jolt awake, a gasp caught in my throat, my body flushed and trembling with a need so intense it's almost painful. For a moment, I'm disoriented, the dream still vivid in my mind as reality slowly reasserts itself.

I'm lying on the hard ground of a cave. Not surrounded by

golden light, no kneeling Tharn, and no mouth between my legs.

Oh, thank God.

And also, *damn it.*

I squeeze my eyes shut, trying to will away the lingering arousal, the phantom sensation of his hands on my thighs, his mouth—

Nope. Not going there. Not thinking about it.

When I open my eyes again, the first thing I see is Tharn, standing near the cave entrance, his massive silhouette outlined against the growing light of dawn. He's perfectly still, except for his head, which turns slightly toward me, those amber eyes finding mine across the distance with unerring accuracy.

Did he... could he have somehow sensed my dream? Felt what I was feeling?

Oh God, please no.

I quickly look away, heat flooding my face as I sit up, pretending to be very interested in smoothing out the wrinkles in my grimy clothes. But I can still feel his gaze on me, making something low in my belly clench with a combination of embarrassment and lingering desire.

This is ridiculous. I'm a grown woman. And I'm having wet dreams about an alien on a desert planet in the middle of nowhere. My life has officially gone off the rails.

"We need to get moving," Justine announces, already awake and preppy. Blast her. "That guy from last night might come back with friends."

Right. The rival clan member. The threat. Reality comes crashing back, and I'm almost grateful for the distraction from my hormonal chaos.

"You two go ahead," Justine says to Rok, gesturing between them. "Scout the path. Jacqui and I will follow."

Rok nods, hesitating only briefly before moving ahead with long, fluid strides. Tharn remains rooted in place, his gaze flickering between me and the distant horizon with obvious reluctance.

"He doesn't want to leave you," Justine murmurs beside me. "It's physically painful for him."

I swallow hard, guilt tempering my embarrassment. "The bond thing?" I ask, though I already know the answer.

She nods, her expression softening. "It's getting worse for him. You've noticed, right? The pain?"

I think of the way he collapsed yesterday, the tremors that ran through his massive frame, the way my touch seemed to ease his suffering. "Yeah," I admit quietly. "I've noticed." A knot of guilt and something unexpected—a fierce, protective anger—tightens in my stomach. *He's suffering because of me.*

"So how do I fix it?" I ask, voice low. "Can that firebloom stuff help? Some other alien medicine? What do I do?"

Justine stops and turns to face me, her expression completely serious. She looks me dead in the eye.

"You fuck him," she says, her voice flat and devoid of any humor. "That's how you fix it. You complete the bond."

I stare at her, unable to respond. The words hang in the hot desert air between us. "That can't be the only way."

"It is," she says, then turns and starts walking again, leaving me standing there, completely stunned.

I swallow hard, my throat suddenly as dry as the sand at my feet. My gaze automatically flicks to Tharn, who is watching us with a curious tilt of his head. He has no idea we're discussing the intimate details of his... recovery plan.

Fuck him.

The words echo in my head, part medical prescription, part command. A sudden, inappropriate warmth pools low in my belly, and I have to clench my thighs together to stop it from spreading.

"EXPLAIN IT TO ME AGAIN LIKE I'M IN KINDERGARTEN." THIS IS certainly not the type of birds and the bees talk I'd thought I'd be getting at my big age. "His dick is exactly like you've always imagined your perfect guy's dick being...and you're *sure* it's not a coincidence?"

Alright, so away with being queasy about discussing my sister's alien boyfriend's goods. Curiosity is too much, and I have to know what I'm getting into.

I kick at the loose sand as we walk, trying not to look over my shoulder at Tharn as we talk about this specific part of his and Rok's anatomy.

Justine snorts, clearly amused by my awkwardness. "It's definitely not a coincidence," she says. "Rok was like Tharn. He didn't have a visible thing. He wasn't... equipped like that when we first met. It happened when he suddenly changed. As if his body was reshaping itself to be exactly what *I*... needed."

She glances at me and sees my dumbfounded expression.

"Hey, I thought it was crazy too at first. But I've thought about it over and over again. It's the only thing that makes sense." She shrugs.

I nearly trip over my own feet. "That's... that's crazy," I stammer. "How is that even possible?"

She shrugs, her expression thoughtful. "I don't know for sure. Maybe it's the particles I dreamt about. Maybe we really are these mythic Daughters of Ain. Or maybe it's the bond itself, somehow. All I know is that one day, Rok was just like Tharn—flat pouch, nothing obviously... you know. And then, after we got closer, after the bond strengthened, things... changed."

I can't help it—my eyes dart to Tharn's figure, specifically to the flat pouch at his groin that I've mostly been trying not to think about. As if on cue, something shifts beneath the skin, a subtle movement that sends a jolt of heat through my core.

Oh. God.

My steps falter as blood rushes to my face, and other places I'm trying desperately to ignore. This is not happening. I'm not getting turned on by watching Tharn's junk twitch. I'm not that far gone.

Except, apparently, I am.

"What does that mean?" I whisper, tearing my gaze away from Tharn. "For me, I mean. If the bond is doing the same thing to him that it did to Rok..."

Justine's expression turns serious. "It means his body is preparing to be compatible with yours," she says quietly. "It means the bond is progressing, whether you're ready for it or not."

A cold shiver runs down my spine despite the desert heat. "And if I'm not ready?" I hiss. "If I don't want this?"

Justine's hand finds mine, squeezing gently. "Then we'll figure something out," she promises. "No one's going to force you into anything, Jacqui. Not even the bond."

I nod, grateful for her reassurance, though a small, traitorous part of me whispers that *forcing* isn't the issue. The issue is that a growing part of me does want this, whatever "this" is. Wants Tharn, with his fierce protectiveness and his gentle touches and his amber eyes that see right through me.

"So," I say, desperate to change the subject before my thoughts spiral any further, "if what you're saying is true, and his body is changing to be... compatible with mine, does that mean it's customizing itself to what I, specifically, would want?"

Justine's lips twitch with suppressed amusement. "It's just my theory, but yes. Why? Got specific preferences you're worried about?"

"No!" I exclaim, too quickly and too loudly. Ahead of us, Rok's head turns slightly, and I lower my voice. "I just... I mean, if I could design the perfect one, I'd make improvements, you know?"

"Oh?" Justine's eyebrows rise, her expression a mix of amusement and genuine curiosity. "Like what?"

I shouldn't continue this conversation. I really shouldn't. But something about the absurdity of our situation, the stress of the past few days, and the lingering arousal from my dream makes me reckless.

"First, it'd have to be thick," I say, my voice dropping to a near-whisper. "Like, really thick, the kind of thickness that makes your breath catch when it first slides in but leaves you desperate for more. Girthy enough to feel like it's stretching you just right."

Justine's eyes widen slightly, but she doesn't interrupt.

"And ridges," I continue, warming to my topic despite the heat in my cheeks. "There'd have to be ridges. The kind that tease every inch of you as it moves, brushing against places you didn't even know could feel that good."

I'm getting carried away now, describing what is essentially my fantasy penis to my *sister*. But I can't seem to stop.

"And then... then there'd be the part for your clit," I add, my voice barely audible. "Because let's be honest, human anatomy? Not always great at multitasking. Something soft but firm, perfectly curved to press against just the right spot. Something that could move when you did, never losing that perfect pressure, even if things got... enthusiastic."

Justine stares at me for a long moment, then bursts into laughter, the sound echoing across the desert.

"What?" I demand, embarrassment warring with my indignation. "It's a legitimate design improvement!"

"I'm not laughing at your design," she gasps, wiping tears from her eyes. "I'm laughing because you just described Rok's... equipment. Everything except for the...clit thing."

I stop dead in my tracks, horror washing over me. "No," I whisper. "No way."

"Yes way," she confirms, still giggling. "Which means..."

My gaze automatically snaps to Tharn, who's looking at us, his expression curious and slightly concerned. As our eyes meet, I swear I can feel his awareness brush against my mind, a whisper of presence that makes me wonder if he's caught any of my thoughts.

Oh god, please no.

"It means nothing," I insist, starting to walk again, faster this time. "It's just a coincidence. A weird, freaky coincidence."

"Uh-huh," Justine says, clearly not buying it. "Just like it's a coincidence that I dreamed about Rok for days before anything actually happened between us. Vivid dreams about—"

"I do not need to hear about your sex dreams involving my apparent brother-in-law," I interrupt hastily. Because let's just call this what it is. No one is coming to rescue us. We're stuck here. And the way I've seen my sister look at Rok, I don't think she'd choose to leave even if the Xyma did miraculously come back to save us.

Justine's expression turns smug. "I didn't say they were sex dreams. But interesting that your mind went there immediately."

I shoot her my best "I'm so annoyed with you" scowl, but the effect is probably ruined by the dawning horror that's making my eyes go wide. How can there be any real anger when her words have confirmed my worst fear—that the dreams I've been having aren't just dreams. That they're somehow connected to the bond, to Tharn, to whatever is happening between us.

"Just one more day," Justine says, her voice gentler now. "We'll reach the clan caves tomorrow. Things will be easier there."

Will they, though? Somehow, I doubt it. Not when every step takes me closer to a future I never asked for but can't seem to escape. Not when my body betrays me at every turn, responding to Tharn in ways that make it increasingly difficult to deny what's happening between us.

As if summoned by my thoughts, Tharn increases his pace, walking closely behind us now. His amber eyes find mine immediately, intense and questioning, and I wonder again if he's sensed any of my thoughts, any of the confusion and desire warring within me.

"Tharn," I greet him, aiming for casual and probably missing by a mile. "Everything okay at the rear?"

He tilts his head at me then lifts his hand, his massive fingers fumbling into the shape I taught him. The thumbs-up. It's absurdly off-kilter, his claw-tipped thumb jutting off to the side.

Oh no.

It's the most endearing thing I've ever seen.

I offer him a small smile, trying to ignore the way my heart beats faster now. "Good. That's... good."

We fall into step together, a slightly awkward trio as Justine picks up her pace to catch up with Rok.

I steal a glance at him as we walk—and immediately regret it.

Because *fuck*, Tharn is...

Strands of his copper-red hair catch the sunlight, clinging

to the sharp planes of his face. Damn, that jawline could cut glass. And the way his muscles move beneath his golden skin —each flex and shift so fluid, so unfairly predatory—makes my mouth go dry.

But it's his hands that undo me. Those broad palms, the lethal claws currently retracted... imagining what they'd feel like dragging down my bare skin—

Oh. My.

My brain conjures exactly how those callouses might rasp between my thighs.

As if sensing my scrutiny, he turns to look at me, those amber eyes softening in a way that makes me forget how to breathe. His gaze drops briefly to my lips before returning to my eyes, and the heat that passes between us blazes hotter than the too-big sun.

Oh, I'm in trouble. So much trouble.

Because one more day suddenly feels like both too long and not nearly enough time before everything changes. Before I have to face what's happening between us, what's been happening since the moment he found me in the desert.

And the scariest part? A growing part of me doesn't want to resist it. Doesn't want to fight the pull that draws me to him like a magnet to true north.

A growing part of me wants to surrender to whatever this is, consequences be damned.

God help me, but I think I'm falling for an alien.

CHAPTER 24
THE DUST SHIFTS, AND SO DOES MY CONTROL

THARN

The clan caves are close now. Just over the ridge before us.

The thought should bring relief. Safety. The comfort of familiar stone walls and the protection of my clan-brothers.

Instead, it fills me with dread.

I watch Jah-kee as she walks ahead with Jus-teen. The desert wind presses her thin garment against her back, outlining the delicate architecture of her shoulder blades. I count each vertebra like a hunter tracking prey, wondering how they'd feel beneath my claws. My chest aches with a pain that has become so constant I barely notice it anymore. Like the burn of muscles after a long hunt or the sting of dust against skin.

What I cannot ignore is what stirs in my pouch.

My member pulses insistently now, pressing against its

confines, seeking release. Seeking her. The sensation is foreign, uncomfortable. A constant reminder of how my body changes.

Rok has explained it all. In hushed projections while the females slept, he described the transformation that awaits me. The emergence of my stem from its pouch. The claiming. The sealing of the bond.

"Only then will her mind fully open to yours," he projected, his mental voice steady but tinged with memory. *"Only then will the pain ease completely."*

I did not need to ask what he meant by claiming. The images he shared told me everything. His body joined with Jus-teen's, their minds merging completely in the mindspace.

The thought of doing this with Jah-kee consumes me. When I close my eyes, I see her beneath me, her water-blue eyes darkened with need, her soft body yielding to mine. I see our minds intertwining, our thoughts becoming one.

I want nothing more.

And the wanting is driving me mad.

The wanting is a living thing in my chest, gnawing at my ribs with teeth of fire.

Jah-kee walks ahead, unaware of the war she wages in me with every sway of her hips, every loose strand of head-fur that dances in the wind.

If only she knew. If only she could feel the fire in my veins, the desperate need clawing at my insides.

"We are close to clan territory," I project, directing my thoughts to Jus-teen to translate. *"I am... alert for threats."*

It is not entirely a lie. The male from the rival clan has left me wary. But the true threat is not external.

It is the madness growing within me.

Rok slows his pace, falling back to walk beside me while the females continue ahead. His topaz eyes study me with too much understanding.

"*It grows worse,*" he projects privately, not a question but a statement.

I say nothing. There is no need. He can see the truth in the tightness of my movements, the strain in my features, the way my claws flex and unflex at my sides.

"*When we reach the clan caves—*" he begins, but I cut him off with a sharp mental hiss.

"*I know what awaits,*" I project. "*Your warnings are unnecessary.*"

A low rumble starts deep in Rok's chest, a sound of profound weariness. "*Not warnings, brother. Counsel. The others will sense your distress immediately. And they will wonder about a female for themselves.*"

My claws extend fully at the thought of my clan-brothers looking at Jah-kee, at them learning of what stirs between us. A growl builds in my chest, unbidden and uncontrolled.

"*They will not touch her,*" I project, the words edged with a possessiveness that surprises even me.

"*No, they will not,*" Rok agrees, his mental voice soothing. "*But they will watch. They will wonder. They will...hunger.*"

The growl escapes my throat before I can stop it, loud enough that both females turn to look at us. Jah-kee's expression shifts from concern to confusion, her gaze moving between me and Rok as if trying to decipher what caused my reaction.

I cannot meet her eyes. Not now. Not when the mere sight of her makes my member pulse painfully in its pouch, makes my skin glow brighter with need.

"What's going on?" she asks, her voice carrying easily in the still desert air.

Jus-teen glances at Rok, who projects a quick explanation to her. She chin-jerks, then turns to Jah-kee.

"Tharn's just a little... stressed," she vocalizes. "We're getting close to the clan territory. Lots of politics to navigate."

Jah-kee doesn't look convinced, but she doesn't press the issue. Instead, she slows her pace, falling back until she walks beside me while Jus-teen moves ahead with Rok.

My body responds instantly to her proximity. My skin glows brighter, my breaths stutter, my member strains even harder against its pouch. The pain-pleasure of it races through my veins like liquid fire.

"You don't have to pretend with me, you know," she says quietly, her water-blue eyes fixed on the horizon.

Her cheeks flush pink—a reaction I've noticed happens even more regularly now. It makes her even more beautiful, the color highlighting the delicate structure of her face.

"Tharn, you're a mystery," she vocalizes, her voice slightly breathless. "But I'm glad I met you."

I want to touch her. Dust. I want to touch her. To run my claws gently over her skin, to press my forehead to hers and sink into the mindspace where vocalizations are unnecessary. To claim her completely, to make her mine in every way possible.

The wanting drowns out rational thought, obliterates caution, leaves only need in its wake.

Ahead of us, Rok and Jus-teen have paused, their heads bent close in conversation. As we approach, I catch the tail end of their exchange.

Rok's eyes are alive with awareness, his expression grim. "*Sand moved. Recently. Could be nothing. Could be—*"

He breaks off, his nostrils flaring as he scents the air. His posture changes instantly, shifting from relaxed to alert in a heartbeat.

He turns, catches my eye, and makes a series of subtle

gestures with his hand. Warning signs. Used by the clan when stealth is required.

Danger. Below. Move carefully.

But the signals barely register through the haze of need and pain that clouds my mind. I see his movements, recognize them as important, but their meaning slides away before I can grasp it.

All I can focus on is Rok, his hand too near Jah-kee, his presence a violation. A growl builds in my throat at the sight, irrational but unstoppable.

Mine. Not his. *Mine.*

I know it makes no sense. Rok is bonded to Jus-teen. But the beast in my blood does not care for sense. It only cares that another male stands too close to what is mine.

"*Tharn,*" Rok projects sharply, his mental voice cutting through my distraction. "*Focus. Dust serpent.*"

The words finally penetrate the fog in my mind. Dust serpent. One of the most dangerous predators of the deep dust. They tunnel beneath the surface, hunting by vibration, erupting from below to drag their prey under the dust, where they slowly suffocate before being consumed.

I scan the ground, suddenly alert for the telltale signs. The slight ripple on the sand's surface. The thin spout that marks the serpent's passage.

There. A straight line of disturbed sand, barely visible, moving slowly toward our group.

"*Move,*" I project urgently, the word lashing out to include all of them. "*Now. Away from the line!*"

Jus-teen reacts immediately, grabbing Rok's arm and pulling him back. But Jah-kee, unable to hear the mindspace warning, remains where she is, her expression confused.

"What's wrong?" she asks, looking between us. "What's happening?"

The sand beneath her feet shifts subtly. Too subtly for her to notice, but my hunter's eyes catch the movement.

The serpent is directly beneath her.

There is no time for explanation, no time for warnings. I move purely on instinct, lunging forward and shoving Jah-kee aside with all my strength. She flies through the air, landing hard several paces away as the sand where she stood erupts.

The serpent bursts upward, its massive body uncoiling like a whip. Dust-colored plates ripple along its length, and beneath them, black, glistening underscales that seem to drink in Ain's light. Its head is nothing but a mouth. No eyes, no snout, just a circular mouth that blooms open, expanding wider than its own body.

It towers above me, swaying slightly, searching for the prey it sensed moments ago.

Then it strikes.

I dive to the side, but I am slower than usual, my reflexes dulled by pain and distraction. The serpent's head misses me by a claw's width, but I feel the displacement of air as it passes, smell the foul rot from its maw. The ground shudders behind me. A second eruption of sand. The serpent's tail whips through the air, faster than sight, and slams into me, wrapping around my leg with crushing force.

I hear Jah-kee scream, the sound distant and distorted as the serpent drags me backward, toward the hole it created. My claws scrape against sand, seeking purchase, finding none.

Rok is moving, but he is too far. The sand is already closing around my legs, the serpent pulling me down into its tunnel.

In the last moment before the dust swallows me completely, I catch a glimpse of Jah-kee's face. Her water-blue eyes wide with terror, her mouth open in a scream I can no longer hear.

I'm going to lose her, I think as darkness closes around me.

And I never told her. Never claimed her. Never completed the bond.

The serpent's grip tightens, pulling me deeper into the earth. I fight against it, claws extended, slashing blindly at the creature's armored hide. But in the confines of the tunnel, with no room to maneuver, my attacks are ineffective.

My lungs burn for air. The pressure against my chest builds, squeezing mercilessly.

I am going to die here, beneath the dust, unclaimed and unclaiming.

The thought brings a surge of rage so intense it burns through the pain, the lack of air, the crushing pressure. No. I will not die. Not like this. Not before I make Jah-kee mine.

Not before I let her know how much she has come to mean to me.

CHAPTER 25
BURIED ALIVE AND OTHER ROMANTIC GETAWAYS

JACQUI

One second, Tharn is beside me; the next, he's shoving me with enough force to send me flying.

I hit the sand hard, the impact knocking the breath from my lungs, but I barely register the pain because what I see next freezes the blood in my veins.

Where I was standing just moments ago, the ground has exploded upward. Something massive and pale bursts from the sand. A nightmare creature with segmented armor plates and a gaping circular mouth ringed with teeth.

The air vibrates with a hiss I *feel* more than *hear*.

It towers above Tharn, its eyeless head turning as if scenting the air... and then it strikes.

Tharn tries to dodge, but he's not moving right—he hasn't been moving right all day. The creature misses his body, but three body-lengths behind where its head emerged, its tail suddenly whips up from the sand. The armored tip strikes like a scorpion's sting, wrapping around Tharn's thigh with a crack that echoes across the dunes.

I see the moment the barbs sink, just before the creature's head dives back into the sand, burrowing once more.

"THARN!" My scream tears from my throat as the serpent begins dragging him backward toward the hole it created.

Everything happens too fast. Tharn's claws rake desperately at the ground, carving deep furrows as the serpent drags him under. His golden body twists and jerks, trying to find purchase, but the merciless sand shifts and crumbles beneath him.

"Tharn!" I scream again, the sound raw in my throat. His gaze snaps up, locking on mine, even as his claws dig into the sand. The serpent is too strong. He's being pulled deeper, the sand shifting like liquid around him.

To my right, Justine cries out—a sharp, pained sound. It cuts through the chaos like a knife.

I whip my head toward her. She's stumbling, clutching her leg, blood streaking her hand.

Rok is already moving. He's there in an instant, his arms sliding under her, lifting her like she weighs nothing.

"No! Forget about me! We have to help Tharn!" Justine shouts, her voice cracking with pain.

Rok's jaw tightens, and for the first time, I see his glow. It erupts, then falters, flickering unevenly—like a heartbeat gone wrong. It pulses brighter as blood seeps between Justine's fingers, and something about that glow twists in my gut.

HE SETS HER DOWN BEHIND AN OUTCROPPING OF ROCK, HIS movements careful despite the chaos, before spinning and racing back toward Tharn.

I turn back just in time to see Tharn's arms sink deeper. His shoulders are almost gone.

I'm running. I don't remember deciding to, but my legs are moving, the world narrowing to the spot where he's vanishing.

"Jacqui, stop!" Justine's voice is hoarse behind me. "You can't! You'll just get yourself killed!"

I don't hear her. Not really.

Tharn's eyes find mine. For a heartbeat, everything slows. There's something in his gaze I've never seen before. Not fear, but regret. Bone-deep, soul-crushing regret.

And then he's gone.

The sand collapses over him, settling as if he were never there.

"No!"

I'm already on my knees, clawing at the sand. It's hot and coarse, scraping my palms raw, but I don't care. A sound rips from my throat. A raw, tearing scream of pure no. I dig faster, the sound continuing, a wordless howl against the silent, indifferent desert.

Rok crashes down beside me, clawing at the sand where Tharn disappeared.

"Jacqui!" Justine's voice cuts through the haze of my panic. "Stop! Stop, damn it!"

I ignore her. My fingers are bleeding now, the sand swallowing every handful I throw aside, but I don't stop. I can't stop. Tharn is down there, being crushed or suffocated or eaten alive, and it's all my fault. He pushed me out of the way. He saved me. Again.

"Please," I sob as I claw at the unyielding sand. "Please, please, please."

Suddenly, the ground beneath us shudders violently. Rok freezes, his head cocked as if listening. Then he grabs my arm and yanks me backward just as the sand erupts again—not where we were digging, but a few feet away.

Something thrashes beneath the surface, creating ripples in the sand like waves on water. I *feel* its hiss again, buzzing in my ears and rattling deep in my chest. The sand pebbles on the surface, trembling in response to the soundless pressure. The creature. It's hurt.

Tharn's fighting. He's alive.

Rok releases me and dives toward the new disturbance, his powerful arms sinking into the sand up to his shoulders. I scramble after him, my heart pounding so hard I can feel it in my throat.

"Come on, Tharn," I whisper. "Come on."

The sand shifts again, more violently this time.

"Rok!" Justine shouts from somewhere behind me.

But Rok ignores the warning, continuing to dig despite the tremors around us.

I turn to see my sister stumbling, her leg giving way beneath her. There's a deep gash in her calf, bleeding freely into the sand.

I'm torn, my gaze darting between my injured sister and the spot where Tharn is buried. I can't leave him. I can't.

But Justine is falling, her face pale with pain and blood loss.

With a final, desperate look at the churning sand, I rush to Justine's side. She's sitting now, her hands pressed against the wound in a futile attempt to stem the bleeding.

"It's not that bad," she says through gritted teeth, but the pallor of her face tells a different story.

I drop to my knees beside her, grabbing the pouch she's tied to her waist with Rok's herbs. "What happened?"

"Something hit me when that thing came up," she hisses as

I crush the leaves, pushing them against the wound. "Some kind of debris. Hurts like hell."

"We need to get you help," I say, packing the wound with shaking hands. "And Tharn—we need help for Tharn too."

Heart still in my throat, I scan the horizon. "We're close to the clan caves, aren't we? Very close."

Justine grits her teeth, pressing a hand to her bleeding leg. "Just over...there." She jerks her chin toward the rocky ridge ahead. "Rok says we should be able to see it from the top of that next dune."

My eyes follow her gesture to a massive dune that stands between us and the ridge. It doesn't look far on a map, but I know better. That's a wall of loose, shifting sand that will fight me every step of the way.

A plan forms in my mind, desperate and probably stupid, but it's all I've got.

"Okay." I exhale sharply, wiping my palms on my thighs. "Okay, I can do this."

Justine's eyes lock onto mine. "Jaqs?"

"Stay here," I tell her, already standing. "Apply pressure to the wound. I'm going to get help."

"Are you su—" But I'm already moving. "Jacqui, wait—!" Justine's voice wavers, her hand outstretched.

I pause just long enough to meet her eyes, really meet them, and see the fear there. Not just for me, but of this moment. The one where she realizes she can't protect me anymore.

"I've got this," I say softly, squeezing her fingers. "You taught me how."

Her breath catches. She searches my face like she's seeing me for the first time. Then, slowly, she nods.

"Run fast," she whispers.

And I do.

THE SAND CLAWS AT MY BOOTS LIKE IT WANTS TO DRAG ME UNDER. Every breath scorches my throat, but I push harder, arms pumping, heart hammering against my ribs.

It's the firebloom cave all over again, but worse.

Because this time, my head is clear. This time, I know exactly what awaits me if I fail.

The ridge looms—closer, closer—as the sun brands my shoulders. Sweat blurs my vision, but I don't slow. Can't.

Somewhere behind me, Tharn is fighting to breathe under a mountain of sand.

Somewhere behind me, Justine is praying I'll make it.

My foot catches in the sand. I stumble, knees slamming into the ground, but I'm up again before the pain registers.

Almost there.

I crest the dune, my eyes fixed on the distant ridge beyond which I pray the clan caves lie. Just a little further. Just a little—

Movement on the ridge catches my eye. A figure, tall and golden-skinned like Tharn and Rok, but with distinct differences. This alien's skin is a richer bronze-amber color. His hair a dark slash against the yellow sky.

And he is alone. Utterly alone. There is no sign of a hunting party, no sense that he belongs here. He is just... an unknown male, appearing on the ridge as if from nowhere, and that uncertainty alone sends a skitter of fear down my spine.

Another hunter. Not from Tharn's clan?

For a moment, I falter. The rival clan member from yesterday flashes through my mind. His threat. What if this is one of his people?

But there's no time for fear. No time for caution. Tharn is buried alive, and Justine is bleeding out in the sand.

I wave my arms frantically, screaming at the top of my lungs. "HELP! HEEEELP!"

The figure on the ridge goes still, gaze snapping in my direction. Fear skitters down my spine again when, one moment he's frozen still and the next he's running toward me with inhuman speed, covering ground so quickly it seems like he's flying over the sand and rocks.

As he gets closer, I can see more details. The intricate shield-like patterns on his skin that are so like Tharn's patterns but different. The way his crimson eyes seem to glow as they fasten on me. Something about the way he moves tells me he's even more dangerous than he seems.

My hands tremble as I raise them halfway, a pathetic attempt at a truce. "P-please, I mean no harm. I only need your help."

He slows as I speak again, his posture cautious. But unlike when I first met Tharn, this hunter doesn't wince when I speak, which strikes me as odd. Unless...unless he's been around humans! Hope flares in my chest.

"Please," I gasp, pointing back the way I came. "A sand creature attacked us. Tharn is buried. And my sister is hurt."

He stares at me, his crimson eyes unblinking, and I realize with a sinking heart that he can't understand me any more than Tharn could at first. We have no mindspace connection, no translator calibrated to his language.

But I don't need words. Action will speak for itself.

I grab his wrist, ignoring the way he jolts at the contact, and tug urgently in the direction I came from. "*Please*," I say again, pouring every ounce of desperation into my voice. "You *have* to follow me."

For a terrifying moment, I think he's going to refuse. But then he tilts his head in a way that seems like affirmation, a sharp, decisive movement, and gestures for me to lead the way.

Relief floods me so completely my legs nearly buckle. But the sand is already flying beneath my boots as I spin and sprint back toward the others, the bronze hunter shadowing my every step.

The dune fights us. Every stride feels like wading through water. Twice I nearly fall, catching myself on hands already raw from digging. Beside me, the hunter clicks something—whether encouragement or impatience, I can't tell.

The world tilts as we finally crest the rise. Below, Rok's massive form is half-buried in the shifting sand, still clawing desperately at the ground. Justine kneels nearby, her injured leg stretched out as she digs with bare hands.

"HURRY!" I scream, but my voice is lost in the expanse.

The hunter takes in the scene with one swift glance, and something like recognition flashes in his crimson eyes. Without hesitation, he leaves me behind as he sprints toward Rok.

Rok doesn't even look up as he arrives, and I realize they're probably communicating in the mindspace. The newcomer drops to his knees, then they're both digging furiously, their powerful arms throwing sand aside with renewed purpose.

I stagger down the dune, my legs shaking with exhaustion, and drop to my knees beside Justine. Her face is grey with pain, her makeshift poultice soaked through with blood.

"You made it," she whispers, her voice weak. "And apparently...you found..." She glances at the male, her gaze zoning out in that way that tells me they're communicating. "Sarven."

I swallow hard. "Friend?"

Justine nods, deep breaths coming from her chest. "Friend."

The sand shifts violently beneath us, another of those vibrating hisses reaching us through the ground. Both aliens dig faster, their movements becoming frantic.

Suddenly, the bronze hunter lunges forward, plunging his entire upper body into the sand. His legs brace against the ground as he strains, pulling at something beneath the surface.

Rok grabs the hunter around the waist, adding his strength to the effort. For a moment, nothing happens. Then, with a spray of sand and another ear-rending hiss, they heave backward.

And Tharn's head and shoulders break the surface.

"THARN!" I'm scrambling forward before I know I'm moving, my heart in my throat.

He looks terrible—covered in sand, his golden skin dulled to a sickly brown, his eyes closed. For one horrifying moment, I think we're too late.

Then he coughs, a violent spasm that sends sand spraying from his mouth. His eyes fly open, wild and disoriented, his claws flexing weakly as Rok and the bronze hunter drag him fully from the sand.

He's alive. Somehow, impossibly, he's alive.

I fall to my knees beside him, my hands shaking as they hover over his sand-caked skin. I can't seem to touch him, as if he might be a mirage that will vanish. "You're okay," I whisper, but the words are more of a question than a statement. "You're okay. You're okay."

His eyes focus slowly, finding mine with visible effort. "Jah-kee," he rasps. "Saaafe?"

A sob escapes me, half-laugh, half-cry. "Am I safe? Y-you're asking if I'm safe?" Tears stream down my face, feeling wet and sticky.

At the sight, Tharn tries to sit up, but his body seems to rebel, a violent tremor running through his massive frame.

"I'm fine." I sob-laugh. "You saved me."

Tharn collapses backward, eyes on me and only me. One arm trembles as it reaches toward me, and I grab his big fist, curling my fingers into his as I press his hand against my chest.

"Sa—fe," he grunts again.

Safe. I'm safe. Because of him.

Before I can say anything more, movement catches my eye. Figures appear on the distant dune, their silhouettes sharp against the harsh sunlight. A half dozen hunters, their golden skin gleaming like molten metal, sprint down the dune toward us with effortless speed.

They move as one, their steps synchronized, their focus unyielding. Even from this distance, I can feel the weight of their presence. A primal energy that seems to hum through the air as they approach.

Sarven straightens beside Rok, his crimson eyes flickering as silent communication passes between the hunters. But my attention snags on Rok.

His massive hands hover over Jus-teen's injured leg, close enough to feel the heat radiating from her wound but not touching. It's as if he fears breaking her further. His nostrils flare, his chest rising with a sharp inhale, but the sound that escapes him is pained. A low rumble that makes the hairs on my arms rise.

The glow beneath his skin dims and brightens, dims and brightens, pulsing erratically like a struggling flame.

Jus-teen reaches up before he can move. She cups his jaw, her thumb brushing the ridge below his eye—once, twice—a gesture so tender it makes my throat tighten. The moment feels too intimate to watch, but I can't look away.

Rok goes utterly still. The tension in his massive frame holds, his claws flexing against the sand. Then, with aching slowness, he leans forward and presses his forehead to hers.

His claws dig into the sand, carving furrows as he fights to steady his breathing.

No words. None needed.

When they part, Jus-teen's tears glisten on her cheeks—and on his.

The hunters reach the edge where we rest, their movements slowing as their attention shifts. Their eyes sweep over the scene, taking in everything: Jus-teen in Rok's arms, Sarven, Tharn, me.

But it's not Rok or Tharn that seems to hold their focus.

It's us.

Me. Jus-teen.

The newcomers' gazes linger on us longer than feels comfortable, their stares sharp and assessing. My skin prickles, a strange heat rushing to my cheeks under their scrutiny. There's no hostility, but there's something else. Curiosity? Oh God... anticipation? I can't tell, and that only makes it worse.

One of them tilts his head slightly, his nostrils flaring. Another's claws twitch at his sides.

And that's when I notice something strange.

Rok and Tharn are the only ones glowing.

The golden light beneath their skin is unmistakable, pulsing in time with their breathing.

Two of the larger males move toward Tharn. He snarls, a sound that sends a shiver down my spine, his claws slashing the air in warning.

Even now, blood streaking his golden skin, he rises...and reaches for me. His breath comes in ragged heaves, his muscles trembling with exhaustion, but his arms lock around me before anyone else can touch me.

"*Tharn*—" My voice cracks.

He doesn't listen. Just lifts me against his chest with a pained growl, his grip iron-tight.

I don't fight him. *Can't.* Not when his wounds weep fresh

blood with every step. Not when his heartbeat thunders against my ear, too fast, too wrong.

I see another hunter approach us. Tharn doesn't acknowledge him. Just adjusts his hold on me and limps forward.

Behind us, the hunters haul the serpent's corpse from the dunes. Sunlight glints off its segmented plates, casting jagged reflections across the sand. The sight should be triumphant. But all I can hear is the way Tharn's breath whistles through his teeth. The way his muscles tremble with each step, as if he's dragging the weight of the desert itself.

And me?

I press my face into his neck and let the tears come.

CHAPTER 26

THESE ARE MY PEOPLE. THAT IS MY ALIEN

JACQUI

The Drakav settlement comes into view as we crest the final ridge, and I can't decide if it's the most beautiful thing I've ever seen, or the most intimidating.

It's not at all what I expected. Instead of primitive huts or basic shelters, massive stone formations rise against the sky like ancient cathedrals, forming a natural fortress of towering cliffs and hidden crevices. Openings are scattered across the cliff face, some natural, others obviously carved. It's both terrifying and beautiful, and way too epic for a girl who just wants a decent meal and a nap.

I'd probably find it even more impressive if I weren't so focused on the fact that Tharn is barely holding it together.

Each step he takes feels heavier, his chest rising and falling like he's running on fumes. Still, his grip on me doesn't loosen, his arms locked around me like I'm the only thing keeping him upright.

I want to tell him to put me down, to let me walk, but I

know better now. Knew better even before today. His protective instinct is beyond reason or argument, especially when he's injured and vulnerable.

So instead, I press my hand gently against his chest, right above his heart, offering what comfort I can without words. He glances down at me, something softening in his amber eyes despite the pain I know grips him.

I glance over my shoulder at Rok and Justine, who are walking several paces behind us. Justine's leg is bloody but not bleeding, but Rok's expression is grim as he cradles her in his arms.

We're all running on empty.

Sarven leads our procession, his crimson eyes constantly scanning the horizon for threats, while the remaining hunters drag the serpent's massive corpse behind us, its segmented body leaving a deep furrow in the sand.

As we approach the base of the clan caves, I notice movement above us. Figures—tall, gold, and distinctly Drakav—peer down from the ridges, their eyes tracking us like hawks. The weight of their stares makes my skin prickle, but I keep my head high.

I mean, sure, I'm covered in dust, sweat, and probably blood, but I'm not about to let a bunch of glowing alien supermodels intimidate me.

Not much, anyway.

The entrance to the main cave is huge, and I expect it to be dark and creepy inside. Instead, it's surprisingly bright, the light from outside filtering in through natural cracks in the stone.

And it's packed.

My breath hitches as my eyes land on the group of women gathered along one side of the cavern. Human women.

They're sitting on carved stone steps, their faces animated

as they talk and laugh. A spread of food and other offerings—roasted meat, waterskins, and what looks like a pile of shiny rocks—sits below them, clearly laid out by the Drakav.

"Oh my god," I whisper, my hand flying to my mouth. "Justine! They're alive! The others are alive!"

I count quickly—one, two, three... at least a dozen women visible from here, their forms so achingly familiar. Relief crashes through me, bringing tears to my eyes. They made it. They survived.

Mikaela spots us first.

Her braids swing as her head jerks up, a waterskin slipping from her fingers. For one frozen second, she just stares, her lips forming a silent oh my God.

Then—

"JACQUI!"

The scream rips through the cavern. Every head whips toward us.

Chaos erupts.

Feet pound stone. A chorus of shrieks and sobs crashes over me as they surge forward—

"She's alive!"

"AND JUSTINE!"

"—can't believe it—" "—thought you were—" "—look at you both!"

Tharn's arms tighten around me, his growl vibrating through my back as the first hands reach for me.

Mikaela gets there first. Her fingers clutch my face, her dark eyes scanning me frantically. "*You absolute bastard*," she chokes, tears streaking her cheeks.

Her fist thumps my shoulder—once, twice—before she yanks me into a hug so tight it hurts. "*Never do that again*," she hisses in my ear.

I can't speak. Can only grip her back, my fingers twisting in her shirt as the others swarm us.

Erika's arms wrap around us both, her happy squeal muffled against my neck. Tina hovers at the edge, wiping her glasses furiously as if she can't trust her eyes. Pam launches herself at Justine, nearly toppling Rok in the process.

Their voices overlap, a cacophony of questions and scoldings:

"Where have you been?"

"We searched—"

"Wait—is Hannah with you?" Alex, the nurse, asks, her voice cutting through the noise with sharp concern as she scans our small party.

A cold knot forms in my stomach. I shake my head, looking from Alex's worried face to Mikaela's grim one. "Hannah? No. Why would she be with me? I was alone."

Alex's face falls. "Damn it."

"She took off a few days after you did," Mikaela explains, her voice flat and heavy with a grief I haven't heard from her before. "She went in a different direction. Said there had to be something better out there than just... waiting to die. We tried to stop her."

Guilt hits me. HARD. My reckless departure didn't just put me in danger; it inspired another, more desperate one.

"We didn't let her go alone," Justine says, a wince in her voice. She's still in Rok's arms, but her expression is steady. "They sent one of the hunters to track her. His name is Sorn. He's one of their best."

A flicker of hope sparks in my chest. "So you think he found her? That they're okay?"

The hope dies when I see the look on Justine's face. "Neither of them have returned."

The silence that follows is heavy, a stark reminder of the dangers that still lurk beyond these caves. The joy of our reunion is suddenly, painfully, incomplete.

"Your sister nearly killed us—" one of the other women starts, breaking the tense quiet.

Justine snorts. "Lies. I was very patient."

More chatter ensures. Through it all, Tharn doesn't let go.

Not when Mikaela glares up at him, sizing up the alien who carried me home.

Not when Erika accidentally elbows him while reaching for me.

Not even when Pam—bless her—tries to peel me from his arms like he's a particularly stubborn backpack.

"He's not letting go, is he?" Mikaela mutters, eyeing Tharn's claws where they cradle my thighs.

I shake my head, my cheek brushing Tharn's chest.

"He's the one who found you?"

I nod, my hand instinctively moving to rest on Tharn's arm. "This is Tharn. He saved my life. More than once."

Mikaela's gaze sharpens, assessing the massive alien with undisguised skepticism. "You okay?" she whispers. "Because I didn't trust this guy to find and keep you safe. No offense."

I feel a surge of protectiveness that surprises me with its intensity. "He almost died pulling me out of the desert," I almost snap. "And again today, when a sand serpent attacked us. I'm here because of him."

Oh...why...why did I respond like that? That isn't me at all.

But something in my tone registers, because Mikaela's eyebrows rise slightly, her gaze flickering between me and Tharn with new speculation. Her lips press into a thin line, but she nods. "Good. But know that if he didn't bring you back, I'd have kicked his ass. Alien or not."

I don't bother pointing out that she's about half Tharn's

size. Somehow, I think she'd still find a way. Instead, my heart warms. Mikaela cares.

The chaos swirls around us, a blur of familiar faces and happy, crying voices. But my focus narrows on my sister. Rok has set her down gently on a stone bench, and she's looking at me, really looking at me, a million unspoken questions in her eyes.

I wiggle one hand free from Tharn's unyielding grip. I fumble inside my bra, my fingers closing around the two small, hard shapes I've kept safe.

"Jus," I say, my voice thick. "I think... these belong to you."

I hold out the small butterfly earrings. They glint in the cavern's dim light, two tiny, impossible pieces of home.

The chatter around us fades into a dull roar. Justine's breath hitches. Tears well in her eyes, spilling over to trace paths through the grime on her cheeks. "You found it," she chokes out. "My god, Jacqui, you found the other one."

"I did," I say, my own tears starting to fall freely now.

Her trembling fingers take the earrings from my palm. She closes her hand around them, holding them tight, her gaze still locked with mine.

"Our mother's earrings," she sobs. "They're together again."

I reach out, my hand covering hers. "We're together again," I correct softly.

A watery, brilliant smile breaks through her tears. "Yeah," she says. "We are."

It's only then, as the knot of fear I've carried for weeks finally unravels, that I notice something else in my sister's eyes. A new strength. A deep, settled peace I haven't seen in her since before our world fell apart. She's not just a survivor. She's... happy.

Before she can say more, we're engulfed by more women,

their voices a blur of questions and exclamations. Some approach, gripping me in their arms. I hug them back, wordless, tears gathering in my eyes.

They all look different from what I remember. Thinner, tanner, their clothes showing signs of hard wear and creative repairs. But they're alive, and the sight of them fills me with a joy so intense it's almost painful.

We're here. Alive.

Tharn brought me home. His home.

As I look around the massive clan cave, I'm struck by how orderly everything is. Stone platforms line the walls, which I assume are sleeping places. Various implements—tools, weapons, and containers made from unfamiliar materials—hang from pegs driven into the rock. A fire pit burns in the center, the smoke rising through a natural chimney in the ceiling.

The human women have established themselves along one side of the cave, their meager belongings clustered together in what looks like a protective huddle.

Around the edges of the space, Drakav males linger, watching the human commotion with expressions ranging from curiosity to confusion to something that looks uncomfortably like hunger. None of them is glowing like Tharn and Rok, but there's a tension in their postures, an anticipation that makes my skin prickle with awareness.

They remind me of a group of shy teenagers at their first high school dance—hovering near the edges, watching the girls with wide eyes, but too nervous to actually approach. One Drakav steps forward, his chest puffed out and his muscles flexed in an obvious display. He's as tall as Tharn, with a cocky look on his face that somehow translates across species. A low rumble beside me, and I realize Tharn is snarling at the showman.

"That's Haroth," one of the women whispers beside me, her cheeks flushing deeper. "He's always showing off."

Mikaela rolls her eyes, mumbling something about "too much testosterone."

I raise an eyebrow at the woman. "You can understand them?"

She shakes her head quickly. "No, no. Not really. We've just been... observing. Learning patterns."

Tina adjusts her glasses. "Justine was the only one who could actually communicate with them. Before you arrived, I mean."

My gaze shifts back to my sister where Rok is tending to her. She winces as he examines the wound, but her face is composed as the other women cluster around her, peppering her with questions.

"What happened to your leg?"

"How did you find Jacqui?"

"Can you really talk to them with your mind?"

Tharn remains rooted with me in his arms, his massive frame radiating tension. My gaze shifts to find him glaring at the one Tina called Haroth. Sarven is the one to grab Haroth and lead him away, but not before I see how he, too, looks at the other women, his gaze snagging on Mikaela particularly, who scowls.

"Tharn?" His snarl disappears the moment I say his name. Those amber eyes shift to me immediately. I expect him to take me somewhere quieter—somewhere he can finally rest—but he seems to be waiting for something, his gaze shifting to the far side of the cave.

Suddenly, the noise in the cave dims, a hush falling over the human women as they notice the change in the Drakav. Every golden alien has gone still, their attention shifting to the far entrance where a new figure has appeared.

He's enormous, even by Drakav standards, his golden skin etched with patterns. His deep amber eyes burn with intelligence and authority as he scans the cave, his gaze lingering on me and Justine before settling on Tharn.

"That's Kol," Justine whispers toward me. "Their dradam...that means 'clan leader'."

Tharn straightens beside me, his posture shifting subtly despite his injuries. When Kol approaches, Tharn inclines his head in a gesture that's clearly respectful.

The two exchange what I assume is a silent conversation, their expressions shifting minutely as they communicate in the mindspace. After a moment, Kol turns to address the entire cave, his gaze sweeping over the assembled humans and Drakav.

Justine's voice rises, translating for the benefit of us human women. "Kol welcomes us all and says he's pleased with Tharn's success in bringing Jacqui safely to the clan caves." She pauses, listening to something none of us can hear. "He's declaring a feast tonight to celebrate our arrival and... um, the victory over the dust serpent. Apparently, its meat is considered a delicacy."

Sand serpent meat. Delightful. The thing that almost killed Tharn is now going to be dinner. I guess there's a certain poetic justice to that, but the thought of eating the creature that nearly dragged him to his death makes my stomach turn.

No, thank you. I'd rather eat sand.

After a few more exchanges that Justine doesn't bother to translate, Kol steps back, gesturing for Tharn to proceed. I feel Tharn's chest expand with a deep breath before he finally turns toward one of the smaller passages leading from the main cave.

"Where are we going?" I ask quietly as he carries me away from the reunion.

He makes a low sound in his throat as he continues moving.

The passage is darker than the main cave, but Tharn's flickering glow lights the way. After several turns, the passage widens into a small chamber that Tharn steps into. It's simple, with a large stone platform covered in what looks like furs or hides, a small alcove containing various weapons and tools, and a natural basin filled with clear water.

Tharn gently sets me down on the edge of the stone platform. The tenderness in his touch makes my heart ache, especially with the fact he must be in so much pain.

The moment I'm safely settled, his legs finally give out. He collapses onto the bedding beside me, his massive body making the stone platform seem suddenly small. He doesn't lose consciousness, but his breathing is ragged, his eyes half-closed with exhaustion.

"Tharn," I whisper, my hand hovering over his shoulder. "What can I do? How can I help?"

His eyes open fully, finding mine with visible effort. He doesn't demand, doesn't beg. Just looks at me like I'm the moon, the stars, the world itself.

My chest aches.

I move quickly, finding a soft fur beside the basin and soaking it in the cool water. When I return to his side, I begin gently cleaning the sand and blood from his wounds, starting with the worst injuries on his legs where the serpent's barbs had entered his skin.

The punctures are deep, the edges ragged and still seeping his dark, almost metallic-looking blood. Sand is ground into the wounds, and I work carefully to clean each one, wincing in sympathy when his muscles tense beneath my touch.

"I'm sorry," I murmur, though I know the cleaning is necessary. "I'm trying to be gentle."

His hand finds mine, engulfing it completely. His touch is warm despite his injuries, his fingers curling around mine.

"*Good.*" The word drops like water in my mind, and my eyes widen.

Heat rises to my cheeks at the simple praise, and I duck my head, focusing on his wounds again to hide my reaction. In the alcove near his weapons, I spot a familiar blue and orange plant. Firebloom. I reach for it, crushing the petals between my fingers.

Some of the tension eases from his frame as I apply the poultice, and the fact makes my heart ease a little.

When I've treated the worst of his injuries, I reach for a waterskin hanging nearby, offering it to him. "You should drink," I say, helping him lift his head slightly. "You've lost a lot of blood."

He takes a few sips, a single droplet escaping. I catch it with my finger without thinking, the casual intimacy of the gesture only registering when his eyes lock onto mine.

"Thank you," I say softly, lowering the waterskin. "For saving me. *Again.* You seem to make a habit of that."

His hand rises so slowly, as if I might vanish. Calloused fingers cradle my cheek, his thumb brushing my skin with a reverence that liquefies my bones.

No one has ever touched me like this. Like I'm the last drop of water in the desert.

I don't think. Don't hesitate. Don't second-guess. I just act on the feeling that's been building inside me since he first held me in the desert.

Leaning forward, I press my lips to his.

For a moment, Tharn goes completely still, his body rigid with surprise. Clearly, kissing isn't a thing Drakav do. But before I can pull back, before embarrassment can overtake me, his arms slide around me, and then—

—fire.

A sound rips from his chest, something between a growl and a prayer, as his arms band around me. His kiss is clumsy at first, all sharp teeth and panting breaths, until I nip his lower lip in guidance.

Oh.

The moment he learns, he *conquers.*

His tongue sweeps into my mouth, hot and wicked, stealing my gasp. The glow beneath his skin erupts, painting us in molten gold as his claws skate down my spine—*careful, so careful*—but the hunger in them?

Unhinged.

I'm drowning. Burning. Alive.

I'm kissing an alien. And it feels like coming home.

Just as the thought forms, Tharn stiffens suddenly, breaking the kiss with a sharp intake of breath. His gaze shoots to mine, filled not with desire but with alarm.

"Tharn?" I pull back slightly, confusion and concern replacing the haze of desire. "What's wrong?"

He doesn't answer, but his expression tells me something is *very* wrong. His body goes rigid, his back arching as a sound of pure agony tears from his throat. The glow beneath his skin flares blindingly bright, then pulses erratically like a malfunctioning light.

"Tharn!" I grab his shoulders, panic rising as his body begins to convulse. "What's happening? What's wrong?"

But even as I ask...I know. He's changing.

The golden light beneath his skin surges one final time, so bright I have to shield my eyes, and then it abruptly shifts—no, explodes—into something unnatural. The glow fractures, splintering like shards of lightning under his skin, and then morphs into streaks of black that ripple across him like living ink.

"Tharn?" I whisper, my voice trembling.

He jerks suddenly, his entire body twisting as if something inside him is breaking and remaking itself all at once. His claws rake against the stone floor, carving deep gouges as a guttural snarl tears from his throat.

I stumble back, my heart hammering as I watch his body convulse. His golden skin darkens, the glow fading into an eerie, star-speckled black, shifting like constellations in motion. His eyes snap open, and they're no longer the warm amber-gold I've grown used to. They burn with a violent, molten light, glowing so brightly they seem untamed.

"Tharn!" I cry, reaching out, but he rears back, his movements jerky and unnatural, like he's fighting something unseen. His head snaps toward me, his lips curling back to reveal sharp teeth, a sound somewhere between a growl and a roar erupting from deep in his chest.

The air around him feels charged, heavy, like a storm is building inside the room. His claws curl and uncurl, his body writhing in agony as he snarls, his gaze flickering between me and something I can't see.

"Help!" I scream, my voice cracking. "Somebody help!"

He lunges forward suddenly, but not at me—at the wall, his claws tearing into the stone like it's nothing. His entire body is trembling, his muscles straining as if they're trying to contain something too big for him to handle.

"Tharn, stop!" I shout, but it's like he can't hear me.

He turns again, his glowing eyes locking onto me, and for one terrifying moment, I think he's going to attack. But then his expression changes—just for a second. His snarl falters, replaced by something raw and desperate.

"*Jah-kee,*" he rasps, his voice distorted and broken, like it's being pulled from the depths of his soul.

His body twists again, a strangled sound escaping him as

he staggers back, his hand clawing at his chest. The black patterns on his skin pulse violently, the pinpricks of light shifting and swirling like a living galaxy.

Then he collapses to his knees, his head thrown back as a roar of pain tears from his throat.

CHAPTER 27

MY GLOW-UP GOT A LITTLE TOO LITERAL

THARN

Fire.

My blood is liquid fire racing through veins too small to contain it. My bones crack and reform with each heartbeat. My skin—my skin is wrong. The familiar gold that has marked me since birth is gone, replaced by something darker, colder, yet somehow... more.

I can't see Jah-kee anymore, though I hear her screaming my name. My vision has fractured, the world splitting into shards of light and shadow.

"Tharn!"

Jah-kee's voice pierces the haze of pain, but I can't answer. Can't speak. Can barely think past the agony tearing through me.

Her soft lips against mine. She shared water from her lips. That was the trigger. That small connection unlocked something beyond my control.

This is wrong. Rok warned me it would be intense, but this

—this is like dying and being reborn at once. The stone floor cracks beneath my claws as they extend involuntarily, sharper than they've ever been.

I can feel the change spreading through me like a fast-acting venom, a dark fire racing through my blood, remaking me from the inside out.

"Help! Somebody help!"

No. No one can help. No one should come. I am dangerous like this. Uncontrolled.

Must get away. Must protect Jah-kee... from me.

I lurch to my feet, staggering toward the chamber entrance. Jah-kee steps toward me, her hand outstretched, her water-blue eyes wide with fear. Fear of me. The realization cuts deeper than any physical pain.

"Jah-kee," I try to say, but it comes out as a guttural snarl. "*Stay... back.*"

She doesn't understand. How could she? We have no mind-space connection, no way to communicate the danger.

But I need her to understand. Need her to run, to hide, to get away from me until this passes. Because if she stays—

My claws gouge the stone floor as another wave of trans-formation crashes through me. My senses sharpen impossibly. Suddenly, I can hear her heartbeat, smell the salt of her tears, feel the heat radiating from her skin.

And something else. Something new.

Her thoughts.

Not foggy like before, but impressions, clear in the mind-space. Emotions, fears swirling like mist.

...terrified he's dying...

...my fault. The kiss was my fault...

...please don't leave me...

The intensity of her concern slams into me, doubling me

over. She's afraid *for* me, not *of* me. The distinction matters, though I can't focus on why.

Another spasm rocks through me, my back arching as my muscles seize. Something is pushing against the flat pouch at my groin, demanding release, the pressure building to unbearable levels. I know what this is. Rok described this, but experiencing it—dust and stars, there are no thoughts for this.

I need to get away. Now. Before the final stage hits, before I lose what little control I have left.

With a roar that shakes dust from the ceiling, I lunge toward the tunnel entrance. Jah-kee cries out, reaching for me, but I evade her grasp. My limbs are uncoordinated, my movements jerky, but fueled by desperation.

"Tharn, stop!" she cries, her voice raw and cracking with the force of the sound. "Please, let me help you!"

I can't stop. Can't explain. Can only run.

The tunnels blur past me as I crash through the passages, my body careening off the walls, leaving streaks of blood in my wake. I'm barely aware of the direction. I just need to go.

Away from her. Away from everyone. I am dangerous. Unstable. A beast breaking free of its cage.

The deeper tunnels are cooler, darker, less traveled. Perfect. My legs finally give out, sending me sprawling onto the hard stone floor of a small chamber. I curl into myself, trembling as the next wave hits.

JACQUI

"Tharn! Answer me!" My voice bounces off the stone walls, echoing back to me with no response.

I've been following the trail of blood smears and gouges in the stone. What the hell is happening to him?

The kiss—it had to be the kiss that triggered this. One moment he was looking at me like I hung the moon; the next he was convulsing, his skin turning black and starry like the night sky.

And then he ran. Bolted like a wounded animal seeking somewhere dark to hide.

I turn another corner, the shadows getting darker as I venture deeper into the mountain. It's getting harder to see, and the tunnels are branching in multiple directions. I'm going to get lost if I'm not careful.

"Tharn, please," I call again. "I just want to help!"

"Jacqui!"

I whirl around at the sound of my name, relief flooding me when I see Justine hobbling toward me, supported by Rok. Her injured leg is hastily bandaged, but she's clearly in pain.

"What are you doing down here?" I ask, rushing to help steady her. "Your leg—"

"Forget my leg," she cuts me off. "It's happened, hasn't it? Everyone heard the commotion."

Before I can answer, two more figures emerge from the shadows behind them. One is Sarven, his crimson eyes gleaming in the dim light. The other is another Drakav.

My worry bubbles to the surface. "He was in agony, Justine. And his skin—it turned black, with these pinpricks of light like stars."

Justine doesn't look surprised. She nods, turning to Rok, who straightens. "It happened to Rok too," she says softly. "Back then, I had no clue what was going on." Her eyes find mine, understanding filling them. "He needs you, Jaqs..." She pauses. "If you'll help him."

She thinks I'll reject Tharn. The realization hits me

suddenly—that Justine went through this with Rok, alone and clueless, and somehow they made it through. She's worried I might not do the same.

I turn back to the tunnel. "We have to find him."

Sarven steps forward, nostrils flaring as he scents the air. He points confidently down the leftmost passage, then starts walking, clearly expecting us to follow.

The tunnel narrows as we descend deeper into the mountain. The air grows cooler, damper. Sarven moves with silent grace despite his size, while the other Drakav follows closely behind him. Rok supports Justine, who's limping badly but refuses to turn back.

Then I hear it—a low, pained growl that raises the hair on my arms.

"Tharn," I whisper, pushing past Sarven to run ahead.

The tunnel opens into a small chamber, and there, curled against the far wall, is Tharn. Or what used to be Tharn.

His golden skin is still entirely black.

But what stops me in my tracks is the change to his body. He's larger somehow, his muscles more defined, his claws longer and sharper. And between his legs, where there was once just a smooth, flat pouch, there's now... well, something decidedly not flat.

"Oh," I breathe, heat rushing to my face.

Tharn snarls, backing further against the wall, his gaze wild and unfocused. He doesn't seem to recognize any of us. His body shudders with another wave of pain.

Behind me, I hear Sarven move. A subtle shift of weight, the sound of muscle and bone settling into a coiled, ready stance.

I take a step forward, but Sarven moves quickly, blocking my path with his massive arm. His crimson eyes flick between me and Tharn, clearly concerned I'm about to get myself killed.

"Let me pass," I say, meeting his gaze directly.

He doesn't budge, just gives me a firm stare.

"Sarven," Justine calls out. "It's okay. She needs to try."

"Be careful," she adds to me, her voice tight with worry.

Sarven hesitates, his expression conflicted. I fix him with my best don't-mess-with-me glare, and after a moment, he reluctantly steps aside.

Tharn's growl deepens as I approach, his teeth bared in warning. I freeze, then force myself to breathe slowly, to project calm I don't feel.

"Hey," I say softly, taking another careful step. "Hey, Tharn. It's me. It's Jacqui."

His growl falters slightly, his head tilting as if the sound of my voice penetrates the haze of pain and instinct.

"That's it," I whisper, inching closer. "You know me. You carried me through the desert, remember?" My voice shakes only slightly. "You fought shadow creatures and sand serpents and every nightmare this planet could throw at us."

Another step.

Now I'm close enough to see it—really see it.

The stars beneath his skin aren't just glowing.

They're moving.

Tiny pinpricks of light swirl like distant galaxies, forming and reforming constellations across his arms, his chest. Patterns that feel familiar, though I've never seen them before in my life.

"You're okay," I continue, my voice low and steady. "Look at me. That's all you have to do. Just stay with me. Look at me."

His growls stop entirely, his breathing still harsh but less frantic. His pupils are blown. They track my every movement as I kneel in front of him.

"It's me," I whisper, my voice shaking despite my best

efforts. "Tharn, it's me. You're okay. Just breathe, okay? Just breathe."

Slowly, so slowly, I extend my hand, palm up. For a long moment, Tharn just stares at it, his chest heaving with each labored breath.

Then, with a movement so careful it breaks my heart, his much larger hand covers mine.

The contact is electric. Heat surges between us, and Tharn gasps, his back arching as if struck by lightning. His grip on my hand tightens painfully, but I don't pull away, don't break the connection.

"It's okay," I whisper, ignoring the pinch of his claws against my skin. "I'm here."

Recognition floods his features, followed by something that looks almost like relief.

The starry patterns beneath his skin pulse faster. Terrifying. Beautiful. I can't look away.

"Jacqui," Justine calls softly from behind me. "I think he's stabilizing. Keep going."

I have no idea what "keep going" means, but I'm not about to let go of his hand. Not when he's looking at me like I'm his only lifeline in a storm.

Slowly, carefully, I move closer, my free hand reaching up to cup his face. The moment my palm touches his cheek, he leans into it with a sound that's half-growl, half-sigh.

"There you are," I murmur, a small smile tugging at my lips despite everything. "Coming back to me?"

He doesn't answer, but the wild look in his eyes dims further, replaced by the Tharn I know. *My* Tharn.

Then, without warning, his entire body goes rigid. The stars beneath his skin freeze in place, then flare brightly.

I'm dimly aware of Sarven and the other Drakav stepping forward as if to shield me, of Justine gasping. But all I can focus on is Tharn's face—his jaw clenched in pain, his eyes squeezed shut as if bracing against some final, terrible impact.

And then, just as suddenly, it's over.

The light fades, the stars settling, slowly being replaced by his usual golden bronze, but without the glow that's been under his skin from the first moment we met. For a heartbeat, he stares at me, eyes wide with wonder and exhaustion.

Then he collapses, his massive frame crumpling forward. I catch him as best I can, though his weight nearly crushes me. It takes Sarven and the other Drakav rushing forward to keep us both from hitting the stone floor.

"Tharn?" I pat his cheek, panic rising again. "Tharn, can you hear me?"

His chest rises and falls in a steady rhythm, but his eyes remain closed. Unconscious, but alive.

"It's okay," Justine says, hobbling closer with Rok's support. "He's just exhausted. The transformation takes everything they have."

I look up at her, a thousand questions on my lips, but only one thing makes it out. "He's changed."

She shares a look with Rok, then turns back to me with a small, knowing smile. "The same thing that happened to Rok. He's... evolved. Adapted. For you."

I glance down at Tharn's unconscious form, at the new body he now inhabits. The more defined muscles. The... addition between his thighs that I'm trying very hard not to stare at.

"For me," I echo, the weight of those two simple words hitting me like a meteor. "This is because of me."

Sarven makes a series of gestures to the other Drakav.

"They need to get him back to his alcove," Justine explains. "He'll be more comfortable there, and safer."

I nod, but my fingers tighten around Tharn's shoulders.

Then I notice it—the way the hunters stare at his lower half, their expressions a mix of awe and alarm.

Oh.

His transformation has left him... exposed.

Without hesitation, I yank off my thin blouse, leaving only my bra on. The fabric tears easily in my hands as I fashion a crude loincloth, my fingers brushing the strange new ridges along his hips as I secure it.

"That was...necessary," Justine says.

"*Very.*" But I can't ignore the little delightful shiver that runs down my belly.

When I finally lean back, my hands linger for one last second against Tharn's chest. I don't want to let go of him, but I know it's for the best.

"I'm coming too," I say, my tone making it clear this isn't a request.

Justine just nods, as if she expected nothing less.

It takes both Sarven and the other Drakav to lift Tharn's unconscious form. He's deadweight, his limbs hanging limply as they carry him through the tunnels. I follow closely, one hand never leaving contact with his skin—his arm, his shoulder, whatever I can reach.

I'm not even sure why I feel compelled to maintain the connection. I just know that when I think about breaking it, letting him go completely, my chest tightens with something like panic.

We return to Tharn's alcove, the same place where this all started. Was it only minutes ago? It feels like hours.

The Drakav lay Tharn on his fur-covered platform, arranging his limbs before stepping back. Sarven gives me a long, assessing look, then inclines his head slightly—respect, I think, or maybe approval—before turning to leave.

CHAPTER 28

MY MATE'S IN A COMA AND ALL I GET IS THIS LOUSY LANGUAGE LESSON (VRAL = KNIFE. COOL. COOLCOOLCOOL.)

JACQUI

It's been three days since Tharn collapsed.

Three days of pacing the tunnels, staring at the darkened alcove where he lies unconscious, and pretending I'm not losing my mind with worry.

Three days of trying to adjust to life in the clan caves. A life so strange and different that it should feel like stepping into another world. And it *does*, but I can't enjoy it. My thoughts are always elsewhere, circling back to him.

Every time I pass his alcove or catch a glimpse of Rok or the other hunters, I want to ask if there's any change. But I don't. The answer is always the same. No.

The clan caves are... fascinating, I'll give them that. There are even more chambers than I first realized, with ceilings so high they disappear into the shadows, the walls lined with alcoves and tunnels leading to who-knows-where. The Drakav move through the space with silent grace, their eyes tracking everything, their presence so alien yet oddly comforting.

The human women's section of the cave is now filled with furs and strange cushions made from some kind of woven plant fiber. It's almost cozy. Almost.

The Drakav have been nothing but accommodating, though their fascination with us can sometimes feel... intense. They watch us constantly, studying our movements, our speech, even the way we eat. It's like we're some new, exotic species they're trying to understand.

Every day, Justine gathers the women and a handful of Drakav for what she calls "language classes." It's slow going. The translators are doing their best, but the process is painstaking.

"Okay," Justine says, holding up a small, carved tool. "This is... uh..." She glances at Rok, who projects the word into her mind. "'Vral.' It's a knife. Vral."

"Vral," Pam repeats, her voice lilting with exaggerated enthusiasm.

Rok nods, his expression stoic as always.

Mikaela snorts from the back of the group. "Great. Now I know how to say 'knife.' That's useful when I'm trying to ask where the bathroom is."

"You're not wrong," I mutter, earning a laugh from a few of the women.

The lessons are slow, frustrating, and occasionally hilarious. Some of the women, like Pam and Tina, throw themselves into it with gusto, while others, like Mikaela, are more skeptical.

"It's like magic," Erika says one afternoon, shaking her head as she tries to wrap her mind around the concept of the mindspace. "You're telling me they can just... *project thoughts* into our brains? How is that even possible?"

"It's not magic," Justine replies patiently, though I can see the strain in her expression. "It's just... different. They evolved this way."

"Uh-huh," Mikaela mutters. "Magic."

The caves have their perks. One of them is the bathing area —a natural pool fed by an underground spring. The water is cool and clear, the surface reflecting the bioluminescent fungi that grow along the walls. It's the first real bath I've had in... I don't even know how long.

I sink into the pool with a sigh, the tension in my muscles easing as the water laps at my skin. A few other women are doing the same, scattered around the pool. Any sense of modesty we might have had back on Earth had been scrubbed away by sand and desperation weeks ago. Beside me, Tina is scrubbing her hair with something that looks like a flattened scale.

"These things are amazing," she says, holding up the scale. "They get all foamy when you rub them with water."

"Smell good too," Pam adds, sniffing her armpit.

I grab one of the scales and start working it through my hair. Sure enough, it lathers into a rich foam, leaving my hair feeling cleaner than it's been in weeks.

For a moment, I close my eyes, letting myself enjoy the sensation. The sound of water splashing, the faint hum of the caves—it's almost peaceful.

Almost.

Because no matter how hard I try to relax, my mind keeps drifting back to Tharn.

And my body? Oh, it's not drifting. It's marching.

There's this... persistent warmth between my thighs, like a second heartbeat. At first, I thought it was just stress. Then dehydration. Then I realized—with no small amount of horror —that my traitorous anatomy has apparently decided to sync up with whatever cosmic nonsense our bond is doing while Tharn's unconscious.

I desperately need a distraction.

Fortunately, the Drakav excel at those. They've got systems for everything, including the less glamorous aspects of life.

"Okay," Justine says, leading a small group of us to one of the side tunnels. "This is... uh... the bathroom."

The "bathroom" is a small, enclosed space filled with what looks like gourd-like plants. Justine explains that for, uh, number one, you basically pee into the plant, which absorbs it.

"For number two," she continues, gesturing to a primitive toilet dug into the ground, "there's this." She picks up a handful of what looks like broad, velvety leaves, their surfaces covered in a soft, downy fuzz. "And you use these to, uh, clean up."

"They smell nice," Pam says, sniffing the leaves.

"No toilet paper?" Alex deadpans.

"Just some sand in your hand, baby," Mikaela quips, earning a chorus of groans.

"Mikaela," Tina mutters. Mikaela grins and shrugs.

"It's not that bad," I say, though I'm not entirely convinced myself.

Still, it's better than nothing. And the Drakav seem genuinely proud of their system, so who am I to judge?

This is our life now. Life in the caves is busy, strange, and surprisingly comfortable. The Drakav are endlessly curious about us, and we're slowly learning to adapt to their way of life.

But I can't focus on any of it.

Not when Tharn is still unconscious.

Every time I go to his alcove, I have the unrelenting urge to stay there. So I limit myself to short visits, or not going to the alcove at all. But whenever I look that way, my gaze lingers. I keep expecting to see him emerge, striding into the main chamber with that quiet confidence that's so uniquely him.

But he doesn't.

I try to distract myself. Help Justine with the language lessons. Take long baths in the pool. Chat with the other women about anything and everything.

But my thoughts always circle back to him.

What if he doesn't wake up? What if the transformation took too much out of him? What if—

"Jacqui!"

Pam's voice snaps me out of my spiral. I blink, realizing I've been standing in the middle of the main chamber, staring at nothing.

"What?" I ask, shaking my head.

"You've been standing there for, like, five minutes," she says, her brows furrowed. "Are you okay?"

"Yeah," I lie, forcing a smile. "Just tired."

Pam doesn't look convinced, but she lets it go.

I glance toward the tunnel again, my chest tightening.

———

I'M IN THE MIDDLE OF ONE OF JUSTINE'S LESSONS WHEN IT HAPPENS.

A gasp echoes through the chamber, followed by a flurry of whispers.

I turn, my heart leaping into my throat.

Tharn is standing at the tunnel entrance, his gaze sweeping the room until it locks onto me.

His eyes burn with intensity, his expression unreadable.

But it's the way he moves that sends my heart racing.

He strides toward me with single-minded purpose, his gaze never wavering.

The room falls silent, all eyes on him.

"Tharn," I whisper.

He doesn't speak. Just stops in front of me, his eyes searching mine.

For a moment, the world narrows to just the two of us.

Tharn moves closer, his massive frame lowering until he's crouched in front of me.

One large hand rises, his palm cupping my face with a gentleness that makes my breath hitch. His touch is warm, grounding, and so achingly familiar that I feel the tension in my chest begin to unravel.

Around us, the women gasp, their murmurs barely audible over the pounding of my heart. But I don't look away from him. I can't.

His eyes burn into mine, their amber-gold brighter than ever, and then his lips part.

"Mine," he growls in English, the word so clear, so final, it leaves no room for doubt.

The word hits me like a lightning strike.

Before I can even process it, he bends forward and captures my lips in a kiss that steals the air from my lungs.

It's not tentative or soft. It's consuming. Heat and desperation and relief all rolled into one. His claws graze the edge of my jaw before they close around my throat.

I'm vaguely aware of the stunned silence around us, of the Drakav shifting, their gazes darting between us and the other women. But none of it matters.

All I can feel is Tharn.

When he finally pulls back, his forehead pressing lightly against mine, I'm left breathless, my hands clutching at his arms for stability.

"*Mine, Jacqui. For this sol and the next.*" I hear his thoughts as clear as day.

"Tharn," I manage, my voice trembling.

But he doesn't give me a chance to say more. In one swift motion, he scoops me into his arms, cradling me against his chest as if I weigh nothing.

Tharn strides toward the tunnel leading to his alcove, his steps sure and steady. He doesn't look at anyone but me.

And in the stunned, watching faces of my friends and his entire clan, I realize what he's just done.

He didn't just kiss me.

He claimed me.

CHAPTER 29
ALIEN ANATOMY 101: EXTRA CREDIT

JACQUI

I barely register the journey to Tharn's alcove.

His arms are warm and strong around me, his chest a solid wall of muscle against my side. Each step he takes sends a faint jolt through me, and I'm acutely aware of the steady rise and fall of his breathing, the heat of his body, the possessive way his claws curl just enough to hold me securely but not hurt me.

The world feels distant, muffled. All I can hear is my own heartbeat pounding in my ears and the echo of his voice in my mind.

Mine.

It wasn't just the word itself—it was the way he said it. Like a vow. Like a promise.

And now here we are. Alone.

He steps into the alcove, the dim light casting shadows across his sharp features.

He lowers me gently onto the fur-covered platform, his hands lingering on my waist for a moment before pulling back.

I sit up, my pulse racing as he steps back, those intense eyes scanning me like he's committing every inch of me to memory.

"Tharn," I whisper, but it comes out shaky.

He doesn't answer. He doesn't need to.

The intensity in his gaze says everything.

He's not just looking at me. He's devouring me, his gaze sliding over my body like he's stripping me bare with his eyes alone.

It should feel intimidating. Overwhelming.

Instead, it's thrilling.

Because for the first time in days, I don't feel lost or unsure. I feel wanted. *Needed.*

And then he moves.

Tharn crouches in front of me, his massive frame making the small alcove feel impossibly intimate. Slowly, so slowly, he reaches out, his clawed hands skimming over the fabric of my top—which is really just a bandeau cut from my skirt—before curling around the hem.

There's no hesitation in his movements, no uncertainty. He pulls the top over my head in one swift motion, leaving me in just my bra.

His breath hitches, his eyes locked on me like I'm the only thing in the universe.

"Tharn," I murmur again, watching as he leans in, his nose brushing against the curve of my neck as he inhales deeply, a low growl rumbling from his chest.

The sound sends a shiver down my spine, heat pooling low in my belly.

His hands move to my waist, his claws grazing my skin as he explores my body with a reverence that leaves me breathless. Every touch feels like he's savoring the moment, committing it to memory.

And then his mouth is on me.

His lips brush against my collarbone, soft and warm, before trailing lower. He pauses at the edge of my bra, tilting his head as if confused by the straps. He makes a low, impatient sound, then hooks his claws under the bottom band and just shoves the entire thing upward, pulling it over my head to be discarded along with my top.

The moment I'm bare before him, Tharn freezes. His entire body goes rigid, a statue of bronze muscle and stunned stillness.

"You've never seen breasts before, have you," I whisper, my cheeks flushing under his intense, unblinking stare.

A low, guttural sound rumbles in his chest, and he leans closer.

His clawed hand comes up, hovering over my breast for a long, silent moment. Then, his fingers make contact. His broad palm cups the weight of me, his thumb brushing over the soft swell of skin.

My breath hitches, my nipple hardening instantly into a tight, aching point against his palm.

Tharn's reaction is immediate. A tremor runs through his hand. His gaze snaps from my breast to my face, his pupils flaring wide, swallowing the amber. The air in the alcove shifts, the quiet curiosity in his posture instantly consumed by a raw, dawning hunger. He felt that. He saw my body respond.

And then his mouth is on me. His mouth closes on my nipple. He tastes me. A deep, guttural rumble vibrates from his chest, and his other hand slams down on the furs beside my hip, his claws extending and digging in as if to anchor himself.

The sensation is electric, a bolt of pleasure that shoots straight to my core. My hands tangle in his hair, my breath hitching as his mouth suckles tentatively at first, then grows stronger as my body arches into his.

He learns fast. And he doesn't stop there.

He moves lower, his lips trailing down my stomach, his claws hooking into the waistband of my skirt and panties, pulling them off with ease.

I'm bare beneath him now, fully exposed, but instead of feeling vulnerable, I feel... powerful.

Because the way he's looking at me—like I'm something sacred, something he can't resist—makes me feel like I could set the world on fire.

His hands clamp around my thighs, *forcing them wider*, fingers digging in hard enough to leave bruises. *Good.* I *want* the marks. I want to feel him tomorrow, even after this is over.

His breath is hot between my legs, but he doesn't move. Not yet. Just watches me, eyes black with hunger, while I squirm. *Begging without words.*

His tongue drags over me in one long, filthy stroke. Mouth searing against my skin, licking into me like he's starving.

I cry out, back arching, fingers clawing at the furs. "*Fuck*—!"

A deep, satisfied growl vibrates against me, his grip tightening, keeping me pinned. He doesn't let me move. Doesn't let me catch my breath. Just *devours.* Rough licks, sharp nips of his fangs, that relentless fucking tongue circling, thrusting, *deep into me.*

Every sound I make only drives him harder.

"Tharn—!" My voice cracks, thighs shaking. He groans against me, the sound dark, *possessive*, and then his mouth seals over me, sucking hard, tongue working mercilessly.

I come so fast it's like falling. Violent, gasping, my whole body seizing. He doesn't stop. Doesn't slow. Just licks me through it, wrings out every last shudder, until I'm sobbing, wrung out, *destroyed*.

Only then does he pull back, lips wet, gaze feral. A single, possessive thought brands my mind.

"*Again.*"

THARN

Her taste is ruinous.

The first time my tongue drags over her, it's like the ground has dropped out from under me.

Sweet.

Salt.

Heat.

Mine.

I will never get enough of this.

I groan against her, sheathing my claws as they sink deeper into the soft flesh of her thighs.

She whimpers, her hips jerking, but I hold her down.

"*Tharn—!*"

Her voice cracks, and something dark and *hungry* uncoils in my chest.

I don't answer.

I *devour*.

My tongue presses deep, licking into her like I'm trying to memorize every inch, every shudder, every pulse of her body around me.

I don't know what I'm doing.

But her gasps, her moans—they teach me.

When I flick my tongue here, her thighs tighten. When I suck there, her back bows off the furs.

I learn fast. This is more than just sharing water. This...this is sharing *life.*

And Jah-kee is drowning in it. Her back arches, her fingers twist in the furs, her breath comes in broken, gasping cries.

I growl low, the sound thrumming through her, and she shakes, her thighs trembling against my face.

Dust.

I could stay here forever.

Buried between her legs, lost in the taste of her, the way her body clenches for me, the way she shatters when I curl my tongue—

But it's *not enough.*

I need *more.*

I need *everything.*

I pull back just enough to look at her. Her heaving chest, her parted lips, her eyes *wild* with pleasure.

She is slick on my mouth, on my chin. I drag my tongue slowly over my own lips, tasting her again. Sweet. Salt. *Mine.*

Her breath hitches at the sight, a fresh wave of heat washing over her skin.

Beautiful.

Her skin is flushed, her scent *thick* in the air, and when my claws trail up her thighs, she jerks—

"W-Wait—"

I don't.

I drag my tongue over her again, *slow,* savoring the way her whole body *tightens,* the way her chest stutters...

Then I *suck.*

Hard.

She screams, the sound piercing the stone walls.

Her hands fly to my head, fingers fisting in the copper-red strands at my scalp, her back bowing off the furs as something rips through her.

I don't stop.

I *can't*.

I keep my mouth on her, drinking in every pulse, every shudder, until she's sobbing, her fingers tugging weakly at me.

"Please—I can't—!"

But she *can*.

And I *won't* let her go.

I press my forehead against her thigh, my breath ragged, my new member aching so badly I can barely *think*.

When her fingers brush my jaw, I freeze.

Her touch is soft, her eyes hazy but locked on mine.

Hers.

The realization *burns* through me.

I shift my weight, moving over her with an aching slowness that is its own kind of violence. My body settles over hers as my member throbs against her stomach, thick and slick and *dripping*.

A hot, viscous fluid beads at the tip, spilling over in a slow, shameless leak. A waste of water? Something my body has never done before.

But no, not a waste. Somehow, instinctively, I know it's for her.

I shudder, my hips jerking involuntarily, smearing the slickness between us.

Her breath hitches as she feels it. The heat, the wetness, the way my member pulses against her.

Then her gaze drops.

I watch her eyes widen, her lips parting as she takes in the changes. The ridges along the underside, raised and sensitive. And the base—

Ain.

A swollen, curved protrusion rises there, like a second, smaller shaft, but flatter, curved like a dust serpent's scale with ridges of its own. It curves toward my shaft like a strange extension.

What the dust is that?

I don't know. But my body does.

It's for her, too.

Jah-kee inhales deeply, her legs spreading wider, welcoming me. My hips stutter. I've seen this before. In her dreams. I know what she wants. I know what she *needs* me to do.

I drag the thick head of my shaft through her slick, *teasing*, watching her face. Her whole body jerks, a single, sharp tremor that runs from her shoulders to her toes.

"Tharn."

Her voice is *broken*.

I growl, pressing forward slowly, so drakking slowly, just to feel every inch of her stretch around me. My mind screams a warning, and I remember the vision of my strength tearing her apart. *She is not prey. Do not break her.*

But Jah-kee meets my gaze, her water-blue eyes hazy with a trust that shatters my fear. She is not afraid. She wants this. She wants me.

Tight.

Hot.

Perfect.

The world, the entirety of Xiraxis, centers on this moment.

Jah-kee's nails dig into my shoulders, her breath coming in sharp, shallow gasps.

"H-Harder—"

A snarl rips from my chest, and I *obey*.

I bury myself to the hilt in one brutal thrust, filling her so *completely* I see stars.

Dust.

Ain.

What is this?

Her body is scalding around me, clenching, pulsing. And it does not break. It holds me. It welcomes the very savagery I feared would destroy it. The beast inside me does not wish to consume her; it wishes to be consumed *by* her. Sheathing myself inside her is not an act of destruction. It is an act of completion.

I've never felt anything like it.

Never dreamed anything could feel this good.

I freeze, shuddering, my claws sinking into the furs as pleasure blows through me like a dust storm.

Is this...

Is this what mating is?

Then Jah-kee moans, her hips jerking, her walls fluttering around me—and I lose myself.

I pound into her, deep, rough, my hips snapping against hers with every ravenous thrust.

She cries out, her body arching. "Yes—!"

Every slam of my hips drives me deeper, her heat milking me, her body begging for more.

She's so soft.

So wet.

So tight.

I look down between us, drawn by a sight so beautiful. Female. *My* female. Stretched around me.

The swollen curve of shaft sprouting from the base of my member grinds against her soft center, perfectly molding to her slick folds.

She wails.

Her back bows off the furs, her thighs clamping around my hips as the dual sensation destroys her.

I growl, possessive, my thrusts turning purposeful, savage,

angling my hips to drag that swollen curve against her with every snap of my body.

She sobs.

"T-Tharn—*fuck*—!"

Her voice cracks, her fingers clawing at my shoulders as pleasure wrecks her.

And I can *feel* it.

I don't slow.

I can't.

Every slam of my hips drives my rod deeper, my ridges rubbing her folds in tight, maddening thrusts just like my body was made to do.

Made for her.

Her breath comes in shallow, broken gasps, her eyes rolling back as something unseen builds within her. Something momentous.

"I'm—I'm gonna—!"

She shatters, screaming my name as her body clenches around me, squeezing my shaft like she never wants me to leave.

I roar.

Something shoots up through me, an unstoppable tide, culminating at the tip of my shaft—

And then—

I waste water.

A flood of it. Hot, thick, relentless, spilling into her in pulsing waves.

A betrayal.

Of the dust. Of my blood.

Survival is water. Wasting it is death.

But this...this is not waste.

This is purpose.

My body knows. Some gnawing instinct screams that this

water belongs inside her. That I must *fill* her, brand her, drown her in every drop.

My hips stutter, driving deeper, spilling into her until my vision whites out, until I'm empty, until my body is shaking with the force of it.

Even so, I need more.

I need to do it again.

"*Mine.*"

"*Mine.*"

"*MINE.*"

Jah-kee's eyes fly open, wide, stunned.

"*Yours.*" Her voice meets mine in the mindspace, clear as the sky across the dust.

And I know—

I will never let her go.

CHAPTER 30
NAKED AND (NOT) AFRAID

JACQUI

I wake the way a planet might wake to its first sunrise. Slow, dazed, irrevocably changed.

My body feels different. Not just the pleasant ache between my thighs, the ghost of his teeth on my neck, the places where his claws left possessive marks. Something deeper. Like my bones have been reforged. Like my blood sings.

Tharn is wrapped around me—a furnace of muscle and heat, his arm slung heavy over my waist, his chest pressed flush against my back. His breath stirs my hair with each exhale, and for one reckless moment, I consider pretending to sleep forever.

But the light shifting through the cave is too bright, the air too thick with the scent of us. Salt and musk and something electric that makes me inhale even deeper. I turn carefully, my movement barely a whisper, but his arm tightens instinctively.

"*Mine.*"

My gaze flies to his, but he's still resting. A soft huff of a chuckle brushes through my nose, my cheeks warming even as everything else within me warms. Even unconscious, he won't let me go.

Good.

His face is softer in sleep, the usual intensity smoothed into something softer, almost vulnerable.

I lift my arm, tracing with my finger, following the curve down his shoulder.

He's beautiful.

Alien.

Mine.

A month ago, that thought would've sent me into a panic. Now? After the way he ruined me, after the way our minds collided at the peak of pleasure—*after feeling his soul knit to mine*—it's the only truth left.

This is why Justine will never leave. This is why *I* will never leave...

Tharn's eyes open suddenly, catching me mid-trace. His lips slowly curve into a smile.

That same damn smile that sent me scrambling backward the first time he tried it. Back when his unfamiliar facial muscles had twisted the expression into something feral, when I'd mistaken bared teeth for threat instead of tentative affection.

Now, heat crawls up my neck for entirely different reasons.

"*You look,*" his mental voice slides into my mind, a low rumble that vibrates through the bone. I blink. We're not touching. The connection is just... open. "*Your thoughts are loud.*"

Oh, this is new.

And terrible. Because Tharn with a direct line to my brain is apparently Tharn with no damn filter. "*And you're smug,*" I shoot back.

His grin widens, all fangs. *"Your pleasure made me so."*

The bluntness makes my face flame. I press my palm against his chest to shove him—or maybe climb him. *"You're imagining things."*

He catches my wrist easily, his thumb brushing my racing pulse. His eyes darken. *"I am not imagining this,"* he projects, the thought a low thrum against my skin. He brings my knuckles to his mouth, his fangs grazing them lightly. *"You taste of me. I want to taste me on you again."*

A low growl rumbles in his chest. He rolls, covering my body with his. His mouth finds mine, not asking but taking, a deep, slow kiss that tastes of possession. His hands are heavy on my sides, his thumbs finding the soft swell of my breasts, pressing in, learning my shape. I shudder.

His tongue flicks against mine, once, and I forget to breathe.

I'm arching into him, gripping his broad shoulders, when—

Clatter.

Stone on stone. Distant voices approaching.

Reality crashes in.

I break the kiss with a gasp, but Tharn chases my lips, growling when I turn my face away.

"We should probably go out there," I murmur, though every cell in my body screams protest.

Tharn makes a sound—half snarl, half plea—and drops his forehead to my collarbone, his breath ragged. For a heartbeat, I think he'll ignore the world and take me, anyway.

Then, with obvious grievance, he rolls away.

Cheeks flaming like the desert outside, I sit up, and pretend to have a modicum of decency as my gaze shifts over the cave floor for my bra. Stretching, I freeze.

Something's wrong.

No. Wait.

Something's *right*.

The exhaustion that's clung to me like a second skin since landing on this cursed planet? Gone. The low-grade fever, the bone-deep ache, the fog that made every step feel like wading through syrup? Vanished.

I flex my hands. My muscles sing with strength I haven't felt in months. My mind is clear, sharp, like I've been doused in ice water and sunlight all at once.

What the hell?

My gaze shoots to Tharn just as he reaches for me. "Tharn, I'm...stronger."

His massive hands pull me back against his chest, my bare spine flush with the furnace-heat of him. His breath ghosts warm across my shoulder as he speaks.

"*You were never weak.*" His mental voice wraps around me like another embrace. "*Your body fought a war. Every breath here was a battle. And still—*" His arms tighten. "*Still, you burned brighter than Ain herself.*"

I turn in his grasp, needing to see his face. Those golden-amber eyes meet mine, their usual intensity softened by something that makes my throat tight.

"*I have words now,*" his thoughts murmur, calloused thumbs tracing my hipbones. "*So many words I couldn't say in the dust.*"

He pauses, eyes searching mine.

"*When you showed me your world—all that water, all the green —I tasted your longing. And feared...*" His gaze searches mine. "*Feared you'd choose that sky over mine.*"

My breath stops in my chest. His claws extend just enough to prick warning against my skin as he leans down, forehead pressing to mine.

"*Know this, Jah-kee...I will tear apart this desert to keep you.*

Shatter every law. Flood the wastes with lifeblood if that is what it takes."

His vow hangs between us, terrifying in its certainty. I should be alarmed. Maybe I am. But my traitorous heart pounds against his chest in answer.

I press closer, until his next breath fills my lungs too. "You idiot," I whisper against his lips. *"Did you ever consider I might choose you back?"*

Tharn goes utterly still at my words.

A snarl tears from his chest, and suddenly I'm on my back, his body crushing me into the furs, his mouth claiming mine in a kiss that's more battle than affection. His hands are everywhere. Kneading my thighs, gripping my hips, dragging me against him until I feel the thick, aching length of him pressed between us.

"You. Choose. Me?"

The words are guttural, disbelieving, like he's tasting them for the first time.

I don't get to answer.

His claws sink into the furs beside my head as he slides into me. Slow, torturous, his golden eyes locked on mine, watching every flinch, every gasp, every shudder as he fills me completely.

"Say it again," he growls.

I can't. Not when he moves, his hips rolling in a deep, devastating rhythm that makes my vision blur. The ridges along his shaft drag against me, the swollen curve at his base grinding ruthlessly against my clit with every thrust.

"Jah-kee." My name is a warning spreading from his mind to mine.

I sob, my legs locking around his waist as I pull him deeper inside, and my heels find them. The strange, raised ridges along the sides of his hips. They are perfect handholds, but for my feet. My heels slot into the grooves as if they were carved for me, allowing me to pull him impossibly deeper with every returning thrust. "*I choose you, you bastard*—!"

His roar shakes the cave as his climax ruptures through him, his cock pulsing inside me, his hips jerking as he spills deep. The bond between us ignites, and I'm coming with him, my back arching off the furs as pleasure obliterates every thought.

For one fractured moment, we're not two bodies. We're starlight, collision, the last two survivors of a dying universe.

Then Tharn collapses over me, his forehead pressed to mine, his breath ragged.

"*My female. My beautiful, perfect Jah-kee.*"

MY CLOTHES—OR MORE ACCURATELY, THE FABRIC GHOSTS OF WHAT used to be clothes—lie in tattered ruins across the alcove floor.

I hold up what might have once been a shirt sleeve. "Fantastic. At this rate, I'll be fashioning pasties from cave lichen by next week."

Tharn watches from the furs, propped on one elbow like some golden desert god, utterly unrepentant. Sunlight catches his skin, painting him like he's Zeus himself.

"*We Drakav do not cover,*" he projects, his mental voice syrup-smooth. The bastard even has the audacity to gesture at his own naked glory, as if his stupidly perfect physique is a compelling argument.

I fling a scrap of fabric at his head. It flutters pathetically to the ground halfway. "*You're wearing my blouse as a loincloth.*"

He glances down at the makeshift garment—stretched taut over his hips, the fabric barely containing him—and has the nerve to look pleased. "*It smells like you.*"

Heat floods my cheeks. "That's not—*That's not the point!*"

Tharn moves, a blur of golden muscle, closing the distance before I can draw a breath. His hands clamp onto my bare waist, his grip firm, possessive. His gaze drops to my mouth, his own lips parting slightly.

"*Better this way,*" his thought is a low, guttural rumble. "*No coverings. Easier to taste.*" His head dips, his fangs grazing my bottom lip like a promise. A brand.

Corn on the cob.

It's a dirty tactic. Effective, but dirty.

I shove at his chest—or try to. My newfound strength doesn't even cause him to budge. When, after a second, he stumbles back a step, I know he did that for my benefit.

I roll my eyes, but my humor dies when his gaze catches on the marks along my neck. His pupils blow wide, his breathing stutters.

"*Jah-kee—*" His claws hover over the bruises like he's afraid to touch them. "*I hurt you.*"

"It's fine, they don't even—Tharn!"

He's already halfway across the cave, bolting for the entrance.

Two minutes later, he explodes back into the alcove, clutching a fistful of firebloom, already crushed.

"*Eat,*" he orders, shoving the petals at my mouth.

"I don't need—mmph!" He stuffs some between my lips.

"*And these.*" He crushes the remaining petals in his palm, then smears the paste over my neck.

The effect is instantaneous. The firebloom stings, but soon there's a soothing coolness spreading over my skin.

I stare at him.

He stares back, chest heaving, eyes wild with guilt.

Silence.

"Oh, Tharn," I whisper.

He collapses against me, his forehead pressed to mine, his arms locking around my waist like I might vanish. "*You are hurt. I fix it.*"

"They're hickies, Tharn. Not stab wounds."

"*Same thing.*"

"Jaqs? Are you awake?" Justine's voice winds through the caves to our alcove, and my eyes widen.

"Shit. Time to face the music." I just had sex with an alien, *my* alien, and I liked it.

My gaze falls back to the floor, scanning for my clothes. "Yeah, coming, just...just give me a second." I find what's left of my skirt and sigh. "I need actual clothing. These won't last for much longer."

Tharn tilts his head, watching me. After a moment of consideration, he crosses to the far side of the alcove, retrieving something from a small storage niche.

It's a hide. Soft, well-tanned, and surprisingly supple. He offers it to me.

"*A covering,*" he projects, his thought simple. "*For now.*"

I take the hide, touched by his thoughtfulness. It's large enough to wrap around my torso and tie at the shoulder, creating a makeshift dress that covers everything essential.

"Thank you," I say, standing on tiptoe to press a kiss to his jaw. "It's perfect for now."

His hands clamp onto my waist, his grip firm, possessive. His gaze drops to the hide I'm now wearing.

"*It is temporary,*" his thought is a low rumble. "*I will tear it off you in the dark.*"

CHAPTER 31
THE WALK OF VERY LITTLE SHAME

JACQUI

We emerge from the alcove hand-in-hand. Me in my makeshift hide dress, Tharn in my goddamn blouse like it's some kind of trophy.

The main cavern buzzes with morning activity, and at least a dozen heads swivel our way.

Oh god.

I brace for disgust. Judgment. At the very least, some awkward coughing.

Instead?

The women exchange glances—not shocked, but... knowing. A few smothered smiles appear. Alex actually winks at me.

Huh.

Tharn's frame brushes against mine. *"They heard,"* he projects, shameless.

My face ignites.

Justine leans against a rock column, arms crossed. "Took

you long enough," she calls, grinning like the cat who got the cream. And the canary. *And the whole damn pet store.*

I flip her off. She toasts me with her waterskin.

Tharn exhales sharply. His version of a laugh, I realise. But his claws tighten around mine when I try to pull away. As his gaze shifts to his brothers, the mindspace hums between us, thrumming with his reluctance like a second pulse beneath my skin.

My focus slides to them too. All watching us. In the back of my mind, I can feel them. A soft insistence.

Oh.

I can sense them.

And not just them...but who they are...

Haroth's restless energy buzzes against my consciousness like static. Sarven's amusement curls at the edges like smoke. The leader, Kol's, steady presence anchors them all. I don't recognize their faces—but I recognize *them*, as if I've always known the shape of their thoughts.

Oh fuck. No wonder Tharn struggled with the translator.

My fingers rise instinctively to the device in my ear. Such a clumsy, limited thing compared to this—this depth, this intimacy of shared silence. I pluck it out, staring at the tiny tech in my palm. All those misunderstandings, all those halting conversations...

A warm breath gusts against my temple as Tharn leans in. "*Jah-kee?*"

I look up, gaze on the Drakav.

"*I think...they want to congratulate you.*" I glance at Tharn.

As if I opened a door, the mental chorus of the Drakav hits me all at once.

"*—he's transformed—*"

"*—got a Daughter to claim him—*"

"*—and she gave him hide coverings—*"

"*—lucky drakki-spawn—*"

My lips twitch. Tharn's growl vibrates through my bones as he glares at the last thought-speaker. Across the firepit, Haroth has the decency to look abashed—for all of three seconds, before he resumes his ridiculous flexing.

"*They're... enthusiastic,*" I project carefully, realizing now that if I can hear them, perhaps they can hear me, too.

Tharn's fingers twitch against mine. "*They're ka'vrakts.*" That word comes across as "mindless creature" in my brain. I snort. He's calling them idiots, but the warmth in his thought betrays him.

I squeeze his hand, marveling at how easily the meaning flows between us now. Just knowing.

Across the cavern, the other unmated males linger near the human women's area, their golden skin bare, their movements just a little too deliberate as they pretend to be busy.

Haroth is still flexing while "sorting" fire stones. Another is stretching his back in a way that definitely isn't necessary. Sarven is dramatically testing the edge of his blade, though he's not even looking at the sharp edge. His eyes are on... Mikaela. Who is focusing on everyone except him. In the mind-space, their thoughts are loud and obvious.

"*Why hasn't any human wanted to share water with **me**?*"

"*Do I need to hunt better prey? Is that the trick?*"

"*Rok wears the scent of his female. Tharn wears his female's scent. Where is my scent to wear?*"

Tharn's mental groan vibrates through me. "*Pathetic.*"

When Haroth—who has migrated near Tina—suddenly flexes so hard his biceps practically ripple in the firelight, even Tharn's patience snaps.

I squeeze his fingers. "*Go. Before they start a war over who deserves scraps of cloth.*"

His amber eyes burn, but he finally releases me—only after

dragging my knuckles to his fangs for one claiming nip. The moment our hands part, the mindspace erupts:

"ASK HIM HOW HE DID IT!"

*"—does the female give coverings **after** the claiming?—"*

"—maybe if I bring her a kill, she'll—"

Tharn stalks toward his brothers, radiating warning. The others immediately crowd him, their bare forms making his blouse-loincloth stand out even more.

Sarven reaches out, fingers twitching toward the fabric. *"Is it... soft?"*

Tharn's answering snarl shakes the cave. *"Mine."*

The others freeze. Tharn's chest puffs out like a preening bird, his spine straightening as if wearing human scraps is the highest honor their people know.

In the mindspace, the jealousy is palpable.

"He won't even let us touch it."

"I want one."

Justine stares at the scene before turning back to me, grinning. "Are they... pouting?"

I bite back a laugh.

Across the cave, Mikaela pats the stone beside her. I join them, suddenly hyperaware of two undeniable facts. I have an alien mate. And said mate is currently preening before his brothers like a prize-winning rooster.

No one mentions it.

Mikaela just passes me a waterskin. "So. Alien sex." Her eyebrow arcs. "Do you now have the whole..." She wiggles her fingers near her temples.

"Telepathy thing?" I take a slow sip, buying time before passing it back to her. The mindspace thrums with Tharn's smug satisfaction and the answering growls of his nosy brothers. "Yeah."

The women's eyes lock onto me. Pam's piece of meat

hovers halfway to her lips. Erika leans forward, curiosity etched in her expression.

Silence.

"Are you okay?" Mikaela blurts. "Like, actually okay? Because we heard—" Her cheeks flush. "Well. We heard everything."

Alex snorts. "The whole damn canyon heard everything."

My face burns.

"But more importantly," Erika cuts in, "you're *telepathic* now. And you're not the first." Her gaze flicks to Justine.

Pam bites a bit of her meat. "What's it like?"

Her question catches me off guard. How do I explain it? How do I explain something that rewires your entire understanding of connection? That the translator in my hand suddenly feels like a child's toy compared to the depth of the mindspace.

"It's..." I struggle for human words, absently rubbing my sternum. "Like realizing you've been deaf your whole life and suddenly hearing music. But the music is... emotions. Memories. The shape of someone's thoughts rather than the words."

Pam's chewing slows. Mikaela's fingers tighten around her waterskin.

"Tharn tried to talk to me through the translator..." I continue. "But this? When we're connected?" A laugh escapes me. "I knew his brothers' names before they even told me." I jerk my chin toward Sarven. "Sarven's thinking about hunting, and I...can taste the blood in my mouth."

Sarven's head snaps up—and he's not the only one. Half the Drakav nearby are now staring at me, their golden eyes bright with something like wonder. I stiffen, suddenly afraid I've breached some unspoken boundary.

But then it hits me. Their awe.

One warrior tilts his head in that distinct Tharn-like

gesture of affirmation. Another touches his chest, over his heart. And Sarven...

Oh.

His hesitant thoughts brush against mine. A raw, aching need from a male trying to be brave. An image floats between us: Mikaela laughing by the firelight, her braids swinging. Then a wordless question.

"Her name?"

The request is so tender, so human in its vulnerability, that my throat tightens. In the mindspace, I cradle the answer gently.

"Mikaela."

The reaction is instantaneous.

Sarven's entire body shudders. The name echoes through him like a struck bell, sending ripples of possessiveness-awe-love-attraction so potent it steals my breath. For a heartbeat, I'm drowning in the sheer rightness he feels. As if he's been waiting his whole life to shape that sound in his mind.

Beside me, Mikaela frowns at her suddenly trembling waterskin. "Why's it getting windy in here?"

Sarven jerks back, the connection snapping as his pointy ears flatten to the sides of his head. But the wonder remains. In his eyes, in the soft growl building in his chest, in the way his claws carefully retract as he looks at her.

"Turns out sleeping with the locals is the universal translator," Erika hums, scratching her chin.

Mikaela follows my gaze to Sarven, who is now vibrating with poorly contained devotion. "Oh no," she murmurs. "Why is *Stabby McGoldy* looking at me like I'm breakfast, lunch, and dinner?"

CHAPTER 32
THARN'S SECRET (BUT NOT REALLY SECRET) CLUB

JACQUI

Mornings begin with the sharp, rhythmic clinking of stone on chitin. The massive corpse of the dust serpent is gone, its meat already cut into strips that hang smoking and curing deep within the cavern, filling the air with a savory scent. What remains is the prize: the creature's immense hide, stretched out on a massive frame just outside the cave.

They work with a reverence I find strangely compelling, their stone knives scraping away the last of the meat before they carefully pry each massive, dust-colored plate free. I watch one Drakav proudly present a cleaned scale to Alex. He sets it on the ground before her, then mimes placing a waterskin and a piece of meat on its surface. He gestures to her, then pats the space beside the scale, a clear offering of a personal eating surface. Then he points to a growing stack where other scales are being meticulously polished.

Progress.

But the main activity for the human women is centered around several large stone frames. Hunters return from patrols with bundles of tough, fibrous vines, which are then stretched across the frames to be woven into surprisingly comfortable sleeping mats and privacy screens.

I watch Erika in surprise as she shows another woman how to work the shuttle—a smooth, heavy piece of polished bone —back and forth, her movements quick and sure. The Drakav leader, Kol, lingers just a little too close, his golden eyes fixed on her hands with an intensity that makes me wonder if he's planning to propose to her fingers.

Only Tharn and Rok are absent most afternoons, vanishing into the tunnel network with that stupid, synchronized casualness.

I notice.

"Where are they going?" I whisper, turning the meat before me.

Sarven—who's become Mikaela's shadow—goes unnaturally still, his crimson eyes fixed on a point somewhere over my shoulder. His ears twitch. Guilty.

Justine hides a smile behind her waterskin. "Maybe they're building you a palace."

I hurl a pebble at her. It bounces off her knee.

Evenings bring the best changes. The Drakav have started partitioning the cavern with those woven drapes, creating semi-private spaces. Tonight, two wrestle one between stone pillars while their brothers "supervise" with unhelpful growls.

It's... almost sweet. These lethal warriors, meticulously measuring drapes like nervous tailors.

"*Privacy,*" Kol declares to no one in particular, stabbing a finger at the hanging divider. Right before his gaze shifts to Erika as if seeking her approval.

When the first divider sways into place, separating the

human sleeping area from the main cavern, Erika's stern expression softens.

The caves still smell of curing meat and cooking. The food's still questionable at best. But as I watch my sister lean into Rok's touch, as I note the way Sarven carefully stacks extra meat near Mikaela's share, I realize...

This might just become home.

And not just for me and Justine. All of us.

Nightfall belongs to the bonds.

I hear Justine's quiet laughter through the mindspace as Rok leads her away. Back in our little 'room' in the caves, Tharn presses a warm bundle into my hands. It's another firebloom salve he's become obsessed with making. The sharp herbal scent makes my nose wrinkle.

"You realize I'm not actually injured, right?" I tease.

His only response is a stubborn rumble as he kneels before me. His claws trace the scar on my calf, his touch sending a familiar shiver through me. He checks my hands, my arms, every inch of exposed skin with a ridiculous, painstaking delicacy. His concern is so earnest it's almost comical, and my heart does a stupid little flip.

When he is finally satisfied that I am not, in fact, secretly broken, he rises to his full height. His gaze lingers on my face for a moment, a silent conversation passing between us that I am only just beginning to understand.

Then, with a final, almost reluctant dip of his head, he turns and begins to walk away. He's leaving. Again.

I wait until he's nearly at the tunnel entrance, until the tension in his shoulders eases just slightly, assuming he's made a clean escape.

"Where do you keep going?" I project, my thought a sharp, clear arrow in the quiet of the cavern.

He freezes mid-stride. The mindspace floods with frantic

not-hiding images: hunting parties, patrol routes, completely unconvincing rock formations.

"*Water. Meat,*" he projects too quickly. "*For the clan.*"

I step closer, crossing my arms. "*Funny.* Because Haroth just brought back two sandfins. And Kol's weaving another mat right now."

A flicker of panic crosses his face. Then the panic is gone, replaced by something much darker.

Before I can blink, he's on me. One arm bands around my waist like a steel trap, hauling me flush against him. His other hand fists in my hair, tilting my head back.

"*No more questions.*" His thought is a low, guttural growl, a pure command that vibrates through my bones.

The raw dominance of it sparks through me. "*But where—*"

His mouth crashes down on mine, swallowing the word. A brutal, possessive claiming meant to obliterate all thought. I gasp as his claws scrape down my spine.

His mouth leaves mine, his breathing a harsh sound in the quiet tunnel. The mindspace between us floods with images. *His* images.

Him pushing me down onto the furs. His mouth on my breasts, his teeth on my neck. His hands on my thighs, pushing them apart. Him sinking into me, filling me, our bodies moving in a frantic rhythm.

My knees go weak at the sheer, savage honesty of his need.

Somehow we're moving. The alcove's furs hit my back as Tharn follows me down, his body a delicious weight. "Cheater," I pant as his mouth finds my neck.

His desire vibrates in a rumble against my skin.

By the time coherent thought returns—by the time I remember there was ever anything to question—dawn light streaks through the cavern. And Tharn is gone again.

That sneaky, beautiful, irresistible bastard.

CHAPTER 33
IT'S THE THOUGHT (AND THE STABBING YOURSELF REPEATEDLY) THAT COUNTS

JACQUI

The answer starts to come together a few days later, when I notice something strange during one of Justine's language lessons.

Tharn's fingers are covered in tiny puncture marks, like he's been repeatedly stabbed with something small and sharp. When I reach for his hand, concerned, he pulls away with uncharacteristic shyness.

"*I am fine, my dear Jah-kee,*" he projects, his mental voice dismissive. "*Just... hunting.*"

Yeah, right. Last I checked, hunting didn't involve getting stabbed in the fingers repeatedly. Unless the local wildlife has developed a taste for Drakav digits.

That night, when Tharn slips away again, I decide to follow him. It's not that I don't trust him—I do, implicitly. But the mystery is killing me, and if he won't tell me what he's up to, I'll just have to find out for myself.

I wait until he's disappeared down one of the lesser-used

tunnels, then slip after him, keeping to the shadows. The tunnels are dark but somehow, my eyes adjust much easier than they would have months ago. I can see better.

The tunnel winds deeper into the cliff, branching off in several directions. I pause at a junction, unsure which way Tharn went, when I hear a soft annoyed click echo from the left passage.

I follow the sound, creeping along the wall until I reach a small chamber lit by a soft golden glow.

Tharn's glow.

And there, sitting cross-legged on the floor with his back to me, is Tharn.

But it's what he's doing that stops me in my tracks.

He's hunched over something on the floor. One of the smaller underscales from the dust serpent, its surface gleaming in the dim light. A bone needle is clutched awkwardly in his massive hand as he painstakingly pushes it through a tough, cord-like strap.

He's sewing the straps onto the scale, threading them through holes he must have painstakingly drilled near the edges. The straps themselves are woven from the same fibrous vines the women use for their sleeping mats. The "thread" he's using looks suspiciously like a thin, dried piece of serpent gut.

My brain struggles to process the image. The fearsome alien hunter is sitting in a cave, trying to attach woven vine straps to a piece of monster armor using a needle made of bone and thread made of guts. And by the looks of it, he's not very good at it.

The stitching is thick and uneven. Beside him on the floor are several frayed, discarded straps, clear evidence of his repeated, frustrated attempts. What he's making is... well, I have no idea. Some kind of bizarre shield with handles?

Then it clicks.

Tharn isn't making a weird shield. He's trying to fashion a dress for me. One set of scales for the front and one for the back, held together by the woven straps he's fighting with. A crude, alien-style dress. Impractical, probably uncomfortable, but unmistakably made for me.

My heart melts at the sight. He's making *clothes*. His version of clothes, from the only materials he knows. For me.

I must make some small sound, because Tharn's head snaps up, his amber eyes finding mine in the dim light. For a moment, he looks startled, almost embarrassed, before his expression shifts to one of resignation.

"*Jah-kee*," he projects, setting the half-finished garment aside. "*You followed me.*"

"*You were being mysterious*," I counter, stepping into the chamber. "*You've been sneaking off to... sew?*"

For the first time, I see Tharn's ears flatten to the sides of his head.

I step closer, kneeling beside him, my fingers reaching out to trace the stitching. A dark smudge on one scale matches the pigment staining his fingertips.

"*You bled making this.*" I catch his hand, turning his palm up to reveal the needle-pricked pads.

He rumbles, defensive. "*Bone needle was... small.*"

"*You hate clothes*," my thought whispers.

"*Females need coverings.*" He says it like a simple fact, but the mindspace betrays him. It floods with memories of me adjusting the hide over myself and even his memory of that night out in the desert. The one when I'd peed and he watched. How I'd tried to hide myself.

He gestures to the pile of scales, his mental voice grumpy but endearingly so. "*It is... difficult*," he admits, holding up the lopsided garment. "*Your people cover. So... I cover you.*"

The simple statement, delivered with such matter-of-fact sincerity, hits me right in the heart.

I throw my arms around his neck, kissing him with all the emotion welling up inside me. He responds immediately, his arms wrapping around my waist as he pulls me onto his lap.

When we finally break apart, I'm breathless and smiling so wide my cheeks hurt. "*It's perfect,*" I tell him, touching the surprisingly soft scales with reverent fingers.

Tharn stills. His claws hover near the garment, as if seeing it anew through my eyes. I can feel his emotions swirling faintly in the mindspace. Uncertainty and hope, layered beneath the quiet pride he's trying to keep hidden.

"I've never had anything like this," I add softly, running my hand over the smooth scales. They feel durable, and Tharn has clearly made the entire thing with care. The seams are tight, the edges reinforced, and even the faint, jagged patterns etched into the scales by his claws give it a strange, artistic beauty.

His claws drop slightly, his posture almost hesitant. "*It is... useful,*" he projects.

"*Useful?*" I repeat, arching a brow, a teasing smile tugging at the corners of my lips. "*Tharn, you made this for me. It's more than useful—it's beautiful.*"

He watches me for a long moment, unmoving, his glowing eyes tracing every line of my face. I feel the faintest pull in the mindspace, his awe cresting like a soft wave and washing over me.

"*You honor my claws' work,*" he projects at last.

I can't stop my smile from widening. On impulse, I reach out, brushing my fingers against his hand. His claws twitch, and I feel a tremor run through him at my touch.

Tharn exhales slowly. The awe in his expression shifts, the warmth in his eyes sharpening into something hotter, more mischievous. His gaze drops from my face to the scale-and-vine creation lying between us. Then his eyes meet mine again, and a slow, predatory grin spreads across his face.

My heart stutters. I know that look.

Before I can react, he moves. He doesn't reach for the new garment. He reaches for the ties of the hide dress I'm already wearing.

"Thar—?" I gasp as he yanks the knot loose with one sharp tug.

I catch his hands, a breathless laugh escaping me. *"Wait, wait! I want to try it on first!"*

A low rumble vibrates in his chest—a sound of pure, smug satisfaction. He releases my dress, his hands settling on my hips as he watches me with undisguised interest.

I slip out of my current garment, my skin prickling under his intense gaze. I pick up his creation. The scales are cool and soft against my skin, the woven straps surprisingly soft. It's awkward to put on, but it covers me—more or less. The fact that his hands made this, that he bled for it, makes it feel more precious than the finest silk.

"Well?" I ask, rising and turning in a slow circle for his inspection. *"What do you think?"*

His eyes darken, that now-familiar hunger blazing in their amber depths.

"Beautiful," he projects. *"But still unnecessary."*

I step closer, settling back onto his lap with my arms draped over his shoulders. *"Thank you,"* I murmur, pressing a soft kiss to his jaw. *"It's the nicest thing anyone's ever made for me."*

He makes a sound that's half growl, half purr, his hands settling on my hips once more. *"I will make more,"* he promises. *"Better ones."*

"*I'd like that,*" I say, smiling against his skin. "*But right now...*"

His grip tightens, breaths ceasing as I trail kisses down his neck. "*Right now?*" he prompts.

I pull back just enough to meet his gaze, my fingers toying with the edge of my new tunic. "*Right now, I think you should help me take this off.*"

Tharn's hands still beneath mine. Then his fingers tighten on the scales.

The ripping sound echoes off the stone as the tunic splits clean down the middle.

My gasp morphs into laughter. "*Was that really necessary?*"

"*Yes.*" He palms my bare waist, his other hand spearing into my hair. "*You honored my gift. Now I honor your skin.*"

The first kiss brands. The second conquers. By the third, Tharn spins me effortlessly, my back pressed flush to his chest, before lowering us onto the scattered scales. His arm bands across my ribs, holding me upright while his other hand splays possessively over my abdomen.

"*You...are so beautiful,*" he projects into the mindspace.

My gaze slides down myself, and I gasp as the thick ridge of his shaft notches at my entrance. One slow thrust and he's halfway in, the stretch delicious. Then there's that unfamiliar pressure against my behind. The new, swollen part of him, nestles perfectly between my cheeks, pulsing with heat as he finally sheathes himself completely.

"Tharn—!" My cry is breathless as my body struggles to accommodate both sensations.

Then he moves.

The dual sensation is ruinous. His length strokes deep while that wicked protrusion rubs relentless circles where I'm oh so sensitive. The mindspace fractures into blinding light as my body arches like a drawn bowstring.

"*Jah-kee.*" His teeth graze my shoulder, the warning vibrating through my bones.

Every nerve sings as he adjusts the angle, that clever ridge finding new ways to wring pleasure from me. His breath comes ragged against my neck, his hips moving in slow, deliberate rolls that make my thighs tremble.

"*You make me ache,*" he projects. The mindspace floods with his restraint, the effort it costs him not to lose control. The sensation is intoxicating.

I rock back against him, reveling in his choked growl. The movement sends sparks through my veins, that perfect pressure building until my vision whites at the edges.

I know the moment Tharn senses I'm close. He leans in, breaths brushing my skin. I feel his claws, sharp against my hips for a barest second before he sheathes them. His hands splay wide across my hips, his palms pressing hard against me, holding me flush against his power.

"*Let me see you shine.*"

The command undoes me. My climax crashes through me, wave after wave of pleasure so intense it borders on pain. The mindspace sings with our shared rapture as Tharn follows me over, his roar shaking dust from the cavern walls.

When awareness returns, I'm cradled against his chest, his heartbeat a steady drum beneath my ear. His claws trace idle patterns along my spine, the touch sending fresh delicious shivers through me.

"*This,*" he projects, his thought a low growl as he presses his body fully against mine, "*is the only covering you will ever need.*"

Later, when our breathing has steadied, he gathers the shredded remains of the tunic.

"*The next one,*" he vows against my shoulder, "*will be*

stronger." His hand skims my bare hip in clear contradiction. "*It will have to be*."

CHAPTER 34
WHEN LIFE GIVES YOU SPACE LEMONS,
MAKE SPACE-ADE (OR JUST GET BONDED)

JACQUI

Morning starts with a scream.

Not the fun kind. Not the Tharn-has-discovered-a-new-way-to-make-me-see-stars kind. The panicked, something-is-very-wrong kind that jolts me awake with my heart in my throat.

I scramble upright, nearly kneeing Tharn in the process. He's already alert, his body coiled tight beside me, claws extended.

"What is it?" I gasp, fumbling for the tunic he made me yesterday—the one that miraculously survived the night despite his best efforts.

But Tharn doesn't answer. His head is cocked, listening to something I can't hear. Something in the mindspace that doesn't include me.

Another scream cuts through the air, followed by urgent voices. Female voices.

I'm on my feet in an instant, tunic half-secured as I rush

from our alcove. Tharn follows silently, his presence a reassuring shadow at my back as we emerge into the main cavern.

The scene that greets us is chaos.

Women cluster near the sleeping area, their voices rising in panicked bursts. At the center of the commotion lies Mikaela, a thin sheen of sweat cresting her dark skin, her chest heaving with labored breaths.

Alex kneels beside her, fingers pressed to Mikaela's wrist. "Her pulse is racing," she says, her nurse's training evident in her clipped, efficient tone. "And she's burning up."

I push through the crowd, dropping to my knees beside them. "What happened?"

"She just collapsed," Tina explains, her voice shaking. "We were getting ready for the day, and she said she felt dizzy, and then—" She gestures helplessly at Mikaela's prone form.

I place my palm on Mikaela's forehead and jerk back immediately. She's not just warm—she's scorching hot.

"She needs water," I say, looking up at the worried faces surrounding us. "And something to bring the fever down."

"I've tried giving her water," Alex says, frustration evident in her tone. "She can't keep it down. And we don't exactly have a medicine cabinet around here."

I glance over my shoulder at Tharn, who stands at the edge of the group, his expression unreadable but his posture alert. In the mindspace, I can sense his concern, a steady pulse of vigilance that's oddly reassuring.

"*Firebloom*," I project to him, recalling how the herb helped reduce my own fever during our journey. "*Would it help?*"

Tharn's gaze sharpens, and he nods once before disappearing down one of the tunnels, presumably to fetch the medicinal plant.

I turn back to Mikaela, whose breathing has grown more labored.

"We need to cool her down," I say, looking around for something we can use. "Is there any cool water nearby?"

"The bathing pool," Pam jumps up, already moving toward the tunnel that leads to it. "I'll get some."

As she hurries away, I notice Erika swaying slightly where she stands, her hand rising to her temple.

"Are you okay?" I ask, concern spiking.

She waves me off. "Just a headache. I've been having them on and off."

"Me too," Tina admits, adjusting her glasses. "And I've been feeling kind of... weird. Hot, then cold."

A murmur ripples through the gathered women as several others nod in agreement.

"I've been nauseous," one woman confesses.

"My joints ache," adds another.

"I can't sleep without having these *crazy* dreams," a third chimes in.

The pieces start to click together in my mind. Dreams. Fever. Aches. Exactly what I experienced before Tharn. Before the bond.

Justine catches my eye across the group, her expression mirroring my dawning realization. In the mindspace, I can feel her thoughts brushing against mine, tentative but clear.

"*It's this planet,*" she projects. "*It's affecting them like it did us.*" I know Justine. She isn't the woo-woo kind. And frankly, I'm not superstitious either. But how else can we explain everything else that's happened so far?

Before I can respond, Tharn returns, a handful of crushed firebloom in his palm. He kneels beside me, offering the herb with a solemnity that makes my heart squeeze.

"Thank you," I murmur, taking the plant matter and turning back to Mikaela. "Alex, help me get this into her."

Together, we manage to mix the firebloom with a small

amount of water and coax Mikaela to swallow it. She coughs, turning her head away, but we persist until most of the mixture is down.

Pam returns with a gourd of cool water and a piece of fur. "Will this help?"

"Yes," I say, taking the fur and dipping it in the water. "We need to cool her gradually."

As I place the damp fur on Mikaela's forehead, I become aware of a shift in the energy of the cavern. The Drakav males have gathered at the periphery, their golden forms unnaturally still as they observe our ministrations. Their concern radiates through the mindspace like heat waves, making it hard to focus.

I glance up to find Kol at the forefront, his amber eyes fixed not on Mikaela, but on me. In the mindspace, I catch a fragment of his thought—not directed at me, but loud enough to overhear.

"*The unclaimed ones sicken,*" he projects, his mental voice deep and resonant. "*The dust rejects them.*"

Justine's head snaps up, her gaze meeting mine across Mikaela's prone form. We don't need to speak aloud—or even through the mindspace—to understand the implication.

Neither of us is sick like the others. Not anymore. We've both been claimed by Drakav. And the dust, as they call this planet, has accepted us fully.

Perhaps if the other women were claimed too...

I shake my head slightly, cutting off the thought. It's not that simple. What happened with Tharn and me, with Justine and Rok—it wasn't just physical. The other women can't just mate with random Drakav and expect it to solve everything.

But we do need to do something. Looking around at the worried faces of the women, at Mikaela's flushed, pained expression, I know we can't just let this continue.

I take a deep breath, centering myself, drawing on the strange new confidence that has settled in my bones since leaving the group weeks ago on that reckless mission to find my sister.

"Okay," I say, my voice steady despite the flutter of anxiety in my chest. "Here's what we're going to do. Alex, you and I will stay with Mikaela. Keep applying the cool fur and give her more firebloom if her fever spikes again."

Alex nods.

"Erika, Pam—I need you to organize water shifts. Everyone needs to stay hydrated, especially those of you who are feeling symptoms."

They straighten, purpose replacing some of the fear in their expressions.

"Justine," I continue, "can you coordinate with Rok and the other hunters? We need more firebloom and any other medicinal herbs they might know about."

"On it," Justine says, already moving toward Rok, who waits at the edge of the gathering.

I turn to address the rest of the women. "I know this is scary. But we've survived a crash landing, a desert crossing, and living with aliens who communicate telepathically. We can handle this too."

A ripple of nervous laughter passes through the group, the tension easing slightly.

"We'll take shifts caring for Mikaela and anyone else who gets worse," I add. "No one handles this alone, okay?"

Nods all around, some more confident than others.

As the women disperse to their assigned tasks, I feel a presence at my back. Warm, solid, reassuring. Tharn.

"You lead well," he projects, a note of pride coloring his mental tone.

I lean back slightly, taking comfort in his nearness without needing to look at him. "*I'm making it up as I go.*"

His hand brushes my lower back, a touch so light I barely feel it through my scale-tunic, but the warmth spreads through me, nonetheless.

"*The best hunters adapt,*" he projects simply. "*You adapt.*"

Coming from Tharn, it's high praise indeed.

THE DAY STRETCHES ENDLESSLY, A BLUR OF DAMP FURS AND WHISPERED reassurances. Mikaela's fever rises and falls like a cruel tide, never quite breaking but never spiking dangerously high again either. The firebloom helps, but it's clearly not enough on its own.

Other women begin to show symptoms too. By midday, three more have taken to their sleeping platforms, their bodies wracked with chills despite the cavern's warmth. Alex and Mira move between them with tireless efficiency, and I'm so happy they're here. Their medical training has proven invaluable.

The Drakav respond in their own way. They bring fresh water without being asked, delivering it in silence before melting back to the periphery. They hunt with renewed vigor, returning with not just meat but various plants and roots that Rok assures me and Justine have medicinal properties.

And they watch. Always watching, their amber eyes tracking our every move, their postures tense and alert as if expecting an attack from an unseen enemy.

I'm checking Mikaela's fever for what feels like the hundredth time when I sense Kol approaching. His presence in the mindspace is distinct. So different from the others. It's a steady pressure, like the weight of stone.

"*Jah-kee,*" he projects, using my name with careful precision. "*A word.*"

I glance up, meeting his gaze directly. Unlike most of the Drakav, who defer to Tharn when they need to communicate with me, Kol addresses me directly through the mindspace. It's both unsettling and oddly flattering.

"*Go ahead,*" I project back, keeping my mental voice calm and open.

Kol's amber eyes shift to Mikaela's prone form, then back to me. "*The sickness spreads,*" he projects. "*It will claim more of your females.*"

There's no judgment in his mental voice, just a statement of fact, but it stings nonetheless.

"*We're doing everything we can,*" I respond, a defensive edge creeping into my thoughts despite my best efforts.

Kol tilts his head. "*There is... another way,*" he projects carefully. "*A faster way.*"

My suspicion rises immediately. "*What way?*"

"*The bond. The claim.*" He projects simply. "*It protects. You and Jus-teen do not sicken. The others—*" He gestures toward the women who've fallen ill. "*—they resist the dust. It fights them.*"

I sit back on my heels, studying him. "*You're suggesting that all the women bond with Drakav males? Just like that?*"

"*It would save them,*" he projects, the certainty in his mental voice absolute.

I shake my head, frustration building. "*It's not that simple, Kol. The bond isn't just... physical. Rok's glow lit up. Tharn's did, too. None of the other Drakav have showed that first signal. I don't think it can be forced or rushed.*"

"*No,*" he agrees, surprising me. "*But it can be... encouraged.*"

Before I can ask what he means by that cryptic statement, Tharn appears at the entrance to the cavern, his massive frame silhouetted against the daylight outside. Even at this distance,

I can feel his awareness lock onto me, his presence in the mindspace a warm pressure against my consciousness.

Kol straightens, acknowledging Tharn with a slight inclination of his head before stepping back. "*Consider my words, Jah-kee,*" he projects. "*For the sake of your female-kin.*" He turns as if to leave, then pauses. Kol's claws flex at his sides, the only outward sign of tension before his mental voice rasps through the mindspace. "*Three thousand orbits, believing your kind no longer existed. Then you fell from the sky. I will not watch you vanish again.*"

As he leaves, Tharn approaches, his gaze tracking Kol with barely concealed suspicion. "*What did the dra-dam want?*" he projects, the possessive edge in his mental voice impossible to miss.

"To suggest a solution," I reply, carefully keeping my tone neutral. "*He thinks the women are sick because they haven't bonded with Drakav.*"

Tharn's expression tightens minutely.

I look down at Mikaela, her face flushed with fever despite our best efforts to cool her. "*I think he's partly right,*" I continue. "*This planet is affecting them like it affected me before we bonded. But I don't think we can just pair everyone off and expect it to work.*"

Tharn crouches beside me, his massive frame eclipsing mine. "*The bond comes when it comes,*" he projects, his mental voice soft but certain. "*Like water in the dust. It cannot be forced.*"

"*That's what I told him,*" I say, relieved that Tharn understands. "*But we still need to do something. Mikaela's getting worse, and others are showing symptoms too.*"

Tharn is silent for a moment, his gaze thoughtful as he studies Mikaela. Then, without warning, he places his palm on her forehead, his golden skin stark against her flushed complexion.

"*What are you doing?*"

He doesn't answer immediately, his eyes half-closed in concentration. Then, just as suddenly as he touched her, he withdraws his hand.

"*The dust fights her body with fire,*" he projects, confirming Kol's assessment. "*But there is... hope. The firebloom will help.*"

I nod, reaching for another cool fur to place on Mikaela's forehead. "*I hope you're right. I really do.*"

FOR THREE DAYS, WE TAKE SHIFTS WATCHING OVER MIKAELA AND THE other women who've fallen ill. The cave settles into a strange rhythm of hushed voices and worried glances. Tharn and the other hunters bring back more firebloom, and we brew it into a strong tea that seems to help—at least a little.

On the morning of the fourth day, I'm dozing beside Mikaela's sleeping form when a soft gasp jolts me awake.

"Whoa," Mikaela murmurs, her voice raspy but stronger than it's been in days. "That was... intense."

I bolt upright, nearly knocking over the gourd beside her in my haste. "Mikaela? You're awake!"

She blinks at me, her expression confused but alert. "Of course, I'm awake. Why wouldn't I be?" She glances around, taking in the makeshift sickbed and the concerned faces gathering around us. "Wait, what happened? Why is everyone looking at me like that?"

"You've been out for *three* days," I explain, pressing my palm to her forehead. The fever is gone, her skin cool and dry beneath my touch. "You collapsed with a fever. We've been worried sick."

Mikaela's eyes widen. "Three days? But that's impossible. I

feel fine." She sits up, wincing slightly as her muscles protest. "Okay, maybe a little stiff, but otherwise normal."

"How do you really feel?" Alex asks as she checks Mikaela's pulse.

"Fine. *Really*," Mikaela insists. "Just... confused. And I had the *wildest* dream." Her cheeks flush suddenly, her gaze darting involuntarily toward the group of Drakav males who've gathered at a respectful distance, watching the proceedings with evident interest.

The blush deepens when her eyes land on Sarven. He straightens immediately, red eyes widening a fraction, fists clenching and unclenching at her attention.

"Must have been some dream," Erika comments dryly, catching the exchange.

Mikaela's blush deepens. "It was... vivid," she admits, her voice dropping to a whisper. "And weird. But not in a bad way."

Justine and I exchange knowing glances.

"The firebloom tea must have worked," Alex says, relief evident in her voice as she checks Mikaela's eyes, seemingly oblivious to the undercurrents.

"Maybe," Justine says, her tone thoughtful. "When this happened to me, I noticed I'd feel better after eating or drinking something that originated on this world. But the effect lessened gradually over time. Like my body was adapting, but not quite fast enough."

A shadow crosses her face, and I know we're thinking the same thing. If the firebloom's effectiveness is temporary, and the women's bodies can't adapt quickly enough on their own...

"We're running out of time," I project at her.

"This isn't normal," Erika suddenly says. "And listen, a lot of things aren't normal here, but this? The fevers? The other illnesses that appear and disappear? It's worrisome." She stands, folding her arms over her chest. "We need to know more about what's happening here. About the Drakav," she gestures to them and the males close by straighten, "where they came from, why there are no females among them."

"Do you think this sickness might be related?" Alex asks, catching on quickly. "That maybe whatever is affecting us... affected their females too?"

The thought sends a chill down my spine.

Tina swallows hard and steps forward. "Are you saying that whatever is making us sick once wiped out an entire population of female Drakav? That maybe that's why they're all male, all seemingly without mates of their own kind?"

A sudden silence settles over the group.

The implications are staggering. Some of the women start whispering. I catch a few of the sentences. Worry about dying here and whether those blasted Xyma that caused us to be here will be coming back.

"We need answers," I say, my resolve hardening. "Real answers, not just guesswork."

That's when Tharn's presence blooms in my mind. He steps up beside Kol and Rok, his amber eyes finding mine across the space.

"*Jah-kee,*" he projects, but there's something in his tone, something that feels like stillness in the mindspace. Something that makes me straighten. "*I can show you.*"

I swallow hard, almost afraid of his next response. "*Show me what?*"

His gaze doesn't waver, his mental voice resonating with a significance I can't quite grasp.

"*Where we came from,*" he projects simply. "*The beginning of all Drakav.*"

CHAPTER 35
HOW TO EXPLAIN YOUR SPECIES' ORIGIN STORY WITHOUT SOUNDING LIKE A CULT

THARN

I lead Jah-kee through passages few Drakav walk anymore.

Her small hand is clasped in mine, her breathing steady despite the steep descent. The carved stone steps wind deeper beneath the clan caves, beyond the reach of Ain's light from the surface. Only our glow lights the way, casting off the stone.

Kol follows behind me while Rok and Jus-teen bring up the rear of our small procession, their footsteps echoing against the ancient stone.

"*Are we almost there?*" Jah-kee asks, squeezing my hand. "*Or is this just an elaborate ploy to get me alone in the dark?*"

I rumble softly, her humor warming me despite the solemnity of our journey. "*If I wanted that,*" I project, "*I would have found a closer cave.*"

She snorts, the sound bouncing off the narrow walls. Behind us, I hear Jus-teen stifle a laugh.

The tunnel widens suddenly, opening into a vast chamber that makes even Jah-kee fall silent in awe. The ceiling soars high above us, the walls curving in a perfect dome. But it's not the size that matters.

It's what covers every surface.

Carvings. Thousands of them. Flowing across the stone like water. In the center of the chamber stands a raised dais with a single stone column, worn smooth by the passage of countless claws.

"*This,*" Kol projects, his mental voice feeling like it reverberates through the chamber, "*is the Hall of Knowing.*"

Jah-kee releases my claw, stepping forward with wonder etched on her face. "It's beautiful," she whispers, turning slowly to take in the panorama of images. "*How old is it?*"

"*Older than memory,*" Kol answers. "*Older than the clan.*"

I watch her closely as she approaches the nearest wall, her fingers hovering just above the surface. I know what she sees —what all see when they first enter this sacred space.

The beginning.

"These figures," she vocalizes, tracing the air above an elaborate carving before switching back to mindspeak. "*They're... different. Not Drakav.*"

"*The Daughters of Ain,*" I project, moving to stand beside her. "*The First Ones.*"

The carving shows tall, slender figures with flowing head-fur like Jah-kee's that seems to move even in stone. Unlike the angular, muscular forms of Drakav, these beings appear soft, curved, almost luminous. Their eyes are large, their features delicate, and around them swirl what look like small particles.

"*They look... almost human,*" Jus-teen comments, joining us. "*But not quite.*"

"*The Daughters of Ain,*" Kol projects. "*Sacred. Divine.*"

I point to the next panel, where the figures stand with arms outstretched, the particles flowing from their fingertips toward what appear to be stone columns.

"*The Giving Stones,*" I project, the sacred words flowing naturally despite their weight. "*Where all Drakav emerge into the dust.*"

Jah-kee's brow furrows. "*Emerge? You mean... You weren't born? You were created?*"

Born. The word has no edges. No meaning. It is a sound without a shape in my mind.

"*We emerge,*" I confirm. "*The Daughters shaped us from the dust and the light. Then we wake in the stone.*"

Her eyes widen, darting between me and the carving. "*That's... that's not how reproduction usually works.*"

Re-production...

The word floats through the mindspace. I tilt my head, trying to grasp the concept. Before I can ask, a flash of Jah-kee's thoughts hits me. Vivid and hot and disorienting.

Me. Her. In my alcove. Her legs spread, my body pressing into hers, slow and deep.

Heat surges through me instantly, my member stiffening at the memory of claiming her. My loincloth tents and Kol notices immediately. His gaze drops to his unchanged pouch, before shifting to Rok's loincloth, too.

But Kol's confusion is easy to ignore because my own confusion follows just as quickly. I cannot imagine how sheathing myself in Jah-kee could create a new Drakav. The thought makes no sense. She is not a Giving Stone.

"*I do not understand. You are not... stone.*"

Jah-kee goes still, her lips parting as her face floods with color. Her thoughts scatter wildly in the mindspace, making it impossible to follow a single thread.

Behind us, Jus-teen makes a strangled sound, somewhere between a gasp and a groan. I glance back at her in concern, but Rok is already at her side, his claws brushing her arm.

"*Jus-teen,*" he rumbles softly, his golden eyes scanning her face. "*You are unwell?*"

"No," she squeaks, her vocalization even higher than usual. Her gaze darts to Jah-kee. "No, I'm fine. Totally fine."

Kol steps forward, his gaze shifting between them. "*Reproduction,*" he repeats slowly, tasting the word like foreign prey. "*What does this mean?*"

"It's not important," Jah-kee shakes her head. But even though she does not communicate it, her mental space does. Her voice is tight and strained.

"*It is important,*" I counter, turning back to her. "*You said it works differently. Jah-kee, please explain.*"

Her cheeks darken further, her body going stiff as she looks anywhere but at me. "It's, uh... humans don't emerge from stones, okay? We, um... we make babies through..." She hesitates, her projections drop to a whisper. "Sex."

The word lands in the mindspace like a spine striker's tail piercing the dust.

Kol's gaze sharpens. Rok tilts his head, his expression one of quiet confusion. The silence stretches, heavy with unspoken questions.

"*Sex,*" I echo, the thought rough.

Jah-kee groans, pressing her hands to her face. "Oh my god, I want to die."

Her words alarm me.

Every muscle in my body locks. "*Why?*" My claws unsheathe instinctively. "*What is this 'sex'? How does it steal life?*" My panicked gaze darts to Rok, who immediately crowds Jus-teen, sniffing for traces of this mortal threat.

Jah-kee peeks through her fingers. "No! I don't actually want to—It's a human expression. For... embarrassment."

317

Kol steps forward with the measured grace of a leader seeking understanding. When he speaks, his projection resonates with calm.

"The Daughters shaped us. If this is how humans shape life... then this 'sex' is sacred too."

Jah-kee groans louder, her hands dragging down her face. *"It's not the same thing, okay? Different species. Different methods. Can we please just move on?"*

I frown, my confusion deepening. *"You enjoy it when I sheathe myself in you. Is it not the same?"*

Jah-kee lets out a strangled noise, her hands flying back up to cover her face again. "Tharn!" She hisses out loud. *"Not here! Not in front of everyone!"*

"Why not?" Kol asks, his head tilting. *"This is sacred knowledge. If this... sex is how humans shape life, we must understand it."*

"It is more than knowledge," I project, my mind grappling with the implications. *"It is a new law. A hunter knows his prey. I know the shadowmaw, the dust serpent, the sandfin. They do not join. They do not... make life within their bodies. They emerge. From the deep caves, from the hot sands, from the cracked earth. All life on this dust emerges. All except... you."*

Rok jerks his chin as his arms circle Jus-teen. *"If this knowledge helps us protect you, it is worth knowing."*

Jus-teen makes another strangled sound, shooting Jah-kee a desperate look. "Help me," she whispers.

Jah-kee groans again, her shoulders slumping in defeat. And then, a thought—sharp and clear and not meant for me—slips through the mindspace.

"They won't stop until they understand. And if they don't understand, they can't protect us. Fine."

The thought is not soft. It is not the thought of prey. It is the thought of a hunter choosing the best path through dangerous ground. My respect for my Jah-kee deepens.

"Okay, look," she starts. *"Humans don't reproduce like Drakav. We don't... emerge from stones. We... join together. Physically. And sometimes that creates babies. But not always."*

Kol's brow furrows. *"Physically? How?"*

Jah-kee winces. *"I'd really rather not—"*

"Show us," Kol interrupts, gesturing toward her frame.

Jah-kee chokes. *"I am not showing you!"*

Kol tilts his head further, clearly baffled by her reaction. *"Why not? If this is how your species survives, it is vital knowledge."*

"It's private!" Jah-kee's face is so red I fear she might overheat. *"Okay. Okay. I guess we're doing this right here, right now. Here's how it works. When a man's... um..."* She hesitates, her hands flailing slightly. *"When a man's happy juice meets a woman's egg, then a baby can be formed. That's just how humans create new humans."*

"Happy juice?" Kol echoes, his head tilting further.

Jah-kee groans, gaze darting to Jus-teen. *"It's called sperm."*

Kol's expression doesn't change, though I sense his curiosity sharpening in the mindspace. *"And this... sperm,"* he projects slowly, *"is a fluid your males produce?"*

"Yes," she mutters, her mental voice strained. *"It's like... little swimmers. Tiny cells that carry half the genetic material needed to make a human."*

Kol looks genuinely intrigued now, his golden eyes narrowing in thought. *"And the female provides the other half?"*

"Exactly!" Jah-kee vocalizes. *"The egg comes from the woman, the sperm comes from the man, and when they meet, they can create a baby."*

Kol's gaze sharpens, his head tilting further as he digests this. *"And this fluid is... released during the act of joining?"*

"Yes," Jah-kee projects.

I freeze.

The fluid released during the act of joining.

My mind flashes back to the many times I have filled her, the heat of my release spilling into her again and again. The memory burns through me.

"*Jah-kee?*" I project slowly. "*This is the fluid my member produces when I... fill you?*"

Her gaze snaps to mine, her eyes widening slightly, but her expression remains composed.

"*Yes,*" she projects carefully. "*That's sperm.*"

The word resonates in the mindspace, heavy with meaning I'm only beginning to grasp.

A strange mix of emotions surges through me. Understanding, confusion, and something deeper, more primal. "*Then every time I have filled you...*" I trail off, my thoughts tangling.

Her brow furrows, her tone softening. "*It's not the same, Tharn. You're Drakav. I'm human. It's hard enough to get pregnant on Earth. There's no way our genetic material is compatible.*"

Her words are logical, reasonable. They should soothe the strange tension building in my chest.

But they don't.

Behind us, Jus-teen shifts uncomfortably. I hear her swallow audibly, her vocalization quiet but edged with something uncertain. "Aliens who... transformed to be perfectly compatible with us."

I stare at Jah-kee, my thoughts spinning. *Compatible.* The dust reshaped me. Altered me in ways I do not fully understand.

Beside me, I feel a flash of sharp, panicked thought from Jah-kee, directed entirely at her sister. It is too fast for me to grasp fully, a jumble of human words and a chemical name I do not recognize.

Jus-teen's response is a wave of pure, cold dread.

Could it be possible? Could I create life with Jah-kee?

My chest tightens with awe and wonder, the thought spiraling through me. A new Drakav. A progeny. *My* progeny.

My focus shifts to Rok, and I see the same realization reflected in his golden eyes. His gaze flicks to Jus-teen and stays there.

But...where would this new Drakav emerge from?

Would it grow beneath Jah-kee's soft skin, hidden from sight? Would she crack open like a Giving Stone, revealing new life within?

I do not want my mate to crack open.

Jah-kee exhales sharply, breaking the silence. "We're not down here to discuss making babies," she vocalizes.

Her words snap me back to the present, though the thoughts still churn in my mind.

"*We're here to figure out why the women are getting sick, and where you came from,*" she continues.

Kol gestures to the carvings. "*The answers lie here. In the Hall of Knowing.*"

Jah-kee follows his gaze, her jaw tightening as her resolve solidifies. "*Then let's figure it out.*"

Jah-kee continues along the wall, her expression shifting from confusion to fascination as she takes in more of the story. The first carvings are clear. They show the Daughters of Ain working in large structures, gathering particles of light, shaping them with gestures that seem almost like dance. Then the Daughters approach the stone columns, placing their creations inside before sealing them with a touch.

Further along, the carvings depict Drakav emerging fully formed from the columns, the Daughters welcoming them with outstretched arms.

"This is incredible," Jah-kee murmurs. "*So the Daughters of Ain... created your entire species?*"

"*Yes,*" Kol projects.

321

I watch her closely as she studies a panel showing Drakav kneeling before the Daughters, offering them water, meat, shelter. The reverence in the carved faces is unmistakable.

"*You worshipped them,*" she projects.

"*They were our makers,*" Kol projects simply.

She moves to the next section, where the story shifts. Here, the carvings are less clear, the meaning harder to grasp. She points to a panel that shows several Drakav clustered around a single Daughter of Ain, all reaching for her, their stone faces a confusing mix of devotion and possession.

"Look at this," Jah-kee murmurs to Jus-teen, who has stepped closer. "Doesn't this look like…"

"A harem?" Jus-teen suggests, her eyebrows rising as she takes in the carving.

"*Harem?*" I project, the unfamiliar word strange in the mindspace. "*What does this mean?*"

Neither female answers immediately, their attention caught by the next panels.

"*What happened here?*" Jah-kee's brow knits.

The wall is a mess. A huge section of the story is simply gone, the stone either intentionally smashed into rubble or worn away by some ancient cataclysm, leaving a gaping hole in the history of our people. Fragments of images remain—a broken spear here, a fallen Drakav there—but there is no context, no story. Only the ghost of a great violence.

"*What happened?*" Jah-kee's mental projection is filled with horror. "*The story… it's just… gone.*"

Kol steps forward. "*Some stories are too painful to carve,*" he projects, his thought resonating with an ancient sorrow. "*And some are lost to the dust forever.*"

Jah-kee turns to him, waiting. But Kol merely gestures to the far wall, where the carvings resume, clear and pristine once more.

The final image is stark. The few remaining Daughters stand together, their arms raised toward a blazing Ain carved at the apex of the chamber. Around them, swirling particles of light rise upward.

"*They went back to Ain*," Kol projects, his mental voice heavy with finality. "*They left the dust.*"

Jah-kee stares at the image. "*But... why? Because of whatever happened here?*" She gestures to the ruined section of the wall.

"*We do not know the whole truth*," Kol admits. "*We know only that they were gone. And we were left alone.*"

Jus-teen's gaze flicks over the carvings. "*That's why you thought we were these mythic Daughters of Ain. You thought they returned.*"

Neither I nor Rok nor Kol reply. Because she is right.

"*I don't know if we're your Daughters of Ain*," she projects. "*I'm pretty sure we're just humans who, through some kind of luck, crashed on your planet.*"

Jah-kee nods. "*It doesn't matter what we believe right now. What matters is keeping the women alive while they adapt—or bond, or whatever needs to happen.*"

Her practical approach fills me with pride.

"*I want to bring the other women here*," she continues. "*They should see this, understand the history. It might help them make their own choices about bonding, if that's what it comes to.*"

Kol stiffens slightly. "*The Hall of Knowing is sacred. Few are permitted to enter.*"

"*If you truly believe we're your Daughters returned*," Jah-kee projects, her voice firm despite her respectful tone, "*then this is our history too. We have a right to know it.*"

A tense silence falls. Then, unexpectedly, Kol's mental voice fills the mindspace with what can only be described as a laugh —rich, deep, and genuinely amused.

"*You speak like a Daughter,*" he projects, satisfaction evident in his tone. "*Commanding even to clan leaders.*"

Jah-kee blinks, clearly not expecting this reaction.

"*The females may come,*" Kol projects. "*In small groups. With proper reverence.*"

"*Thank you,*" Jah-kee projects, relief evident. "*I promise they'll be respectful.*"

As we prepare to leave the Hall, Jah-kee lingers by the carving, her fingers hovering over the Drakav lying broken in the stone.

"Three thousand years," she murmurs. "*You've been waiting three thousand years for the Daughters to return.*"

"*Yes,*" Kol projects simply.

She turns to look at him, her expression softer now. "*That's a long time to keep faith.*"

Kol regards Jah-kee for a long moment, his glow steady and warm in the dim chamber. When he finally speaks, his mental voice resonates with quiet strength.

"*A hunter does not count the sols he waits in the dust,*" he projects. "*He is judged only by the hunger that drives him through the dark. Our hunger for their return has never faded.*"

Jah-kee's lips part slightly. She doesn't reply, simply nodding in acknowledgment.

Kol dips his head in return, a gesture of mutual respect that seems to bridge the vast gulf between us. Then he steps aside, motioning for us to leave the Hall.

As we ascend the winding steps, the air grows warmer the closer we get to the main cavern, but my thoughts remain heavy, anchored in the Hall and the revelations we unearthed within it.

Ahead of me, Jah-kee walks with sure steps, her small fingers brushing the stone wall to steady herself. Her resilience is unmistakable—her fire, her strength. She commands even Kol, a clan leader, as though she were born to it.

But as I watch her, a strange thought curls in the back of my mind.

The Daughters made us to adapt. To survive. To be compatible.

The thought twists through me, vivid and unsettling. My mind flashes to the Giving Stones, the way they crack open to reveal new life.

I clench my claws.

No. Jah-kee is strong, but she is not stone. She would not —*could not*—split open like that.

She glances back at me as we near the top of the steps, her expression curious. "*You okay, big guy?*"

I nod once, forcing my thoughts to quiet. "*Yes,*" I project, keeping the thought steady.

She flashes me a small, teasing smile. "*Good. Because we still have a lot of work to do.*"

I say nothing, but as we step into the main cavern, my gaze lingers on her.

My Jah-kee. Strong, fierce, unyielding.

Still, one thought refuses to leave me:

If she ever cracked open like a Giving Stone, I'd lose my mind completely.

CHAPTER 36
YEAH, I'M KEEPING HIM. NO TAKE-BACKS

JACQUI

Mikaela's laughter is the first sign that things are finally looking up.

Three days ago, she was flushed with fever, her body wracked with chills. Now, she's sitting cross-legged near the central fire, sorting through the meager pile of Earth belongings we've managed to salvage—some tattered clothing and a handful of personal items that somehow survived the crash and our trek across the desert.

"Look what I found!" she exclaims, holding up a cracked but still faintly glowing smartwatch. "Useless now, but..." She taps the screen, making it flicker weakly.

"Keep it," Tina says, pausing from her work sorting through the last of the Xyma supplies they brought with them from the wreckage. "You never know when we might need tech from home."

The firebloom tea seems to be working. Now, we consume it even when not showing symptoms. It's not a permanent fix, but enough to buy us time. Mikaela's fever broke first, and since then, the others have shown signs of improvement too.

Around us, the clan caves hum with activity. Near the eastern wall, several Drakav work with the massive hide of the dust serpent Tharn took down. The pale, glistening underbelly leather is stretched taut across massive stone frames. The warriors' sharp stone knives scrape the last of the fat and sinew from the inner surface.

Rok kneels beside a freshly scraped section, his claws testing the texture of the hide. Nearby, Tharn is working with a smaller piece, cutting it into long, thin strips.

Mikaela glances over and wrinkles her nose. "Smells like old saddle leather."

Justine snorts. "Better than smelling like *dead* leather."

In the mindspace, one Drakav's focus sharpens as he watches me inspect the hide.

"*She touches it like it might bite*," he observes, amused.

"*Because the last time she saw these, they were biting*," Tharn deadpans.

Kol, overseeing the work, flicks his claws in a dismissive gesture. "*We need more. One serpent is not enough for a clan our size, now.*" His gaze sweeps over the human women. "*We need more hides. More meat. More of everything.*"

A ripple of agreement passes through the warriors, followed immediately by Haroth's dry projection: "*I volunteer to hunt more. Immediately.*" His gaze lingers just a beat too long on the women behind me.

Tharn's lips curl in disapproval. "*You just want to impress the small one.*"

"*You shaped an entire garment for your female,*" Haroth counters. "*Do not deny me a single scale's worth of praise.*"

Rok exhales sharply through his nose. "*Careful, brother. Human thoughts don't light up in the mindspace. You'll have to interpret...*" He gestures vaguely at Alex's frown of concentration as she prods the hide. "*... that.*"

Haroth's answering growl is pure theatrics. "*Then I'll hunt the largest serpent in the wastes. Surely that earns—*"

"*A scolding for recklessness,*" Kol interrupts, though even his mental voice carries reluctant amusement.

My gaze shifts back to our little group, just in time to see Mikaela shudder and rub her temples.

"Ugh," she mutters, shooting a glare toward the Drakav. "Are they doing that... mental chest-thumping again?"

Pam blinks. "Wait, you felt that too? I just got this weird urge to roll my eyes."

Across the circle, Tina tilts her head. "Huh. I thought I imagined someone thinking about serpents."

Justine and I exchange glances. Not full mindshare, not yet —just emotional echoes slipping through. They're not just surviving here anymore. They're becoming part of this place. Part of them. Like me and Justine.

The thought sends a shiver through me. The memory of the carvings in the Hall of Knowing flashes in my mind—the Giving Stones, Tharn's confusion at the word "born," his story of how all life on this dust emerges. It all collides with the sickness, with the way our human bodies are fighting this world.

Everything here is... grown. Made.

Everything except us. We are the only things on this planet that know how to give birth.

It explains everything. The fevers. The dreams. The way the planet seems to be trying to either reject us or... remake us.

The thought stays with me as my eyes drift across the cavern where two warriors sharpen bone blades against smooth stones, the rhythmic scraping a counterpoint to the low conversations happening throughout the cavern.

Nearby, Erika has somehow convinced a stoic Drakav to

show her how they cure meat, and she's watching intently as he demonstrates the precise cuts that allow the flesh to dry evenly in the hot, dry air.

It's strange how quickly the impossible becomes routine. A month ago, the idea of living in a cave with giant golden aliens would have been a fever dream. Now, the rhythmic scrape of their knives and the low murmur of their thoughts in the mindspace is just... the background noise of my afternoon.

I glance over at Tharn, who's now wrapping the scraped skin around a stone pillar, his sharp golden eyes tracking my every move in that quiet, intense way he has. His presence in the mindspace suddenly gives me a pulse of warmth that wraps around me like sunlight through an open window.

He's proud of me. I can feel it, even without him saying a word.

"Stop staring at me like that," I project, teasing.

"Why?" he projects back, his voice tinged with amusement. *"You are mine. I will look whenever I wish."*

I roll my eyes, but can't help the way my lips curve into a smile.

Beside me, Mikaela's laughter cuts off abruptly, and I follow her gaze to the group of Drakav males entering the main chamber. Most are returning from a hunt, their golden skin dusted with fine sand that seems to cling to everything outside. But Mikaela's focus has zeroed in on one in particular.

Sarven.

His red eyes are locked on her like she's the only person in the room. He doesn't move, doesn't say anything, but his claws flex at his sides, and I recognize the tension in his stance.

It's the same way Tharn used to look at me before I realized this whole bond thing was happening between us.

Mikaela flushes, her gaze darting away as if trying to escape his intensity. But her hands tremble slightly as she sets

AG WILDE

down the smartwatch, and I don't miss the way her eyes flicker back to him, like a moth drawn to a flame.

Interesting.

I make a mental note to follow up on that later, but for now, there's something else I want to focus on.

"*Tharn,*" I project, turning to him. "*Come with me.*"

He straightens immediately, pushing off the pillar with fluid grace. "*Where?*"

I don't answer, just grab his hand and start walking.

He follows without hesitation, his larger frame blocking out the light briefly as we pass through the tunnel that leads to our alcove. The moment we're alone, I stop and turn to face him.

"Thank you," I say softly, my voice barely above a whisper.

His head tilts, confusion rippling through the mindspace. "*For what, my light?*"

"*For everything,*" I say, stepping closer. "*For helping the women. For helping me. For being... you.*"

His claws flex at his sides, the only outward sign of tension before he reaches for me, his hands settling on my waist.

"*You do not need to thank me,*" he projects, his voice rough with emotion. "*You already know...I would tear this world apart for you.*"

The words steal my breath.

"*I know,*" I whisper, leaning into him.

His claws dig into my hips as he backs me against the cave wall. The soft dust-serpent scales of my dress scrape against the rough stone.

"*Off,*" he growls, already tugging at the sinew ties along my shoulder. I help him, fingers fumbling from how he's biting a path down my throat, how his hands are everywhere at once.

The loincloth is gone before I can blink, tossed aside with a flick of his claws. He doesn't give me time to think, to breathe.

330

Just lifts me effortlessly, my legs wrapping around his waist as he pins me to the wall.

One thrust and he's buried to the hilt, his snarl vibrating through my chest as I gasp.

Beyond our alcove, the caves hum with life.

But here?

Here, there's only the punishing grip of his hands, the scrape of stone against my back, and the mindspace roaring with a single, savage truth:

Mine.

EPILOGUE

IT'S NOT FLIRTING IF YOU SCOWL WHILE DOING IT (AN IDIOT'S GUIDE TO INTERSPECIES ROMANCE)

MIKAELA

A chill that has nothing to do with the cavern air snakes down my spine. I wrap my arms around myself, trying to ignore the low thrum of a headache building behind my eyes. It's happening more often now. The fevers, the aches. The feeling that this planet is trying to reject us, one cell at a time.

Across the cavern, the other women are integrating, finding their places among our giant, golden hosts. They accept the gifts, the help, the soft purrs of approval. They see kindness.

I see a tactic.

My gaze slides to the shadows near the weapon's cache. And of course, he's there. Sarven. While the other males hover and offer, he just... watches. His stillness is unnerving, his crimson eyes fixed on me with a predator's focus. He's not trying to court me. He's trying to...solve me?

It should be terrifying. It is. But underneath the fear is a hot spark of anger. He thinks I'm a puzzle? Fine. Let him try to figure me out. I've been underestimated before.

I meet his stare across the firelight, and for a moment, the rest of the cavern fades away. The headache pulses in time with my heartbeat. *Make your move,* I think. *I'm ready.*

SARVEN

My glow does not erupt.

This is the thought that grinds in my mind like stone on stone. Rok and Tharn said that is the first sign. But for me, there is nothing but a dull, unresponsive emptiness in my chest.

Is it me? Am I broken?

I watch her. She shivers, though the cavern is warm. A tremor of weakness runs through her, and a possessive rage washes through me. The sickness. It is a rival hunter, stalking my prey.

She feels my gaze and turns. Her chin lifts. Her eyes narrow, not with fear, but with challenge. The quick, angry pulse in her throat beats a rhythm that makes my own lifeblood heat.

This is the puzzle. The others see a female to be gifted, to be soothed. I see a fire that the sickness is trying to smother. My glow may be silent, but my instincts are not.

In my dreams, she does not reach for me. She turns and bares her teeth. A worthy mate.

I will not let the sickness take her. I will solve the mystery of my own broken body. I will learn the language of her strength, and I will make my skin burn for her. The fever is a hunter, but I am the better predator. And I will not lose what is mine.

AFTERWORD

❀☆❅☆❀

Dear Reader,

Well, hello again!

You survived the Great Sand Serpent Attack and officially learned that **alien D is custom-made.** If you *still* want more, well hell yeah! I'm not done yet!

Thank you. Seriously. The journey was intense, but watching our big, beautiful, bewildered Tharn finally claim his mate was worth every moment of his chest pain.

(Yes, I cried when Jacqui told him she chose him. Yes, I know I'm the one that wrote it. No, I am not okay.)

We didn't head back to the Silent Valley this time but the story in the dust is far from over. Mikaela has officially caught the eye of a certain crimson-eyed hunter who is very, very patient.

Next is Book 3, **SARVEN'S OATH.** Ready to find out if the most guarded human falls for the most watchful alien?

• Don't forget to join my newsletter (https://agwilde.com/newsletter-sign-up/) for new release updates.

• Follow me on social media. I *am* present on there. Pardon my introverted silence.

• Leave a review if you swooned, laughed, or now have a very, *very* specific list of design improvements for the male anatomy.

Most of all, thank you for making the journey. The real treasure was the alien anatomy we explored along the way.

See you in the Dust,

🩶 A.G.

NEXT IN THE SERIES

Sarven's Oath

I don't trust aliens. Especially not the seven-foot-tall, golden-skinned warrior assigned to "protect" me.

So when our only water source is suddenly contaminated, I don't buy their story. I volunteer for the mission to find a new well, because the only person I can rely on to keep my friends safe is me. My guide? Sarven, the clan's shadow. Silent. Watchful. And way too observant for my liking.

He doesn't speak much. Doesn't need to.

Not when the air between us crackles every time I get too close.

He thinks he's my protector. I know he's my keeper.

But when we're stranded and the desert itself tries to kill us, the lines start to blur.

And suddenly, the heat in his crimson eyes feels less like a threat...

And the unspoken promise on his fangs feels a lot like a claim.

(First-contact sci-fi romance with forced proximity, survival stakes, and a possessive but devoted alien hero. She's sure he has a hidden agenda. He's sure she's his mate.)

Also By

Captured by Aliens

Xul

Crex

Yce

Kyris

Kyro

Riv's Sanctuary

Riv's Sanctuary

Sohut's Protection

Ka'Cit's Haven

The Restitution

Ajos

V'Alen

Akur

A New Home

An Alien for the Farm

An Alien for Her Heart

An Alien for the Future

Captured Earth

Arrival

Base Zero

Cataclysm

War

Rebirth

Fated Mates of the Atari

Claiming His Mate

Craving His Mate

Fighting for His Mate

Guarding His Mate

The Midnight Seven

<u>Outlaw</u>

Barbarians of the Dust

Rok's Captive

Tharn's Hunt

Sarven's Oath

Scan the QR code to view all books

About the Author

A. G. Wilde is an avid reader, a gamer, a lover of all things space, alien, and sci-fi.

She is addicted to intense romance, irresistible heroes, and deliciously naughty things.

- facebook.com/agwilde
- instagram.com/authoragwilde
- tiktok.com/@authoragwilde
- x.com/authoragwilde
- bookbub.com/profile/a-g-wilde
- amazon.com/author/agwilde